Q.

Dead Man's Rock

A Romance

Q.

Dead Man's Rock
A Romance

ISBN/EAN: 9783337019754

Printed in Europe, USA, Canada, Australia, Japan

Cover: Foto ©Andreas Hilbeck / pixelio.de

More available books at **www.hansebooks.com**

DEAD MAN'S ROCK:

A Romance.

BY

Q.

—·••·— —

CASSELL & COMPANY, Limited:

LONDON, PARIS, NEW YORK, & MELBOURNE.

1887.

To

THE MEMORY OF

MY FATHER

I DEDICATE THIS BOOK.

CONTENTS.

---·:·---

DEAD MAN'S ROCK.

Book I.

THE QUEST OF THE GREAT RUBY.

CHAPTER I.

TELLS OF THE STRANGE WILL OF MY GRANDFATHER, AMOS TRENOWETH.

WHATEVER claims this story may have upon the notice of the world, they will rest on no niceties of style or aptness of illustration. It is a plain tale, plainly told: nor, as I conceive, does its native horror need any ingenious embellishment. There are many books that I, though a man of no great erudition, can remember, which gain much of interest from the pertinent and appropriate comments with which the writer has seen fit to illustrate any striking situation. From such books an observing man may often draw the exactest rules for the regulation of life and conduct, and their authors may therefore be esteemed public benefactors. Among these I, Jasper Trenoweth, can claim no place; yet I venture to think my history will not altogether lack interest—

B

and this for two reasons. It deals with the last chapter
(I pray Heaven it be the last) in the adventures of a
very remarkable gem—none other, in fact, than the
Great Ruby of Ceylon; and it lifts, at least in part, the
veil which for some years has hidden a certain mystery
of the sea. For the moral, it must be sought by the
reader himself in the following pages.

To make all clear, I must go back half a century,
and begin with the strange and unaccountable Will made
in the year of Grace 1837 by my grandfather, Amos
Trenoweth, of Lantrig in the County of Cornwall. The
old farm-house of Lantrig, heritage and home of the
Trenoweths as far as tradition can reach, and Heaven
knows how much longer, stands some few miles N.W.
of the Lizard, facing the Atlantic gales from behind a
scanty veil of tamarisks, on Pedn-glâs, the northern point
of a small sandy cove, much haunted of old by smugglers,
but now left to the peaceful boats of the Polkimbra
fishermen. In my grandfather's time however, if tales
be true, Ready-Money Cove saw many a midnight cargo
run, and many a prize of cognac and lace found its way
to the cellars and store-room of Lantrig. Nay, there is
a story (but for its truth I will not vouch) of a struggle
between my grandfather's lugger, the *Pride of Heart*,
and a certain Revenue cutter, and of an unowned shot
that found a Preventive Officer's heart. But the whole
tale remains to this day full of mystery, nor would I
mention it save that it may be held to throw some light
on my grandfather's sudden disappearance no long time

after. Whither he went, none clearly knew. Folks said, to fight the French; but when he returned suddenly some twenty years later, he said little about seafights, or indeed on any other subject; nor did many care to question him, for he came back a stern, taciturn man, apparently with no great wealth, but also without seeming to want for much, and at any rate indisposed to take the world into his confidence. His father had died meanwhile, so he quietly assumed the mastership at Lantrig, nursed his failing mother tenderly until her death, and then married one of the Triggs of Mullyon, of whom was born my father, Ezekiel Trenoweth.

I have hinted, what I fear is but the truth, that my grandfather had led a hot and riotous youth, fearing neither God, man, nor devil. Before his return, however, he had "got religion" from some quarter, and was confirmed in it by the preaching of one Jonathan Wilkins, as I have heard, a Methodist from "up the country," and a powerful mover of souls. As might have been expected in such a man as my grandfather, this religion was of a joyless and gloomy order, full of anticipations of hell-fire and conviction of the sinfulness of ordinary folk. But it undoubtedly was sincere, for his wife Philippa believed in it, and the master and mistress of Lantrig were alike the glory and strong support of the meeting-house at Polkimbra until her death. After this event, her husband shut himself up with the tortures of his own stern conscience, and was seen by few. In this dismal self-communing

B 2

he died on the 27th of October, 1837, leaving behind
him one mourner, his son Ezekiel, then a strong and
comely youth of twenty-two.

This brings me to my grandfather's Will, discovered
amongst his papers after his death; and surely no
stranger or more perplexing document was ever penned,
especially as in this case any Will was unnecessary, seeing that only one son was left to claim the inheritance.
Men guessed that those dark years of seclusion and
self-repression had been spent in wrestling with memories
of a sinful and perhaps a criminal past, and predicted
that Amos Trenoweth could not die without confession.
They were partly right, from knowledge of human
nature; and partly wrong, from ignorance of my
grandfather's character.

The Will was dated "June 15th, 1837," and ran as
follows:—

*"I, Amos Trenoweth, of Lantrig, in the Parish of
"Polkimbra and County of Cornwall, feeling, in this year
"of Grace Eighteen hundred and thirty-seven, that my
"Bodily Powers are failing and the Hour drawing near
"when I shall be called to account for my Many and
"Grievous Sins, do hereby make Provision for my Death
"and also for my son Ezekiel, together with such Descend-
"ants as may hereafter be born to him. To this my
"son Ezekiel I give and bequeath the Farm and House
"of Lantrig, with all my Worldly Goods, and add my
"earnest hope that this may suffice to support both him
"and his Descendants in Godliness and Contentment,*

"*knowing how greatly these excell the Wealth of this
"World and the Lusts of the Flesh. But, knowing also
"the mutability of earthly things, I do hereby command
"and enjoin that, if at any time He or his Descendants
"be in stress and tribulation of poverty, the Head of our
"Family of Trenoweth shall strictly and faithfully obey
"these my Latest Directions. He shall take ship and go
"unto Bombay in India, to the house of Elihu Sanderson,
"Esquire, or his Heirs, and there, presenting in person
"this my last Will and Testament, together with the Holy
"Bible now lying in the third drawer of my Writing Desk,
"shall duly and scrupulously execute such instructions
"as the said Elihu Sanderson or his Heirs shall lay upon
"him.*

"*Also I command and enjoin, under pain of my
"Dying Curse, that the Iron Key now hanging from the
"Middle Beam in the Front Parlour be not touched or
"moved, until he who undertakes this Task shall have
"returned and have crossed the threshold of Lantrig,
"having duly performed all the said Instructions. And
"furthermore that the said Task be not undertaken lightly
"or except in direst Need, under pain of Grievous and
"Sore Affliction. This I say, knowing well the Spiritual
"and worldly Perils that shall beset such an one, and
"having myself been brought near to Destruction of Body
"and Soul, which latter may Christ in His Mercy avert.*

"*Thus, having eased my mind of great and pressing
"Anguish, I commend my soul to God, before Whose
"Judgment Bar I shall be presently summoned to stand,*

" the greatest of sinners, yet not without hope of Ever-
" lasting Redemption, for Christ's sake. Amen.

"AMOS TRENOWETH."

Such was the Will, written on stiff parchment in
crabbed and unscholarly characters, without legal forms
or witnesses; but all such were needless, as I have
pointed out. And, indeed, my father was wise, as I
think, to show it to nobody, but go his way quietly as
before, managing the farm as he had managed it during
the old man's last years. Only by degrees he broke
from the seclusion which had been natural to him
during his parents' lifetime, so far as to look about for
a wife—shyly enough at first—until he caught the
dark eyes of Margery Freethy one Sunday morning in
Polkimbra Church, whither he had gone of late for
freedom, to the no small tribulation of the meeting-
house. Now, whether this tribulation arose from the
backsliding of a promising member, or the loss of the
owner of Lantrig (who was at the same time unmarried),
I need not pause here to discuss. Nor is it necessary
to tell how regularly Margery and Ezekiel found themselves in church, nor how often they caught each
other's eyes straying from the prayer-book. It is
enough that at the year's end Margery answered
Ezekiel's question, and shortly after came to Lantrig
" for good."

The first years of their married life must have been
very happy, as I gather from the hushed joy with

which my mother always spoke of them. I gather also that my first appearance in this world caused more delight than I have ever given since—God forgive me for it! But shortly after I was four years old everything began to go wrong. First of all, two ships in which my father had many shares were lost at sea; then the cattle were seized with plague, and the stock gradually dwindled away to nothing. Finally, my father's bank broke—or, as we say in the West, "went scat!"—and we were left all but penniless, with the prospect of having to sell Lantrig, being without stock and lacking means to replenish it. It was at this time, I have since learnt from my mother, that Amos Trenoweth's Will was first thought about. She, poor soul! had never heard of the parchment before, and her heart misgave her as she read of peril to soul and body sternly hinted at therein. Also, her best-beloved brother had gone down in a squall off the Cape of Good Hope, so that she always looked upon the sea as a cruel and treacherous foe, and shuddered to think of it as lying in wait for her Ezekiel's life. It came to pass, therefore, that for two years the young wife's tears and entreaties prevailed; but at the end of this time, matters growing worse and worse, and also because it seemed hard that Lantrig should pass away from the Trenoweths while, for aught we knew, treasure was to be had for the looking, poverty and my father's wish prevailed, and it was determined, with the tearful assent of my mother, that he should start to seek this Elihu Sanderson, of Bombay, and, with good fortune, save the failing house of the Trenoweths. Only he waited until the worst of the winter was over, and then, having commended us both to the care of his aunt, Elizabeth Loveday, of Lizard Town, and provided us with the largest sum he could scrape together (and small indeed it was), he started for the port of Plymouth one woeful morning in February, and thence sailed away in the good ship *Golden Wave* to win his inheritance.

CHAPTER II.

So my father sailed away, carrying with him—sewn
for safety in his jersey's side—the Will and the small
clasped Bible; nor can I think of stranger equipment
for the hunting of earthly treasure. And the great
iron key hung untouched from the beam, while the
spiders outvied one another in wreathing it with their
webs, knowing it to be the only spot in Lantrig where
they were safe from my mother's broom. It is with
these spiders that my recollections begin, for of my
father, before he sailed away, remembrance is dim
and scanty, being confined to the picture of a tall fair
man, with huge shoulders and wonderful grey eyes,
that changed in a moment from the stern look he must
have inherited from Amos to an extraordinary depth of
love and sympathy. Also I have some faint memories
of a pig, named Eleazar (for no well-explained reason),
which fell over the cliff one night and awoke the household with its cries. But this I mention only because it
happened, as I learn, before my father's going, and not
for any connection with my story. We must have

lived a very quiet life at Lantrig, even as lives go on
our Western coast. I remember my mother now as she
went softly about the house contriving and scheming
to make the two ends of our small possessions meet.
She was a woman who always walked softly, and,
indeed, talked so, with a low musical voice such as I
shall never hear again, nor can ever hope to. But I
remember her best in church, as she knelt and prayed
for her absent husband, and also in the meeting-house,
which she sometimes attended, more to please Aunt
Elizabeth than for any good it did her. For the religion there was too sombre for her quiet sorrow; and
often I have seen a look of awful terror possess her
eyes when the young minister gave out the hymn and
the fervid congregation wailed forth—

> "In midst of life we are in death,
>   Oh! stretch Thine arm to save,
> Amid the storm's tumultuous breath
>   And roaring of the wave,"

which, among a fishing population, was considered a
particularly appropriate hymn; and, truly, to hear the
unction with which the word "tu-mult-u-ous" was
rendered, with all strength of lung and rolling of
syllables, was moving enough. But my mother would
grow all white and trembling, and clutch my hand
sometimes, as though to save herself from shipwreck;
whilst I too often would be taken with the passion of
the chant, and join lustily in the shouting, only half

comprehending her mortal anguish. It was this, perhaps, and many another such scene, which drew upon me her gentle reproof for pointing one day to the text above the pulpit and repeating, " How dreadful is this place ! " But that was after I had learned to spell.

It had always been my father's wish that I should grow up "a scholar," which, in those days, meant amongst us one who could read and write with no more than ordinary difficulty. So one of my mother's chief cares was to teach me my letters, which I learnt from big A to "Ampusand" in the old hornbook at Lantrig. I have that hornbook still,

> ———— " covered with pellucid horn,
> To save from fingers wet the letters fair."

The horn, alas! is no longer pellucid, but dim, as if with the tears of the many generations that have struggled through the alphabet and the first ten numerals and reached in due course the haven of the Lord's Prayer and Doxology. I had passed the Doxology, and was already deep in the "Pilgrim's Progress" and the "Holy War" (which latter book, with the rude taste of childhood, I greatly preferred, so that I quickly knew the mottoes and standards of its bewildering hosts by heart), when my father's first letter came home. In those days, before the great canal was cut, a voyage to the East Indies was no light matter, lying as it .did around the treacherous Cape and through seas where a ship may lie becalmed for weeks. So it was little wonder that my father's letter, written from Bombay, was some time on its way. Still, when the news came it was good. He had seen Mr. Elihu Sanderson, son of the Elihu mentioned in my grandfather's Will, had presented his parchment and Testament, and received some notes (most of which he sent home), together with a sealed packet, directed in Amos Trenoweth's handwriting: "To the Son of my House, who, having Counted all the Perils, is Resolute." This packet, my father went on to say, contained much mysterious matter, which would keep until he and his dear wife met. He added that, for himself, he could divine no peril, nor any cause for his dear wife to trouble, seeing that he had but to go to the island of Ceylon, whence, having accomplished the commands contained in the packet, he purposed to take ship and return with all speed to England. This was the substance of the letter, wrapped around with many endearing words, and much tender solicitude for Margery and the little one, as that he hoped Jasper was tackling his letters like a real scholar, and comforting his mother's heart, with more to this effect; which made us weep very sorrowfully when the letter was read, although we could not well have told why. As to the sealed packet, my father would have been doubtless more explicit had he been without a certain distrust of letters and letter-carriers, which, amid much faith in the miraculous powers of the Post

Office, I have known to exist among us even in these later days.

Than this blessed letter surely no written sheet was ever more read and re-read; read to me every night before prayers were said, read to Aunt Elizabeth and Uncle Loveday, read (in extracts) to all the neighbours of Polkimbra, for none knew certainly why Ezekiel had gone to India except that, somewhat vaguely, it was to "better hisself." How many times my mother read it, and kissed it, and cried over it, God alone knows; I only know that her step, which had been failing of late, grew firmer, and she went about the house with a light in her face like "the face of an angel," as the vicar said. It may have been: I have never since seen its like upon earth.

After this came the great joy of sending an answer, which I wrote (with infinite pains as to the capital letters) at my mother's dictation. And then it was read over and corrected, and added to, and finally directed, as my father had instructed us, to "Mr. Ezekiel Trenoweth; care of John P. Eversleigh, Esq., of the East India Company's Service, Colombo, Ceylon." I remember that my mother sealed it with the red cornelian Ezekiel had given her when he asked her to be his wife, and took it with her own hands to Penzance to post, having, for the occasion, harnessed old Pleasure in the cart for the first time since we had been alone.

Then we had to wait again, and the little store of money grew small indeed. But Aunt Elizabeth was a wonderful contriver, and tender of heart besides, although in most things to be called a "hard" woman. She had married, during my grandfather's long absence, Dr. Loveday, of Lizard Town—a mild little man with a prodigious vanity in brass buttons, and the most terrific religious beliefs, which did not in the least alter his natural sweetness of temper. My aunt and uncle (it was impossible to think of them except in this order) would often drive or walk over to Lantrig, seldom without some little present, which, together with my aunt's cap-box, would emerge from the back seat, amid a *duetto* something after this fashion :—

My Aunt.—"So, my dear, we thought as we were driving in this direction we would see how you were getting on; and by great good fortune, or rather as I should say (Jasper, do not hang your head so; it looks so deceitful) by the will of Heaven (and Heaven's will be done, you know, my dear, which must be a great comfort to you in your sore affliction), as Cyrus was driving into Cadgwith yesterday—were you not, Cyrus?"

My Uncle.—"To be sure, my dear."

My Aunt.—"Well, as I was saying, as Cyrus was driving into Cadgwith yesterday to see Martha George's husband, who was run over by the Helston coach, and she such a regular attendant at the Prayermeeting, but in the midst of life (Jasper, don't fidget)—well, whom should he see but Jane Ann Collins, with the finest pair of ducks, too, and costing a mere nothing. Cyrus will bear me out."

My Uncle.—"Nothing at all, my dear. Jasper, come here and talk to me. Do you know, Jasper, what happens to little boys that tell lies? You do? Something terrible, eh? Soul's perdition, my boy; soul's ev-er-last-ing perdition. There, come and show me the pig."

What agonies of conscience it must have cost these two good souls thus to conspire together for benevolence, none ever knew. Nor was it less pathetic that the fraud was so hollow and transparent. I doubt not that the sin of it was washed out with self-reproving tears, and cannot think that they were shed in vain.

So the seasons passed, and we waited, till in the late summer of 1849 (my father having been away nineteen months) there came another letter to say that he was about to start for home. He had found what he sought, so he said, but could not rightly understand its value, or, indeed, make head or tail of it by himself, and dared not ask strangers to help him. Perhaps, however, when he came home, Jasper (who was such a scholar) would help him; and maybe the key would be some aid. For the rest, he had been stricken with a fever—a malady common enough in those parts—but was better, and would start in something over a week, in the *Belle Fortune*, a barque of some 650 tons register, homeward bound with a cargo of sugar, spices, and coffee, and having a crew of about eighteen hands, with, he thought, one or two passengers. The letter was full of strong hope and love, so that my mother, who trembled a little when she read about the fever, plucked up courage to smile again towards the close. The ship would be due about October, or perhaps November. So once more we had to resume our weary waiting, but this time with glad hearts, for we knew that before Christmas the days of anxiety and yearning would be over.

The long summer drew to a glorious and golden September, and so faded away in a veil of grey sky; and the time of watching was nearly done. Through September the skies had been without cloud, and the sea almost breathless, but with the coming of October came dirty weather and a strong sou'-westerly wind, that gathered day by day, until at last, upon the evening of October 11th, it broke into a gale. My mother for days had been growing more restless and anxious with the growing wind, and this evening had much ado to sit quietly and endure. I remembered that as the storm raged without and tore at the door-hinges, while the rain lashed and smote the tamarisk branches against the panes, I sat by her knee before the kitchen fire and read bits from my favourite "Holy War," which, in the pauses of the storm, she would explain to me.

I was much put to it that night, I recollect, by the questionable morality at one point of Captain Credence, who in general was my favourite hero, dividing that honour with General Boanerges for the most part, but exciting more sympathy by reason of his wound—so grievously I misread the allegory, or rather saw no allegory at all. So my mother explained

it to me, though all the while, poor creature, her
heart was racked with terror for *her* Mansoul, beaten,
perhaps, at that moment from its body by the fury
of that awful night. Then when the fable's meaning
was explained, and my difficulty smoothed away, we
fell to talking of father's home-coming, in vain
endeavours to cheat ourselves of the fears that rose
again with every angry bellow of the tempest, and
agreed that his ship could not possibly be due yet
(rejoicing at this for the first time), but must, we
feigned, be lying in a dead calm off the West Coast
of Africa; until we almost laughed—God pardon us!
—at the picture of his anxiety to be home while such
a storm was raging at the doors of Lantrig. And
then I listened to wonderful stories of the East Indies
and the marvels that men found there, and wondered
whether father would bring home a parrot, and if it
would be as like Aunt Loveday as the parrot down
at the "Lugger Inn," at Polkimbra, and so crept upstairs to bed to dream of Captain Credence and parrots,
and the "Lugger Inn" in the city of Mansoul, as
though no fiends were shouting without and whirling
sea and sky together in one devil's cauldron.

How long I slept I know not; but I woke with
the glare of a candle in my eyes, to see my mother,
all in white, standing by the bed, and in her eyes an
awful and soul-sickening horror.

"Jasper, Jasper! wake up and listen!"

I suppose I must have been still half asleep, for I

c

lay looking at her with dazzled sight, not rightly knowing whether this vision were real or part of my strange
dreams.

"Jasper, for the love of God wake up!"

At this, so full were her words of mortal fear, I
shook off my drowsiness and sat up in bed, wide awake
now and staring at the strange apparition. My mother
was white as death, and trembling so that the candle
in her hand shook to and fro, casting wild dancing
shadows on the wall behind.

"Oh, Jasper, listen, listen!"

I listened, but could hear nothing save the splashing of spray and rain upon my window, and above it
the voice of the storm; now moaning as a creature
in pain, now rising and growing into an angry roar
whereat the whole house from chimney to base
shook and shuddered, and anon sinking slowly with
loud sobbings and sighings as though the anguish of
a million tortured souls were borne down the blast.

"Mother, I hear nothing but the storm."

"Nothing but the storm! Oh, Jasper, are you
sure you hear nothing but the storm?"

"Nothing else, mother, though that is bad enough."

She seemed relieved a little, but still trembled
sadly, and caught her breath with every fresh roar.
The tempest had gathered fury, and was now raging
as though Judgment Day were come, and earth about
to be blotted out. For some minutes we listened
almost motionless, but heard nothing save the furious

elements; and, indeed, it was hard to believe that any sound on earth could be audible above such a din. At last I turned to my mother and said—

"Mother dear, it is nothing but the storm. You were thinking of father, and that made you nervous. Go back to bed—it is so cold here—and try to go to sleep. What was it you thought you heard?"

"Dear Jasper, you are a good boy, and I suppose you are right, for you can hear nothing, and I can hear nothing now. But, oh, Jasper! it was so terrible, and I seemed to hear it so plainly; though I daresay it was only my——Oh, God! there it is again! listen! listen!"

This time I heard—heard clearly and unmistakably, and, hearing, felt the blood in my veins turn to very ice.

Shrill and distinct above the roar of the storm, which at the moment had somewhat lulled, there rose a prolonged wail, or rather shriek, as of many human voices rising slowly in one passionate appeal to the mercy of Heaven, and dying away in sobbing, shuddering despair as the wild blast broke out again with the mocking laughter of all the fiends in the pit— a cry without similitude on earth, yet surely and awfully human; a cry that rings in my ears even now, and will continue to ring until I die.

I sprang from bed, forced the window open and looked out. The wind flung a drenching shower of spray over my face and thin night-dress, then tore

c 2

past up the hill. I looked and listened, but nothing could be seen or heard; no blue light, nor indeed any light at all; no cry, nor gun, nor signal of distress— nothing but the howling of the wind as it swept up from the sea, the thundering of the surf upon the beach below; and all around, black darkness and impenetrable night. The blast caught the lattice from my hand as I closed the window, and banged it furiously. I turned to look at my mother. She had fallen forward on her knees, with her arms flung across the bed, speechless and motionless, in such sort that I speedily grew possessed with an awful fear lest she should be dead. As it was, I could do nothing but call her name and try to raise the dear head that hung so heavily down. Remember that I was at this time not eight years old, and had never before seen a fainting fit, so that if a sight so like to death bewildered me it was but natural. How long the fit lasted I cannot say, but at last, to my great joy, my mother raised her head and looked at me with a puzzled stare that gradually froze again to horror as recollection came back.

" Oh, Jasper, what could it be?—what could it be?"

Alas! I knew not, and yet seemed to know too well. The cry still rang in my ears and clamoured at my heart; while all the time a dull sense told me that it must have been a dream, and a dull desire bade me believe it so.

" Jasper, tell me—it cannot have been——"

She stopped as our eyes met, and the terrible sus-

picion grew and mastered us, numbing, freezing, paralysing the life within us. I tried to answer, but turned
my head away. My mother sank once more upon her
knees, weeping, praying, despairing, wailing, while the
storm outside continued to moan and sob its passionate
litany.

CHAPTER III.

TELLS OF TWO STRANGE MEN THAT WATCHED THE SEA UPON POLKIMBRA BEACH.

MORNING came at last, and with the first grey light the storm had spent its fury. By degrees my mother had grown calmer, and was now sleeping peacefully upon her bed, worn out with the passion of her terror. I had long ago dressed; but even had I wished to sleep again, curiosity to know the meaning of that awful cry would have been too strong for me. So, as soon as I saw that my mother was asleep, I took my boots in my hand and crept down-stairs. The kitchen looked so ghostly in the dim light, that I had almost resolved to give up my plan and go back, but reflected that it behoved me to play the man, if only to be able to cheer mother when I came back. So, albeit with my heart in my mouth, I drew back the bolt—that surely, for all my care, never creaked so loudly before or since—and stepped out into the cool air. The fresh breeze that smote my cheeks as I sat down outside to put on my boots brought me back to the every-day world—a world that seemed to make the events of the night unreal and baseless, so that I had, with boyish elasticity of temper, almost forgotten all fear as I began to descend the cliff towards Ready-Money Cove.

Before I go any further, it will be necessary to describe in a few words that part of the coast which is the scene of my story. Lantrig, as I have said, looks down upon Ready-Money Cove from the summit of Pedn-glâs, its northern arm. The cove itself is narrow, running in between two scarred and rugged walls of serpentine, and terminating in a little beach of whitest sand beneath a frowning and precipitous cliff. It is easy to see its value in the eyes of smugglers, for not only is the cove difficult of observation from the sea, by reason of its straitness and the protection of its projecting arms, but the height and abruptness of its cliffs also give it seclusion from the land side. For Pedn-glâs on the north rises sheer from the sea, sloping downwards a little as it runs in to join the mainland, but only enough to admit of a rough and winding path at its inmost point, while to the south the cove is guarded by a strange mass of rock that demands a somewhat longer description.

For some distance the cliff ran out as on the north side, but, suddenly breaking off as if cleft by some gigantic stroke, left a gloomy column of rock, attached to it only by an isthmus that stood some six or seven feet above high-water mark. This separate mass went by the name of Dead Man's Rock—a name dark and dreadful enough, but in its derivation innocent, having been but Dodmên, or "the stony headland," until common speech perverted it. For this reason I suppose I ought not to ·call it Dead Man's

Rock, the " Rock " being superfluous, but I give it the name by which it has always been known, being to a certain extent suspicious of those antiquarian gentlemen that sometimes, in their eagerness to restore a name, would deface a tradition.

Let me return to the rock. Under the neck that joins it to the main cliff there runs a natural tunnel, which at low water leads to the long expanse of Pol-kimbra Beach, with the village itself lying snugly at its further end ; so that, standing at the entrance of this curious arch, one may see the little town, with the purple cliffs behind framed between walls of glistening serpentine. The rock is always washed by the sea, except at low water during the spring tides, though not reaching out so far as Pedn-glâs. In colour it is mainly black as night, but is streaked with red stains that bear an awful likeness to blood; and, though it may be climbed—and I myself have done it more than once in search of eggs — it has no scrap of vegetation save where, upon its summit, the gulls build their nests on a scanty patch of grass and wild asparagus.

By the time I had crossed the cove, the western sky was brilliant with the reflected dawn. Above the cliffs behind, morning had edged the flying wrack of indigo clouds with a glittering line of gold, while the sea in front still heaved beneath the pale yellow light, as a child sobs at intervals after the first gust of passion is over-past. The tide was at the ebb, and the fresh breeze dropped as I got under the shadow of Dead Man's

Rock and looked through the archway on to Polkimbra Sands.

Not a soul was to be seen. The long stretch of beach had scarcely yet caught the distinctness of day, but was already beginning to glisten with the gathering light, and, as far as I could see, was desolate. I passed through and clambered out towards the south side of the rock to watch the sea, if perchance some bit of floating wreckage might explain the mystery of last night. I could see nothing.

Stay! What was that on the ledge below me, lying on the brink just above the receding wave? A sailor's cap! Somehow, the sight made me sick with horror. It must have been a full minute before I dared to open my eyes and look again. Yes, it was there! The cry of last night rang again in my ears with all its supreme agony as I stood in the presence of this silent witness of the dead—this rag of clothing that told so terrible a history.

Child as I was, the silent terror of it made me faint and giddy. I shut my eyes again, and clung, all trembling, to the ledge. Not for untold bribes could I have gone down and touched that terrible thing, but, as soon as the first spasm of fear was over, I clambered desperately back and on to the sands again, as though all the souls of the drowned were pursuing me.

Once safe upon the beach, I recovered my scattered wits a little. I felt that I could not repass that dreadful

rock, so determined to go across the sands to Polkimbra, and homewards around the cliffs. Still gazing
at the sea as one fascinated, I made along the length of
the beach. The storm had thrown up vast quantities of
weed, that lined the water's edge in straggling lines
and heaps, and every heap in turn chained and riveted
my shuddering eyes, that half expected to see in each
some new or nameless horror.

I was half across the beach, when suddenly I looked
up towards Polkimbra, and saw a man advancing towards me along the edge of the tide.

He was about two hundred yards from me when I
first looked. Heartily glad to see any human being
after my great terror, I ran towards him eagerly, thinking to recognise one of my friends among the Polkimbra fishermen. As I drew nearer, however, without
attracting his attention—for the soft sand muffled all
sound of footsteps—two things struck me. The first
was that I had never seen a fisherman dressed as this
man was; the second, that he seemed to watch the sea
with an absorbed and eager gaze, as if expecting to find
or see something in the breakers. At last I was near
enough to catch the outline of his face, and knew him
to be a stranger.

He wore no hat, and was dressed in a red shirt and
trousers that ended in rags at the knee. His feet were
bare, and his clothes clung dripping to his skin. In
height he could not have been much above five feet six
inches, but his shoulders were broad, and his whole

appearance, cold and exhausted as he seemed, gave evidence of great strength. His tangled hair hung over a somewhat weak face, but the most curious feature about the man was the air of nervous expectation that marked, not only his face, but every movement of his body. Altogether, under most circumstances, I should have shunned him, but fear had made me desperate. At the distance of about twenty yards I stopped and called to him.

I had advanced somewhat obliquely from behind, so that at the sound of my voice he turned sharply round and faced me, but with a terrified start that was hard to account for. On seeing only a child, however, the hesitation faded out of his eyes, and he advanced towards me. As he approached, I could see that he was shivering with cold and hunger.

"Boy," he said, in an eager and expectant voice, "what are you doing out on the beach so early?"

"Oh, sir!" I answered, "there was such a dreadful storm last night, and we—that is, mother and I—heard a cry, we thought; and oh! I have seen——"

"What have you seen?"—and he caught me by the arm with a nervous grip.

"Only a cap, sir," I said, shrinking—"only a cap; but I climbed up on Dead Man's Rock just now—the rock at the end of the beach—and I saw a cap lying there, and it seemed——"

"Come along and show it to me!" and he began

to run over the sands towards the rock, dragging me helpless after him.

Suddenly he stopped.

"You saw nothing else?" he asked, facing round and looking into my eyes.

"No, sir."

"Nor anybody?"

"Nobody, sir."

"You are sure you saw nobody but me? You didn't happen to see a tall man with black hair, and rings in his ears?"

"Oh, no, sir."

"You'll swear you saw no such man? Swear it now; say, 'So help me, God, I haven't seen anybody on the beach but you.'"

I swore it.

"Say, 'Strike me blind if I have!'"

I repeated the words after him, and, with a hurried look around, he set off running again towards the rock. I had much ado to keep from tumbling, and even from crying aloud with pain, so tight was his grip. Fast as we went, the man's teeth chattered and his limbs shook; his wet clothes flapped and fluttered in the cold morning breeze; his face was drawn and pinched with exhaustion, but he never slackened his pace until we reached Dead Man's Rock. Here he stopped and looked around again.

"Is there any place to hide in hereabouts?" he suddenly asked.

The oddness of the question took me aback; and, indeed, the whole conduct of the man was so strange that I was heartily frightened, and longed greatly to run away. There was no help for it, however, so I made shift to answer—

"There is a nice cave in Ready-Money Cove, which is the next cove to this, sir. The smugglers used to use it because it was hidden so, but——"

I suppose my eyes told him that I was wondering why he should want to hide, for he broke in again—

"Well, show me this cap. Out on the face of this rock, you say—what's the name? Dead Man's Rock, eh? Well, it's an ugly name enough, and an ugly rock enough!" he added, with a shiver.

I climbed up the rock, and he after me, until we gained the ledge where I had stood before. I looked down. The cap was still lying there, and the tide had ebbed still further.

My companion looked for a moment, then, with a short cry, scrambled quickly down and picked it up. To me it had looked like any ordinary sailor's cap, but he examined it, fingered it, and pulled it about, muttering all the time, so that I imagined it must be his own, though at a loss to know why he made so much of recovering it. At last he climbed up again, holding it in his hands, and still muttering to himself—

"His cap, sure enough; nothing in it, though. But he was much too clever a devil. However, he's gone right enough; I knew he must, and this proves it, curse him! Well, I'll wear it. He's not left behind as much as he thought, but mad enough he'd be to think I was his heir. I'll wear it for old acquaintance' sake. Sit down, boy," he said aloud to me; "we're safe here, and can't be seen. I want to talk with you."

The rocky ledge on which we stood was about seven feet long and three or four in breadth. On one side of it ran down the path by which we had ascended; the other end broke off with a sheer descent into the sea of some forty feet in the present state of the tide. High above us rose an unscaleable cliff; at our feet lay a short descent to the ledge on which the cap had rested, and after that another precipice. It was not a pleasant position in which to be left alone with this strange companion, but I was helpless, and perhaps the trace of weakness and a something not altogether evil in his face, gave me some courage. Little enough it was, however, and in mere desperation I sat down on the side by the path. My companion flung himself down on the other side, with his legs dangling over the ledge, and so sat for a minute or two watching the sea.

The early sun was now up, and its oblique rays set the waves dancing with a myriad points of fire. Above us the rock cast its shadow into the green depths below, making them seem still greener and deeper. To my left I could see the shining sands of Polkimbra, still desolate, and, beyond, the purple line of cliffs towards Kynance; on my right the rock hid everything from

view, except the open sea and the gulls returning after
the tempest to inspect and pry into the fresh masses of
weed and wreckage. I looked timidly at my companion. He was still gazing out towards the sea,
apparently deep in thought. The cap was on his head,
and his legs still dangled, while he muttered to himself
as if unconscious of my presence. Presently, however,
he turned towards me.

"Got anything to eat?"

I had forgotten it in my terror, but I had, as I
crossed the kitchen, picked up a hunch of bread to serve
me for breakfast. This, with a half-apologetic air, as
if to deprecate its smallness, I produced from my pocket
and handed to him. He snatched it without a word,
and ate it ravenously, keeping his eye fixed upon me in
the most embarrassing way.

"Got any more?"

I was obliged to confess I had not, though sorely
afraid of displeasing him. He turned still further
towards me, and stared without a word, then suddenly
spoke again.

"What is your name?"

Truly this man had the strangest manner of
questioning. However, I answered him duly—

"Jasper Trenoweth."

"God in heaven! What?"

He had started forward, and was staring at me
with a wild surprise. Unable to comprehend why my
name should have this effect on him, but hopeless of

understanding this extraordinary man's behaviour, I repeated the two words.

His face had turned to an ashy white, but he slowly took his eyes off me and turned them upon the sea, almost as though afraid to meet mine. There was a pause.

"Father by any chance answering to the name of Ezekiel—Ezekiel Trenoweth?"

Even in my fright I can remember being struck with this strange way of speaking, as though my father were a dog; but a new fear had gained possession of me. Dreading to hear the answer, yet wildly anxious, I cried—

"Oh, yes. Do you know him? He was coming home from Ceylon, and mother was so anxious; and then, what with the storm last night and the cry that we heard, we were so frightened! Oh! do you know —do you think——"

My words died away in terrified entreaty; but he seemed not to hear me. Still gazing out on the sea, he said—

"Sailed in the *Belle Fortune*, barque of 600 tons, or thereabouts, bound for Port of Bristol? Oh, ay, I knew him—knew him well. And might this here place be Lantrig?"

"Our house is on the cliff above the next cove," I replied. "But, oh! please tell me if anything has happened to him!"

"And why should anything have happened to

Ezekiel Trenoweth? That's what I want to know. Why should anything have happened to him?"

He was still watching the waves as they danced and twinkled in the sun. He never looked towards me, but plucked with nervous fingers at his torn trousers. The gulls hovered around us with melancholy cries, as they wheeled in graceful circles and swooped down to their prey in the depths at our feet. Presently he spoke again in a meditative, far-away voice—

"Ezekiel Trenoweth, fair, broad, and six foot two in his socks; why should anything have happened to him?"

"But you seem to know him, and know the ship he sailed in. Tell me—please tell me what has happened. Did you sail in the same ship? And, if so, what has become of it?"

"I sailed," said my companion, still examining the horizon, "from Ceylon on the 12th of July, in the ship *Mary Jane*, bound for Liverpool. Consequently, if Ezekiel Trenoweth sailed in the *Belle Fortune* we couldn't very well have been in the same ship, and that's logic," said he, turning to me for the first time with a watery and uncertain smile, but quickly withdrawing his eyes to their old occupation.

But he had lifted a great load from my heart, so that for very joy at knowing my father was not among the crew of the *Mary Jane* I could not speak for a time, but sat watching his face, and thinking how I should question him next.

D

"Sailed in the *Mary Jane*, bound for Liverpool," he repeated, his face twitching slightly, and his hands still plucking at his trousers, "sailed along with—never mind who. And this boy's Ezekiel Trenoweth's son, and I knew him; knew him well." His voice was husky, and he seemed to have something in his throat, but he went on: "Well, it's a strange world. To think of him being dead!" looking at the cap—which he had taken off his head.

"What! Father dead?"

"No, my lad, t'other chap: him as this cap belonged to. Ah, he was a devil, he was. Can't fancy him dead, somehow; seemed as though the water wasn't made as could have drowned him; always said he was born for the gallows, and joked about it. But he's gone this time, and I've got his cap. 'Tis a hard thought that I should outlive him; but, curse him, I've done it, and here's his cap for proof—why, what the devil is the lad staring at?"

During his muttered soliloquy I had turned for a moment to look across Polkimbra Beach, when suddenly my eyes were arrested and my heart again set violently beating by a sight that almost made me doubt whether the events of the morning were not still part of a wild and disordered dream. For there, at about fifty yards' distance, and advancing along the breakers' edge, was another man, dressed like my companion, and also watching the sea.

"What's the matter, boy? Speak, can't you?"

"It's a man."

"A man! Where?"

He made a motion forwards to look over the edge, but checked himself, and crouched down close against the rock.

"Lie down!" he murmured in a hoarse whisper. "Lie down low and look over."

My arm was clutched as though by a vice. I sank down flat, and peered over the edge.

"It's a man," I said, "not fifty yards off, and coming this way. He has on a red shirt, and is watching the sea just as you did. I don't think that he saw us."

"For the Lord's sake don't move. Look; is he tall and dark?"

His terrified excitement was dreadful. I thought I should have had to shriek with pain, so tightly he clutched me, but found voice to answer—

"Yes, he seems tall, and dark too, though I can't well see at——"

"Has he got earrings?"

"I can't see; but he walks with a stoop, and seems to have a sword or something slung round his waist."

"God defend us! that's he! Curse him, curse him! Lie down—lie down, I say! It's death if he catches sight of us."

We cowered against the rock. My companion's face was livid, and his lips worked as though fingers were plucking at them, but made no sound. I never

D 2

saw such abject, hopeless terror. We waited thus for a full minute, and then I peered over the ledge again.

He was almost directly beneath us now, and was still watching the sea. At his side hung a short sheath, empty. I could not well see his face, but the rings in his ears glistened in the sunlight.

I drew back cautiously, for my companion was plucking at my jacket.

"Listen," he said—and his hoarse voice was sunk so low that I could scarcely catch his words—"Listen. If he catches us it's death—death to me, but perhaps he may let you off, though he's a cold-blooded, murderous devil. However, there's no saying but you might get off. Any way, it'll be safest for you to have this. Here, take it quick, and stow it away in your jacket, so as he can't see it. For the love of God, look sharp!"

He took something out of a pocket inside his shirt, and forced it into my hands. What it was I could not see, so quickly he made me hide it in my jacket. But I caught a glimpse of something that looked like brass, and the packet was hard and heavy.

"It's death, I say; but you may be lucky. If he does for me, swear you'll never give it up to him. Take your Bible oath you'll never do that. And look here: if I'm lucky enough to get off, swear you'll give it back. Swear it. Say, 'Strike me blind!'"

He clutched me again. Shaking and trembling, I gave the promise.

"And look, here's a letter; put it away and read it

after. If he does for me—curse him!—you keep what I've given you. Yes, keep it; it's my last Will and Testament, upon my soul. But you ought to go half shares with little Jenny; you ought, you know. You'll find out where she lives in that there letter. But you'll never give it up to him. Swear it. Swear it again."

Again I promised.

"Mind you, if you do, I'll haunt you. I'll curse you dying, and that's an awful thing to happen to a man. Look over again. He mayn't be coming—perhaps he'll go through to the next beach, and then we'll run for it."

Again I peered over, but drew back as if shot; for just below me was a black head with glittering earrings, and its owner was steadily coming up the path towards us.

CHAPTER IV.

THERE was no escape. I have said that the ascent of
Dead Man's Rock was possible, but that was upon the
northern side, from which we were now utterly cut off.
Hemmed in as we were between the sheer cliff and the
precipice, we could only sit still and await the man's
coming. Utter fear had apparently robbed my companion of all his faculties, for he sat, a stony image of
despair, looking with staring, vacant eyes at the spot
where his enemy would appear; while as for me,
dreading I knew not what, I clung to the rock and
listened breathlessly to the sound of the footsteps as
they came nearer and nearer. Presently, within about
fifteen feet, as I guess, of our hiding-place, they
suddenly ceased, and a full, rich voice broke out in
song—

"Sing hey! for the dead man's eyes, my lads;
　　Sing ho! for the dead man's hand;
　For his glittering eyes are the salt sea's prize,
　And his fingers clutch the sand, my lads—
　　Sing ho! how they grip the land!

"Sing hey! for the dead man's lips, my lads;
　　Sing ho! for the dead man's soul.
　At his red, red lips the merrymaid sips
　For the kiss that his sweetheart stole, my lads—
　　Sing ho! for the bell shall toll!"

The words were full and clear upon the morning air—so clear that their weird horror, together with the strangeness of the tune (which had a curious catch in the last line but one) and, above all, the sweetness of the voice, held me spellbound. I glanced again at my companion. He had not changed his position, but still sat motionless, save that his dry lips were again working and twitching as though they tried to follow the words of the song. Presently the footsteps again began to advance, and again the voice broke out—

"So it's hey! for the homeward bound, my lads,
  And ho! for the drunken crew.
For his messmates round lie dead and drowned,
And the devil has got his due, my lads—
  Sing ho! but he——"

He saw us. He had turned the corner, and stood facing us; and as he faced us, I understood my companion's horror. The new-comer wore a shirt of the same red colour as my comrade, and trousers of the same stuff, but less cut and torn with the rocks. At his side hung an empty sheath, that must once have held a short knife, and the handle of another knife glittered above his waistband. But it was his face that fascinated all my gaze. Even had I no other cause to remember it, I could never forget the lines of that wicked mouth, or the glitter in those cruel eyes as their first sharp flash of surprise faded into a mocking and evil smile.

For a minute or so he stood tranquilly watching our

confusion, while the smile grew more and more devilishly bland. Not a word was spoken. What my comrade did I know not, but, for myself, I could not take my eyes from that fiendish face.

At last he spoke: in a sweet and silvery voice, that in company with such eyes was an awful and fantastic lie, he spoke—

"Well, this is pleasant indeed. To run across an old comrade in flesh and blood when you thought him five fathom deep in the salt water is one of the pleasantest things in life, isn't it, lad? To put on sack-cloth and ashes, to go about refusing to be comforted, to find no joy in living because an old shipmate is dead and drowned, and then suddenly to come upon him doing the very same for you—why, there's nothing that com-pares with it for real, hearty pleasure; is there, John? You seem a bit dazed, John: it's too good to be true, you think? Well, it shows your good heart; shows what I call real feeling. But you always were a true friend, always the one to depend upon, eh, John? Why don't you speak, John, and say how glad you are to see your old friend back, alive and hearty?"

John's lips were trembling, and something seemed working in his throat, but no sound came.

"Ah, John, you were always the one for feeling a thing, and now the joy is too much for you. Considerate, too, it was of you, and really kind—but that's you, John, all over—to wear an old shipmate's cap in affectionate memory. No, John, don't deprive yourself of it."

The wretched man felt with quivering fingers for the cap, took it off and laid it on the rock beside me, but never spoke.

"And who is the boy, John? But, there, you were always one to make friends. Everybody loves you; they can't help themselves. Lucy loved you when she wouldn't look at me, would she? You were always so gentle and quiet, John, except perhaps when the drink was in you: and even then you didn't mean any harm; it was only your play, wasn't it, John?"

John's face was a shade whiter, and again something worked in his throat, but still he uttered no word.

"Well, anyhow, John, it's a real treat to see you— and looking so well, too. To think that we two, of all men, should have been on the jib-boom when she struck! By the way, John, wasn't there another with us? Now I come to think of it, there must have been another. What became of him? Did he jump too, John?"

John found speech at last. "No; I don't think he jumped." The words came hoarsely and with difficulty. I looked at him; cold and shivering as he was, the sweat was streaming down his face.

"No? I wonder why."

No answer.

"You're quite sure about it, John? Because, you know, it would be a thousand pities if he were thrown up on this desolate shore without seeing the faces of his old friends. So I hope you are quite sure, John; think again."

"He didn't jump."

"No?"

"He fell."

"Poor fellow, poor fellow!" The words came in the softest, sweetest tones of pity. "I suppose there is no mistake about his melancholy end?"

"I saw him fall. He just let go and fell; it's Bible oath, Captain — it's Bible oath. That's how it happened; he just—let go—and fell. I saw it with my very eyes, and——Captain, it was your knife." To this effect John, with great difficulty and a nervous shifting stare that wandered from the Captain to me until it finally rested somewhere out at sea.

The Captain gave a sharp keen glance, smiled softly, set his thin lips together as though whistling inaudibly, and turned to me.

"So you know John, my boy? He's a good fellow, is John; just the sort of quiet, steady, Christian man to make a good companion for the young. No swearing, drinking, or vice about John Railton; and so truthful, too—the very soul of truth! Couldn't tell a lie for all the riches of the Indies. Ah, you are in luck to have such a friend! It's not often a good companion is such good company."

I looked helplessly at the model of truth to see how he took this tribute; but his eyes were still fixed in that eternal stare at the sea.

"And so, John, you saw him fall? 'Who saw him die?'—'I,' said the soul of truth, 'with my little eye'

—and you have very sharp eyes, John. However, the poor fellow's gone; 'fell off,' you say? I don't wonder you feel it so; but, John, with all our sympathy for the unfortunate dead, don't you think this is a good opportunity for reading the Will? We three, you know, may possibly never meet again, and I am sure our young friend—what name did you say? Jasper?—I am sure that our young friend Mr. Jasper would like the melancholy satisfaction of hearing the Will."

The man's eyes were devilish. John, as he faced about and caught their gaze, looked round like a wild beast at bay.

"Will? What do you mean? I don't know—I haven't got no Will."

"None of your own, John, none of your own; but maybe you might know something of the last Will and Testament of—shall we say—another party? Think, John; don't hurry, think a bit."

"Lord, strike me—— "

"Hush, John, hush! Think of our young friend Mr. Jasper. Besides, you know, you were such a friend of the deceased—such a real friend—and knew all his secrets so thoroughly, John, that I am sure if you only consider quietly, you must remember; you who watched his last moments, who saw him—'fall,' did you say?"

No answer.

"Come, come, John; I'm sorry to press you, but really our young friend and I must insist on an answer. For consider, John, if you refuse to join in our conversation, we shall have to go—reluctantly, of course, but still we shall have to go — and talk somewhere else. Just think how very awkward that would be."

" You devil—you devil ! "

John's voice was still hoarse and low, but it had a something in it now that sounded neither of hope nor fear.

" Well, yes ; devil if you like : but the devil must have his due, you know—

> "And the devil has got his due, my lads —
> Sing hey ! but he waits for you !

Yes, John, devil or no devil, *I'm* waiting for you. As to having my due, why, a lucky fellow like you shouldn't grudge it. Why, you've got Lucy, John : what more can you want ? We both wanted Lucy, but you got her, and now she's waiting at home for you. It would be awkward if I turned up with the news that you were languishing in gaol—I merely put a case, John—and little Jenny wouldn't have many sweet-hearts if it got about that her father—and I suppose you are her father—— "

Before the words were well out of his mouth John had him by the throat. There was a short, fierce struggle, an oath, a gleam of light—and then, with a screech of mortal pain and a wild clutch at the air, my companion fell backwards over the cliff.

*　　*　　*　　*　　*

It was all the work of a moment—a shriek, a splash,

and then silence. How long the silence lasted I cannot tell. What happened next—whether I cried or fainted, looked or shut my eyes—is to me an absolute blank. Only I remember gradually waking up to the fact that the Captain was standing over me, wiping his knife on a piece of weed he had picked up on the rock, and regarding me with a steady stare.

I now suppose that during those few moments my life hung in the balance: but at the time I was too dazed and stunned to comprehend anything. The Captain slowly replaced his knife, hesitated, went to the ledge and peered over, and then finally came back to me.

"Are you the kind of boy that's talkative?" His voice was as sweet as ever, but his eyes were scorching me like live coals.

I suppose I must have signified my denial, for he went on—

"You heard what he called me? He called me a devil; a devil, mark you; and that's what I am."

In my state of mind I could believe anything; so I easily believed this.

"Being a devil, naturally I can hear what little boys say, no matter where I am; and when little boys are talkative I can reach them, no matter how they hide. I come on them in bed sometimes, and sometimes from behind when they are not looking; there's no escaping me. You've heard of Apollyon perhaps? Well, that's who I am."

I had heard of Apollyon in Bunyan; and I had no
doubt he was speaking the truth.

"I catch little boys when they are not looking, and
carry them off, and then their fathers and mothers don't
see any more of them. But they die very slowly, very
slowly indeed—you will find out how if ever I catch you
talking."

But I did not at all want to know; I was quite
satisfied, and apparently he was also; for, after staring
at me a little longer, he told me to get up and go down
the rock in front of him.

The agonies I suffered during that descent no pen
can describe. Every moment I expected to feel my
shoulder gripped from behind, or to feel the hands of
some mysterious and infernal power around my neck.
Close behind me followed my companion, humming—

> " And the devil has got his due, my lads—
>   Sing hey! but he waits for you!"

And though I was far from singing hey! at the prospect, I felt that he meant what he said.

Arrived at the foot of the rock, we passed through
the archway on to Ready-Money Cove. Turning down
to the edge of the sea, the Captain scanned the water
narrowly, but there was no trace of the hapless John.
With a muttered curse, he began quickly to climb out
along the north side of the rock, just above the sea-
level, and looked again into the depths. Once more he
was disappointed. Flinging off his clothes, he dived

again and again, until from sheer exhaustion he crept out, bundled on his shirt and trousers, and climbed back to me.

"Curse him! where can he be?"

I now saw for the first time how terribly worn and famished the man was: he looked like a wolf, and his white teeth were bare in his rage. He had cut his foot on the rock. Still keeping his evil eye upon me, he knelt down by the water's edge and began slowly to bathe the wound.

"By the way, boy, what did you say your name was? Jasper? Jasper what?"

"Trenoweth."

"Ten thousand devils!"

He was on his feet, and had gripped me by the shoulder with a furious clutch. I turned sick and cold with terror. The blue sky swam and circled around me: then came mist and black darkness, lit only by the gleam of two terrible eyes: a shout—and I knew no more.

CHAPTER V.

I CAME gradually back to consciousness amid a buzz of
voices. Uncle Loveday was bending over me, his every
button glistening with sympathy, and his face full of
kindly anxiety. What had happened, or how I came to
be lying thus upon the sand, I could not at first remember, until my gaze, wandering over my uncle's
shoulder, met the Captain's eyes regarding me with a
keen and curious stare.

He was standing in the midst of a small knot of
fishermen, every now and then answering their questions
with a gesture, a shrug of the shoulders, or shake of the
head; but chiefly regarding my recovery and waiting,
as I could see, for me to speak.

"Poor boy!" said Uncle Loveday. "Poor boy!
I suppose the sight of this man frightened him."

I caught the Captain's eye, and nodded feebly.

"Ah, yes, yes. You see," he explained, turning to
the shipwrecked man, "your sudden appearance upset
him : and to tell you the honest truth, my friend, in
your present condition—in your present condition, mind

you—your appearance is perhaps somewhat—startling. Shall we say, startling?"

In answer to my uncle's apologetic hesitation the stranger merely spread out his palms and shrugged his shoulders.

"Ah, yes. A foreigner evidently. Well, well, although our coast is not precisely hospitable, I believe its inhabitants are at any rate free from that reproach. Jasper, my boy, can you walk now? If so, Joseph here will see you home, and we will do our best for the —the—foreign gentleman thus unceremoniously cast on our shores."

My uncle seemed to regard magnificence of speech as the natural due of a foreigner : whether from some hazy conception of "foreign politeness," or a hasty deduction that what was not the language of one part of the world must be that of another, I cannot say. At any rate, the fishermen regarded him approvingly as the one man who could—if human powers were equal to it—extricate them from the present deadlock.

"You do not happen, my friend, to be in a position to inform us whether any—pardon the expression—any corpses are now lying on the rocks to bear witness to this sad catastrophe?"

Again the stranger made a gesture of perplexity.

"Dear, dear! I forgot. Jasper, when you get home, read very carefully that passage about the Tower of Babel. Whatever the cause of that melancholy confusion, its reality is impressed upon us when we stand

E

face to face with one whom I may perhaps be allowed
to call, metaphorically, a dweller in Mesopotamia."

As no one answered, my uncle took silence for consent, and called him so twice—to his own great satisfaction and the obvious awe of the fishermen.

"It is evident," he continued, "that this gentleman
(call him by what name you will) is in immediate need
of food and raiment. If such, as I do not doubt, can
be obtained at Polkimbra, our best course is to accompany him thither. I trust my proposition meets with
his approval."

It met, at any rate, with the approval of the fishermen, who translated Uncle Loveday's speech into
gestures. Being answered with a nod of the head and
a few hasty foreign words, they began to lead the
stranger away in their midst. As he turned to go, he
glanced for the last time at me with a strange flickering
smile, at which my heart grew sick. Uncle Loveday
lingered behind to adjure Joe to be careful of me as we
went up the cliff, and then, with a promise that he
would run in to see mother later in the day, trotted
after the rest. They passed out of sight through the
archway of Dead Man's Rock.

For a minute or so we plodded across the sand in
silence. Joe Roscorla was Uncle Loveday's "man," a
word in our parts connoting ability to look after a
horse, a garden, a pig or two, or, indeed, anything
that came in the way of being looked after. At the
present moment I came in that way; consequently,

after some time spent in reflective silence, Joe began
to speak.

"You'm looking wisht."

"Am I, Joe?"

"Mortal."

There was a pause: then Joe continued—

"I don't hold by furriners: let alone they be so
hard to get along with in the way of convarsing, they
be but a heathen lot. But, Jasper, warn't it beautiful?"

"What, Joe?"

"Why, to see the doctor tackle the lingo. Beautiful, I calls it; but there, he's a scholard, and no mistake, and 'tain't no good for to say he ain't. Not as
ever I've heerd it said."

"But, Joe, the man didn't seem to understand
him."

"Durn all furriners, say I; they be so cursed pig-
headed. Understand? I'll go bail he understood fast
enough."

Joe's opinions coincided so fatally with my certainty
that I held my tongue.

"A dweller in—what did he call the spot, Jasper?"

"Mesopotamia."

"Well, I can't azacly say as I've seen any from them
parts, but they be all of a piece. Thicky chap warn't
in the way when prettiness was sarved out, anyhow.
Of all the cut-throat chaps as ever I see—— Mark
my words, 'tain't no music as he's come after."

E 2

This seemed so indisputable that I did not venture to contradict it.

"I bain't clear about thicky wreck. Likely as not 'twas the one I seed all yesterday tacking about: and if so be as I be right, a pretty lot of lubbers she must have had aboard. Jonathan, the coast-guard, came down to Lizard Town this morning, and said he seed a big vessel nigh under the cliffs toward midnight, or fancied he seed her: but fustly Jonathan's a buffle-head, and secondly 'twas pitch-dark; so if as he swears there weren't no blue light, 'tain't likely any man could see, let alone a daft fule like Jonathan. But, there, 'tain't no good for to blame he; durn Government! say I, for settin' one man, and him a born fule, to mind seven mile o' coast on a night when an airey mouse cou'dn' see his hand afore his face."

"What was the vessel like, Joe, that you saw?"

"East Indyman, by the looks of her; and a passel of lubberin' furriners aboard, by the way she was worked. I seed her miss stays twice myself: so when Jonathan turns up wi' this tale, I says to myself, 'tis the very same. Though 'tis terrible queer he never heard nowt; but he ain't got a ha'porth o' gumption, let alone that by time he's been cloppin' round his seven mile o' beat half a dozen ships might go to kingdom come."

With this, for we had come to the door of Lantrig, Joe bid me good-bye, and turned along the cliffs to seek fresh news at Polkimbra.

Instead of going indoors at once I watched his short,

oddly-shaped figure stride away, and then sat down on
the edge of the cliff for a minute to collect my thoughts.
The day was ripening into that mellow glory which is
the peculiar grace of autumn. Below me the sea, still
flaked with spume, was gradually heaving to rest; the
morning light outlined the cliffs in glistening promi-
nence, and clothed them, as well as the billowy clouds
above, with a reality which gave the lie to my morning's
adventure. The old doorway, too, looked so familiar
and peaceful, the old house so reassuring, that I half
wondered if I had not two lives, and were not coming
back to the old quiet everyday experience again.

Suddenly I remembered the packet and the letter.
I put my hand into my pocket and drew them out. The
packet was a tin box, strapped around with a leathern
band : on the top, between the band and the box, was a
curious piece of yellow metal that looked like the half
of a waist-buckle, having a socket but without any
corresponding hook. On the metal were traced some
characters which I could not read. The tin box was
heavy and plain, and the strap soaking with salt water.

I turned to the letter; it was all but a pulp, and in
its present state illegible. Carefully smoothing it out,
I slipped it inside the strap and turned to hide my
prize; for such was my fear of the man who called himself Apollyon, that I could know no peace of mind
whilst it remained about me. How should I hide it?
After some thought, I remembered that a stone or two
in the now empty cow-house had fallen loose. With a

hasty glance over my shoulder, I crept around and into the shed. The stones came away easily in my hand. With another hurried look, I slipped the packet into the opening, stole out of the shed, and entered the house by the back door.

My mother had been up for some time—it was now about nine o'clock—and had prepared our breakfast. Her face was still pale, but some of its anxiety left it as I entered. She was evidently waiting for me to speak. Something in my looks, however, must have frightened her, for, as I said nothing, she began to question me.

"Well, Jasper, is there any news?"

"There was a ship wrecked on Dead Man's Rock last night, but they've not found anything except——"

"What was it called?"

"The *Mary Jane*—that is—I don't quite know."

Up to this time I had forgotten that mother would want to know about my doings that morning. As an ordinary thing, of course I should have told her whatever I had seen or heard, but my terror of the Captain and the awful consequences of saying too much now flashed upon me with hideous force. I had heard about the *Mary Jane* from the unhappy John. What if I had already said too much? I bent over my breakfast in confusion.

After a dreadful pause, during which I felt, though I could not see, the astonishment in my mother's eyes, she said—

" You don't quite know ? "

" No; I think it must have been the *Mary Jane*, but there was a strange sailor picked up. Uncle Loveday found him, and he seemed to be a foreigner, and he said—I mean—I thought—it was the name, but——"

This was worse and worse. Again at my wits' end, I tried to go on with my breakfast. After awhile I looked up, and saw my mother watching me with a look of mingled surprise and reproach.

" Was this sailor the only one saved ? "

" No—that is, I mean—yes; they only found one."

I had never lied to my mother before, and almost broke down with the effort. Words seemed to choke me, and her saddening eyes filled me with torment.

" Jasper dear, what is the matter with you ? Why are you so strange ? "

I tried to look astonished, but broke down miserably. Do what I would, my eyes seemed to be beyond my control; they would not meet her steady gaze.

" Uncle Loveday is coming up later on. He's looking after the Cap—I mean the sailor, and said he would run in afterwards."

" What is this sailor like ? "

This question fairly broke me down. Between my dread of the Captain and her pained astonishment, I could only sit stammering and longing for the earth to gape and swallow me up. Suddenly a dreadful suspicion struck my mother.

"Jasper! Jasper! it cannot be—you cannot mean—that it was *his* ship?"

"No, mother, no! Father is all right. He said—I mean—it was not his ship."

"Oh! thank God! But you are hiding something from me! What is it? Jasper dear, what are you hiding?"

"Mother, I *think* it was the *Mary Jane*. But it was not father's ship. Father's all right. And, mother, don't ask me any more; Uncle Loveday will tell all about it. And—I'm not very well, mother. I think——"

Want of sleep, indeed, and the excitement of the morning, had broken me down. My mother stilled her desire to hear more, and tenderly saw me to bed, guessing my fatigue, but only dimly apprehensive of anything beyond. In bed I lay all that morning, but could get no sleep. The vengeance of that dreadful man seemed to fill the little room and charge the atmosphere with horror. "I come on them in bed sometimes, and sometimes from behind when they're not looking"—the words rang in my ears, and could not be muffled by the bed-clothes; whilst, if I began to doze, the dreadful burthen of his song—

> "And the devil has got his due, my lads—
> Sing ho! but he waits for you!"—

with the peculiar catch of its lilt, would suddenly make me start up, wide awake, with every nerve in my body dancing to its grisly measure.

At last, towards noon, I dozed off into a restless slumber, but only to see each sight and hear each sound repeated with every grotesque and fantastic variation. Dead Man's Rock rose out of a sea of blood, peopled with hundreds of ghastly faces, each face the distorted likeness of John or the Captain. Blood was everywhere — on their shirts, their hands, their faces, in splashes across the rock itself, in vivid streaks across the spume of the sea. The very sun peered through a blood-red fog, and the waves, the mournful gulls, the echoes from the cliff, took up the everlasting chorus, led by one silvery demoniac voice—

"Sing ho! but he waits for you!"

Finally, as I lay tossing and tormented with this phantom horror in my eyes and ears, the sound died imperceptibly away into the soft hush of two well-known voices, and I opened my eyes to see mother with Uncle Loveday standing at my bedside.

"The boy's a bit feverish," said my uncle's voice; " he has not got over his fright just yet."

"Hush! he's waking!" replied my mother; and as I opened my eyes she bent down and kissed me. How inexpressibly sweet was that kiss after the nightmare of my dream!

"Jasper dear, are you better now? Try to lie down and get some more sleep."

But I was eager to know what news Uncle Loveday had to tell, so I sat up and questioned him. There

was little enough; though, delivered with much pomp,
it took some time in telling.   Roughly, it came to
this :—

A body had been discovered—the body of a small
infant — washed up on the Polkimbra Beach. This
would give an opportunity for an inquest; and, in fact,
the coroner was to arrive that afternoon from Penzance
with an interpreter for the evidence of the strange
sailor, who, it seemed, was a Greek.   Little enough
had been got from him, but he seemed to imply that
the vessel had struck upon Dead Man's Rock from the
south-west, breaking her back upon its sunken base,
and then slipping out and subsiding in the deep water.
It must have happened at high tide, for much coffee
and basket-work was found upon high-water line.   This
fixed the time of the disaster at about 4 a.m., and my
mother's eyes met mine, as we both remembered that it
was about that hour when we heard the wild despairing
cry.   For the rest, it was hopeless to seek information
from the Greek sailor without an interpreter; nor
were there any clothes or identifying marks on the
child's body.   The stranger had been clothed and
fed at the Vicarage, and would give his evidence that
afternoon.   Hitherto, the name of the vessel was unknown.

At this point my mother's eyes again sought mine,
and I feared fresh inquiries about the *Mary Jane;* but,
luckily, Uncle Loveday had recurred to the question
of the Tower of Babel, on which he delivered several

profound reflections. Seeing me still disinclined to explain, she merely sighed, and was silent.

But when Uncle Loveday had broken his fast and, rising, announced that he must drive down to be present at the inquest, to our amazement, mother insisted upon going with him. Having no suspicion of her deadly fear, he laughed a little at first, and quoted Solomon on the infirmities of women to an extent that made me wonder what Aunt Loveday would have said had he dared broach such a subject to that strong-minded woman. Seeing, however, that my mother was set upon going, he desisted at last, and put his cart at her service. Somewhat to her astonishment, as I could see, I asked to be allowed to go also, and, after some entreaty, prevailed. So we all set out behind Uncle Loveday's over-fed pony for Polkimbra.

There was a small crowd around the door of the "Lugger Inn" when we drove up. It appeared that the coroner had just arrived, and the inquest was to begin at once. Meanwhile, the folk were busy with conjecture. They made way, however, for my uncle, who, being on such occasions a person of no little importance, easily gained us entry into the Red Room where the inquiry was about to be held. As we stepped along the passage, the landlord's parrot, looking more than ever like Aunt Elizabeth, almost frightened me out of my wits by crying, "All hands lost! All hands lost! Lord ha' mercy on us!" Its hoarse note still sounded in my ears, when the door opened, and we stood in presence of the "crowner's quest."

I suppose the Red Room of the "Lugger" was full; and, indeed, as the smallest inquest involves at least twelve men and a coroner, to say nothing of witnesses, it must have been very full. But for me, as soon as my foot crossed the threshold, there was only one face, only one pair of eyes, only one terrible presence, to be conscious of and fear. I saw him at once, and he saw me; but, unless it were that his cruel eye glinted and his lips grew for the moment white and fixed, he betrayed no consciousness of my presence there.

The coroner was speaking as we entered, but his voice sounded as though far away and faint. Uncle Loveday gave evidence, and I have a dim recollection of two rows of gleaming buttons, but nothing more. Then Jonathan, the coast-guardsman, was called. He had seen, or fancied he saw, a ship in distress near Gue Graze; had noticed no light nor heard any signal of distress; had given information at Lizard Town. The rocket apparatus had been got out, and searchers had scoured the cliffs as far as Porth Pyg, but nothing was to be seen. The search-party were returning, when they found a shipwrecked sailor in company with a small boy, one Jasper Trenoweth, in Ready-Money Cove.

At the sound of my own name I started, and for the second time since our entry felt the eyes of the stranger question me. At the same time I felt my mother's clasp of my hand tighten, and knew that she saw that look.

The air grew closer and the walls seemed to draw nearer as Jonathan's voice continued its drowsy tale. The afternoon sun poured in at the window until it made the little wainscoted parlour like an oven, but still for me it only lit up one pair of eyes. The voices sounded more and more like those of a dream; the scratching of pens and shuffling of feet were, to my ears, as distant murmurs of the sea, until the coroner's voice called—"Georgio Rhodojani."

Instantly I was wide awake, with every nerve on the stretch. Again I felt his eyes question me, again my mother's hand tightened upon mine, as the stranger stood up and in softest, most musical tones gave his evidence. And the evidence of Georgio Rhodojani, Greek sailor, as translated by Jacopo Rousapoulos, interpreter, of Penzance, was this:—

"My name is Georgio Rhodojani. I am a Greek by birth, and have been a sailor all my life. I was seaman on board the ship which was wrecked last night on your horrible coast. The ship belonged to Bristol, and was homeward bound, but I know neither her name nor the name of her captain."

At this strange opening, amazement fell upon all. For myself, the wild incongruity of this foreign tongue from lips which I had heard utter such fluent and flute-like English swallowed up all other wonder.

After a pause, seeing the marvelling looks of his audience, the witness quietly explained—

"You wonder at this; but I am Greek, and cannot master your hard names. I joined the ship at Colombo as the captain was short of hands. I was wrecked in a Dutch vessel belonging to Dordrecht, off Java, and worked my passage to Ceylon, seeking employment. It is not, therefore, extraordinary that I am so ignorant, and my mouth cannot pronounce your English language, but show me your list of ships and I will point her out to you."

There was a rustling of papers, and a list of East Indiamen was handed up to him: he hastily ran his finger over the pages. Suddenly his face lighted up.

"Ah! this is she!—this is the ship that was wrecked last night!"

The coroner took the paper and slowly read out —"The *James and Elizabeth*, of Bristol. Captain— Antonius Merrydew."

"Ah, yes, that is she. The babe here was the captain's child, born on the voyage. There were eighteen men on board, an English boy, and the captain's wife. The child was born off the African coast. We sailed from Colombo on the 22nd of July last, with a cargo of coffee and sugar. Two days ago we were off a big harbour, of which I do not know the name; but early yesterday morning were abreast of what you call, I think, the Lizard. The wind was S.W., and took us into your terrible bay. All yesterday we were tacking

to get out. Towards evening it blew a gale. The
captain had been ill ever since we passed the Bay of
Biscay. We hoisted no signal, and knew not what to
do, for the captain was sick, and the mate drunk. The
mate began to cry when we struck. I alone got on to
the jib-boom and jumped. What became of the others
I know not, but I jumped on to the rock by which you
found me this morning. The vessel broke up in a very
short time. I heard the men crying bitterly, but the
mate's voice was louder than any. The captain of
course was below, and so, when last I saw them, were
his wife and child, but she might have rushed upon
deck. I was almost sucked back twice, but managed
to scramble up. It was not until daylight that I knew
I was on the mainland, and climbed down to the
sands."

As this strange history proceeded, I know not who
in that little audience was most affected. The jury,
fascinated by the sweet voice of the speaker, as well
as the mystery about the vessel and its unwitnessed
disappearance, leant forward in their seats with strained
and breathless attention. My mother could not take
her eyes off the stranger's face. As he hesitated over
the name of the ship, her very lips grew white in
agonised suspense, but when the coroner read "the *James
and Elizabeth*," she sank back in her seat with a low
"Thank God!" that told me what she had dreaded, and
how terribly. I myself knew not what to think, nor if
my ears had heard aright. Part of the tale I knew to

be a lie; but how much? And what of the *Mary
Jane?* I looked round about. A hush had succeeded
the closing words of Rhodojani. Even the coroner was
puzzled for a moment; but improbable as the evidence
might seem, there was none to gainsay it. I alone,
had they but known it, could give this demon the lie—
I, an unnoticed child.

The coroner put a question or two and then summed
up. Again the old drowsy insensibility fell upon me.
I heard the jury return the usual verdict of "Accidental Death," and, as my mother led me from the
room, the voice of Joe Roscorla (who had been on the
jury) saying, "Durn all foreigners! I don't hold by
none of 'em." As the door slammed behind us,
shutting out at last those piercing eyes, a shrill screech
from the landlord's parrot echoed through the house—

"All hands lost! Lord ha' mercy on us!"

CHAPTER VI.

TELLS HOW A FACE LOOKED IN AT THE WINDOW OF
LANTRIG; AND IN WHAT MANNER MY FATHER CAME
HOME TO US.

My mother and I walked homeward together by way of
the cliffs. We were both silent. My heart ached to
tell the whole story, and prove that my tale of the
Mary Jane was no wanton lie; but fear restrained me.
My mother was busy with her own thoughts. She had
seen, I knew, the glance of intelligence which the
stranger gave me; she guessed that his story was a
lie and that I knew it. What she could not guess was
the horror that held my tongue fastened as with a
padlock. So, both busy with bitter thoughts, we walked
in silence to Lantrig.

The evening meal was no better. My food choked
me, and after a struggle I was forced to let it lie almost
untouched. But when the fire was stirred, the candles
lit, and I drew my footstool as usual to her feet by the
hearth, the old room looked so warm and cosy that my
pale fears began to vanish in its genial glow. I had
possessed myself of the "Pilgrim's Progress," and the
volume, a dumpy octavo, lay on my knee. As I read

F

the story of Christian and Apollyon to its end, a new courage fought in me with my morning fears.

"In this combat no man can imagine, unless he has seen and heard as I did, what yelling and hideous roaring Apollyon made all the time of the fight: he *spake like a dragon*; and, on the other side, what sighs and groans burst from Christian's heart. I never saw him all the while give so much as one pleasant look, till he perceived that he had wounded Apollyon with his two-edged sword; then indeed he did smile and look upward! but it was the dreadfullest sight that ever I saw."

I glanced up at my mother, half resolved. She was leaning forward a little and gazing into the fire, that lit up her pale face and wonderful eyes with a sympathetic softness. I can remember now how sweet she looked and how weary—that tender figure outlined in warm glow against the stern, dark room. And all the time her heart was slowly breaking with yearning for him that came not. I did not know it then; but when does childhood know or understand the suffering of later life? I looked down upon the page once more, turned back a leaf or two, and read:

"Then did Christian begin to be afraid, and to cast in his mind whether to go back or stand his ground. But he considered again that he had no armour for his back, and therefore thought that to turn his back to him might give him greater advantage, with ease to pierce him with his darts; therefore he resolved to venture and stand his ground."

"I come on them in bed sometimes, and sometimes from behind." The words of my Apollyon came across my mind. Should I speak and seek counsel?—What was that?

It was a tear that fell upon my hand as it lay across my mother's lap. Since the day when father left us I had never seen her weep. Was it for my deceit? I looked up again and saw that her eyes were brimming with sorrow. My fears and doubts were forgotten. I would speak and tell her all my tale.

" Mother."

Somewhat ashamed at being discovered, she dried her eyes and tried to smile—a poor pitiful smile, with the veriest ghost of joy in it.

" Yes, Jasper."

" Is Apollyon still alive?"

" He stands for the powers of evil, Jasper, and they are always alive."

" But, I mean, does he walk about the world like a man? Is he *really* alive?"

" Why, no, Jasper. What nonsense has got into your head now?"

" Because, mother, I met him to-day. That is, he said he was Apollyon, and that he would come and carry me off if——"

Half apprehensive at my boldness, I cast an anxious look around as I spoke. Nothing met my eyes but the familiar furniture and the dancing shadows on the wall, until their gaze fell upon the window, and rested there,

F 2

whilst my heart grew suddenly stiff with terror, and my tongue clave to my mouth.

As my voice broke off suddenly, mother glanced at me in expectation. Seeing my fixed stare and dropped jaw, she too looked at the window, then started to her feet with a shriek.

For there, looking in upon us with a wicked smile, was the white face of the sailor Rhodojani.

For a second or two, petrified with horror, we stood staring at it. The evil smile flickered for a moment, baring the white teeth and lighting the depths of those wolfish eyes; then, with a fiendish laugh, vanished in the darkness.

He had, then, told the truth when he promised to haunt me. Beyond the shock of mortal terror, I was but little amazed. It seemed but natural that he should come as he had threatened. Only I was filled with awful expectation of his vengeance, and stood aghast at the consequences of my rashness. By instinct I turned to my mother for protection.

But what ailed her? She had fallen back in her chair and was still staring with parted lips at the dark pane that a minute ago had framed the horrid countenance. When at last she spoke, her words were wild and meaningless, with a dreadful mockery of laughter that sent a swift pang of apprehension to my heart.

"Mother, it is gone. What is the matter?"

Again a few meaningless syllables and that awful laugh.

And so throughout that second awful night did she mutter and laugh, whilst I, helpless and terror-stricken, strove to soothe her and recall her to speech and sense. The slow hours dragged by, and still I knelt before her waiting for the light. The slow clock sounded the hours, and still she gave no sign of understanding. The mice crept out of their accustomed holes and jumped back startled at her laugh. The fire died low and the candles died out; the wind moaned outside, the tamarisk branches swished against the pane; the hush of night, with its intervals of mysterious sound, held the house; but all the time she never ceased to gaze upon the window, and every now and then to mutter words that were no echo of her mind or voice. Daylight, with its premonitory chill, crept upon us at last, but oh, how slowly! Daylight looked in and found us as that cruel sight had left us, helpless and alone.

But with daylight came some courage. Had there been neighbours near Lantrig I should have run to summon them before, but Polkimbra was the nearest habitation, and Polkimbra was almost two miles off, across a road possessed by horrors and perhaps tenanted by that devilish face. And how could I leave my mother alone? But now that day had come I would run to Lizard Town and see Uncle Loveday. I slipped on my boots, unbolted the door, cast a last look at my mother still sitting helpless and vacant of soul, and rushed from the house. The sound of her laughter rang in my ears as the door closed behind me.

Weak, haggard and wild of aspect, I ran and stumbled along the cliffs. Dead Man's Rock lay below wrapped in a curtain of mist. Thick clouds were rolling up from seaward; the grey light of returning day made sea, sky and land seem colourless and wan. But for me there was no sight but Polkimbra ahead. As I gained the little village I ran down the hill to the "Lugger" and knocked upon the door. Heavens! how long it was before I was answered. At last the landlady's head appeared at an upper window. With a few words to Mrs. Busvargus, which caused that worthy soul to dress in haste with many ejaculations, I raced up the hill again and across the downs for Lizard Town. My strength was giving way; my head swam, my sides ached terribly, my legs almost refused to obey my will, and a thousand lights danced and sparkled before my eyes, but still I kept on, now staggering, now stumbling, but still onward, nor stopped until I stood before Uncle Loveday's door.

There at last I fell; but luckily against the door, so that in a moment or two I became conscious of Aunt Elizabeth standing over me and regarding me as a culprit caught red-handed in some atrocious crime.

"Hoity-toity! What's the matter now? Why, it's Jasper! Well, of all the freaks, to come knocking us up! What's the matter with the boy? Jasper, what ails you?"

Incoherently I told my story, at first to Aunt Elizabeth alone, but presently, in answer to her call,

Uncle Loveday came down to hear. The pair stood silent and wondering.

They were not elaborately dressed. Aunt Elizabeth, it is true, was smothered from head to foot in a gigantic Inverness cape, that might have been my uncle's were it not obviously too large for that little man. Her nightcap, on the other hand, was ostentatiously her own. No other woman would have had strength of mind to wear such a head-dress. Uncle Loveday's costume was even more singular; for the first time I saw him without a single brass button, and for the first time I understood how much he owed to those decorations. His first words were—

"Jasper, I hope you are telling me the truth. Your mother told me yesterday of some cock-and-bull story concerning the *Anna Maria* or some such vessel. I hope this is not another such case. I have told you often enough where little boys who tell falsehoods go to."

My white face must have been voucher for my truth on this occasion; for Aunt Elizabeth cut him short with the single word "Breakfast," and haled me into the little parlour whilst the pair went to dress.

As I waited, I heard the sound of the pony without, and presently Aunt Elizabeth returned in her ordinary costume to worry the small servant who laid breakfast. Whether Uncle Loveday ever had that meal I do not know to this day, for whilst it was being prepared I saw him get into the little carriage and drive off towards Lantrig. I was told that I could not go until I had

eaten ; and so with a sore heart, but no thought of dis-
obedience, I turned to breakfast.

The meal had scarcely begun when the door opened
and Master Thomas Loveday sauntered into the room.
Master Thomas Loveday, a youth of some eight sum-
mers, was, in default of a home of his own, quartered
permanently upon my uncle, whose brother's son he was.
His early days had been spent in India. After, however, both father and mother had succumbed to the
climate of Madras, he was sent home to England, and
had taken root in Lizard Town. Hitherto, his life had
been one long lazy slumber. Whenever we were sent,
on his rare visits to Lantrig, to "play together," as
old age always rudely puts it, his invariable rule had
been to go to sleep on the first convenient spot. Consequently his presence embarrassed me not a little. He
was a handsome boy, with blue eyes, long lashes, fair
hair, and a gentle habit of speech. When I came to
know him better, I learnt the quick wit and subtle
power that lay beneath his laziness of manner ; but at
present the soul of Thomas Loveday slept.

He was certainly not wide awake when he entered
the room. With a sleepy nod at me, and no trace of
surprise at my presence, he pursued his meal. Occasion-
ally, as Aunt Elizabeth put a fresh question, he would
regard her with a long stare, but otherwise gave no
sign of animation. This finally so exasperated my aunt
that she addressed him—

"Thomas, do not stare."

Thomas looked mildly surprised for a moment, and then inquired, " Why not ? "

" Does the boy think I'm a wild Indian ? " The question was addressed to me, but I could not say, so kept a discreet silence. Thomas relieved me from my difficulty by answering, " No," thoughtfully.

" Then why stare so ? I'm sure I don't know what boys are made of, nowadays."

" Slugs and snails and puppy-dogs' tails," was the dreamy answer.

" Thomas, how dare you ? I should like to catch the person who taught you such nonsense. I'd teach him ! "

" It was Uncle Loveday," remarked the innocent Thomas.

There was an awful pause; which I broke at length by asking to be allowed to go. Aunt Elizabeth saw her way to getting rid of the offender.

" Thomas, you might walk with Jasper over the downs to Lantrig. It will be nice exercise for you."

" It may be exercise, aunt, but——"

" Do not answer me, but go. Where do you expect little boys will go to, who are always idle ? "

" Sleep ? " hazarded Thomas.

" Thomas, you shall learn the whole of Dr. Watts's poem on the sluggard before you go to bed this night."

At this the boy slowly rose, took his cap, stood before her, and solemnly repeated the whole of that melancholy tale, finishing the last line at the door and

gravely bowing himself out.   I followed, awestruck, and
we set out in silence.

At first, anxiety for my mother possessed all my
thoughts, but presently I ventured to congratulate Tom
on his performance.

"She has read it to me so often," replied he, "that
I can't help knowing it.   I hate Dr. Watts, and I love
to go to sleep.   I dream such jolly things.   Sleep is
ever so much nicer than being awake, isn't it?"

I wanted sleep, having had but little for two nights,
and could therefore agree with him.

"You get such jolly adventures when you dream,"
said Tom, reflectively.

I had been rather surfeited with adventures lately,
so held my peace.

"Now, real life is so dull.   If one could only meet
with adventures——"

I caught the sound of wheels behind us, and turned
round.   We had struck off the downs on to the high
road.   A light gig with one occupant was approaching
us.   As it drew near the driver hailed us.

"Hullo! lads, is this the road for Polkimbra?"

The speaker was a short, grizzled, seafaring man,
with a kind face and good-humoured mouth.   He drove
execrably, and pulled his quiet mare right back upon her
haunches.

I answered that it was.

"Are you bound for there?   Yes?   Jump up then.
I'll give you a lift."

I looked at Tom; he, of course, was ready for anything that would save trouble, so we clambered up beside
the stranger.

"There was a wreck there yesterday, I've heard,"
said he, after we had gone a few yards, "and an inquest,
and, by the tale I heard, a lot of lies told."

I started. The man did not notice it, but continued—

"Maybe you've heard of it. Well, it's a rum world,
and a fine lot of lies gets told every day, but you don't
often get so accomplished a liar as that chap—what's
his name? Blessed if I can tackle it; not but what it's
another lie, I'll wager."

I was listening intently. He continued more to
himself than to us—

"An amazing liar, though I wonder what his game
was. It beats me; beats me altogether. The '*James
and Elizabeth*,' says he, as large as life. I take it the
fellow couldn't 'a been fooling who brought the news to
Falmouth. Didn't know me from Adam, and was fairly
put about when he saw how I took it, and, says he,
' 'twas the *James and Elizabeth* the chap said, as sure as
I stand here.' Boy, do you happen to know the name
of the vessel that ran ashore here, night afore last?"

I had grown accustomed to being asked this dreadful
question, and therefore answered as bravely as I could,
"The *James and Elizabeth*, sir."

"Captain's name?"

"Captain Antonius Merrydew."

"Ah, poor chap! He was lying sick below when she struck, wasn't he? And he had a wife aboard, and a child born at sea, hadn't he? Fell sick in the Bay o' Biscay, like any land-lubber, didn't he? Why, 'tis like play-actin'; damme! 'tis better than that."

With this the man burst into a shout of laughter and slapped his thigh until his face grew purple with merriment.

"What d'ye think of it, boy, for a rare farce? Was ever the likes of it heard? Captain Antonius Merrydew sick in the Bay o' Biscay! Ho, ho! Where's play-actin' beside it?"

"Wasn't it true, sir?"

"True? God bless the boy! Look me in the face: look me in the face, and then ask me if it's true."

"But why should it not be true, sir?"

"Because I am Captain Antonius Merrydew!"

For the rest of the journey I sat stunned. Thomas beside me was wide awake and staring, seeing his way to an adventure at last. It was I that dreamed—I heard without comprehension the rest of the captain's tale:— how he had come, after a quick passage from Ceylon, to Falmouth with the barque *James and Elizabeth*, just in time to hear of this monstrous lie; how he was unmarried, and never had a day's illness in his life; how, suspecting foul play, he had hired a horse and gig with a determination to drive over to Polkimbra and learn the truth; how a horse and gig were the most cursedly obstinate of created things; with much besides in the way of oaths and ejaculations. All this I must have heard, for memory brought them back later; but I did not listen. My life and circumstances had got the upper hand of me, and were dancing a devil's riot.

At last, after much tacking and porting of helm, we navigated Polkimbra Hill and cast anchor before the "Lugger." There we alighted, thanked the captain, and left him piping all hands to the horse's head. His cheery voice followed us down to the sands.

We had determined to cut across Polkimbra Beach and climb up to Lantrig by Ready-Money Cliffs, as in order to go along the path above the cliffs we should have to ascend Polkimbra Hill again. The beach was so full of horror to me that without a companion I could not have crossed it; but Tom's presence lent me courage. Tom was nearer to excitement than I had ever seen him; he grew voluble; praised the captain, admired his talk, and declared adventure to be abroad in the air— in fact, threw up his head as though he scented it.

Yes, adventure was in the air. It was not exactly to my taste, however, nor did the thought of my poor mother at home make me more sympathetic with Tom's ecstasy; so whilst he chattered I strode gloomily forward over the beach.

The day was drawing towards noon. October was revelling in an after-taste of summer, and smiled in broad glory over beach and sea. A light breeze bore eastward a few fleecy clouds, and the waves danced and murmured before its breath. Their salt scent was in

our nostrils, and the glitter of the sand in our eyes.
Black and sombre in the clear air, Dead Man's Rock
rose in gloomy isolation from the sea, while the sea-
birds swept in glistening circles round its summit. But
what was that at its base?

Seemingly, a little knot of men stood at the water's
edge. As we drew nearer I could distinguish their
forms but not their occupation, for they stood in a circle,
intent on some object in their midst concealed from our
view. Presently, however, they fell into a rough line
as though making for the archway to Ready-Money
Cove. Something they carried among them, and continually stooped over; but what it was I could not see.
Their pace was very slow, but they turned into the arch
and were disappearing, when I caught sight of the uncouth little figure of Joe Roscorla among the last, and
ran forward, hailing him by name.

At the sound of my voice Joe started, turned round
and made a slow pause; then, with a few words to his
neighbour, came quickly towards me. As he drew
near, I saw that his face was white and his manner full
of embarrassment; but he put on a smile, and spoke
first—

"Why, Jasper, what be doin' along here?"

"I'm going home. Has Uncle Loveday seen mother?
And is she better?"

"Aw iss, he've a seen her an' she be quieter: least-
ways, he be bound to do her a power o' good. But
what be goin' back for? 'Tain't no use botherin' in-

doors wi' your mother in thicky wisht state. Run about an' get some play."

"What were you doing down by the Rock just now, Joe?"

Joe hesitated for a while; stammered, and then said, " Nuthin."

" But, Joe, you were doing something: what were you carrying over to Ready-Money?"

" Look-ee here, my lad, run an' play, an' doan't ax no questions. 'Tain't for little boys to ax questions. Now I comes to think of it, Doctor said as you was to stay over to Lizard Town, 'cos there ain't no need of a passel of boys in a sick house: so run along back."

Joe's voice had a curious break in it, and his whole bearing was so unaccountable that I did not wonder when Tom quietly said—

" Joe, you're telling lies."

Now Joe was, in an ordinary way, the soul of truth: so I looked for an explosion. To my surprise, however, he took no notice of the insult, but turned again to me—

" Jasper, lad, run along back: do'ee now."

His voice was so full of entreaty that a sudden suspicion took hold of me.

" Joe, is—has anything happened to mother?"

" Noa, to be sure: she'll be gettin' well fast enough, if so be as you let her be."

" Then I'll go and see Uncle Loveday, and find out if I am really to go back."

I made a motion to go, but he caught me quickly by the arm.

"Now, Jasper, doan't-'ee go: run back, I tell'ee — run back — I tell'ee you *must* go back."

His words were so earnest and full of command that I turned round and faced him. Something in his eyes filled me with sickening fear.

"Joe, what were you carrying?"

No answer.

"Joe, what were you carrying?"

Still no answer; but an appealing motion of the hand.

"Joe, what was it?"

"Go back!" he said, hoarsely. "Go back!"

"I will not, until I have seen what you were carrying."

"Go back, boy: for God's sake go back!"

I wrenched myself from his grasp, and ran with all speed. Joe and Tom followed me, but fear gave me fleetness. Behind I could hear Joe's panting voice, crying, "Come back!" but the agony in his tone set me running faster. I flew through the archway, and saw the small procession half-way across the cove. At my shout they halted, paused, and one or two advanced as if to stop me. But I dashed through their hands into their midst, and saw—God in heaven! What? The drowned face of my father!

Tenderly as women they lifted me from the body. Gently and with tear-stained faces, they stood around

and tried to comfort me. Reverently, while Joe Roscorla held me in his arms behind, they took up the
corpse of him they had known and loved so well, and
carried it up the cliffs to Lantrig. As they lifted the
latch and bore the body across the threshold, a yell of
maniac laughter echoed through the house to the very
roof.

And this was my father's " Welcome Home ! "

Nay, not all ; for as Uncle Loveday started to his
feet, the door behind him flew open, and my mother, all
in white, with very madness in her eyes, rushed to the
corpse, knelt, caught the dead hand, kissed and fondled
the dead face, cooing and softly laughing the while with
a tender rapture that would have moved hell itself to
pity.

In this manner it was that these two fond lovers
met.

G

CHAPTER VII.

TELLS HOW UNCLE LOVEDAY MADE A DISCOVERY; AND
WHAT THE TIN BOX CONTAINED.

An hour afterwards I was sitting at the bedside of my
dying mother. The shock of that terrible meeting had
brought her understanding — and death: for as her
mind returned her life ebbed away. White and placid
she lay upon her last bed, and spoke no word; but in
her eyes could be read her death-warrant, and by me
that which was yet more full of anguish, a tender but
unfading reproach. This world is full of misunder-
standings, but seldom is met one so desperate. How
could I tell her now? And how could she ever understand? It was all too late. "Too late! too late!"
the words haunted me there as the bright sun struggled
through the drawn blind and illumined her saintly
face. They and the look in her sweet eyes have haunted
me many a day since then, and would be with me yet,
did I not believe she knows the truth at last. There
are too many ghosts in my memories for Heaven to
lightly add this one more.

She was dying—slowly and peacefully dying, and
this was the end of her waiting. He had returned at

last, this husband for whose coming she had watched so
long. He had returned at last, after all his labour, and
had been laid at her feet a dead man. She was free to
go and join her love. To me, child as I was, this was
sorely cruel. Death, as I know now, is very merciful
even when he seems most merciless, but as I sat and
watched the dear life slowly drift away from me, it was
a hard matter to understand.

The pale sunlight came, and flickered, and went ;
but she lay to all seeming unchanged. Her pulse's
beat was failing — failing ; the broken heart feebly
struggling to its rest ; but her sad eyes were still the
same, appealing, questioning, rebuking—all without
hope of answer or explanation. So were they when the
sobbing fishermen lifted her from the body, so would
they be until closed for the last sleep. It was very
cruel.

My father's body lay in the room below, with Uncle
Loveday and Mrs. Busvargus for watchers. Now and
again my uncle would steal softly upstairs, and as softly
return with hopelessness upon his face. The clock
downstairs gave the only sound I heard, as it marked
the footsteps of the dark angel coming nearer and
nearer. Twice my mother's lips parted as if to speak ;
but though I bent down to catch her words, I could
hear no sound.

So, as I sat and watched her waxen face, all the
sweet memories of her came back in a sad, reproachful
train. Once more we sat together by the widowed hearth,

G 2

reading: once more we stood upon the rocky edge of Pedn-glâs and looked into the splendours of the summer sunset "for father's ship:" once more we knelt together in Polkimbra Church, and prayed for his safe return: once more I heard that sweet, low voice—once more? Ah, never, never more!

Uncle Loveday stole into the room on tip-toe, and looked at her; then turned and asked—

"Has she spoken yet?"

"No."

He was about to leave when the lips parted again, and this time she spoke—

"He is coming, coming. Hush! that is his step!"

The dark eyes were ablaze with expectation: the pale cheek aglow with hope. I bent down over the bed, for her voice was very low.

"He is coming, I know it. Listen! Oh, husband, come quicker, quicker!"

Alas! poor saint, the step you listen for has gone before, and is already at the gate of heaven.

"He is here! Oh, husband, husband, you have come for me!"

A moment she sat up with arms outstretched, and glory in her face; then fell back, and the arms that caught her were the arms of God.

*　　*　　*　　*　　*　　*

After the first pang of bereavement had spent itself, Uncle Loveday got me to bed, and there at last I slept.

The very bewilderment of so much sorrow enforced sleep, and sleep was needed : so that, worn out with watching and excitement, I had not so much as a dream to trouble me. It was ten o'clock in the morning when I awoke, and saw my uncle sitting beside the bed. Another sun was bright in the heavens outside : the whole world looked so calm and happy that my first impulse was to leap up and run, as was my custom, to mother's room. Then my eyes fell on Uncle Loveday, and the whole dreadful truth came surging into my awakened brain. I sank back with a low moan upon the pillow.

Uncle Loveday, who had been watching me, stepped to the bed and took my hand.

" Jasper, boy, are you better ? "

After a short struggle with my grief, I plucked up heart to answer that I was.

" That's a brave boy. I asked, because I have yet to tell you something. I am a doctor, you know, Jasper, and so you may take my word when I say there is no good in what is called ' breaking news.' It is always best to have the pain over and done with ; at least, that's my experience. Now, my dear boy, though God knows you have sorrow enough, there is still something to tell : and if you are the boy I take you for, it is best to let you know at once."

Dimly wondering what new blow fortune could deal me, I sat up in bed and looked at my uncle helplessly.

" Jasper, you think—do you not—that your father
was drowned ? "

" Of course, uncle."

" He was not drowned."

" Not drowned ! "

" No, Jasper, he was murdered."

The words came slowly and solemnly, and even with
the first shock of surprise the whole truth dawned upon
me. This, then, explained the effect my name had
wrought upon those two strange men. This was the
reason why, as we sat together upon Dead Man's Rock,
the eyes of John Railton had refused to meet mine : this
was the reason why his murderer had gripped me so
viciously upon Ready-Money Beach. These few words
of my uncle's began slowly to piece together the
scattered puzzle of the last two days, so that I half
guessed the answer as I asked—

" Murdered !   How ? "

" He was stabbed to death."

I knew it, for I remembered the empty sheath that
hung at Rhodojani's waist, and heard again Railton's
words, " Captain, it was your knife." As certainly as
if I had fitted the weapon to its case, I knew that man
had prompted father's murder. Even as I knew it
my terror of him faded away, and a blind and helpless
hate sprang up in its stead : helpless now, but some
day to be masterful and worthy of heed. That the man
who called himself Georgio Rhodojani was guilty of one
death, I knew from the witness of my own eyes : that

he had two more lives upon his black account—for the hand that struck my father had also slain my mother— I knew as surely.

"And the devil has got his due, my lads!"

No, not yet : there was still one priceless soul for him to wait for.

"He was stabbed," repeated Uncle Loveday, "stabbed to the heart, and from behind. I found this blade as I examined your poor father's body. It was broken off close to the hilt, and left in the wound, which can hardly have bled at all. Death must have been immediate. It's a strange business, Jasper, and a strange blade by the look of it."

I took the blade from his hand. It was about four inches in length, sharp, and curiously worked : one side was quite plain, but the other was covered with intricate tracery, and down the centre, bordered with delicate fruit and flowers, I spelt out the legend " RICORDATI."

" What does that word mean ? " I asked, as I handed back the steel. My voice was so calm and steady that Uncle Loveday glanced at me for a moment in amazement before he answered—

" It's not Latin, Jasper, but it's like Latin, and I should think must mean ' Remember,' or something of the sort."

" ' Remember,' " I repeated. " I will, uncle. As surely as father was murdered, I will remember—when the time comes."

They were strange words from a boy. My uncle looked at me again, but doubtless thinking my brain turned with grief, said nothing.

"Have you told anybody?" I asked at length.

"I have seen nobody. There will be an inquest, of course, but in this case an inquest can do nothing. Murderer and murdered have both gone to their account. By the way, I suppose nothing has been seen of the man who gave evidence. It was an unlikely tale; and this makes it the more suspicious. Bless my soul!" said my uncle, suddenly, "to think it never struck me before! Your father was to sail in the *Belle Fortune*, and this man gave the name of the ship as the *James and Elizabeth*."

"It was the *Belle Fortune*, and the man told a falsehood."

"I suppose it must have been."

"I know it was."

"Know? How do you know?"

"Because the *James and Elizabeth* is lying at this moment in Falmouth Harbour, and her captain is down at the 'Lugger.'"

Thereupon I told how I had met with Captain Antonius Merrydew. Nay, more, for my heart ached for confidence, I recounted the whole story of my meeting with John Railton, and the struggle upon Dead Man's Rock. Every word I told, down to the dead man's legacy—the packet and letter which I hid in the cow-house. As the tale proceeded my uncle's eyes grew wider and wider with astonishment. But I held on calmly and resolutely to the end, nor after the first shock of wonderment did he doubt my sanity or truthfulness, but grew more and more gravely interested.

When I had finished my narrative there was a long silence. Finally Uncle Loveday spoke—

"It's a remarkable story—a very remarkable story," he said, slowly and thoughtfully. "In all my life I have never heard so strange a tale. But the man must be caught. He cannot have gone far, if, as you say, he was here at Lantrig only the night before last. I expect they are on the look-out for him down at Polkimbra since they have heard the captain's statement; but all the same I will send off Joe Roscorla, who is below, to make sure. I must have a pipe, Jasper, to think this over. As a general rule I am not a smoker: your aunt does not—ahem!—exactly like the smell. But it collects the thoughts, and this wants thinking over. Meanwhile, you might dress if you feel well enough. Run to the shed and get the packet; we will read it over together when I have finished my pipe. It is a remarkable story," he repeated, as he slowly opened the door, "a most marvellous story. I must have a pipe. A most—remarkable—tale."

With this he went downstairs and left me to dress.

I did so, and ran downstairs to the cow-shed. No one had been there. With eager fingers I tore away the bricks from the crumbling mortar, and drew out my prize. The buckle glittered in the light that stole through the gaping door. All was safe, and as I left it.

Clutching my treasure, I ran back to the house and found Mrs. Busvargus spreading the midday meal. Until that was over, I knew that Uncle Loveday would not attack the mystery. He was sitting outside in the front garden smoking solemnly, and the wreaths of his pipe, curling in through the open door, filled the house with fragrance.

I crept upstairs to my mother's door, and reverently entered the dim-lit room. They had laid the two dead lovers side by side upon the bed. Very peacefully they slept the sleep that was their meeting—peacefully as though no wickedness had marred their lives or wrought their death. I could look upon them calmly now. My father had left his heritage—a heritage far different from that which he went forth to win; but I accepted it nevertheless. Had they known, in heaven, the full extent of that inheritance, would they not, as I kissed their dead lips in token of my acceptance, have given some sign to stay me? Had I known, as I bent over them, to what the oath in my heart would bring me, would I even then have renounced it? I cannot say. The dead lips were silent, and only the dead know what will be.

Uncle Loveday was already at table when I descended. But small was our pretence of eating. Mrs. Busvargus, it is true, had lost no appetite through sorrow; but Mrs. Busvargus was accustomed to such

scenes, and in her calling treated Death with no more
to-do than she would a fresh customer at her husband's
inn.   Long attendance at death-beds seemed to have
given that good woman a perennial youth, and certainly
that day she seemed to have lost the years which I had
gained.   Uncle Loveday made some faint display of
heartiness; but it was the most transparent feigning.
He covered his defection by pressing huge helpings
upon me, so that my plate was bidding fair to become
a new Tower of Babel, when Mrs. Busvargus interposed
and swept the meal away; after which she disappeared
into the back kitchen to " wash up," and was no more
seen ; but we heard loud splashings at intervals as if
she had found a fountain, and were renewing her youth
in it.

Left to ourselves, we sat silent for a while, during
which Uncle Loveday refilled and lit his pipe and
plunged again into thought, with his eyes fixed on the
rafters.   Whether because his cogitations led to something, or the tobacco had soothed him sufficiently, he
finally turned to me and asked—

" Have you got that packet? "

I produced it.   He took his big red handkerchief
from his pocket, spread it on the table, and began slowly
to undo the strap.   Then after arranging apart the
buckle, the letter, and the tin box, he inquired—

" Was it like this when the man gave it to you ? "

" No, the letter was separate.   I slipped it under
the strap to keep it safe."

"It seems to me," said my uncle, adjusting his spectacles and unfolding the paper, "illegible, or almost so. It has evidently been thoroughly soaked with salt water. Come here and see if your young eyes can help me to decipher it."

We bent together over the blurred handwriting. The letter was evidently in a feminine hand; but the characters were rudely and inartistically formed, while every here and there a heavy down-stroke or flourish marred the beauty of the page. Wherever such thick lines occurred the ink had run and formed an illegible smear. Such as it was, with great difficulty, and after frequent trials, we spelt out the letter as follows:—

"The Welc . . . Home, Barbican, Plymo.

"My Deerest Jack,—This to hope it will find You quite well, as it leaves Me at present. Also to say that I hope this voyage . . . *new Leaf* with Simon as Company, who is a *Good Friend*, though, as you well know, I did not think . . . came *courting* me. But it is for the best, and . . . liquor . . . which I pray to Heaven may begin happier Days. Trade is very poor, and I do not know . . . little Jenny, who is getting on *Famously* with her Schooling. She keeps the Books already, which is a great saving . . . looks in often and sits in the parlour. He says as you have Done Well to be . . . *Ware*, but misdoubts Simon, which I tell him must be wrong, for it was him that advised . . . the fuss and warned against liquor, which he never took Himself. Jenny is so Fond of her Books, and says she will *teech you to write* when you come home, which will be a great *Comfort*, you being away so long and never a word. And I am doing wonders under her teaching, which I dare say she will let you know of it all in the letter she is writing to go along with this . . . Simon to write for you, who is a . . . scholar, which is natural . . . in the office. So that I wonder he left it, having no taste for the

you know, he could not possibly have heard of Amos Trenoweth's Will."

"You and aunt were the only people father told of it."

"Quite so; and your father (excuse me, Jasper) not being a born fool, naturally didn't cry his purpose about the streets of Plymouth when he took his passage. Still, it's curious. Your father sailed from Plymouth and this pair of rascals sailed from Plymouth—not that there's anything in that; hundreds sail out of the Sound every week, and we have nothing to show when Simon and John started—it may have been before your father. But look here, Jasper, what do you make of that?"

I bent over the letter, and where my uncle's finger pointed, read, "He says as you have Done Well to be . . . *Ware*."

"Well, uncle?"

"Well, my boy; what do you make of it?"

"I can make nothing of it."

"No? You see that solitary word '*Ware*'?"

"Yes."

"What was the ship called in which your father sailed?"

"The *Golden Wave*."

"That's it, the *Golden Wave*. Now, what do you make of it?"

My uncle leaned back in his chair and looked at me over his spectacles, with the air of one who has played his trump card and watches for its effect. A certain consciousness of merit and expectancy of approbation animated his person; his reasoning staggered me, and he saw it, nor was wholly displeased. After waiting some time for my reply, he added—

"Of course I may be wrong, but it's curious. I do not think I am wrong, when I mark what it proves. It proves, first, that these two ruffians—for ruffians they both were, as we must conclude, in spite of John Railton's melancholy end — it proves, I say, that these two sailed along with your father. They come home with him, are wrecked, and your father's body is found—murdered. Evidence, slight evidence, but still worthy of attention, points to them. Now, if it could be proved that they knew, at starting or before, of your father's purpose, it would help us; and, to my mind, this letter goes far to prove that wickedness of some sort was the cause of their going. What do you think?"

Uncle Loveday cleared his throat and looked at me again with professional pride in his diagnosis. There was a pause, broken only by Mrs. Busvargus splashing in the back kitchen.

"Good heavens!" said my uncle, "is that woman taking headers? Come, Jasper, what do you think?"

"I think," I replied, "we had better look at the tin box."

"Bless my soul! There's something in the boy, after all. I had clean forgotten it."

The box was about six inches by four, and some

four inches in depth. The tin was tarnished by the sea, but the cover had been tightly fastened down and secured with a hasp and pin. Uncle Loveday drew out the pin, and with some difficulty raised the lid. Inside lay a tightly-rolled bundle of papers, seemingly un-injured. These he drew out, smoothed, and carefully opened.

As his eyes met the writing, his hand dropped, and he sank back—a very picture of amazement—in his chair.

" My God ! "

" What's the matter ? "

" It's your father's handwriting ! "

I looked at this last witness cast up by the sea and read, " The Journal of Ezekiel Trenoweth, of Lantrig."

H

CHAPTER VIII.

CONTAINS THE FIRST PART OF MY FATHER'S JOURNAL; SETTING FORTH HIS MEETING WITH MR. ELIHU SANDERSON, OF BOMBAY; AND MY GRANDFATHER'S MANUSCRIPT.

IT was indeed my father's Journal, thus miraculously preserved to us from the sea. As we sat and gazed at this inanimate witness, I doubt not the same awe of an all-seeing Providence possessed the hearts of both of us. Little more than twenty-four hours ago had my dead father crossed the threshold of his home, and now his voice had come from the silence of another world to declare the mystery of his death. It was some minutes before Uncle Loveday could so far control his speech as to read aloud this precious manuscript. And thus, in my father's simple language, embellished with no art, and tricked out in no niceties of expression, the surprising story ran :—

"May 23rd, 1848.—Having, in obedience to the instructions of my father's Will, waited upon Mr. Elihu Sanderson, of the East India Company's Service, in their chief office at Bombay, and having from him received a somewhat singular communication in my father's handwriting, I have thought fit briefly to put

together some record of the same, as well as of the more
important events of my voyage, not only to refresh my
own memory hereafter, if 1 am spared to end my days
in peace at Lantrig, but also being impelled thereto by
certain strange hints conveyed in this same communication.   These hints, though I myself can see no ground
for them, would seem to point towards some grave
bodily or spiritual peril; and therefore it is my plain
duty, seeing that I leave a beloved wife and young son
at home, to make such provision that, in case of mis-
adventure or disaster, Divine Providence may at least
have at my hands some means whereby to inform them
of my fate.   For this reason I regret the want of fore-
sight which prevented my beginning some such record
at the outset ; but as far as I can reasonably judge, my
voyage has hitherto been prosperous and without event.
Nevertheless, I will shortly set down what I can remember as worthy of remark before I landed at this
city of Bombay, and trust that nothing of importance
has slipped my notice.

"On the 3rd of February last I left my home at Lantrig, travelling by coach to Plymouth, where I slept at
the ' One and All ' in Old Town Street, being attracted
thither by the name, which is our Cornish motto.   The
following day I took passage for Bombay in the *Golden
Wave*, East Indiaman, Captain Jack Carey, which, as I
learnt, was due to sail in two days.   It had been my
intention, had no suitable vessel been found at Plymouth, to proceed to Bristol, where the trade is much

H 2

greater; but on the Barbican—a most evil-smelling neighbourhood—it was my luck to fall in with a very entertaining stranger, who, on hearing my case, immediately declared it to be a most fortunate meeting, as he himself had been making inquiries to the same purpose, and had found a ship which would start almost immediately. He had been, it appeared, a lawyer's clerk, but on the death of his old employer (whose name escapes my memory), finding his successor a man of difficult temper, and having saved sufficient money to be idle for a year or two, had conceived the wish to travel, and chosen Bombay, partly from a desire to behold the wonders of the Indies, and partly to see his brother, who held a post there in the East India Company's service. Having at the time much leisure, he kindly offered to show me the vessel, protesting that should I find it to my taste he was anxious for the sake of the company to secure a passage for himself. So very agreeable was his conversation that I embraced the opportunity which fortune thus threw in my way. The ship, on inspection, proved much to our liking, and Captain Carey of so honest a countenance, that the bargain was struck without more ado. I was for returning to the 'One and All,' but first thought it right to acquaint myself with the name of this new friend. He was called Simon Colliver, and lived, as he told me, in Stoke, whither he had to go to make preparation for this somewhat hasty departure, but first advised me to move my luggage from the 'One and

All' (the comfort of which fell indeed short of the promise of so fair a name) to the 'Welcome Home,' a small but orderly house of entertainment in the Barbican, where, he said, I should be within easy distance of the *Golden Wave*. The walk to Old Town Street was not far in itself, but a good step when traversed five or six times a day; and, moreover, I was led to make the change on hearing that the landlord of the 'Welcome Home' was also intending to sail as seaman in this same ship. My new acquaintance led me to the house, an ill-favoured-looking den, but clean inside, and after a short consultation with John Railton, the landlord, arranged for my entertainment until the *Golden Wave* should weigh anchor. This done, and a friendly glass taken to seal the engagement, he departed, congratulating himself warmly on his good fortune in finding a fellow-traveller so much, as he protested, to his taste.

"I must own I was not over-pleased with John Railton, who seemed a sulky sort of man, and too much given to liquor. But I saw little of him after he brought my box from the 'One and All.' His wife waited upon me—a singularly sweet woman, though sorely vexed, as I could perceive, with her husband's infirmity. She loved him nevertheless, as a woman will sometimes love a brute, and was sorry to lose him. Indeed, when I noticed that evening that her eyes were red with weeping, and said a word about her husband's departure, she stared at me for a moment in amazement, and could not guess how I came to hear of it, 'for,' said she, 'the resolution had been so suddenly taken that even she could scarce account for it.' She admitted, however, that it was for the best, and added that 'Jack was a good seaman, and she always expected that he would leave her some day.' Her chief anxiety was for her little daughter, aged seven, whom it was hard to have exposed to the rough language and manners of a public-house. I comforted her as best I could, and doubt not she has found her husband's absence a less misfortune than she anticipated.

"The *Golden Wave* weighed anchor on the 6th of February, and reached Bombay after a tedious voyage of 103 days, on the 21st of May, having been detained by contrary winds in doubling the Cape. I saw little of Simon Colliver before starting, though he came twice, as I heard, to the 'Welcome Home' to inquire for me, and each time found me absent. On board, however, being the only other passenger, I was naturally thrown much into his society, and confess that I found him a most diverting companion. Often of a clear moonlight night would we pace the deck together, or watch in a darker sky the innumerable stars, on which Colliver had an amazing amount of information. Sometimes, too, he would sing—quaint songs which I had never heard before, to airs which I suspect, without well knowing why, were of his own composition. His voice was of large compass—a silvery tenor of surpassing purity and sweetness, inasmuch as I have seen the sailors stand spellbound, and even with tears in their eyes, at some sweet song of love and home. Often, again, the words would be weird and mysterious, but the voice was always delicious whether he spoke or sang. I asked him once why with such a gift he had not tried his fortune on the stage. At which he laughed, and replied that he could never be bound by rules of art, or forced to sing, whatever his humour, to an audience for which he cared nothing. I do not know why I dwell so long upon this extraordinary man. His path of life has chanced to run side by side with my own for a short space, and the two have now branched off, nor in all likelihood will ever meet again. My life has been a quiet one, and has not lain much in the way of extra-ordinary men, but I doubt if many such as Simon Colliver exist. He is a perfect enigma to me. That such a man, with such attainments (for besides his wonderful conversation and power of singing, he has an amazing knowledge of foreign tongues), that such a man, I say, should be a mere attorney's clerk is little short of marvellous. But as regards his past he told me nothing, though an apt and ready listener when I spoke of Lantrig and of Margery and Jasper at home. But he showed no curiosity as to the purpose of my voyage, and in fact seemed altogether careless as well of the fate as of the opinions of his fellow-men. He has passed out of my life; but when I shook hands with him at parting I left with regret the most fasci-nating companion it has been ever my lot to meet.

"Our voyage, as I have said, was without event, though full of wonders to me who had seldom before sailed far out of sight of Pedn-glàs. But on these I need not here dwell. Only I cannot pass without mention the exceeding marvels of this city of Bombay. As I stood upon deck on the evening before last and watched the Bhôr Ghauts (as they are called) rise gradually on the dim horizon, whilst the long ridge of the Malabar Hill with its clustered lights grew swiftly dyed in delicate pink and gold, and as swiftly sank back into night, I confess that my heart was strangely fluttered to think that the wonders of this strange country lay at my feet, and I slept but badly for the excitement. But when, yesterday morning, I disembarked upon the Apollo Bund, I knew not at first whither to turn for very dismay. It was like the play-acting we saw, my dear Margery, one Christmas at Plymouth. Every sight in the strange crowd was unfamiliar to my Cornish eyes, and I felt sorely tempted to laugh when I thought what a figure some of them would cut in Polkimbra, and not less when I reflected that after all I was just as much out of place in Bombay, though of course less noticed because of the great traffic. As I strolled through the Bazaar, Hindoos, Europeans, Jews, Arabs, Malays, and Negro men passed me by. Mr. Elihu Sanderson has kindly taught me to distinguish some of these nations, but at the time I did not know one from another, fancying them indeed all Indians, though at a loss to account for their diversity.

Also the gaudy houses of red, blue, and yellow, the number of beautiful trees that grew in the very streets, and the swarms of birds that crowded every roof-top and ventured down quite fearlessly among the passers-by, all made me gasp with wonder. Nor was I less amazed to watch the habits of this marvellous folk, many of them to me shocking, and to see the cows that abound everywhere and do the work of horses. But of all this I will tell if Heaven be pleased to grant me a safe return to Lantrig. Let me now recount my business with Mr. Elihu Sanderson.

" I said farewell to the captain of the *Golden Wave* and my friend Colliver upon the quay, meaning to ask Mr. Sanderson to recommend a good lodging for the short time I intended to stay in Bombay. Captain Carey had already directed me to the East India Company's office, and hither I tried to make my way at once. Easy as it was, however, I missed it, being lost in admiration of the crowd. When at last I arrived at the doors I was surprised to see Colliver coming out, until I remembered that his brother was in the Company's employ. It seems, however, that he had been transferred to Trichinopoly some months before, and my friend's labour was in vain. I am bound to say that he took his disappointment with great good-humour, and made very merry over our meeting again so soon, protesting that for the future we had better hunt in couples among this outlandish folk ; and so I lost him again.

" After some difficulty and delay I found myself at

length in the presence of this Mr. Elihu Sanderson, on whom I had speculated so often. I was ushered by a clerk into his private office, and as he rose to meet me, judged him directly to be the son of the Elihu Sanderson mentioned in my father's Will—as indeed is the case. A spare, dry, shrivelled man, with a mouth full of determination and acuteness, and a habit of measuring his words as though they were for sale, he is in everything but height the essence of every Scotchman I remember to have seen.

"'Good day,' said he, 'Mr.—— I fancy I did not catch your name.'

"'Trenoweth,' said I.

"'Indeed! Trenoweth!' he repeated, and I fancy I saw a glimmer of surprise in his eyes. 'Do I guess your business?'

"'Maybe you do,' I replied, 'for I take it to be somewhat unusual.'

"'Ah, yes; just so; somewhat unusual!'—and he chuckled drily—'somewhat unusual! Very good indeed! I suppose—eh?—you have some credentials—some proof that you really are called Trenoweth?'— Here Mr. Sanderson looked at me sharply.

"In reply I produced my father's Will and the little Bible from my jersey's side. As I did so, I felt the Scotchman's eyes examining me narrowly. I handed him the packet. The Will he read with great attention, glanced at the Bible, pondered awhile, and then said—

"'I suppose you guess that this was a piece of private business between Amos Trenoweth, deceased, and my father, also deceased. I tell ye frankly, Mr. Trenoweth—by the way, what is your Christian name, eh? So you are the Ezekiel mentioned in the Will? Are you a bold man, eh? Well, you look it, at any rate. As I was saying, I tell ye frankly it is not the sort of business I would have undertaken myself. But my father had his crotchets—which is odd, as I'm supposed to resemble him—he had his crotchets, and among them was an affection for your father. It may have been based on profit, for your father, Mr. Trenoweth, as far as I have heard, was not exactly a lovable man, if ye'll excuse me. If it was, I've never seen those profits, and I've examined my father's papers pretty thoroughly. But this is a family matter, and had better not be discussed in office hours. Can you dine with me this evening?'

"I replied that I should be greatly obliged; but, in the first place, as a stranger, would count it a favour to be told of some decent lodging for such time as I should be detained in Bombay.

"Mr. Sanderson pondered again, tapped the floor with his foot, pulled his short crop of sandy whiskers, and said—

"'Our business may detain us, for aught I know, long into the night, Mr. Trenoweth. Ye would be doing me a favour if ye stayed with me for a day or two. I am a bachelor, and live as one. So much the better, eh? If you will get your boxes sent up to Craigie Cottage, Malabar Hill—any one will tell ye where Elihu Sanderson lives—I will try to make you comfortable. You are wondering at the name " Craigie Cottage "—another crotchet of my father's. He was a Scotchman, I'd have ye know; and so am I, for that matter, though I never saw Scotch soil, being that prodigious phenomenon, a British child successfully reared in India. But I hope to set foot there some day, please God! Save us! how I am talking, and in office hours, too! Good-bye, Mr. Trenoweth, and '—once more his eyes twinkled as I thanked him and made for the door —' I would to Heaven ye were a Scotchman!'

" Although verily broiled with the heat, I spent the rest of the day in sauntering about the city and drinking in its marvels until the time when I was due to present myself at Craigie Cottage. Following the men who carried my box, I discovered it without difficulty, though very unlike any cottage that came within my recollection. Indeed, it is a large villa, most richly furnished, and crowded with such numbers . of black servants, that it must go hard with them to find enough to do. That, however, is none of my business, and Mr. Sanderson does not seem the man to spend his money wastefully; so I suppose wages to be very low here.

" Mr. Sanderson received me hospitably, and entertained me to a most agreeable meal, though the dishes were somewhat hotly seasoned, and the number of servants again gave me some uneasiness. But when, after dinner, we sat and smoked out on the balcony and watched the still gardens, the glimmering houses and, above all, the noble bay sleeping beneath the gentle shadow of the night, I confess to a feeling that, after all, man is at home wherever Nature smiles so kindly. The hush of the hour was upon me, and made me disinclined to speak lest its spell should be broken—disinclined to do anything but watch the smoke-wreaths as they floated out upon the tranquil air.

" Mr. Sanderson broke the silence.

" ' You have not been long in coming.'

" ' Did you not expect me so soon ? '

" ' Why, you see, I had not read your father's Will.'

" I explained to him as briefly as I could the reasons which drove me to leave Lantrig. He listened in silence, and then said, after a pause—

" ' You have not, then, undertaken this lightly ? '

" ' As Heaven is my witness, no, whether there be anything in this business or not.'

" ' I think,' said he, slowly, ' there is something in it. My father had his crotchets, it is true ; but he was no fool. He never opened his lips to me on the matter, but left me to hear the first of it in his last Will and Testament. Oddly enough, our fathers seem both to have found religion in their old age. Mine took his comfort in the Presbyterian shape. But it is all the same. There was some reason for your father to repent, if rumours were true ; but why mine, a respectable servant of the East India Company, should want consolation, is not so clear. Maybe 'twas only another form of egotism. Religion, even, is spelt with an I, ye'll observe.

"'An odd couple,' he continued, musing, 'to be mixed up together! But we'll let them rest in peace. I'd better let you have what was entrusted to me, and then, mayhap, ye'll be better able to form an opinion.'

"With this he rose and stepped back into the lighted room, whilst I followed. Drawing a bunch of keys from his pocket, he opened a heavy chest of some dark wood, intricately carved, which stood in one corner, drew out one by one a whole pile of tin boxes, bundles of papers and heavy books, until, almost at the very bottom of the chest, he seemed to find the box he wanted; then, carefully replacing the rest, closed and fastened the chest, and, after some search among his keys, opened the tin box and handed me two envelopes, one much larger than the other, but both bulky.

"And here, my dear Margery, with my hand upon the secret which had cost us so much anxious thought and such a grievous parting, I could not help breathing to myself a prayer that Heaven had seen fit to grant me at last some means of comforting my wife and little one and restoring our fallen house; nor do I doubt, dear wife, you were at that moment praying on your knees for me. I did not speak aloud, but Mr. Sanderson must have divined my thoughts, for I fancied I heard him utter 'Amen' beneath his breath, and when I looked up he seemed prodigiously red and ashamed of himself.

"The small envelope was without address, and contained £50 in Bank of England notes. These were enclosed without letter or hint as to their purpose, and sealed with a plain black seal.

"The larger envelope was addressed in my father's handwriting—

'To the Son of my House who, having

COUNTED ALL THE PERILS, IS RESOLUTE.

'Mem.—*To be burned in one hundred years from this date, May 4th, in the year of our Lord MDCCCV.*'

"It likewise was sealed with a plain black seal, and contained the manuscript which I herewith pin to this leaf of my Journal."

[Here Uncle Loveday, who had hitherto read without comment, save an occasional interjection, turned the page and revealed, in faded ink on a large sheet of parchment, the veritable writing of my grandfather, Amos Trenoweth. We both unconsciously leaned further forward over the relic, and my uncle, still without comment, proceeded to read aloud as follows :—]

"*From Amos Trenoweth, of Lantriy, in the Parish of Pol-*
"*kimbra and County of Cornwall; to such descendant of mine*
"*as may inherit my wealth.*

"*Be it known to you, my son, that though in this parch-*
"*ment mention is made of great and surpassing Wealth, seem-*
"*ingly but to be won for the asking, yet beyond doubt the dangers*
"*which beset him who would lay his hand upon this accursed*
"*store are in nature so deadly, that almost am I resolved to*
"*fling the Secret from me, and so go to my Grave a Beggar.*
"*For that I not only believe, but am well assured, that not with-*

"out much Spilling of Blood and Loss of Human Life shall
"they be enjoyed, I myself having looked in the Face of Death
"thrice before ever I might set Hand upon them, escaping each
"time by a Miracle and by forfeit of my Soul's Peace. Yet,
"considering that the Anger of Heaven is quick and not re-
"vengeful unduly, I have determined not to do so wholly, but
"in part, abandoning myself the Treasure unrighteously won,
"if perchance the Curse may so be appeased, but committing it to
"the enterprise of another, who may escape, and so raise a fall-
"ing House.

"You then, my Son who may read this Message, I entreat
"to consider well the Perils of your Course, though to you
"unknown. But to me they are known well, who have lived a
"Sinful Life for the sake of this gain, and now find it but as
"the fruit of Gomorrah to my lips. For the rest, my Secret is
"with God, from whom I humbly hope to obtain Pardon, but
"not yet. And even as the Building of the Temple was with-
"held from David, as being a Shedder of Blood, but not from
"Solomon his son, so may you lay your Hand to much Treasure
"in Gold, Silver, and Precious Stones, but chiefly the GREAT
"RUBY OF CEYLON, whose beauty excels all the jewels of the
"Earth, I myself having looked upon it, and knowing it to be, as
"an Ancient Writer saith, 'a Spectacle Glorious and without
"Compare.'

"Of this Ruby the Traveller Marco Polo speaks, saying, 'The
"King of Seilan hath a Ruby the Greatest and most Beautiful
"that ever was or can be in the World. In length it is a palm,
"and in thickness the thickness of a man's arm. In Splen-
"dour it exceedeth the things of Earth, and gloweth like unto
"Fire. Money cannot purchase it.' Likewise Maundevile tells
"of it, and how the Great Khan would have it, but was refused;
"and so Odoric, the two giving various Sizes, and both placing
"it falsely in the Island of Nacumera or Nicoveran. But this
"I know, that in the Island of Ceylon it was found, being lost
"for many Centuries, and though less in size than these Writers
"would have it, yet far exceeding all imagination for Beauty
"and colour.

"Now this Ruby, together with much Treasure beside, you
"may gain with the Grace of Heaven and by following my

"*plain words. You will go from this place unto the Island of*
"*Ceylon, and there proceed to Samanala or Adam's Peak, the*
"*same being the most notable mountain of the Island. From*
"*the Resting House at the foot of the Peak you will then ascend,*
"*following the track of the Pilgrims, until you have passed the*
"*First Set of Chains. Between these and the Second there lies*
"*a stretch of Forest, in which, still following the track, you will*
"*come to a Tree, the trunk of which branches into seven parts*
"*and again unites. This Tree is noticeable and cannot be*
"*missed. From its base you must proceed at a right angle to*
"*the left-hand edge of the track for thirty-two paces, and you*
"*will come to a Stone shaped like a Man's Head, of great size,*
"*but easily moved. Beneath this Stone lies the Secret of the*
"*Great Ruby; and yet not all, for the rest is graven on the*
"*Key, of which mention shall already have been made to you.*

"*These precautions I have taken that none may surprise*
"*this Secret but its right possessor; and also that none may*
"*without due reflection undertake this task, inasmuch as it is*
"*prophesied that ' Even as the Heart of the Ruby is Blood and*
"*its Eyes a Flaming Fire, so shall it be for them that would*
"*possess it : Fire shall be their portion and Blood their inherit-*
"*ance for ever.'*

"*This prophecy I had from an aged priest, whose bones lie*
"*beneath the Stone, and upon whose Sacred clasp is the Secret*
written. This and all else may God pardon. Amen.

"*A. T.*"

"*He visiteth the iniquity of the Fathers upon the Children*
"*unto the third and fourth*
"*generation.*"

[To this extraordinary document was appended a
note in another handwriting.]

"*There is little doubt that the Ruby now in the possession of*
"*Mr. Amos Trenoweth is the veritable Great Ruby of which the*
"*traveller Marco Polo speaks. But, however this may be, I*
"*know from the testimony of my own eyes that the stone is of*
"*inestimable worth, being of the rarest colour, and in size*

I

"greatly beyond any Ruby that ever I saw. The stone is spoken
"of, in addition to such writers as Mr. Tremoweth quotes, by
"Friar Jordanus 'in the fourteenth century, who mentions it
"as 'so large that it cannot be grasped in the closed hand'; and
"Ibn Batuta reckons it as great as the palm of a man's hand.
"Cosmas, as far back as 550, had heard tell of it from Sopater,
"and its fame extended to the sixteenth century, wherein Corsali
"wrote of 'two rubies so lustrous and shining that they seem a
"flame of fire.' Also Hayton, in the thirteenth century, men-
"tions it, telling much the same story as Sir John Maundeville,
"to the effect that it was the especial symbol of sovereignty, and
"when held in the hand of the newly-chosen king, enforced the
"recognition of his majesty. But, whereas Hayton simply calls
"it the greatest and finest Ruby in existence, Maundeville puts it
"at a foot in length and five fingers in girth. Also—for I have
"made much inquiry concerning this stone—it was well known
"to the Chinese from the days of Hwen Tsang downward.

"Mr. Tremoweth has wisely forborne for safety from show-
"ing it to any of the jewellers here; but on the one occasion
"when I saw the gem I measured it, and found it to be, roughly,
"some 3½ inches square and 2 inches in depth; of its weight I
"cannot speak. But that it truly is the Great Ruby of Ceylon,
"the account of the Buddhist priest from whom Mr. Tremoweth
"got the stone puts out of all doubt.

" E. S."

"As I finished my reading, I looked up and saw
Mr. Sanderson watching me across the table. 'Well?'
said he.

"I pushed the parchment across to him, and filled
a pipe. He read the whole through very slowly, and
without the movement of a muscle; then handed it
back, but said never a word.

"'Well,' I asked, after a pause; 'what do you
think of it?'

"'Why, in the first place, that my father was a

marvellously honest man, and yours, Mr. Trenoweth, a very indiscreet one. And secondly, that ye're just as indiscreet as he, and it will be lucky for ye if I'm as honest as my father.'

" I laughed.

"' Aye, ye may laugh; but mark my words, Mr. Trenoweth. Ye've a trustful way with ye that takes my liking; but it would surprise me very much, sir, did ye ever lay hands on that Ruby.' "

CHAPTER IX.

"Sept. 29th, 1818. —It is a strange thing that on
the very next day after reading my father's message I
should have been struck down and reduced to my present
condition. But so it is, and now, four months after my
first entry in this Journal, I am barely able to use the
pen to add to my account. As far as I remember—for
my head wanders sadly at times - it happened thus : On
the 23rd of May last, after spending the greater part
of the day in writing my Journal, and also my first
letter to my dear wife, I walked down in the cool of the
evening to the city, intending to post the latter; which
I did, and was returning to Mr. Sanderson's house,
when I stopped to watch the sun setting in this glorious
Bay of Bengal. I was leaning over a low wall, looking
out on the open sea with its palm-fringed shores, when
suddenly the sun shot out a jagged flame; the sky
heaved and turned to blood—and I knew no more. I
had been murderously struck from behind. That I was
found, lying to all appearance dead, with a hideous zig-
zag wound upon the scalp; that my pockets had been

to all appearance rifled (whether by the assassin or the natives that found me is uncertain); that I was finally claimed and carried home by Mr. Sanderson, who, growing uneasy at my absence, had set out to look for me; that for more than a month, and then again for almost two months, my life hung in the balance; and that I owe my recovery to Mr. Sanderson's unceasing kindness —all this I have learnt but lately. I can write no more at present.

"Oct. 3rd.—I am slightly better. My mental powers are slowly coming back after the fever that followed the wound. I pass my days mostly in speculating on the reason of this murderous attack, but am still unable to account for it. It cannot have been for plunder, for I do not look like a rich man. Mr. Sanderson has his theory, but I cannot agree with him, for nobody but ourselves knew of my father's manuscript. At any rate, it is fortunate that I left it in my chest, together with this Journal, before I went down to Bombay. Margery must have had my letter by this time; Mr. Sanderson very wisely decided to wait the result of my illness before troubling her. As it is she need know nothing about it until we meet.

"Oct. 14th.—Mr. Sanderson is everything that is good; indeed, had I been a brother he could not have shown me more solicitude. But he is obstinate in connecting my attack with the Great Ruby of Ceylon; it is certainly a curious coincidence that this dark chapter of my life should immediately follow my father's warning, but that is all one can say. I shall give up trying to convince him.

"Oct. 31st.— I am now considerably better. My strength is slowly returning, and with it, I am glad to say, my memory. At first it seemed as though I could remember nothing of my past life, but now my recollection is good on every point up to the moment of my attack. Since then, for at least the space of three months, I can recall nothing. I am able to creep about a little, and Mr. Sanderson has taken me for one or two excursions. Curiously enough, I thought I saw John Railton yesterday upon the Apollo Bund. I was probably mistaken, but at the time it caused me no surprise that he should still be here, since I forgot the interval of three months in my memory. If it were really Railton, he has, I suppose, found employment of some kind in Bombay; but it seems a cruel shame for him to desert his poor wife at home. I, alas! am doing little better, but God knows I am anxious to be gone; however, Mr. Sanderson will not hear a word on the subject at present. He has promised to find a ship for me as soon as he thinks I am able to continue my travels.

"Nov. 4th.—I was not mistaken. It was John Railton that I saw on the Apollo Bund. I met him hovering about the same spot to-day, and spoke to him; but apparently he did not hear me. I intended to ask him some news of my friend Colliver, but I daresay he knows as little of his doings as I do. Mr. Sanderson says that in a week's time I shall be recovered sufficiently to start. I hope so, indeed, for this delay is chafing me sorely.

"Nov. 21st.—Mr. Sanderson has found a ship for me at last. I am to sail in five days for Colombo in the schooner *Campaspe*, whose captain is a friend—a business friend, that is—of my host. I shall be the only passenger, and Mr. Sanderson has given Captain Dodge full instructions to take care of me. But I am feeling strong enough now, and fit for anything.

"Nov. 23rd.—I have been down to look at the vessel, and find that a most comfortable little cabin has been set apart for me. But the strangest thing is that I met Colliver also inspecting the ship. He was most surprised at seeing me, and evidently imagined me home in England by this time. I told him of my meeting with John Railton, and he replied—

"'Oh, yes; I have taken him into my service. We are going together to Ceylon, as I have travelled about India enough for the present. I went to visit my brother at Trichinopoly, and have only just returned to Bombay. Unfortunately the captain of the *Campaspe* declares he is unable to take me, so I shall have to wait.'

"I explained the reasons of the captain's reluctance, and offered him a share of my cabin if Captain Dodge would consent to be burdened with Railton's company.

"'Oh, for that matter,' replied he, 'Railton can follow; but he's a handy fellow, and I daresay would make himself useful without payment.'

" We consulted Captain Dodge, who admitted himself ready to take another passenger, and even to accommodate Railton, if that were my wish. Only, he explained, Mr. Sanderson had especially told him that I should wish to be alone, being an invalid. So the bargain was struck.

" Mr. Sanderson did not seem altogether pleased when I informed him that I intended to take a companion. He asked many questions about Colliver, and was especially anxious to know if I had confided anything of my plans to him. So far was this from being the case that Colliver, as I informed my host, had never betrayed the least interest in my movements. At this Mr. Sanderson merely grunted, and asked me when I intended to learn prudence, adding that one crack in the head was enough for most men, but he supposed I wanted more. I admit that, pleasant companion as Colliver is, I should prefer to be entirely alone upon this adventure. But I could not deny the invitation without appearing unnecessarily rude, and I owe him much gratitude for having made the outward voyage so pleasant. Besides, we shall part at Colombo.

" Nov. 25th.—I make this entry (my last upon Indian soil) just before retiring to rest. To-morrow I sail for Colombo in the *Campaspe*. But I cannot leave Bombay without dwelling once more on Mr. Sanderson's great kindness. To-night, as we sat together for the last time upon the balcony of Craigie Cottage, I declare that my heart was too full for words.

My host apparently was revolving other thoughts, for when he spoke it was to say—

" ' Visited his brother in Trichinopoly, eh? Only just returned, too—h'm! What I want to know is, why the devil he returned at all? There are plenty of vessels at Madras.'

" ' But Colliver is not the man who cares to follow the shortest distance between two points,' I answered. ' Why should he not return to Bombay?'

" ' I'll beg ye to observe,' said Mr. Sanderson, ' that the question is not " why shouldn't he?" but " why should he?" '

" ' At any rate,' said I, ' I'll be on my guard.'

" This suspicion on my behalf has become quite a mania with my host. I thought it best to let him grumble his fill, and then endeavoured to thank him for his great kindness.

" ' Don't say another word,' he interrupted. ' I owe ye some reparation for being mixed up in this at all. It's a serious matter, mark ye, for a respectable clerk like myself to be aiding and abetting in this mad chase; and, to tell the truth, Trenoweth, I took a fancy to ye when first I set eyes on your face, and——Don't say another word, I'll ask ye.'

" My friend's eyes were full of tears. I arose, shook him silently by the hand, and went to my room.

" Nov. 26th.—I am off. I write this in my cabin, alone—Colliver having had another assigned to him by Mr. Sanderson's express wish. He saw Colliver for the first time to-day on the quay, and drew me aside at the last moment to warn me against 'that fellow with the devilish eyes.' As I stood on deck and watched his stiff little figure waving me farewell until it melted into the crowd, and Bombay sank behind me as the city of a dream, I wondered with sadness on the little chance we had of ever meeting on this earth again. Colliver's voice at my elbow aroused me.

"'Odd man, that friend of yours—made up of emotion, and afraid of his life to show it. Has he done you a favour?'

"'He has,' I replied, 'as great a favour as one man can do for another.'

"'Ah,' said he, 'I thought as much. That's why he is so full of gratitude.'

"Dec. 6th.—Never shall I forget the dawn out of which Ceylon, the land of my promise, arose into view. I was early on deck to catch the first sight of land. Very slowly, as I stood gazing into the east, the pitch-black darkness turned to a pale grey, and discovered a long, narrow streak, shaped like the shields one sees in Bible prints, and rising to a point in the centre. Then, as it seemed to me, in a moment, the sun was up and as if by magic the shield had changed into a coast fringed with palms and swelling upwards in green and gradual slopes to a chain of mighty hills. Around these some light, fleecy clouds had gathered, but sea and coast were radiant with summer. So clear was the air that I could distinguish the red sand of the beaches and the white trunks of the palms that crowded to the shore; and then before us arose Colombo, its white houses gleaming out one by one.

"The sun was high by the time our pilot came on board, and as we entered the harbour the town lay deep in the stillness of the afternoon. We had cast anchor, and I was reflecting on my next course of action when I heard my name called from under the ship's side. Looking down, I spied a tall, grave gentleman seated in a boat. I replied as well as I could for the noise, and presently the stranger clambered up on deck and announced himself as Mr. Eversleigh, to whom Mr. Sanderson had recommended me. I had no notion until this moment—and I state it in proof of Mr. Sanderson's kindness—that any arrangement had been made for entertaining me at Colombo. It is true that Mr. Sanderson had told me, on the night when our acquaintance began, to send this gentleman's address to Margery, that her letter might safely reach me; but beyond this I knew nothing. Mr. Eversleigh shook me by the hand, and, to my unspeakable joy, handed me my dear wife's letter.

" I say to my unspeakable joy, for no words can tell, dear wife, with what feelings I read your letter as the little boat carried me up to the quay. How often during the idle days of my recovery have I lain wondering how you and Jasper were passing this weary time, and cried out on the weakness that kept me so long dallying. Patience, dear heart, it is but a little time now.

"I have forgotten to speak of Colliver. He has been as delightful and indifferent as ever throughout the voyage. Certainly I can find no reason for crediting Mr. Sanderson's suspicions. In the hurry of landing I missed him, not even having opportunity to ask about his plans. Doubtless I shall see him in a day or two.

"Dec. 10th.—What an entrancing country is this Ceylon! The monsoon is upon us, and hinders my journey: indeed, Mr. Eversleigh advises me not to start for some weeks. He promises to accompany me to the Peak if I can wait, but the suspense is hard to bear. Meantime I am drinking in the marvels of Colombo. The quaint names over the shops, the bright dresses of white and red, the priests with their robes of flaming yellow—all these are diverting enough, but words cannot tell of the beauty of the country here. The roads are all of some strange red soil, and run for miles beneath the most beautiful trees imaginable—bamboos, palms, and others unknown to me, but covered with crimson and yellow blossom. Then the long stretches of rice fields, and again more avenues of palms, with here and there a lovely pool by the wayside—all this I cannot here describe. But most wonderful of all is the monsoon which rages over the country, wrapping the earth sometimes in sheets of lightning which turn sea, sky and earth to one vivid world of flame. The wind is dry and parching, so that all windows are kept carefully closed at night; but, indeed, the mosquitoes are sufficient excuse for that. I have seen nothing of Colliver and Railton.

" Dec. 31st.—New Year's Eve, and, as I hope, the dawn of brighter days for us, dear wife. Mr. Eversleigh has to-night been describing Adam's Peak to me. Truly this is a most marvellous mountain, and its effect upon me I find hard to put into words. To-day I watched it standing solitary and royal from the low hills that surround it. At its feet waved a very sea of green forest, around its summit were gathered black clouds charged with lightning. Mr. Eversleigh tells me of the worship here paid to it, and the thousands of pilgrims that wear its crags with their patient feet. Can I hope to succeed when so many with prayers so much more holy have failed? Even as I write, its unmoved face is mocking the fire of heaven. I dream of the mountain; night and day it has come to fill my life with dark terror. I am not by nature timid or despondent, but it is hard to have to wait here day after day and watch this goal of my hopes—so near, yet seemingly so forbidding of access.

" On looking back I find I have said nothing about the house where I am now staying. It lies in the Kolpetty suburb, in the midst of most lovely gardens, and is called Blue Bungalow, from the colour in which it is painted. I have made many excursions with Mr. Eversleigh on the lagoon; but for me the only object in this land of beauty is the great Peak. I cannot endure this idleness much longer. Colliver seems to have vanished: at least, I have not seen him.

" Jan. 25th, 1849.—I have been in no mood lately

to make any fresh entry in my Journal. But to-morrow I start for Adam's Peak. At the last moment my host finds himself unable to go with me, much as he protests he desires it ; but two of his servants will act as my guides. It is about sixty miles from Colombo to the foot of the Peak, so that in four days from this time I hope to lay my hand upon the secret. The two natives their real names I do not know, but Mr. Eversleigh has christened them Peter and Paul, which I shall doubtless find more easy of mastery than their true outlandish titles) are, as I am assured, trusty, and have visited the mountain before. We take little baggage beyond the necessary food and one of my host's guns. I cannot tell how impatient I am feeling.

" Feb. 1st. — My journey to the Peak is over. Whether from fatigue or excitement I am feeling strangely light-headed to-day ; but let me attempt to describe as briefly as I can my adventure. We set out from Colombo in the early morning of Jan. 26th. For about two-thirds of our journey the road lies along the coast, stretching through swampy rice-fields and interminable cocoanut avenues until Ratnapoora is reached. So far the scenery does not greatly differ from that of Colombo. But it was after we left Ratnapoora that I first realised the true wonders of this land. Our road rose almost continuously by narrow tracks, which in some places, owing to the late heavy rains, were almost impassable ; but Peter and Paul worked hard, and so reduced the delay. We had not left Ratnapoora far behind when we plunged into a tangled forest, so dense as almost to blot out the light of day. On either hand deep ravines plunged precipitately down, or giant trees enclosed us in black shadow. Where the sun's rays penetrated, myriads of brilliant insects flashed like jewels; yellow butterflies, beetles with wings of ruby-red or gold, and dragonflies that picked out the under-growth with fire. In the shadow overhead flew and chattered crowds of green paroquets and glossy crows, while here and there we could see a Bird of Paradise drooping its smart tail-feathers amid the foliage. A little further, and deep in the forest the ear caught the busy tap-tap of the woodpecker, the snap of the toucan's beak, or far away the deep trumpeting of the elephant. Once we startled a leopard that gazed a moment at us with flaming eyes, and then was gone with a wild bound into the thicket. From tree to tree trailed hosts of gorgeous creepers, blossoming in orange, white and crimson, or wreathing round some hapless monarch of the forest and strangling it with their rank growth. Still we climbed.

"The bridle-track now skirted a torrent, now wound dizzily round the edge of a stupendous cliff, and again plunged into obscurity. Here and there the ruins of some ancient and abandoned shrine confronted us, its graceful columns entwined and matted with vegetation; or, again, where the forest broke off and allowed our eyes to sweep over the far prospect, the guides would point to the place where stood, hardly to

be descried, the relics of some dead city, desolate and
shrined in desolation.   Even I, who knew nothing of
the past glories of Ceylon, could not help being possessed
with melancholy thoughts as I passed now a mass of
deserted masonry, now a broken column, the sole witnesses of generations gone for ever. Some were very
richly carved, but Nature's tracery was rapidly blotting
out the handiwork of man, the twining convolvulus
usurping the glories of the patient chisel. Still up we
climbed, where hosts of chattering monkeys swung from
branch to branch, or poised screaming overhead, or a
frightened serpent rose with hissing mouth, and then
glided in a flash back through the undergrowth. One,
that seemed to me of a pure silver-white, started almost
from under my feet, and darted away before I could
recover myself. We hardly spoke; the vastness of
Nature hushed our tongues. It seemed presumption
to raise my gun against any of the inhabitants of this
spot where man seemed so mean, so strangely out of
place. Once I paused to cut back with my knife the
creepers that hid in inextricable tangle a solitary and
exquisitely carved archway. But the archway led no-
where, its god and temple alike had perished, and
already the plants have begun their tireless work again.

"Between the stretches of wilderness our road often
led us across rushing streams, difficult to ford at this
season, or up rocky ravines, that shut in with their
towering walls all but a patch of blue overhead. Emerg-
ing from these we would find ourselves on naked ledges

where the sun's rays beat until the air seemed that of
an oven. At such spots the plain below spread itself
out as a crumpled chart, whilst always above us, domed
in the blue of a sapphire-stone, towered the goal of our
hopes, serene and relentless. But such places were not
many. More often a threatening cliff faced us, or an
endless slope closed in the view, only to give way to
another and yet another as we climbed their weary
length.

"Yet our speed was not trifling. We had passed a
train of white-clothed pilgrims in the morning soon
after leaving Ratnapoora. Since then we had seen no
man except one poor old priest at the ruined resting-
house where we ate our mid-day meal. The shadow of
the forest allowed us to travel through the heat of the
day, and the thirst of discovery would have hurried me
on even had the guides protested. But they were both
sturdy, well-built men, and suffered from the heat far
less than I did. So we hardly paused until, in the first
swift gloom of sunset, we emerged on the grassy lawn
of Diabetne, beneath the very face of the cone.

"We had to rest for the night in the ruined
Ambulam, as it is called; and here, thoroughly tired
but sleepless, I lay for some hours and watched the
innumerable stars creep out and crown that sublime head
which rose at first into a fathomless blue that was
almost black, and then as the moon swept up, flashed
into unutterable radiance. Nothing, I am told, can
compare with the moonlight of Ceylon, and I can

J

well believe it. That night I read clearly once again by the light of its rays my father's manuscript, that no point in it should escape my memory; then sank down upon my rugs and slept an uneasy sleep.

"In an hour or two, as it seemed, I was awakened by Peter, who shook me and proclaimed it time to be stirring if we meant to see the sunrise from the summit. The moon was still resplendent as we started across the three miles or 'league of heaven' that still lay between us and the actual cone. This league traversed, we plunged down a gully and crossed a stream whose waters danced in the silver moonlight until the eyes were dazzled, then swept in a pearly shower down numberless ledges of rock. After this the climb began in good earnest. After a stretch of black forest, we issued on a narrow track that grew steeper at every step. The moon presently ceased to help us here, so that my guides lit torches, which flared and cast long shadows on the rocky wall. By degrees the track became a mere watercourse, up which we could only scramble one by one. So narrow was it that two men could scarcely pass, yet so richly clothed in vegetation that our torches scorched the overhanging ferns. Peter led the way, and I followed close at his heels, for fear of loose stones; but every now and then a crash and a startled cry from Paul behind us told us that we had sent a boulder flying down into the depths. Beyond this and the noise of our footsteps there was no sound. We went but slowly, for the labour of the day before had nearly exhausted us, but at length we scrambled out into the moonlight again upon a rocky ledge half-way up the mountain-side.

" Here a strong breeze was blowing, that made our heated bodies shiver until we were fain to go on. Casting one look into the gulf below, deepened without limit in the moonlight, we lit fresh torches and again took to the path. Before we had scrambled, now we climbed. We had left vegetation behind us, and were face to face with the naked rock that forms the actual Peak. At the foot of this Peter called a halt, and pointed out the first set of chains. Without these, in my weak state I could never have attempted the ascent. Even as it was, my eye was dazed and my head swam and reeled as I hung like a fly upon the dizzy side. But clutching with desperation the chains riveted in the living rock, I hauled myself up after Peter, and sank down thoroughly worn out upon the brink.

" It now wanted but little before daybreak would be upon us. As I gathered myself up for a last effort, I remembered that amid the growth into which we were now to plunge, stood the tree of seven trunks which was to be my mark. But my chance was small of noting it by the light of these flaring torches that distorted every object, and wreathed each tree into a thousand fantastic shapes. Plainly I must stake my hopes on the descent next day ; at any rate, I would scale the summit before I began my search.

" We had plunged into the thicket of rhododendrons,

J 2

whose crimson flowers showed oddly against the torches'
gleam, and I was busy with these thoughts, when
suddenly my ankle gave way, and I fell heavily forward.
My two guides were beside me in an instant, and had
me on my feet again.

"'All's good,' said Peter, 'but lucky it not happen
otherwhere. Only take care for last chain. But what
bad with him?'

"He might well ask; for there, full in front of my
eyes that strained and doubted, glimmered a huge trunk
cleft into seven—yes, seven—branches that met again
and disappeared in a mass of black foliage. It was my
father's tree.

"So far then the parchment had not lied. Here
was the tree, 'noticeable and not to be missed,' and
barely thirty-two paces from the spot where I was
standing lay the key to the treasure which I had
travelled this weary distance to seek. But the time for
search had not yet come. By the clear light of day and
alone I must explore the secret. It would keep for a
few hours longer.

"Dismissing my pre-occupied manner which had
caused no small astonishment to Peter and Paul, I fixed
the position of the tree as firmly as I could in my mind,
and gave the word to advance.

"We then continued in the same order as before,
whilst, to make matters sure, I counted our steps. I had
reached six hundred and twenty—though when I considered the darkness and the rough path I reflected that

this was but little help—when we arrived at the second set of chains. My foot was already beginning to give me pain, but under any circumstances this would have been by far the worst of the ascent. All around us stretched darkness void and horrible, leading, for all that we could see, down through veils of curling mist into illimitable depths. In front the rock was almost perpendicular. The fascination of gazing down was wellnigh resistless, but Peter ahead continually cried 'Hurry!' and the voice of Paul behind repeated 'Hurry!' so that panting, gasping, and fit to faint, with fingers clinging to the chain until the skin was blistered, with every nerve throbbing and every muscle strained to its utmost tension, I clambered, clambered, until with one supreme effort I swung myself up to the brink, staggered rather than ran up the last few feet of rock, and as my guides bent and with outstretched palms raised the cry '*Saadoo! Saadoo!*' I fell exhausted before the very steps of Buddha's shrine.

"When I recovered, I saw just above me the open shrine perched on a tiny terrace and surrounded by low walls of stone ; a yard or two from me the tiny hut in which its guardians live ; and all around the expanse of sky. Dawn was stealing on; already its pale light was creeping up the east, and a bar or two of vivid fire proclaimed the coming of the sun. The priests were astir to receive the early pilgrims, and as Paul led me to the edge of the parapet I could see far away below the torches of the new-comers dotted in thin lines of fire down the mountain-side. Some pilgrims had arrived before us, and stood shivering in their thin white garments about the summit.

"Presently the distant sound of measured chanting came floating up on the tranquil air, sank and died away, and rose again more loudly. Paler and paler grew the heavens, nearer and nearer swept the chanting; and now the first pilgrim swung himself up into our view, quenched his torch and bowed in homage. Others following did the same, all adoring, until the terrace was crowded with worshippers gazing eager and breathless into the far east, where brighter and brighter the crimson bars of morning were widening.

"Then with a leap flashed up the sun, the dazzling centre of a flood of golden light. Godlike and resplendent he rode up on wreaths of twirling mist, and with one stroke sent the shadows quivering back to the very corners of heaven. As the blazing orb topped the horizon, every head bent in worship, every hand arose in welcome, every voice broke out in trembling adoration, ' Saadoo! Saadoo!' Even I, the only European there, could not forbear from bowing my head and lifting up my hands, so carried away was I with the aching fervour of this crowd. There they stood and bent until the whole fiery ball was clear, then turning, paced to the sound of chanting up the rough steps and laid their offerings on the shrine. Thrice at each new offering rang out a clattering gong, and the worshipper stepped reverently back to make way for another; while all the time the newly-risen sun blazed aslant on their robes of dazzling whiteness.

"As I stood watching this strange scene, Peter plucked me by the sleeve and pointed westward. I looked, and all the wonders I had yet viewed became as nothing. For there, disregarded by the crowd, but plain and manifest, rose another Peak, graven in shadow upon the western sky. Bold and confronting, it soared into heaven and, whilst I gazed in silent awe, came striding nearer through the void air, until it seemed to sweep down upon me—and was gone! For many a day had the shadow of this mighty cone lain upon my soul; here, on the very summit, that shadow took visible form and shape, then paled into the clear blue. Has its invisible horror left me now at last? I doubt it.

But by this time the sun was high, and the last pilgrim with a lingering cry of ' Saadoo !' was leaving the summit. So, although my ankle was now beginning to give me exquisite pain, I gave the order to return. Before leaving, however, I looked for a moment at the sacred footprint, to my mind the least of the wonders of the Peak, and resembling no foot that ever I saw. We had gone but a few steps when I plainly guessed from the state of my ankle that our descent would be full of danger, but the guides assured me of their carefulness; so once more we attacked the chains.

"How we got down I shall never fully know; but at last and after infinite pain we stood at the foot of the cliff and entered the forest of rhododendrons. And here, to the wild astonishment of my guides who plainly thought me mad, I bade them leave me and proceed ahead, remaining within call. They were full of protestations and dismay, but I was firm. Trusty they might be, but it was well in this matter to distrust everything and everybody. Finally, therefore, they obeyed, and I sat watching until their white-clad forms disappeared in the thicket.

" As soon as I judged them to have gone a sufficient distance, I arose and followed, cautiously counting my footsteps. But this was needless; my father had described the tree as ' noticeable and not to be missed,' nor was he wrong. Barely had I counted five hundred paces when it rose into view, uncouth and monstrous. All around it spread the crimson blossoms of huge rhododendrons; but this strange tree was at once unlike any of its fellows and of a kind altogether unknown to me. Its roots were partly bare, and writhed in fantastic coils across the track. Above these rose and spread its seven trunks matted with creepers, and then united about four feet below the point where the branches began. Its foliage was of a dark, glossy green, particularly dense, and its height, as I should judge, some sixty feet.

"Taking out my compass, I started from the left-hand side of the narrow track, and at a right angle to it. The undergrowth gave me much trouble, and once I had to make a circuit round a huge rhododendron; but I fought my way through, and after going, as I reckoned, thirty-two paces, pulled up full in front of—another rhododendron.

"There must be some mistake. My father had spoken of a 'stone shaped like a man's head,' but said nothing of a rhododendron tree, and indeed this particular tree was in nowise different from its companions. I looked around; took a few steps to the right, then to the left; went round the tree; walked back a few paces; returned to the tree to see if it concealed anything; then sought the track to begin my measurement afresh.

"I was just starting again in a very discomposed mood, when a thought struck me. I had been behaving like a fool. The parchment said 'at a right angle to the left-hand edge of the track.' I had started from my left hand, but I was descending the mountain, whereas the directions of course supposed the explorer to be ascending. Almost ready to laugh at my stupidity, I tried again.

"Facing round, I got the needle at an angle of ninety degrees, and once more began counting. My heart was beginning to beat quickly by this time, and I felt myself trembling with excitement. The course was now more easily followed. True, the growth was as thick as ever, but no rhododendrons blocked my passage. Beating down the creepers that swung across my face, twined around my legs, and caught at my cap, I measured thirty-two paces as nearly as I could, and then stopped.

" Before me was a patch of velvet grass, some twelve feet square and bare of the undergrowth that crowded elsewhere ; but not a trace of a stone. I looked right and left, crossed the tiny lawn, peered all about, but still saw nothing at all resembling what I sought.

" As it began to dawn on me that all my hopes had been duped, my journey vain, and my father's words an empty cheat, a sickening despair got hold of me. My knees shook together, and big drops of sweat gathered on my forehead. I roused myself and searched again ; again I was baffled. Distractedly I beat the bushes round and round the tiny lawn, then flung myself down on the turf and gave way to my despair. To this, then, it had all come ; this was the end for which I had abandoned my wife and child ; this the treasure that had dangled so long before my eyes. Fool that I had been ! I cursed my madness and the hour when I was born ; never before had I heartily despised myself, never until now did I know how the lust for this treasure had eaten into my soul. The secret, if secret indeed there were, and all were not a lie, was in the keeping of the silent Peak.

" I almost wept with wrath. I tore the turf in my frenzy, and felt as one who would fain curse God and die. But after a while my passion spent itself. I sat up and reflected that after all my first direction might have been the right one; at any rate, I would try it again and explore it thoroughly. The instructions were precise, and had been confirmed in the matter of the tree. Evidently the person that wrote them had been upon the Peak, and what, if they were lies, was to be gained by the cheat?

"I pulled out the parchment again and read it through; then started to my feet with fresh energy. I was just leaving the little lawn and returning down my path, when it struck me that the bush on my left hand was of a curious shape. It seemed a mere tangled knot of creepers covered with large white blossom, and rose to about my own height. Carelessly I thrust my stick into the mass, when its point jarred upon — stone!

" Yes, stone! In a moment my knife was out and I was down on hands and knees cutting and tearing at the tendrils. Some of them were full three inches thick, but I slashed and tugged, with breath that came and went immoderately fast, with bleeding hands and thumping heart, until little by little the stone was bared and its outlines revealed themselves.

" But as they grew distinct and I saw what I had uncovered, I fell back in terror. The stone was about five feet ten inches in height, and was roughly shaped to represent a human head and neck. But the face it was that froze my heated blood in horror. Never until I die shall I forget that hellish expression. It was the smoothly-shaven face of a man of about fifty years of age, roughly carved after the fashion of many of the ruins on this mountain. But whoever fashioned it, the artist must have been a fiend.

If ever malignant hate was expressed in form, it stood before me. Even the blank pupils made the malevolence seem but the more undying. Every feature, every line was horrible, every touch of the chisel had added a fresh grace of devilish spite. It was simply Evil petrified.

"As this awful face, bared of the innocent creeper that for years had shrouded its ugliness from the light of day, confronted me, a feeling of such repulsion overcame me that for several minutes I could not touch it. The neck was loosely set in a sort of socket fixed in the earth; this was all the monster's pedestal. I saw that it barely needed a man's strength to send it toppling over. Yet for a moment I could summon up none. At length I put my hands to it and with an effort sent it crashing over amid the brushwood.

"The trough in which this colossal head had rested was about four feet in depth, and narrowed towards the bottom. I put down my hand and drew out—a human thigh-bone. The touch of this would have turned me sick again, had not the statue's face already surfeited me with horror. As it was, I was nerved for any sight. The passion of my discovery was upon me, and I tossed the mouldering bones out to right and left.

"But stay. There seemed a great many in the trough. Surely this was the third thigh-bone that I held now in my hand. Yes, and below, close to the bottom of the trough, lay two skulls side by side. There were two, then, buried here. The parchment had only

spoken of one.   But I had no time to consider about
this.   What I sought now was the Secret, and as I took
up the second skull I caught the gleam of metal under-
neath it.   I put in my hand and drew out a Buckle of
Gold.

"This buckle is formed of two pieces, bound to
either end of a thin belt of rotten linen, and united by
hook and socket.   Its whole dimensions are but 3 in.
× 2 in., but inside its curiously carved border it is entirely covered with writing in rude English character.
The narrowing funnel of the trough had kept it from
being crushed by the statue, which fitted into a rim
running round the interior.   Beyond the buckle and the
two skeletons there was nothing in the trough; but I
looked for nothing else.   Here, in my hands, lay the
secret of the Great Ruby of Ceylon; my fingers clutched
the wealth of princes.   My journey had ended and the
riches of the earth were in my grasp.

"Forgetful of my guides, forgetful of the flight of
time, mindful of nothing but the Golden Buckle, I sat
down by the rim of the trough and began to decipher
the writing.   The inscription, as far as I could gather,
ran right across the clasp.   It could be read easily enough
and contained accurate directions for searching in some
spot, but where that spot was it did not reveal.   It
might be close to the statue; and I was about to start
up and make the attempt when I thought again of
the parchment.   Pulling it from my pocket, I read:
'   .   .   .   *beneath this stone lies the secret of the Great*

*Ruby; and yet not all, for the rest is graven on the Key
which shall be already entrusted to you. These precautions have I taken that none may surprise this Secret
but its right possessor. . . .'*

"Now my father's Will had expressly enjoined, on
pain of his dying curse, that this key should not be
moved from its place until the Trenoweth who went to
seek the treasure should have returned and crossed the
threshold of Lantrig. Consequently the ruby was not
buried on Adam's Peak, or to return for the key would
have been so much labour wasted. Consequently, also,
the Golden Buckle was valueless to anybody but him
who knew the rest of my father's injunctions. Although not yet in my hand, the Great Ruby was mine.
I was folding up the buckle with the parchment before
rejoining the guides, when a curious thing happened.

"The sun had climbed high into heaven whilst I
was absorbed in my search, and was now flooding the
little lawn with light. In my excitement I had heard
and seen nothing, nor noted that the heat was growing
unbearable beneath the vertical rays. But as I was
folding up the parchment a black shadow suddenly fell
across the page. I started and looked up.

"Above me stood Simon Colliver.

"He was standing in the broad light of the sun
and watching me intently, with a curious smile which
grew as our eyes met. How long he had been there I
could not guess, but the strangeness of meeting him on
this spot, and the occupation in which I was surprised,

discomposed me not a little. Hastily thrusting back the buckle and the parchment into my pocket, I scrambled to my feet and stood facing him. Even as I did so, all Mr. Sanderson's warnings came flashing into my mind.

" For full a minute we stood confronting each other without a word. He was still standing in the full blaze of the sunlight, with the same odd smile upon his face, and a peculiar light in his dark eyes that never swerved for a moment. Finally he gave a low laugh and nodding lightly, said—

"'Odd thing our meeting like this, eh? Hand of Fate or some such thing might be mixed up in it from the way we run across each other's path.'

" I assented.

"'Queer too, you'll allow, that we should both be struck with the fancy for ascending this mountain. Very few Europeans do it, so I'm told. I'm on my way up, are you? No? Coming down and taking things easily, to judge by the way I found you occupied.'

" Was the man mocking me? Or had he, after all, no suspicions? His voice was soft and pleasant as ever, nor could I detect a trace of irony in its tone. But I was on my guard.

"'This Peak seems strewn with the handiwork of the heathen,' he continued. 'But really you seem to be in luck's way. I congratulate you. What's this? Skeletons, eh? Upon my word, Trenoweth, you've unearthed a treasure. And this? A statue? Well, it's a queer place to come hunting for statues, but you've picked up an ugly-looking beggar in all conscience!'

"He had advanced to the head, which lay in the rank herbage staring up in hideous spite to heaven. Presently he turned to me and said—

"'Well, this is very remarkable. The fellow who carved this seems to have borrowed my features—not very complimentary of him, I must say. Don't you see the likeness?'

"It was solemn truth. Feature by feature that atrocious face was simply a reproduction of Colliver's. As I stared in amazement, it seemed more and more marvellous that I had not noticed the resemblance before. True, each feature was distorted and exaggerated to produce the utter malignity of its expression. But the face was the face of Colliver. Nobody could have called him a handsome man, but before this I had found Colliver not unpleasant to look upon. Now the hate of the statue's face seemed to have reflected itself upon him I leant against a tree for support and passed my hand across my brow as if to banish a fearful dream. But it was no dream, and when he turned to speak again I could see lurking beneath the assumed expression of the man all the evil passions and foul wickedness engraved upon the stone.

"'Well,' he remarked, 'stranger things than this have happened, but not much. You seem distressed,

Trenoweth. Surely I, if any one, have the right to be annoyed. But you let your antiquarian zeal carry you too far. It's hardly fair to dig these poor remains from their sepulchre and leave them to bleach beneath this tropical sun, even in the interest of science.'

"With this he knelt down and began to gather— very reverently, as I thought—the bones into a heap, and replace them in their tomb. This done, he kicked up a lump or two of turf from the little lawn and pressed it down upon them, humming to himself all the while. Finally he rose and turned again towards me—

"'You'll excuse me, Trenoweth. It's sentimental, no doubt, but I have conceived a kind of respect for these remains. Suppose, for example, this face was really a portrait of one of this buried pair. Why, then the deceased was very like me. I forgive him for caricaturing my features now; were he alive, it might be different. But this place is sufficiently out of the way to prevent the resemblance being noted by many. By the way, I forgot to ask how you chanced on this spot. For my part, I thought that I heard something moving in the thicket, so I followed the sound out of pure curiosity, and came upon you. Well, well! it's a strange world; and it's a wonderful thought too, that this may be the grave of some primæval ancestor of mine who roamed this Peak for his daily food—an ancestor of some importance too, in his day, to judge by the magnificence of his tomb. A poet might make something out of this: to-day face to face with the day

K

before yesterday. But that's the beauty of archæology.
I did not know it was a pursuit of yours, and am glad
to see you are sufficiently recovered of your illness to
take it up again. Good-bye for the present. I am
obliged to be cautious in taking farewell of you, for we
have such a habit of meeting unexpectedly. So, as I
have to be up and moving for the summit, I'll say
"Good-bye for the present." We may as well leave
this image where it is ; the dead won't miss it, and it's
handy by, at any rate. *Addio*, Trenoweth, and best of
luck to your future researches.'

" He was gone. I could hear him singing as he
went a strange song which he had often sung on the
outward voyage—

> " 'Sing hey ! for the dead man's lips, my lads ;
> Sing ho ! for the dead man's soul.
> At his red, red lips . . . . . .'

" The song died away in the distance before I moved.
I had hardly opened my lips during the interview, and
now had much ado to believe it a reality. But the
newly-turfed grave was voucher enough for this. A
horror of the place seized me ; I cast one shuddering
look at the giant face and rushed from the spot, leaving
the silent creepers to veil once more that awful likeness
from the eyes of day.

" As I emerged upon the track again I came upon
Peter and Paul, who were seeking me high and low,
with dismay written upon their faces. Excusing my
absence as best I could, I declared myself ready, in spite

of my ankle, to make all haste in the descent. Of our journey down the Peak I need say little, except that, lame as I was, I surprised and exhausted my guides in my hurry. Of the dangers and difficulties which had embarrassed our ascent I seemed to feel nothing. Except in the cool of the forest, the heat was almost insufferable; but I would hear of no delay until we reached Ratnapoora. Here, instead of returning as we had come, we took a boat down the Kalu-ganga river to Cattura, and thence travelled along the coast by Pantura to Colombo.

"The object of my journey is now accomplished: and it only remains to hasten home with all speed. But I am feeling strangely unwell as I write this. My head has never fully recovered that blow at Bombay, and I think the hours during which I remained exposed to the sun's rays, by the side of that awful image, must have affected it. Or perhaps the fatigue of the journey has worn me out. If I am going to sicken I must hide my secret. It would be safer to bury it with the Journal, at any rate for the time, somewhere in the garden here. I have a tin box that will just answer the purpose. My head is giving me agony. I can write no more."

K 2

CHAPTER X.

CONTAINS THE THIRD AND LAST PART OF MY FATHER'S JOURNAL; SETTING FORTH THE MUTINY ON BOARD THE *BELLE FORTUNE.*

"June 19th.—Strange that wherever I am hospitably entertained I recompense my host by falling ill in his house. Since my last entry in this Journal I have been lying at the gate of death, smitten down with a sore sickness. It seems that the long exposure and weariness of my journey to the Peak threw me into a fever; but of this I should soon have recovered, were it not for my head, which I fear will never be wholly right again. That cowardly blow upon Malabar Hill has made a sad wreck of me; twice, when I seemed in a fair way to recovery, has my mind entirely given way. Mr. Eversleigh, indeed, assures me that my life has more than once been despaired of—and then what would have become of poor Margery? I hope I am thankful to God for so mercifully sparing my poor life, the more so because conscious how unworthy I am to appear before Him.

"I trust I did not betray my secret in my wanderings. Mr. Eversleigh tells me I talked the strangest stuff at times — about rubies and skeletons, and a certain dreadful face from which I was struggling to escape. But the security of my Journal and the golden clasp, which I recovered to-day, somewhat reassures me. I am allowed to walk in the garden for a short space every day, but not until to-day have I found strength to dig for my hoard. I can hardly describe my emotions on finding it safe and sound.

"Poor Margery! How anxious she must be getting at my silence. I will write her to-morrow—at least I will begin my letter to-morrow, for I shall not have strength to finish it in one day. Even now I ought not to be writing, but I cannot forbear making an entry in my recovered Journal, if only to record my thankfulness to Heaven for my great deliverance.

"June 22nd.—I have written to Margery, but torn the letter up on second thoughts, as I had better wait until I hear news of a vessel in which I can safely travel home. Mr. Eversleigh (who is very kind to me, though not so hearty as Mr. Sanderson) will not hear of my starting in my present condition. I wonder in what part of the world Colliver is travelling now.

"July 1st.—Oh, this weary waiting! Shall I never see the shores of England again? The doctor says that I only make myself worse with fretting; but it is hard to linger so—when at my journey's end lies wealth almost beyond the imagination, and (what is far more to me) the sight of my dear ones.

"July 4th.—In answer to my entreaties, Mr. Eversleigh has consented to make inquiries about the homeward-bound vessels starting from Colombo. The result is that he has at once allayed my impatience, and compassed his end of keeping me a little longer, by selecting —upon condition that I approve his choice—an East Indiaman due to sail in about a fortnight's time. The name of the ship is the *Belle Fortune*, and of the captain, Cyrus Holding. In spite of the name the ship is English, and is a barque of about 600 tons register. Her cargo consists of sugar and coffee, and her crew numbers some eighteen hands. To-morrow I am going down with Mr. Eversleigh to inspect her, but I am prepared beforehand to find her to my liking. The only pity is that she does not start earlier.

"July 6th.—Weak as I am, even yesterday's short excursion exhausted me, so that I felt unable to write a word last night. I have been over the *Belle Fortune*, and am more than pleased, especially with her captain, whose honest face took my fancy at once. I have a most comfortable cabin next to his set apart for me, at little cost, since it had been fitted up for a lady on the outward voyage: so that I shall still have a little money in pocket on my return, as my living, both here and at Bombay, has cost me nothing, and the doctor's bills have not exhausted my store. I wrote to Margery to-day, making as light of my illness as I could, and saying nothing of the business on Malabar Hill. That will best be told her when she has me home again, and can hold my hand feeling that I am secure.

"July 8th.—I have been down again to-day to see

the *Belle Fortune.* I forgot to say that she belongs to
Messrs. Vincent and Hext, of Bristol, and is bound for
that port. The only other passengers are a Dr. Concanen
and his wife, who are acquaintances of Mr. Eversleigh.
Dr. Concanen is a physician with a good practice in
Colombo, or was—as his wife's delicate health has forced
him to throw up his employment here and return to
England. Mr. Eversleigh introduced me to them this
morning on the *Belle Fortune.* The husband is almost
as tall as my host, and looks a man of great strength :
Mrs. Concanen is frail and worn, but very lovely.
To-day she seemed so ill that I offered to give up my
cabin, which is really much more comfortable than
theirs. But she would not hear of it, insisting that I
was by far the greater invalid, and that a sailing vessel
would quickly set her right again—especially a vessel
bound for England. Altogether they promise to be most
pleasant companions. I forgot to say that Mrs. Concanen is taking a native maid home to act as her nurse.

" July 11th.—We start in a week's time. I had a
long talk with Captain Holding to-day; he hopes to
make a fairly quick passage, but says he is short of
hands. I have not seen the Concanens since.

" July 16th.—We sail to-morrow afternoon. I have
been down to make my final preparations, and find my
cabin much to my liking. Captain Holding is still
short of hands.

" July 17th., 7.30 p.m.—We cast off our warps
shortly after four o'clock, and were quickly running

homeward at about seven knots an hour. The Concanens stood on deck with me watching Ceylon grow dim on the horizon. As the proud cone of Adam's Peak faded softly and slowly into the evening mist, and so vanished, as I hope, for ever out of my life, I could not forbear returning thanks to Providence, which has thus far watched over me so wonderfully. There is a fair breeze, and the hands, though short, do their work well to all appearances. There were only fifteen yesterday, three having been missed for about a week before we sailed; but I have not yet seen Captain Holding to ask him if he made up his number of hands at the last moment. Mrs. Concanen has invited me to their cabin to have a chat about England.

"July 18th.—I am more disturbed than I care to own by a very curious discovery which I made this morning. As I issued on deck I saw a man standing by the forecastle, whose back seemed familiar to me. Presently he turned, and I saw him to be Simon Colliver. He has most strangely altered his appearance, being dressed now as a common sailor, and wearing rings in his ears as the custom is. Catching sight of me, he came forward with a pleasant smile and explained himself.

"'It is no manner of use, Trenoweth; we're fated to meet. You did not expect to see me here in this get-up; but I learnt last night you were on board. You look as though you had seen a ghost! Don't stare so, man—I should say "sir" now, I suppose—it's only another of fortune's rubs. I fell ill after that journey to the Peak, and although Railton nursed me like a woman—he's a good fellow, Railton, and not as rough as you would expect—I woke up out of my fever at last to find all the money gone. I'm a fellow of resource, Trenoweth, so I hit on the idea of working my passage home; by good luck found the *Belle Fortune* was short of hands, offered my services, was accepted —having been to sea before, you know—sold my old clothes for this costume—must dress when one is acting a part—and here I am.'

" ' Is Railton with you ? ' I asked.

" ' Oh, yes, similarly attired. I did not see you yesterday, being busy with the cargo, so that it's all the more pleasant to meet here. But work is the order of the day now. You'll give me a good character to the captain, won't you? Good-bye for the present.'

" I cannot tell how much this meeting has depressed me. Certainly I have no reason for disbelieving the man's story, but the frequency and strangeness of our meetings make it hard to believe them altogether accidental. I saw Railton in the afternoon : he is greatly altered for the worse, and, I should think, had been drinking heavily before he shipped; but the captain was evidently too short of hands to be particular. I think I will give the Concanens my tin box to hide in their cabin. Of course I can trust them, and this will baffle theft; the clasp I will wear about me. This is a happy idea; I will go to their cabin now and ask them. It is 9.30 p.m., and the wind is still fair, I believe.

"July 20th.—We have so far kept up an average speed of seven and a half knots an hour, and Captain Holding thinks we shall make even better sailing when the hands are more accustomed to their work. I spend my time mostly with the Concanens—who readily, by the way, undertook the care of my tin box—and find them the most agreeable of fellow-travellers. Mrs. Concanen has a very sweet voice, and her husband has learnt to accompany it on the guitar, so that altogether we spend very pleasant evenings.

"July 21st, 22nd, 23rd.—The weather is still beautiful, and the breeze steady. Last night, at about six in the evening, it freshened up, and we ran all night under reefed topsails in expectation of a squall; but nothing came of it. I trust the wind will last, not only because it brings me nearer home, but also because without it the heat would be intolerable. The mention of home leads me to say that Mrs. Concanen was most sympathetic when I spoke of Margery. It is good to be able to talk of my wife to this kind creature, and she is so devoted to her husband that she plainly finds it easy to sympathise. They are a most happy couple.

"July 24th.—Our voyage, hitherto so prosperous, has been marred to-day by a sad accident. Mr. Wilkins, the mate, was standing almost directly under the mainmast at about 4.30 this afternoon, when Railton, who was aloft, let slip a block, which descended on the mate's head, striking it with fearful force and killing him instantly. He was an honest, kindly man, to judge from the little I have seen of him, and, as Captain Holding assures me, an excellent navigator. Poor Railton was dreadfully upset by the effects of his clumsiness; although I dislike the man, I have not the heart to blame him when I see the contrition upon his face.

"July 25th, midnight.—We buried Wilkins to-day. Captain Holding read the burial service, and was much affected, for Wilkins was a great friend of his; we then lowered the body into the sea. I spent the evening with the Concanens, the captain being on deck and too depressed to receive consolation. Nor was it much better with us in the cabin. Although we tried to talk we were all depressed and melancholy, and I retired earlier than usual to write my Journal.

"July 26th to August 4th.—There has been nothing to record. The wind has been fair as yet throughout, though it dropped yesterday (Aug. 3rd), and we lay for some hours in a dead calm. We have recovered our spirits altogether by this time.

"August 5th.—One of our hands, Griffiths, fell overboard to-day and was drowned. He and Colliver were out upon the fore-yard when Griffiths slipped, and missing the deck, fell clear into the sea. The captain was below at the time, but rushed upon deck on hearing Colliver's alarm of 'Man overboard!' It was too late, however. The vessel was making eight knots an hour at the time, and although it was immediately put about, there was not the slightest hope of finding the poor fellow. Indeed, we never saw him again."

[At this point the Journal becomes strangely meagre, consisting almost entirely of disconnected jottings about the weather, while here and there occurs merely a date with the latitude and longitude entered opposite. Only two entries seem of any importance: one of August 20th, noting that they had doubled the Cape, and a second written two days later and running as follows :—]

"August 22nd.—Dr. Concanen came into my cabin early this morning and told me that his wife had just given birth to a son. He seemed prodigiously elated, and I congratulated him heartily, as this is the first child born to them. He stayed but a moment or so with me, and then went back to attend to his wife. I spent most of the day on deck with Captain Holding, who is unceasingly vigilant now. Wind continues steadily S.E."

[After this the record is again scanty, but among less important entries we found the following : —]

"August 29th.—Mrs. Concanen rapidly recovering. The child is a fine boy: so, at least, the doctor says, though I confess I should have thought it rather small. However, it seems able to cry lustily.

"Sept. 6th.—Sighted Ascension Island.

"Sept. 8th, 9th. —Wind dropping off and heat positively stifling. A curious circumstance occurred to-day (the 9th), which shows that I did well to be careful of my Journal. I was sitting on deck with the Concanens, beneath an awning which the doctor has rigged up to protect us from the heat, when our supply of to-

bacco ran short. As I was descending for more I met
Colliver coming out of my cabin. He was rather dis-
concerted at seeing me, but invented some trivial excuse
about fetching a thermometer which Captain Holding
had lent me. I am confident now that he was on the
look-out for my papers, the more so as I had myself
restored the thermometer to the captain's cabin two
days ago. It is lucky that I confided my papers to the
Concanens. As for Railton, the hangdog look on that
man's face has increased with his travels. He seems
quite unable to meet my eye, and returns short, surly
answers if questioned. I cannot think his dejection
is solely due to poor Wilkins' death, for I noticed something very like it on the outward voyage."

[Here follow a few jottings on weather and speed,
which latter—with the exception of five days during
which the vessel lay becalmed—seems to have been very
satisfactory. On the 17th they caught a light breeze
from N.E., and on the 19th passed Cape Verde. Soon
after this the Journal becomes connected again, and so
continues.]

"Sept. 24th.—Just after daybreak, went on deck,
and found Captain Holding already there. This man
seems positively to require no sleep. Since Wilkins'
death he has managed the navigation almost entirely
alone. He seemed unusually grave this morning, and
told me that four of the hands had been taken ill during
the night with violent attacks of vomiting, and were
lying below in great danger. He had not seen the

doctor yet, but suspected that something was wrong with the food. At this point the doctor joined us and took the captain aside. They conversed earnestly for about three minutes, and presently I heard the captain exclaiming in a louder tone, ' Well, doctor, of course you know best, but I can't believe it for all that.' Shortly after the doctor went below again to look after his patients. He was very silent when we met again at dinner, and I have not seen him since.

" Sept. 25th. One of the hands, Walters, died during the night in great agony. We sighted the Peak of Teneriffe early in the afternoon, and I remained on deck with Mrs. Concanen, watching it. The doctor is below, analysing the food. I believe he is completely puzzled by this curious epidemic.

" Sept. 26th.—Wind N.E., but somewhat lighter. Three more men seized last night with precisely the same symptoms. With three deaths and five men ill, we are now left with but nine hands (not counting the captain) to work the ship. Walters was buried to-day. I learned from Mrs. Concanen that her husband has made a *post mortem* examination of the body. I do not know what his conclusions are.

" I open my Journal again to record another disquieting accident. It is odd, but I have missed one of the pieces of my father's clasp. I am positive it was in my pocket last night. I now have an indistinct recollection of hearing something fall whilst I was dressing this morning, but although I have searched both cabin and state-room thoroughly, I can find nothing. However, even if it has fallen into Colliver's hands, which is unlikely, he can make nothing of it, and luckily I know the words written upon it by heart. Still the loss has vexed me not a little. I will have another search before turning in to-night.

"Sept. 27th.—Wind has shifted to N.W. The doctor was summoned during the night to visit one of the men taken ill two nights before. The poor fellow died before daybreak, and I hear that another is not expected to live until night. The doctor has only been on deck for a few minutes to-day, and these he occupied in talk with the captain, who seems to have caught the prevailing depression, for he has been going about in a state of nervous disquietude all the afternoon. I expect that want of sleep is telling upon him at last. The clasp is still missing.

"Sept. 28th.—A rough day, and all hands busily engaged. Wind mostly S.W., but shifted to due W. before nightfall. Three of the invalids are better, but the other is still lying in a very critical state.

"Sept. 29th, 30th, Oct. 1st, 2nd.—Weather squally, so that we may expect heavy seas in the Bay of Biscay. All the invalids are by this time in a fair way of recovery, and one of them will be strong enough to return to work in a couple of days. Doctor Concanen is still strangely silent, however, and the captain's cheerfulness seems quite to have left him. Oh, that this gloomy voyage were over!

"Oct. 3rd.—Weather clearer.   Light breeze from
S.S.W.

"Oct. 5th.—Let me roughly put down in few words
what has happened, not that I see at present any chance
of leaving this accursed ship alive, but in the hope that
Providence may thus be aided—as far as human aid
may go—in bringing these villains to justice, if this
Journal should by any means survive me.

"Last night, shortly before ten, I went at Doctor
Concanen's invitation to chat in his cabin.   The doctor
himself was busily occupied with some medical works,
to which, as his wife assured me, he had been giving his
whole attention of late.   But Mrs. Concanen and I sat
talking together of home until close upon midnight,
when the baby, who was lying asleep at her side, awoke
and began to cry.   Upon this she broke off her conversation and began to sing the little fellow to sleep.
'Home, Sweet Home' was the song, and at the end of
the first verse—so sweetly touching, however hack-
neyed, to all situated as we—the doctor left his books,
came over, and was standing behind her, running his
hands, after a trick of his, affectionately through her
hair, when the native nurse, who slept in the next cabin
and had heard the baby crying, came in and offered to
take him.   Mrs. Concanen, however, assured her that it
was not necessary, and the girl was just going out of
the door when suddenly we heard a scream and then the
captain's voice calling, 'Trenoweth! Doctor! Help,
help!'

"The doctor immediately rushed past the maid and up the companion. I was just following at his heels when I heard two shots fired in rapid succession, and then a heavy crash. Immediately the girl fell with a shriek, and the doctor came staggering heavily back on top of her. Quick as thought, I pulled them inside, locked the cabin door, and began to examine their wounds. The girl was quite dead, being shot through the breast, while Concanen was bleeding terribly from a wound just below the shoulder: the bullet must have grazed his upper arm, tearing open the flesh and cutting an artery, passed on and struck the nurse, who was just behind. Mrs. Concanen was kneeling beside him and vainly endeavouring to staunch the flow of blood.

"Oddly enough, the attack, from whatever quarter it came, was not followed up; but I heard two more shots fired on deck, and then a loud crashing and stamping in the fore part of the vessel, and judged that the mutineers were battening and barricading the forecastle. I unlocked the door and was going out to explore the situation, when the doctor spoke in a weak voice—

"'Quick, Trenoweth! never mind me. I've got the main artery torn to pieces and can't last many more minutes—but quick for the captain's cabin and get the guns. They'll be down presently, as soon as they've finished up there.'

"Opening the door and telling Mrs. Concanen—who although white as a sheet never lost her presence of mind for a moment—to lock it after me, I stole along

L

the passage, gained the captain's cabin, found two guns, a small keg of powder (to get at which I had to smash in a locker with the butt-end of one of the guns), and some large shot, brought I suppose for shooting gulls.

"I found also a large packet of revolver cartridges, but no revolver; and it suddenly struck me that the shots already fired must have been from the captain's revolver, taken probably from his dead body. Yes, as I remembered the sound of the shots I was sure of it. The mutineers had probably no other ammunition, and so far I was their master.

"Fearful that by smashing the locker I had made noise enough to be heard above the turmoil on deck, I returned swiftly and had just reached the door of Concanen's cabin, when I heard a shout above, and a man whom I recognised by the voice as Johnston, the carpenter, came rushing down the steps crying, 'Hide me, doctor, hide me!' As Mrs. Concanen opened the door in answer to my call, another shot was fired, the man suddenly threw up his hands and we tumbled into the cabin together. I turned as soon as I had locked and barricaded the door, and saw him lying on his face —quite dead. He had been shot in the back, just below the shoulder-blades.

"The doctor also was at his last gasp, and the floor literally swam with blood. As we bent over him to catch his words he whispered, 'It was Railton—that— I saw. Good-bye, Alice,' and fell back a corpse. I carried the body to a corner of the cabin, took off my jacket and covered up his face, and turned to Mrs. Concanen. She was dry-eyed, but dreadfully white.

"'Give me the guns,' she said quietly, 'and show me how to load them.'

"I was doing so when I heard footsteps coming slowly down the companion. A moment after, two crashing blows were struck upon the door-panel and Colliver's voice cried—

"'Trenoweth, you dog, are you hiding there? Give me up those papers and come out.'

"For answer I sent a charge of shot through the cabin door, and in an instant heard him scrambling back with all speed up the stairs.

"By this time it was about 3 a.m., and to add to the horrors of our plight the lamp suddenly went out and left us in utter darkness. I drew Mrs. Concanen aside—after strengthening the barricade about the door —put her and the child in a corner where she would be safe if they attempted to fire through the skylight, and then sat down beside her to consider.

"If, as I suspected, the mutineers had only the revolver which they had taken from the captain, they had but one shot left, for I had already counted five, and it was not likely that Holding—who always, as I knew, carried some weapon with him—would have any loose cartridges upon him at a time when no one suspected the least danger.

"Next, as to numbers. Excluding Captain Holding —now dead—and including the cook I reckoned that

L 2

there were fourteen hands on board. Of these, five
were sick and probably at this moment barricaded in
the forecastle. One, the carpenter, was lying here dead,
and from the shriek which preceded the captain's cry,
another had already been accounted for by the mutineers.

"This reduced the number to eight. The next
question was, how many were the mutineers? I had
guessed at once that Colliver and Railton had a hand in
the business, for (in addition to my previous distrust of
the men) it was just upon midnight when we heard the
first cry, that is to say, the time when the watch was
changed, and I knew that these two belonged to the
captain's watch. But could they be alone?

"It seemed impossible, and yet I knew no others
among the crew to distrust, and certainly Davis, who
was acting as mate at present, was, although an indifferent navigator, as true as steel. Moreover, the
fact that the mutineers' success in shooting the doctor
had not been followed up, made my guess seem more
likely. Certainly Colliver and Railton were the only
two of whom we could be sure as yet. Nevertheless the
supposition was amazing.

"I had arrived at this point in my calculations
when a yell which I recognised, told me that they had
caught Cox the helmsman and were murdering him.
After this came dead silence, which lasted all through
the night.

"I must hasten to conclude this, for we have no
light in the cabin, and I am writing now by the faint

evening rays that struggle in through the sky-light.
As soon as morning broke I determined to reconnoitre.
Cautiously removing the barricade, I opened the cabin
door and stole up the companion ladder. Arrived at the
top I peered cautiously over and saw the mutineers
sitting by the foreward hatch, drinking. They were
altogether four in number—Colliver, Railton, a seaman
called Rogerson, who had lately been punished by
Captain Holding for sleeping when on watch, and the
cook, a Chinaman. Rogerson was not with the rest, but
had hold of the wheel and was steering. The vessel at
the time was sailing under crowded canvas before a stiff
sou'-westerly breeze. I kept low lest Rogerson should
see me, but he was obviously more than half drunk, and
was chiefly occupied in regarding his comrades with
anything but a pleasant air. Just as I was drawing a
beautiful bead however, and had well covered Colliver,
he saw me and gave the alarm; and immediately the
three sprang to their feet and made for me, the Chinaman first. Altering my aim I waited until he came
close and then fired. I must have hit him, I think in
the ankle, for he staggered and fell with a loud cry
about ten paces from me. Seeing this, I made all speed
again down the ladder, turning at the cabin door for a
hasty shot with the second barrel, which, I think,
missed. The other two pursued me until I gained the
cabin, and then went back to their comrade. The rest
of the day has been quite quiet. Luckily we have a
large tin of biscuits in the cabin, so as far as food goes

we can hold out for some time. Mrs. Concanen and I are going to take turns at watching to-night.

"Oct. 6th, 1 p.m.—At about 1.30 a.m. I was sleeping when Mrs. Concanen woke me on hearing a noise by the skylight. The mutineers, finding this to be the only point from which they could attack us with any safety, had hit upon the plan of lashing knives to the end of long sticks and were attempting to stab us with these clumsy weapons. It was so dark that I could hardly see to aim, but a couple of shots fired in rapid succession drove them quickly away. The rest of the night was passed quietly enough, except for the cries of the infant, which are very pitiable. The day, too, has been without event, except that I have heard occasional sounds in the neighbourhood of the forecastle, which I think must come from the sick men imprisoned there, and attempting to cut their way out.

"Oct. 7th.—We are still let alone. Doubtless the mutineers think to starve us out or to lull us into a false security and catch us unawares. As for starvation, the box of biscuits will last us both for a week or more; and they stand little chance of taking us by surprise, for one of us is always on the watch whilst the other sleeps. They spent last night in drinking. Railton's voice was very loud at times, and I could hear Colliver singing his infernal song—

"'Sing hey! for the dead man's lips, my lads.'

That man must be a fiend incarnate. I have but little

time to write, and between every word have to look about for signs of the mutineers. I wonder whither they are steering us.

"Oct. 8th.—A rough day evidently, by the way in which the vessel is pitching, but I expect the crew are for the most part drunk. We must find some way of getting rid of the dead bodies soon. I hardly like to speak to Mrs. Concanen about it. Words cannot express the admiration I feel for the pluck of this delicate woman. She asked me to-day to show her how to use a gun, and I believe will fight to the end. Her child is ailing fast, poor little man! And yet he is happier than we, being unconscious of all these horrors.

"Oct. 9th, 3.30 p.m.—Sick of this inaction I made another expedition up the companion to-day. Rogerson was steering, and Railton standing by the wheel talking to him. He had a bottle in his hand and seemed very excited. I could not see Colliver at first, but on glancing up at the rigging saw a most curious sight. There was a man on the main-top, the boatswain, Kelly, apparently asleep. Below him Colliver was climbing up, knife in mouth, and was already within a couple of yards of him. I fired and missed, but alarmed Kelly, who jumped up and seized a block which he had cut off to defend himself with. At the same moment Railton and Rogerson made for me. As I retreated down the ladder I stumbled, the gun went off and I think hit Rogerson, who was first. We rolled down the stairs together, he on top and hacking at me furiously with a knife. At this moment I heard the report of a gun, and my assailant's grasp suddenly relaxed. He fell back, tripping up Railton who was following unsteadily, and so giving me time to gain the cabin door, where Mrs. Concanen was standing, a smoking gun in her hand. Before we could shut the door, however, Colliver, who by this time had gained the head of the stairs, fired, and she dropped backwards inside the cabin. Locking the door, I found her lying with a wound just below the heart. She had just time to point to her child before she died. Was ever so ghastly a tragedy?

"Oct. 10th.—Awake all night, trying to soothe the cries of the child, and at the same time keeping a good look-out for the mutineers. The sea is terribly rough, and the poor corpses are being pitched from side to side of the cabin. At midday I heard a cry on deck, and judged that Kelly had dropped from the rigging in pure exhaustion. The noise in the forecastle is awful. I think some of the men there must be dead.

"Oct. 11th, 5 p.m.—The child is dying. There is a fearful storm raging, and with this crew the vessel has no chance if we are anywhere near land. God help——"

CHAPTER XI.

TELLS OF THE WRITING UPON THE GOLDEN CLASP; AND
HOW I TOOK DOWN THE GREAT KEY.

So ended my father's Journal—in a silence full of
tragedy, a silence filled in with the echo of that awful
cry borne landwards on the wings of the storm; and
now, in the presence of this mute witness, shaping itself
into the single word "Murder." Of the effect of the
reading upon us, I need not speak at any length. For
the most part it had passed without comment; but the
occasional choking of Uncle Loveday's voice, my own
quickening breath as the narrative continued, and the
tears that poured down the cheeks of both of us as we
heard the simple loving messages for Margery—messages so vainly tender, so pitifully fond—were evidence
enough of our emotion.

I say that we both wept, and it is true. But though,
do what I could, my young heart would swell and ache
until the tears came at times, yet for the most part I
sat with cold and gathering hate. It was mournful
enough when I consider it. That the hand which
penned these anxious lines should be cold and stiff, the
ear for which they were so lovingly intended for ever
deaf: that all the warm hopes should end beside that

bed where husband and wife lay dead—surely this was
tragic enough. But I did not think of this at the time
—or but dimly if at all. Hate, impotent hate, was
consuming my young heart as the story drew to its end;
hate and no other feeling possessed me as Uncle Loveday broke abruptly off, turned the page in search of
more, found none, and was silent.

Once he had stopped for a moment to call for a
candle. Mrs. Busvargus brought it, trimmed the wick,
and again retired. This was our only interruption. Joe
Roscorla had not returned from Polkimbra; so we were
left alone to the gathering shadows and the horror of
the tale.

When my uncle finished there was a long pause.
Finally he reached out his hand for his pipe, filled it,
and looked up. His kindly face was furrowed with the
marks of weeping, and big tears were yet standing in
his eyes.

"Murdered," he said, "murdered, if ever man was
murdered."

"Yes," I echoed, "murdered."

"But we'll have the villain," he exclaimed, bringing
his fist down on the table with sudden energy. "We'll
have him for all his cunning, eh, boy?"

"Not yet," I answered; "he is far away by this
time. But we'll have him: oh, yes, we'll have him."

Uncle Loveday looked at me oddly for a moment,
and then repeated—

"Yes, yes, we'll have him safe enough. Joe Roscorla

must have given the alarm before he had time to go far.
And to think," he added, throwing up his hand, "that
I talked to the villain only yesterday morning as though
he were some unfortunate victim of the sea!"

I am sure that my uncle was regretting the vast
deal of very fine language he had wasted: and, indeed,
he had seldom more nobly risen to an occasion.

"Pearls, pearls before swine! Swine did I say?
Snakes, if it's not an insult to a snake to give its name
to such as Colliver. What did you say, Jasper?"

"We'll have him."

"Jasper, my boy," said he, scanning me for a second
time oddly, "maybe you'll be better in bed. Try to
sleep again, my poor lad—what do you think?"

"I think," I answered, "that we have not yet
looked at the clasp."

"My dear boy, you're right: you're right again.
Let us look at it."

The piece of metal resembled, as I have said, the
half of a waist-buckle, having a socket but no corresponding hook. In shape it was slightly oblong, being
about 2 in. by 1½ in. It glittered brightly in the
candle's ray as Uncle Loveday polished it with his
handkerchief, readjusted his spectacles, and bent over it.

At the end of a minute he looked up, and said—

"I cannot make head or tail of it. It seems plain
enough to read, but makes nonsense. Come over here
and see for yourself."

I bent over his shoulder, and this is what I saw—

The edge of the clasps wa engraved with a border of flowers and beasts, all exquisitely small. Within this was cut, by a much rougher hand, an inscription which was plain enough to read, though making no sense whatever. The writing was arranged in five lines of three words apiece, and ran thus :—

MOON . END . SOUTH.
N.N.W. . . 22 . FEET.
NORTH . SIDE . 4.
DEEP . AT . POINT.
WATER . $1\frac{1}{2}$. HOURS.

I read the words a full dozen times, and then, failing of any interpretation, turned to Uncle Loveday—

" Jasper," said he, " to my mind those words make nonsense."

" And to mine, uncle."

" Now attend to me, Jasper. This is evidently but one half of the clasp which your father discovered. That's as plain as daylight. The question is, what has become of the other half, of the hook that should fit into this eye ? Now, what I want you to do is to try and remember if this was all that the man Railton gave you."

" This was all."

" You are quite certain ? "

" Quite."

" You did not leave the other piece behind in the cow-shed by any chance ? "

"No, for I looked at the packet before I hid it, and there was only one piece of metal."

"Very well. One half of the golden clasp being lost, the next question is, what has become of it?"

I nodded.

"To this," said Uncle Loveday, bending forward over the table, "two answers are possible. Either it lies at the bottom of the sea with the rest of the freight of the *Belle Fortune,* or it is in Colliver's possession."

"It may lie beneath Dead Man's Rock, in John Railton's pocket," I suggested.

"True, my boy, true ; you put another case. But anyhow it makes no difference. If it lies at the bottom of the sea, whether in Railton's pocket or not, the secret is safe. If it is in Colliver's possession the secret is safe, unless he has seen and learnt by heart this half of the inscription. In any case, I am sorry to tell you— and this is what I was coming to—the secret is closed against us for the time."

"That is not certain," said I.

"Excuse me, Jasper, it is quite certain. You admit yourself that this writing is nonsense. Well and good. But besides this, I would have you remember," pursued Uncle Loveday, turning once more to my father's Journal, "that Ezekiel expressly says, 'The inscription ran right across the clasp.' It could be read easily enough and contained accurate directions for searching in some spot, but where that spot was it did not reveal——"

"Quite so," I interrupted, "and that is just what we have to discover."

" How ? "

"Why, by means of the key, as the parchment and the Will plainly show. We may still be beaten, but even so, we shall know whereabouts to look, if we can only catch Colliver."

"Bless the boy!" said Uncle Loveday, "he certainly has a head."

"Uncle," continued I, rising to my feet, "the secret of the Great Ruby is written upon my grandfather's key. That key was to be taken down when he that undertook the task of discovering the secret should have returned and crossed the threshold of Lantrig. Uncle, my father has crossed the threshold of Lantrig—"

"Feet foremost, feet foremost, my boy. Oh, poor Ezekiel!"

"Feet foremost, yes," I continued — "dead and murdered, yes. But he has come: come to find my mother dead, but still he has come. Uncle, I am the only Trenoweth left to Lantrig; think of it, the only one left——"

"Poor Ezekiel! Poor Margery!"

"Yes, uncle, and all I inherit is the knife that murdered my father, and this key. I have the knife, and I will take down the key. We are not beaten yet."

I drew a chair under the great beam, and mounted it. When first my grandfather returned he had hung the iron key upon its hook, giving strict injunctions that no one should touch it. There ever since it had hung, the centre of a host of spiders' webs. Even my poor mother's brush, so diligent elsewhere, had never invaded this sacred relic, and often during our lonely winter evenings had she told me the story of it : how that Amos Trenoweth's dying curse was laid upon the person that should touch it, and how the spiders' days were numbered with every day that brought my father nearer home.

There it hung now, scarcely to be seen for cobwebs. Its hour had come at last. Even as I stretched out my hand a dozen horrid things hurried tumultuously back into darkness. Even as I laid my hand on it, a big ungainly spider, scared but half incredulous, started in alarm, hesitated, and finally made off at full speed for shelter.

This, then, was the key that should unlock the treasure—this, that had from the first hung over us, the one uncleansed spot in Lantrig : this was the talisman —this grimy thing lying in my hand. The spiders had been jealous in their watch.

Stepping down, I got a cloth and brushed away the cobwebs. The key was covered thickly with rust, but even so I could see that something was written upon it. For about a minute I stood polishing it, and then carried it forward to the light.

Yes, there was writing upon it, both on the handle and along the shaft—writing that, as it shaped itself

before my eyes, caused them to stare in wrathful in-
credulity, caused my heart to sink at first in dismay
and then to swell in mad indignation, caused my blood
to turn to gall and my thoughts to very bitterness. For
this was what I read :—

On the handle were engraved in large capitals the
initials A. T. with the date MDCCCXII. Along the
shaft, from handle to wards, ran on either side the
following sentence in old English lettering :—

**THY HOUSE IS SET UPON THE SANDS:
AND THY HOPES BY A DEAD MAN.**

This was all. This short sentence was the sum of
all the vain quest on which my father had met his end.
"Thy house is set upon the sands," and even now had
crumbled away beneath Amos Trenoweth's curse. "Thy
hopes by a dead man," and even now he on whom our
hopes had rested, lay upstairs a pitiful corpse. Was
ever mockery more fiendish? As the full cruelty of the
words broke in upon me, once again I seemed to hear
the awful cry from the sea, but now among its voices
rang a fearful laugh as though Amos Trenoweth's soul
were making merry in hell over his grim jest—the
slaughter of his son and his son's wife.

White with desperate passion, I turned and hurled
the accursed key across the room into the blazing
hearth.

END OF BOOK I.

𝔅ook II.

THE FINDING OF THE GREAT RUBY.

CHAPTER I.

TELLS HOW THOMAS LOVEDAY AND I WENT IN SEARCH OF
FORTUNE.

SEEING that these pages do not profess to be an auto-
biography, but rather the plain chronicle of certain
events connected with the Great Ruby of Ceylon, I
conceive myself entitled to the reader's pardon if I do
some violence to the art of the narrator, and here ask
leave to pass by, with but slight allusion, some fourteen years. This I do because the influence of this
mysterious jewel, although it has indelibly coloured my
life, has been sensibly exercised during two periods
alone—periods short in themselves, but nevertheless
long enough to determine between them every current
of my destiny, and to supply an interpretation for my
every action.

I am the more concerned with advertising the reader
of this, as on looking back upon what I have written
with an eye as far as may be impartial, I have not failed

M

to note one obvious criticism that will be passed upon
me. "How," it will be asked, "could any boy barely
eight years of age conceive the thoughts and entertain
the emotions there attributed to Jasper Trenoweth?"

The criticism is just as well as obvious. As a solitary man for ever brooding on the past, I will not deny
that I may have been led to paint that past in colours
other than its own. Indeed, it would be little short of
a miracle were this not so. A morbid soul—and I will
admit that mine is morbid—preying upon its recollections, and nourished on that food alone, cannot hope to
attain the sense of proportion which is the proper gift
of varied experience. I readily grant, therefore, that
the lights and shades on this picture may be wrong,
as judged by the ordinary eye, but I do claim them
to be a faithful reproduction of my own vision. As I
look back I find them absolutely truthful, nor can I
give the lie to my own impressions in the endeavour to
write what shall seem true to the rest of the world.

This must be, therefore, my excuse for asking the
reader to pass by fourteen years and take up the tale far
from Lantrig. But before I plunge again into my
story, it is right that I should briefly touch on the chief
events that occurred during this interval in my life.

They buried my father and mother in the same
grave in Polkimbra Churchyard. I remember now
that crowds of fisher-folk lined the way to their last
resting-place, and a host, as it seemed to me, of tear-
stained faces watched the coffins laid in the earth.

But all else is a blurred picture to me, as, indeed, is the time for many a long day after.

Colliver was never found. Captain Merrydew raised the hue and cry, but the sailor Georgio Rhodojani was never seen again from the moment when his evil face leered in through the window of Lantrig. A reward was offered, and more than once Polkimbra was excited with the news of his arrest, but it all came to nothing. Failing his capture, Uncle Loveday was wisely silent on the subject of my father's Journal and the secret of the Great Ruby. He had not been idle, however. After long consultation with Aunt Elizabeth he posted off to Plymouth to gain news of Lucy Railton and her daughter, but without success. The "Welcome Home" still stood upon the Barbican, but the house was in possession of new tenants, and neither they nor their landlord could tell anything of the Railtons except that they had left suddenly about two months before (that being the date of the wreck of the *Belle Fortune*) after paying their rent to the end of the Christmas quarter. The landlord could give no reasons for their departure —for the house had a fair trade—but supposed that the husband must have returned from sea and taken them away. Uncle Loveday, of course, knew better, but on this point held his peace. The one result of all his inquiries was the certainty that the Railtons had vanished utterly.

So Lantrig, for the preservation of which my father had given his life, was sold to strangers, and I went to

M 2

live with Aunt and Uncle Loveday at Lizard Town.
The proceeds of the sale (and they were small indeed)
Uncle Loveday put carefully by until such time as I
should be cast upon the world to seek my fortune. For
twelve uneventful years my aunt fed me, and uncle
taught me—being no mean scholar, especially in Latin,
which tongue he took great pains to make me perfect in.
Thomas Loveday was my only companion, and soon
became my dear friend. Poor Tom! I can see his
handsome face before me now as it was in those old days
—the dreamy eyes, the rare smile with its faint sugges-
tion of mockery, the fair curls in which a breeze seemed
for ever blowing, the pursed lips that had a habit of saying such wonderful things. In my dreams—those few
dreams of mine that are happy—we are always boys
together, climbing the cliffs for eggs, or risking our
lives in Uncle Loveday's boat—always boys together.
Poor Tom! Poor Tom!

So the unmarked time rolled on, until there came a
memorable day in July on which I must touch for a
moment. It was evening. I was returning with Tom
to Lizard Town from Dead Man's Rock, where we had
been basking all the sunny afternoon, Tom reading, and
I simply staring vacantly into the heavens and wondering when the time would come that should set me
free to unravel the mystery of this ill-omened spot.
Finally, after taking our fill of idleness, we bathed as
the sun was setting; and I remember wondering, as
I dived off the black ledge, whether beneath me there

lay any relic of the *Belle Fortune*, any fragment that might preserve some record of her end. I had dived here often enough, but found nothing, nor could I see anything to-day but the clean sand twinkling beneath its veil of blue, though here, as I guessed, must still lie the bones of John Railton. But I must hasten. We were returning over the Downs when suddenly I spied a small figure running towards us, and making frantic signals of distress.

"That," said I, "from the shape of it, must be Joe Roscorla."

And Joe Roscorla it was, only by no means the Joe Roscorla of ordinary life, but a galvanised and gesticulating Joe, whereas the Joe that we knew was of a lethargic bearing and slow habit of speech. Still, it was he, and as he came up to us he stayed all questioning by gasping out the word "Missus!" and then falling into a violent fit of coughing.

"Well, what is amiss?" asked Tom.

"Took wi' a seizure, an' maister like a thing mazed," blurted Joe, and then fell to panting and coughing worse than ever.

"What! a seizure? paralysis do you mean?" I asked, while Tom turned white.

"Just a seizure, and I ha'n't got time for no longer name. But run if 'ee want to see her alive."

We ran without further speech, Joe keeping at our side for a minute, but soon dropping behind and fading into distance. As we entered the door Uncle Loveday met us, and I saw by his face that Aunt Elizabeth was dead.

She had been in the kitchen busied with our supper, when she suddenly fell down and died in a few minutes. Heart disease was the cause, but in our part people only die of three complaints—a seizure, an inflammation, or a decline. The difference between these is purely one of time, so that Joe Roscorla, learning the suddenness of the attack, judged it forthwith a case of "seizure," and had so reported.

My poor aunt was dead; and until now we had never known how we loved her. Like so many of the Trenoweths she seemed hard and reserved to many, but we who had lived with her had learnt the goodness of her soul and the sincerity of her religion. The grief of her husband was her noblest epitaph.

He, poor man, was inconsolable. Without his wife he seemed as one deprived of most of his limbs, and moved helplessly about, as though life were now without purpose. Accustomed to be ruled by her at every turn, he missed her in every action of the day. Very swiftly he sank, of no assigned complaint, and within six months was laid beside her.

On his death-bed my uncle seemed strangely troubled about us. Tom was to be a doctor. My destiny was not so certain; but already I had renounced in my heart an inglorious life in Lizard Town. I longed to go with Tom; in London, too, I thought I should be free to follow the purpose of my life. But the question was, how should I find the money? For I knew that the sum obtained by the sale of Lantrig was miserably insufficient. So I sat with idle hands and waited for destiny; nor did I realise my helplessness until I stood in the room where Uncle Loveday lay dying.

"Tom," said my uncle, "Tom, come closer."

Tom bent over the bed.

" I am leaving you two boys without friends in this world. You have friends in Lizard Town, but Lizard Town is a small world, Tom. I ought to have sent you to London before, but kept putting off the parting. If one could only foresee—could only foresee."

He raised himself slightly on his elbow, and continued with pain—

" You will go to Guy's, and Jasper, I hope, may go with you. Be friends, boys; you will want friendship in this world. It will be a struggle, for there is barely enough for both. But it is best to share equally; *she* would have wished that. She was always planning that. I am doing it badly, I know, but she would have done it better."

The chill December sun came stealing in and illumined the sick man's face with a light that was the shadow of heaven. The strange doctor moved to the blind. My uncle's voice arrested him—

" No, no. Leave it up. You will have to pull it down very soon—only a few moments now. Tom, come closer. You have been a good boy, Tom, a good boy, though "—with a faint smile—" a little trying at times.

Ah, but she forgave you, Tom. She loved you dearly; she will tell me so—when we meet."

My uncle's gaze began to wander, as though anticipating that meeting; but he roused himself and said—

"Kiss me, Tom, and send Jasper to me."

Bitterly weeping, Tom made room, and I bent over the bed.

"Ah, Jasper, it is you. Kiss me, boy. I have been telling Tom that you must share alike. God has been stern with you, Jasper, to His own good ends—His own good ends. Only be patient, it will come right at the last. How dark it is getting; pull up the blind."

"The blind is up, uncle."

"Ah, yes, I forgot. I have often thought—do you remember that day—reading your father's paper—and the key?"

"Yes, uncle."

"I have often thought—about that key—which you flung into the fire—and I picked out—your father Ezekiel's key—keep it. Closer, Jasper, closer——"

I bent down until my ear almost touched his lips.

"I have—often—thought—we were wrong that night—and perhaps—meant—search—in . . ."

For quite a minute I bent to catch the next word, then looking on his face withdrew my arm and laid the grey head back upon the pillow.

My uncle was dead.

    *   *   *   *   *   *

So it happened that a few weeks after Tom and I,

having found Uncle Loveday's savings equally divided between us, started from Lizard Town by coach to seek our fortunes in London. In London it is that I must resume my tale. Of our early mishaps and mis-adventures I need not speak, the result being discernible as the story progresses. We did not find our fortunes, but we found some wisdom. Neither Tom nor I ever confessed to disappointment at finding the pavements of mere stone, but certainly two more absolute Whit-tingtons never trod the streets of the great city.

But before I resume I must say a few words of myself. No reader can gather the true moral of this narrative who does not take into account the effect which the cruel death of my parents had wrought on me. From the day of the wreck hate had been my constant companion, cherished and nursed in my heart until it held complete mastery over all other passions. I lived, so I told myself over and over again, but to avenge, to seek Simon Colliver high and low until I held him at my mercy. Thousands of times I rehearsed the scene of our meeting, and always I held the knife which stabbed my father. In my waking thoughts, in my dreams, I was always pursuing, and Colliver for ever fleeing before me. In every crowd I seemed to watch for his face alone, at every street-corner to listen for his voice—that face, that voice, which I should know among thousands. I had read De Quincey's "Opium-Eater," and the picture of his unresting search for his lost Ann somehow seized upon my imagination. Night after night it was to Oxford Street that my devil drove me, night after night I paced the "never-ending terraces," as did the opium-eater, on my tireless quest—but with feelings how different! To me it was but one long thirst of hatred, the long avenues of gaslight vistas of an avenging hell, all the multitudinous sounds of life but the chorus of that song to which my footsteps trod—

"Sing ho! but he waits for you."

To London had Simon Colliver come, and somewhere, some day, he would be mine. Until that day I sought a living face in a city of dead men, and down that illimitable slope to Holborn, and back again, I would tramp until the pavements were silent and deserted, then seek my lodging and throw myself exhausted on the bed.

In a dingy garret, looking out, when its grimy panes allowed, above one of the many squalid streets that feed the main artery of the Strand, my story begins anew. The furniture of the room relieves me of the task of word-painting, being more effectively described by catalogue, after the manner of the ships at Troy. It consisted of two small beds, one rickety washstand, one wooden chair, and one tin candlestick. At the present moment this last held a flickering dip, for it was ten o'clock on the night of May the ninth, eighteen hundred and sixty-three. On the chair sat Tom, turning excitedly the leaves of a prodigiously imposing manuscript. I was sitting on the edge of the bed nearest the candle, brooding on my hate as usual.

Fortune had evidently dealt us some rough knocks. We were dressed, as Tom put it, to suit the furniture, and did it to a nicety. We were fed, according to the same authority, above our income; but not often. I also quote Tom in saying that we were living rather fast : we certainly saw no long prospect before us. In short, matters had reached a crisis.

Tom looked up from his reading.

"Do you know, Jasper, I could wish that our wash-stand had not a hole cut in it to receive the basin. It sounds hyper-critical. But really it prejudices me in the eyes of the managers. There's a suspicious bulge in the middle of the paper that is damning."

I was absorbed in my own thoughts, and took no notice. Presently he continued—

"Whittington is an overrated character, don't you think? After all he owed his success to his name. It's a great thing for struggling youth to have a three-syllabled name with a proparoxyton accent. I've been listening to the bells to-night and they can make nothing of Loveday, while as for Trenoweth, it's hopeless."

As I still remained silent, Tom proceeded to an-nounce—

"The House will now go into the Question of Supply."

"The Exchequer," I reported, "contains exactly sixteen and eightpence halfpenny."

"Rent having been duly paid to-day and receipt given."

"Receipt given," I echoed.

"Really, when one comes to think of it, the situation is striking. Here are you, Jasper Trenoweth, inheritor of the Great Ruby of Ceylon, besides other treasure too paltry to mention, in danger of starving in a garret. Here am I, Thomas Loveday, author of 'Francesca: a Tragedy,' and other masterpieces too numerous to catalogue, with every prospect of sharing your fate. The situation is striking, Jasper, you'll allow."

"What did the manager say about it?" I asked.

"Only just enough to show he had not looked at it. He was more occupied with my appearance; and yet we agreed before I set out that your trousers might have been made for me. They are the most specious articles in our joint wardrobe: I thought to myself as walked along to-day, Jasper, that after all it is not the coat that makes the gentleman—it's the trousers. Now, in the matter of boots, I surpass you. If yours decay at their present rate, your walks in Oxford Street will become a luxury."

I was silent again.

"I do not recollect any case in fiction of a man being baulked of his revenge for the want of a pair of boots. Cheer up, Jasper, boy," he continued, rising and placing a hand on my shoulder. "We have been fools, and have paid for it. You thought you could find your enemy in London, and find the hiding-place too big. I thought I could write, and find I cannot. As for legitimate work, sixteen and eightpence halfpenny, even with economy, will hardly carry us on for three years."

I rose. " I will have one more walk in Oxford Street," I said, "and then come home and see this miserable farce of starvation out."

" Don't be a fool, Jasper. It is difficult, I know, to perish with dignity on sixteen and eightpence halfpenny : the odd coppers spoil the effect. Still we might bestow them on a less squeamish beggar and redeem our pride."

"Tom," I said, suddenly, " you lost a lot of money once over *rouge-et-noir.*"

" Don't remind me of that, Jasper."

" No, no ; but where did you lose it ? "

"At a gambling hell off Leicester Square. But why——"

" Should you know the place again ? Could you find it ? "

" Easily."

" Then let us go and try our luck with this miserable sum."

" Don't be a fool, Jasper. What mad notion has taken you now ? "

" I have never gambled in my life," I answered, "and may as well have a little excitement before the end comes. It's not much of a sum, as you say ; but the thought that we are playing for life or death may make up for that. Let us start at once."

"It is the maddest folly."

"Very well, Tom, we will share this. There may may be some little difficulty over the halfpenny, but I don't mind throwing that in. We will take half each, and you can hoard whilst I tempt fortune."

"Jasper," said Tom, his eyes filling with tears, "you have said a hard thing, but I know you don't mean it. If you are absolutely set on this silly freak, we will stand or fall together."

"Very well," said I, "we will stand or fall together, for I am perfectly serious. The six and eightpence halfpenny, no more and no less, I propose to spend in supper. After that we shall be better prepared to face our chance. Do you agree?"

"I agree," said Tom, sadly.

We took our hats, extinguished the candle, and stumbled down the stairs into the night.

We ordered supper at an eating-house in the Strand, and in all my life I cannot recall a merrier meal than this, which, for all we knew, would be our last. The very thought lent a touch of bravado to my humour, and presently Tom caught the infection. It was not a sumptuous meal in itself, but princely to our ordinary fare; and the unaccustomed taste of beer loosened our tongues, until our mirth fairly astonished our fellow-diners. At length the waiter came with the news that it was time for closing. Tom called for the bill, and finding that it came to half-a-crown apiece, ordered two sixpenny cigars, and tossed the odd eightpence halfpenny to the waiter, announcing at the same time that this was our last meal on earth. This done, he gravely handed me four half-crowns, and rose to leave. I rose also, and once more we stepped into the night.

Since the days of which I write, Leicester Square has greatly changed. Then it was an intricate, and, by night, even a dangerous quarter, chiefly given over to foreigners. As we trudged through innumerable by-streets and squalid alleys, I wondered if Tom had not forgotten his way. At length, however, we turned up a blind alley, lit by one struggling gas-jet, and knocked at a low door. It was opened almost immediately, and we groped our way up another black passage to a second door. Here Tom gave three knocks very loud and distinct. A voice cried, " Open," the door swung back before us, and a blaze of light flashed in our faces.

CHAPTER II.

TELLS OF THE LUCK OF THE GOLDEN CLASP.

As the door swung back I became conscious first of a
flood of light that completely dazzled my eyes, next of
the buzz of many voices that confused my hearing. By
slow degrees, however, the noise and glare grew familiar
and my senses were able to take in the strange scene.

I stood in a large room furnished after the fashion
of a drawing-room, and resplendent with candles and
gilding. The carpet was rich, the walls were hung with
pictures, which if garish in colour were not tasteless in
design, and between these glittered a quantity of gilded
mirrors that caught and reflected the rays of a huge
candelabrum depending from the centre of the ceiling.
Innumerable wax candles also shone in various parts of
the room, while here and there rich chairs and sofas
were disposed ; but these were for the most part un-
occupied, for the guests were clustered together beneath
the great candelabrum.

They were about thirty in number, and from their
appearance I judged them to belong to very different
classes of society. Some were poorly and even miserably
attired, others adorned with gorgeous, and not a few
with valuable, jewellery. Here stood one who from his

clothes seemed to be a poor artisan ; there lounged a
fop in evening dress. There was also a sprinkling of
women, and not a few wore masks of some black stuff
concealing the upper part of their faces.

But the strangest feature of the company was
that one and all were entirely and even breathlessly
watching the table in their midst. Even the idlest
scarcely raised his eyes to greet us as we entered, and
for a moment or two I paused at the door as one who
had no business with this strange assemblage. During
these few moments I was able to grasp the main points
of what I saw.

The guests were grouped around the table, some
sitting and others standing behind their chairs. The
table itself was oblong in shape, and at its head sat the
most extraordinary woman it had ever been my lot to
behold. She was of immense age, and so wrinkled that
her face seemed a very network of deeply-printed lines.
Her complexion, even in the candle-light, was of a deep
yellow, such as is rarely seen in the most jaundiced
faces. Despite her age, her features were bold and bore
traces of a rare beauty outlived ; her eyes were of a
deep yet glittering black, and as they flashed from the
table to the faces of her guests, seemed never to wink or
change for an instant their look of intense alertness.

But what was most noteworthy in this strange
woman was neither her eyes, her wrinkles, nor her
curious colour, but the amazing quantity of jewels that
she wore. As she sat there beneath the glare of the

N

candelabrum she positively blazed with gems. With
every motion of her quick hands a hundred points of
fire leapt out from the diamonds on her fingers; with
every turn of her wrinkled neck the light played upon
innumerable facets; and all the time those cold, lustrous
eyes scintillated as brightly as the stones. She was engaged in the game as we entered, and turned her gaze
upon us for an instant only, but that momentary flash
was so cold, so absolutely un-human, that I doubted if
I looked upon reality. The whole assembly seemed
rather like a room full of condemned spirits, with this
woman sitting as presiding judge.

As we still stood by the door a hush fell on the
company; men and women seemed to catch their breath
and bend more intently over the table. There was a
pause; then someone called the number "Thirty-one,"
and the buzz of voices broke out again—a mixture of
exclamations and disappointed murmurs. Then, and not
till then, did the woman at the head of the table speak,
and when she spoke her words were addressed to us.

"Come in, gentlemen, come in. You have not
chosen your moment well, for the Bank is winning;
but you are none the less welcome."

Her eyes as she turned them again upon us did
not alter their expression. They were—though I can
scarcely hope that this description will be understood
—at once perfectly vigilant and absolutely impassive.
But even more amazing was the voice that contradicted
both these impressions, being most sweetly and delicately

modulated, with a musical ring that charmed the ear as the notes of a well-sung song. The others, hearing us addressed, turned an incurious gaze upon us for a moment, and then fastened their attention anew upon the table.

Thus welcomed, we too stepped forward to the centre of the room and began to watch the game. I have never seen roulette played elsewhere, so do not know if its accessories greatly vary, but this is what I saw.

The table, which I have described as oblong, was lined to the width of about a foot around the edge with green baize, and on this were piled heaps of gold and silver, some greater, some less. Sunk in the centre was a well, in which a large needle revolved upon a pivot at a turn of the hand. The whole looked like a large ship's compass, but instead of north, south, east, and west, the table around the well, and at a level with the compass, was marked out into alternate spaces of red and black, bearing—one on each space—the figures from 1 to 36, and ending in 0, so that in all there were thirty-seven spaces, the one bearing the cipher being opposite to the strange woman who presided. As the game began again the players staked their money on one or another of these spaces. I also gathered that they could stake on either black or red, or again on one of the three dozens—1 to 12, 13 to 24, 25 to 36. When all the money was staked, the woman bent forward, and with a sweep of her arm sent the needle spinning round upon its mission.

N 2

Thrice she did this, thrice the eager faces bent over the revolving needle, and each time I gathered from the murmurs around me that the bank had won heavily. At the end of the third round the hostess looked up and said to Loveday—

"You have been here before, and, if I remember rightly, were unfortunate. Come and sit near me when you have a chance, and perhaps you may break this run of luck. Even I am tiring of it. Or better still, get that dark handsome friend of yours to stake for you. Have you ever played before?" she asked, turning to me.

I shook my head.

"All the better. Fortune always favours beginners, and if it does I shall be well recompensed to have so handsome a youth beside me," and with this she turned to the game again.

At her right sat a grey-headed man with worn face and wolfish eyes, who might have been expected to take this as a hint to make way. But he never heard a word. All his sense was concentrated on the board before him, and his only motion was to bend more closely and eagerly over the play. Tom whispered in my ear--

"You have the money, Jasper; take her advice if you really mean to play this farce out. Take the seat if you get a chance, and play your own game."

"You have been here before," I answered, "and know more about the game."

"Here before! Yes, to my cost. No, no, the idea

of play is your own and you shall carry it out. I am always unlucky, and as for knowledge of the game, you can pick that up by watching a round or two; it's perfectly simple."

Again the bank had won. At the left hand of our hostess stood a stolid man holding a small shovel with which he gathered in the winnings. All around were faces as of souls in torture; even the features of the winners (and these were few enough) scarcely expressed a trace of satisfaction, but seemed rather cast into some horrible trance in which they saw nothing but the piles of coin, the spinning needle, and the flashing hands of the woman that turned it. She all the while sat passionless and cold, looking on the scene as might some glittering and bejewelled sphinx.

As I gazed, as the needle whirled and stopped and once more whirled, the mad excitement of the place came creeping upon me. The glittering fingers of our hostess fascinated me as a serpent holds its prey. The stifling heat, the glare, the confused murmurs mounted like strong wine into my brain. The clink and gleam of the gold as it passed to and fro, the harsh voice of the man with the shovel calling at intervals, "Put on your money, gentlemen," the mechanical progress of the play, confused and staggered my senses. I forgot Tom, forgot the reason of our coming, forgot even where I was, so absorbed was I, and craned forward over the hurrying wheel, as intent as the veriest gambler present.

I was aroused from my stupor by a muttered curse, as the grey-headed man before me staggered up from his chair, and left the table with desperate eyes and stupid gait. As he rose the jewelled fingers made a slight motion, and I dropped into the vacant seat.

The bank was still winning. At our hostess' left hand rose a swelling pile of gold and silver that time after time absorbed all the smaller heaps upon the black and red spaces. Meanwhile the woman had scarcely spoken, but as the needle went round once more, slackened and stopped—this time amid deep and desperate execrations—she turned to me and said—

"Now is your time to break the bank if you wish. Play boldly; I should like to lose to so proper a man."

I looked back at Tom, who merely nodded, and put my first half-crown upon the red space marked 19. My neighbour, without seeming to notice the smallness of the sum, bent over the table and sent the wheel spinning on its errand. I, too, bent forward to watch, and as the wheel halted, saw the coin swept, with many more valuable, into the great pile.

"A bad beginning," said the sweet voice beside me. "Try again."

I tried again, and a third time, and two more half-crowns went to join their fellow.

There was one more chance. White with desperation I drew out my last half-crown, and laid it on the black. A flash, and my neighbour's hand sent the needle whirling. Round and round it went, as though it would never cease; round and round, then slackened, slackened, hesitated and stopped—where?

Where but over the red square opposite me?

For a moment all things seemed to whirl and dance before me. The candles shot out a million glancing rays, the table heaved, the rings upon the woman's fingers glittered and sparkled, while opposite me the devilish finger of Fortune pointed at the ruin of my hopes, and as it pointed past them and at me, called me very fool.

I clutched the table's green border and sank back in my seat. As I did so I heard a low curse from Tom behind me. The overwhelming truth broke in upon my senses, chasing the blood from my face, the hope from my heart. Ruined! Ruined! The faces around me grew blurred and misty, the room and all my surrounding seemed to fade further and yet further away, leaving me face to face with the consequences of my folly. Scarce knowing what I did, I turned to look at Tom, and saw that his face was white and set. As I did so the musical voice beside me murmured—

"The game is waiting : are you going to stake this time?"

I stammered out a negative.

"What? already tired? A faint heart should not go with such a face," and again she swept the pointer round.

"Is it," she whispered in my ear, "is it that you cannot?"

"It is."

"Ah, it is hard with half-a-sovereign to break the bank. But see, have you nothing—nothing? For I feel as if my luck were going to leave me."

"Nothing," I answered, "nothing in the world."

"Poor boy!"

Her voice was tender and sympathetic, but in her eyes there glanced not the faintest spark of mercy. I sat for a moment stunned and helpless, and then she resumed.

"Can I lend to you?"

"No, for I have no chance of repaying. This was my all, and it has gone. I have not one penny left in the world."

"Poor boy!"

"I thank you. I could not expect you to pity me, but ——"

"Ah, but you are wrong. I pity you: I pity you all. Fools, fools, I call you all, and yet I make my living out of you. So you cannot play," she added, as she set the game going once again. "What will you do?"

"Go, first of all."

"And after?"

I shrugged my shoulders.

"No, do not go yet. Sit beside me for a while and watch: it is only Fortune that makes me your enemy. I would willingly have lost to you."

She looked so curious, sitting there with her yellow

face, her wrinkles and her innumerable diamonds, that I could only sit and stare.

"I have seen many a desperate boy," continued this extraordinary woman, "sitting beside me in that very chair. Ah, many a young life have I murdered in this way. I am old, you see, very old; older even than you could guess, but I triumph over youth none the less. Sometimes I feel as if I fed on the young lives of others."

She delivered these confidences without a change in her emotionless face, and still I stared fascinated.

"Ah, yes, they sit here for a moment, and then they go—who knows where? You will be going presently, and then I shall lose you for ever, without a thought of what happens to you. Money is my blood: you see its colour in my face. Here they all come, and I suck their blood and fling them aside. They win sometimes; but I can wait. I wait and wait, and they come back here as surely as there is a destiny. They come back, and I win in the end. I always win in the end."

She turned her attention to the game for a moment and then went on :—

"It is a rare drink, this yellow blood: and all the sweeter when it comes from youth. I have had but a drop from you, but I like you nevertheless. Oh, yes, I can pity, my heart is always full of pity as I sit here drinking gold. Your friend is a charming boy, but I like you better : and now you will go. These partings are very cruel, are they not?"

There was not a trace of mockery in her voice, and her eyes were the same as ever. I merely looked up in reply, but she divined my thoughts.

"No, I am not mocking you. I should like you to win—once : I say it, and am perfectly honest about it. You would be beaten in the end, but it would please me while it lasted. Has your friend no money?"

"No, this was all we had between us."

"So he came back and got you to play with your money. That was strange friendship."

"You are wrong," I answered, "he was set against coming; but I persuaded him—or rather, I insisted. It is all my own fault."

"Well," she said, musingly, "I suppose you must go; but it is a pity. You are too handsome a boy to—to do what you will probably do : but the game does not regard good looks, or it would fare badly with me. Good-bye."

Still there was no shadow of pity in those unfathomable eyes. I looked into them for a moment, but their shining jet revealed nothing below the surface—nothing but inexorable calm.

"Good-bye," I said, and rose to go, for Tom's hand was already on my shoulder. I dared not look in his face. All hope was gone now, all wealth, all——Stay ! I put my fingers in my waistcoat-pocket and drew out the Golden Clasp. Worthless to me as any sign of the hiding-place of the Great Ruby, it might yet be worth something as metal. I had carried it ever since the day

when Uncle Loveday and I read my father's Journal.
But what did it matter now? In a few hours I should
be beyond the hope of treasure. Might I not just as
well fling this accursed clasp after the rest? For aught
I knew it might yet win something back to me—that
is, if anyone would accept it as money. At least I
would try.

I sank back into my chair again. The woman
turned her eyes upon me carelessly, and said—

" What, back again so soon? "

" Yes," said I, somewhat taken aback by her cold-
ness, " if you will give me another chance."

" I give nothing, least of all chance," she replied.

" Well, can you tell me if this is worth anything? "

As I said this I held out the clasp, which flashed
brightly as it caught the rays of the large candelabrum
overhead. She turned her eyes upon it, and as she did
so, for the first time I fancied I caught a gleam of
interest within them. It was but a gleam, however,
and died out instantly as she said—

" Let me look at it."

I handed it to her. She bent over it for a moment,
then turned to me and asked—

" Is this all of it? I mean that it seems only one
half of a clasp. Have you not the other part? "

I shook my head, and she continued—

" It is beautifully worked, and seems valuable. Do
you wish me to buy it? "

" Not exactly that," I explained ; " but if you think

it worth anything I should like to stake it against an equivalent."

"Very well; it might be worth three pounds—perhaps more : but you can stake it for that if you will. Shall it be all at once?"

"Yes, let me have it over at once," I said, and placed it on the red square marked 13.

She nodded, and bending over the table, set the pointer on its round.

This time I felt quite calm and cool. All the intoxication of play had gone from me and left my nerves steady as iron. As the needle swung round I scarcely looked at it, but fell to watching the faces of my fellow-gamblers with idle interest. This stake would decide between life and death for me, but I did not feel it. My passion had fallen upon an anti-climax, and I was even yawning when the murmur of many voices, and a small pile of gold and silver at my side, announced that I had won.

"So the luck was changed at last," said the woman. "Be brave whilst it is with you."

In answer I again placed the clasp upon the number 13.

Once more I won, and this time heavily. Tom laid his hand upon my shoulder and said, "Let us go," but I shook my head and went on.

Time after time I won now, until the pile beside me became immense. Again and again Tom whispered in my ear that we had won enough and that luck would change shortly, but I held on. And now the others surrounded me in a small crowd and began to stake on the numbers I chose. Put the clasp where I would the needle stopped in front of it. They brought a magnet to see if this curious piece of metal had any power of attraction, but our hostess only laughed and assured them at any rate there was no steel in the pointer, as (she added) some of them ought to know by this time. When eight times I had put the buckle down and eight times had found a fresh heap of coin at my side, she turned to me and said—

"You play bravely, young man. What is your name?"

"Jasper Trenoweth."

Again I fancied I caught the gleam in her eyes; and this time it even seemed as though her teeth shut tight as she heard the words. But she simply laughed a tranquil laugh and said—

"A queer-sounding name, that Trenoweth. Is it a lucky one?"

"Never, until now," said I.

"Well, play on. It does my heart good, this fight between us. But you are careful, I see; why don't you stake your pile as well while this wonderful run lasts?"

Again Tom's hand was laid upon my shoulder, and this time his voice was urgent. But I was completely deaf.

"As you please," said I, coldly, and laid the whole pile down upon the black.

It was madness. It was worse than madness. But I won again; and now the heap of my winnings was enormous. I glanced at the strange woman; she sat as impassive as ever.

"Play," said she.

Thrice more I won, and now the pile beside her had to be replenished. Yet she moved not a muscle of her face, not a lash of her mysterious eyes.

At last, sick of success, I turned and said—

"I have had enough of this. Will it satisfy you if I stake it all once more?"

Again she laughed. "You are brave, Mr. Trenoweth, and indeed worth the fighting. You may win to-night, but I shall win in the end. I told you that I would readily lose to you, and so I will; but you take me at my word with a vengeance. Still, I should like to possess that clasp of yours, so let it be once more."

I laid the whole of my winnings on the red. By this time all the guests had gathered round to see the issue of this conflict. Not a soul put any money on this turn of the wheel, so engrossed were they in the duel. Every face was white with excitement, every lip quivered. Only we, the combatants, sat unmoved —I and the strange woman with the unfathomable eyes.

"Red stands for many things," said she, as she lightly twirled the needle round, "blood and rubies and lovers' lips. But black is the livery of Death, and Death shall win them all in the end."

As the pointer of fortune circled on its last errand, I could catch the stifled breath of the crowd about me, so deep was the hush that fell upon us all. I felt Tom's hand tighten its clutch upon my shoulder. I heard, or fancied I heard, the heart of the man upon my right thump against his ribs. I could feel my own pulse beating all the while with steady and regular stroke. Somehow I knew that I should win, and somehow it flashed upon me that she knew it too. Even as the idea came darting across my brain, a multitude of pent-up cries broke forth from thirty pairs of white lips. I scarcely looked to see the cause, but as I turned to our hostess her eyes looked straight into mine and her sweet voice rose above the din—

"Gentlemen, we have played enough to-night. The game is over."

I had broken the bank.

I stood with Tom gathering up my winnings as the crowd slowly melted from the room, and as I did so, cast a glance at the woman whom I had thus defeated. She was leaning back in her chair, apparently indifferent to her losses as to her gains. Only her eyes were steadily fixed upon me as I shovelled the coin into my pockets. As she caught my eye she pulled out a scrap of paper and a pencil, scribbled a few words, tossed the note to the man with the shovel, who instantly left the room, and said—

"Is it far from this place to your home?"

"Not very."

"That's well; but be careful. To win such a sum is only less dangerous than to lose it. I shall see you again—you and your talisman. By the way, may I look at it for a moment?"

We were alone in the room, we three. She took the clasp, looked at it intently for a full minute, and then returned it. Already the dawn of another day was peering in through the chinks in the blinds, giving a ghastly faintness to the expiring candles, throwing a grey and sickening reality over the scene—the disordered chairs, the floor strewn with scraps of paper, the signs and relics of the debauchery of play. Ghastlier than all was the yellow face of the woman in the pitiless light. But there she sat, seemingly untired, in all the splendour of her flashing gems, as we left her—a very goddess of the gaming-table.

We had reached the door and were stepping into the darkness of the outer passage, when Tom whispered—

"Be on your guard; that note meant mischief."

I nodded, swung open the door, and stepped out into the darkness. Even as I did so, I heard one quick step at my left side, saw a faint gleam, and felt myself violently struck upon the chest. For a moment I staggered back, and then heard Tom rush past me and deal one crashing blow.

"Run, run! Down the passage, quick!"

In an instant we were tearing through the black darkness to the outer door, but in that instant I could see, through the open door behind, in the glare of all the candles, the figure of the yellow woman still sitting motionless and calm.

We gained the door, and plunged into the bright daylight. Up the alley we tore, out into the street, across it and down another, then through a perfect maze of by-lanes. Tom led and I followed behind, panting and clutching my bursting pockets lest the coin should tumble out. Still we tore on, although not a footstep followed us, nor had we seen a soul since Tom struck my assailant down. Spent and breathless at last we emerged upon the Strand, and here Tom pulled up.

" The streets are wonderfully quiet," said he.

I thought for a moment and then said, " It is Sunday morning."

Scarcely were the words out of my mouth when I heard something ring upon the pavement beside me. I stooped, and picked up—the Golden Clasp.

" Well," said I, " this is strange."

" Not at all," said Tom. " Look at your breast-pocket."

I looked and saw a short slit across my breast just above the heart. As I put my hand up, a sovereign, and then another, rolled clinking on to the pavement.

Tom picked them up, and handing them to me, re-marked—

" Jasper, you may thank Heaven to-day, if you are in a mood for it. You have had a narrow escape."

" What do you mean ? "

O

"Why, that you would be a dead man now had you not carried that piece of metal in your breast-pocket. Let me see it for a moment."

We looked at it together, and there surely enough, almost in the centre of the clasp, was a deep dent. We were silent for a minute or so, and then Tom said—

"Let us get home. It would not do for us to be seen with this money about us."

We crossed the Strand, and turned off it to the door of our lodgings. There I stopped.

"Tom, I am not coming in. I shall take a long walk and a bathe to get this fearful night out of my head. You can take the money upstairs, and put it away somewhere in hiding. Stay, I will keep a coin or two. Take the rest with you."

Tom looked up at the gleam of sunshine that touched the chimney-pots above, and decided.

"Well, for my part, I am going to bed; and so will you if you are wise."

"No. I will be back this evening, so let the fatted calf be prepared. I must get out of this for a while."

"Where are you going?"

"Oh, anywhere. I don't care. Up the river, perhaps."

"You don't wish me to go with you?"

"No, I had rather be alone. Tom, I have been a fool. I led you into a hole whence nothing but a marvellous chance has delivered us, and I owe you an apology. And—Tom, I also owe you my life."

"Not to me, Jasper; to the Clasp."

"To you," I insisted. "Tom, I have been a thoughtless fool, and—Tom, that was a splendid blow of yours."

He laughed, and ran upstairs, while I turned and gloomily sauntered down the deserted street.

CHAPTER III.

WHEN Tom asked me where I was going, I had suggested an excursion up the river; though, to tell the truth, this answer had come with the question. Be that as it may, the afternoon of that same Sunday found me on the left bank of the Thames between Streatley and Pangbourne; found me, with my boat moored idly by, stretched on my back amid the undergrowth, and easefully staring upward through a trellis-work of branches into the heavens. I had been lying there a full hour wondering vaguely of my last night's adventure, listening to the spring-time chorus of the birds, lazily and listlessly watching a bough that bent and waved its fan of foliage across my face, or the twinkle of the tireless kingfisher flashing down-stream in loops of light, when a blackbird lit on a branch hard by my left hand, and, all unconscious of an audience, began to pour forth his rapture to the day.

Lying there I could spy his black body and yellow bill, and drink in his song with dreamy content. So sweetly and delicately was he fluting, that by degrees slumber crept gently and unperceived upon my tired brain; and as the health-giving distillation of the melody stole upon my parched senses, I fell into a deep sleep.

 * * * * *

What was that? Music? Yes, but not the song of my friend the black-bird, not the mellow note that had wooed me to slumber and haunted my dreams. Music? Yes, but the voice was human, and the song articulate. I started, and rose upon my elbow to listen. The voice was human beyond a doubt—sweetly human: it was that of a girl singing. But where? I looked around and saw nobody. Yet the singer could not be far off, for the words, though softly and gently sung, dwelt clearly and distinctly upon my ear. Still half asleep, I sank back again and listened.

> " Flower of the May,
> Saw ye one pass ?
> ' Love passed to-day
> While the dawn was,
> O, but the eyes of him shone as a glass.' "

The low, delicate notes came tremulous through the thicket. The blackbird was hushed, the trees overhead swayed soundlessly, and when the voice fell and paused, so deep was the silence that involuntarily I held my breath and waited. Presently it broke out again—

> " Bird of the thorn,
> What his attire ?
> ' Lo ! it was torn,
> Marred with the mire,
> And but the eyes of him sparkled with fire.' "

Again the voice died away in soft cadences, and again all was silence. I rose once more upon my elbow, and gazed into the green depths of the wood; but saw only the blackbird perched upon a twig and listening with head askew.

> "Flower of the May,
> Bird of the —"

The voice quivered, trailed off and stopped. I heard a rustling of leaves to the right, and then the same voice broke out in prose, in very agitated and piteous prose— "Oh, my boat! my boat! What shall I do?"

I jumped to my feet, caught a glimpse of something white, and of two startled but appealing eyes, then tore down to the bank. There, already twenty yards downstream, placidly floated the boat, its painter trailing from the bows, and its whole behaviour pointing to a leisurely but firm resolve to visit Pangbourne.

My own boat was close at hand. But when did hot youth behave with thought in a like case? I did as ninety-nine in a hundred would do. I took off my coat, kicked off my shoes, and as the voice cried, "Oh, please, do not trouble," plunged into the water. The refractory boat, once on its way, was in no great hurry, and allowed itself to be overtaken with great good-humour. I clambered in over the stern, caught up the sculls which lay across the thwarts, and, dripping but triumphant, brought my captive back to shore.

"How can I thank you?"

If my face was red as I looked up, it must be remembered that I had to stoop to make the boat fast. If my eyes had a tendency to look down again, it must be borne in mind that the water from my hair was dripping into them. They gazed for a moment, however, and this was what they saw :—

At first only another pair of eyes, of dark grey eyes twinkling with a touch of merriment, though full at the same time of honest gratitude. It was some time before I clearly understood that these eyes belonged to a face, and that face the fairest that ever looked on a summer day. First, as my gaze dropped before that vision of radiant beauty, it saw only an exquisite figure draped in a dress of some white and filmy stuff, and swathed around the shoulders with a downy shawl, white also, across which fell one ravishing lock of waving brown, shining golden in the kiss of the now drooping sun. Then the gaze fell lower, lighted upon a little foot thrust slightly forward for steadiness on the bank's verge, and there rested.

So we stood facing one another—Hero and Leander, save that Leander found the effects of his bath more discomposing than the poets give any hint of. So we stood, she smiling and I dripping, while the blackbird, robbed of the song's ending, took up his own tale anew, and, being now on his mettle, tried a few variations. So, for all power I had of speech, might we have stood until to-day had not the voice repeated—

"How can I thank you ?"

I looked up. Yes, she was beautiful, past all

criticism—not tall, but in pose and figure queenly beyond words. Under the brim of her straw hat the waving hair fell loosely, but not so loosely as to hide the broad brow arching over lashes of deepest brown. Into the eyes I dared not look again, but the lips were full and curling with humour, the chin delicately poised over the most perfect of necks. In her right hand she held a carelessly-plucked creeper that strayed down the white of her dress and drooped over the high firm instep. And so my gaze dropped to earth again. Pity me. I had scarcely spoken to woman before, never to beauty. Tongue-tied and dripping I stood there, yet was half inclined to run away.

"And yet, why did you make yourself so wet? Have you no boat? Is not that your boat lying there under the bank?" There was an amused tremor in the speech.

Somehow I felt absurdly guilty. She must have mistaken my glance, for she went on:—"Is it that you wish——?" and began to search in the pocket of her gown.

"No, no," I cried, "not that."

I had forgotten the raggedness of my clothes, now hideously emphasised by my bath. Of course she took me for a beggar. Why not? I looked like one. But as the thought flashed upon me it brought unutterable humiliation. She must have divined something of the agony in my eyes, for a tiny hand was suddenly laid on my arm and the voice said—

" Please, forgive me ; I was stupid, and am so sorry."

Forgive her ?   I looked up for an instant and now
her lids drooped in their turn.   There was a silence
between us for a moment or two, broken only by the
blackbird, by this time entangled in a maze of difficult
variations.   Presently she glanced up again, and the
grey eyes were now chastely merry.

" But it was odd to swim when your boat was close
at hand, was it not ? "

I looked, faltered, met her honest glance, and we
both broke out into shy laughter.   A mad desire to seize
the little hand that for a moment had rested on my arm
caught hold of me.

" Yes, it was odd," I answered slowly and with
difficulty ; " but it seemed—the only thing to do at the
time."

She laughed a low laugh again.

" Do you generally behave like that ? "

" I don't know."

There was a pause and then I added—

" You see, you took me by surprise."

" Where were you when I first called ? " she asked.

" Lying in the grass close by."

" Then "—with a vivid blush—" you must have—"

" Heard you singing ?   Yes."

" Oh ! "

Again there was a pause, and this time the blackbird
executed an elaborate exercise with much delicacy and
finish.   The brown lashes drooped, the lovely eyes were

bent on the grass, and the little hand swung the creeper nervously backward and forward.

"Why did you not warn me that I had an audience?"

"Because, in the first place, I was too late. When you began I was——"

"What?" she asked as I hesitated.

"Asleep."

"And I disturbed you. I am so sorry."

"I am not."

I was growing bolder as she became more embarrassed. I looked down upon her now from my superior height, and my heart went out to worship the grace of God's handiwork. With a touch of resentment she drew herself up, held out her hand, and said somewhat proudly—

"I thank you, sir, for this service."

I took the hand, but not the hint. It was an infinitesimal hand as it lay in my big brown one, and yet it stung my frame as with some delicious and electric shock. My heart beat wildly and my eyes remained fixed upon hers.

The colour on the fair face deepened a shade: the little chin was raised a full inch, and the voice became perceptibly icy.

"I must go, sir. I hope I have thanked you as far as I can, and——"

"And what?"

"Forgive me that I was about to offer you money."

The hat's brim bent now, but under it I could see the honest eyes full of pain.

" Forgive you ! " I cried. " Who am I to forgive you ? You were right : I am no better than a beggar."

The red lips quivered and broke into a smile ; a tiny dimple appeared, vanished and reappeared ; the hat's brim nodded again, and then the eyes sparkled into laughter—

" A sturdy beggar, at any rate."

It was the poorest little joke, but love is not exacting of wit. Again we both laughed, but this time with more relief, and yet the embarrassment that followed was greater.

" Must you go ? " I asked as I bent down to pull the boat in.

" I really must," she answered shyly ; and then as she pulled out a tiny watch at her waist—" Oh ! I am late—so late. I shall keep mother waiting and make her lose the train. What shall I do ? Oh, pray, sir, be quick ! "

A mad hope coursed through me ; I pointed to the boat and said—

" I have made it so wet. If you are late, better let me row you. Where are you going ? "

" To Streatley ; but I cannot——"

" I also am going to Streatley. Please let me row you : I will not speak if you wish it."

Over her face, now so beautifully agitated, swept the rarest of blushes. " Oh no, it is not that, but I

can manage quite well "—her manner gave the lie to
her brave words—" and I shall not mind the wet."

" If I have not offended you, let me row."

" No, no."

" Then I have offended."

" Please do not think so."

" I shall if you will not let me row."

Before my persistency she wavered and was conquered. " But my boat ? " she said.

" I will tow it behind "—and in the glad success of
my hopes I allowed her no time for further parley, but
ran off for my own boat, tied the two together, and
gently helped her to her seat. Was ever moment so
sweet ? Did ever little palm rest in more eager hand
than hers in mine during that one heavenly moment ?
Did ever heart beat so tumultuously as mine, as I pushed
the boat from under the boughs and began to row ?

Somehow, as we floated up the still river, a hush fell
upon us. She was idly trailing her hand in the stream
and watching the ripple as it broke and sparkled
through her fingers. Her long lashes drooped down
upon her cheek and veiled her eyes, whilst I sat drinking in her beauty and afraid by a word to break the
spell.

Presently she glanced up, met my burning eyes, and
looked down abashed.

" Forgive me, I could not help it."

She tried to meet the meaning of that sentence with
a steady look, but broke down, and as the warm blood

surged across her face, bent her eyes to the water again. For myself, I knew of nothing to say in extenuation of my speech. My lips would have cried her mercy, but no words came. I fell to rowing harder, and the silence that fell upon us was unbroken. The sun sank and suddenly the earth grew cold and grey, the piping of the birds died wholly out, the water-flags shivered and whispered before the footsteps of night. Slowly, very slowly the twilight hung its curtains around us. Swiftly, too swiftly the quiet village drew near, but my thoughts were neither of the village nor the night. As I sat and pulled silently upwards, life was entirely changing for me. Old thoughts, old passions, old aims and musings slipped from me and swept off my soul as the darkening river swept down into further night.

"Streatley! So soon! We are in time, then."

Humbly my heart thanked her for those words, "So soon." I gave her my hand to help her ashore, and, as I did so, said—

"You will forgive me?"

"For getting wet in my service? What is there to forgive?"

Oh, cruelly kind! The moon was up now and threw its full radiance on her face as she turned to go. My eyes were speaking imploringly, but she persisted in ignoring their appeal.

"You often come here?"

"Oh, no! Sunday is my holiday; I am not so idle always. But mother loves to come here on Sundays.

Ah, how I have neglected her to-day!" There was a world of self-reproach in her speech, and again she would have withdrawn her hand and gone.

"One moment," said I, hoarsely. "Will you—can you—tell me your name?"

There was a demure smile on her face as the moon kissed it, and—

"They call me Claire," she said.

"Claire," I murmured, half to myself.

"And yours?" she asked.

"Jasper—Jasper Trenoweth."

"Then good-bye, Mr. Jasper Trenoweth. Good-bye, and once more I thank you."

She was gone; and standing stupid and alone I watched her graceful figure fade into the shadow and take with it the light and joy of my life.

     *   *   *   *   *

"Jasper," said Tom, as I lounged into our wretched garret, "have you ever known what it is to suffer from the responsibility of wealth? I do not mean a few paltry sovereigns; but do you know what it is to live with, say, three thousand four hundred and sixty-five pounds thirteen and sixpence on your conscience?"

"No," I said; "I cannot say that I have. But why that extraordinary sum?"

"Because that is the sum which has been hanging all day around me as a mill-stone. Because that is the exact amount which at present makes me fear to look my fellow-man in the face."

I simply stared.

"Jasper, you are singularly dense, or much success has turned your brain. Say, Jasper, that success has not turned your brain."

"Not that I know of," I replied.

"Very well, then," said Tom, stepping to the bed and pulling back the counterpane with much mystery. "Oblige me by counting this sum, first the notes, then the gold, and finally the silver. Or, if that is too much trouble, reflect that on this modest couch recline bank-notes for three thousand one hundred and twenty pounds, gold sovereigns to the number of three hundred and forty-two, whence by an easy subtraction sum we obtain a remainder of silver, in value three pounds thirteen and sixpence."

"But, Tom, surely we never won all that?"

"We did though, and may for the rest of our days settle down as comparatively honest medical students. So that I propose we have supper, and drink—for I have provided drink—to the Luck of the Golden Clasp."

Stunned with the events of the last twenty-four hours, I sat down to table, but could scarcely touch my food. Tom's tongue went ceaselessly, now apologising for the fare, now entertaining imaginary guests, and always addressing me as a man of great wealth and property.

"Jasper,' he remarked at length, "either you are ill, or you must have been eating to excess all day."

"Neither."

"Do I gather that you wish to leave the table, and pursue your mortal foe up and down Oxford Street?"

I shook my head.

"What! no revenge to-night? No thirst for blood?"

"Tom," I replied, solemnly, "neither to-night nor any other night. My revenge is dead."

"Dear me! when did it take place? It must have been very sudden."

"It died to-day."

"Jasper," said Tom, laying his hand on my shoulder, "either wealth has turned yo r brain, or most remarkably given you sanity."

CHAPTER IV.

TELLS HOW I SAW THE SHADOW OF THE ROCK; AND HOW
I TOLD AND HEARD NEWS.

A WEEK passed, and in the interval Tom and I made several discoveries. In the first place, to our great relief, we discovered that the bank-notes were received in Threadneedle Street without question or demur. Secondly, we found our present lodgings narrow, and therefore moved westward to St. James's. Further, it struck us that our clothes would have to conform to the "demands of more Occidental civilisation," as Tom put it, and also that unless we intended to be medical students for ever it was necessary to become medical men. Lastly, it began to dawn upon Tom that "Francesca: a Tragedy" was a somewhat turgid performance, and on me that a holiday on Sunday was demanded by six days of work.

I do not know that we displayed any remarkable interest in the *Materia Medica*, or that the authorities of Guy's looked upon us as likely to do them any singular credit. But Tom, who had now a writing-desk, made great alterations in "Francesca," while I consumed vast quantities of tobacco in the endeavour to reproduce a certain face in my note-book; and I am certain that

P

the resolution to take a holiday on Sunday was as strong at the end of the first week as though I had wrought my faculties to the verge of brain fever.

I did not see her on that Sunday, or the next, though twice my boat explored the river between Goring and Pangbourne from early morning until nightfall. But let me hasten over heart-aching and bitterness, and come to the blessed Sunday when for a second time I saw my love.

Again the day was radiant with summer. Above, the vaulted blue arched to a capstone of noonday gold. Hardly a fleecy cloud troubled the height of heaven, or blotted the stream's clear mirror; save here and there where the warm air danced and quivered over the still meadows, the season's colour lay equal upon earth. Before me the river wound silently into the sunny solitude of space untroubled by sight of human form.

But what was that speck of white far down the bank—that brighter spot upon the universal brightness, moving, advancing? My heart gave one great leap; in a moment my boat's bows were high upon the crumbling bank, and I was gazing down the tow-path.

Yes, it was she! From a thousand thousand I could tell that perfect form as it loitered—how slowly—up the river's verge. Along heaven's boundary the day was lit with glory for me, and all the glory but a golden frame for that white speck so carelessly approaching. Still and mute I stood as it drew nearer—so still, so mute, that a lazy pike thrust out its wolfish jaws just under my

feet and, seeing me, splashed under again in great dis-
composure ; so motionless that a blundering swallow all
but darted against me, then swept curving to the water,
and vanished down the stream.

She had been gathering May-blossom, and held a
cluster in one hand. As before, her gown was purest
white, and, as before, a nodding hat guarded her fair face
jealously.

Nearer and nearer she came, glanced carelessly at me
who stood bare-headed in the sun's glare, was passing,
and glanced again, hesitated for one agonising moment,
and then, as our eyes met, shot out a kindly flash of
remembrance, followed by the sweetest of little blushes.

"So you are here again," she said, as she gave her
hand, and her voice made exquisite music in my ear.

"Again?" I said, slowly releasing her fingers as a
miser might part with treasure. "Again? I have
been here every Sunday since."

"Dear me! is it so long ago? Only three weeks
after all. I remember, because——"

The fleeting hope possessed me that it might be
some recollection in which I had place, but my illusion
was swiftly shattered.

"Because," the pitiless sentence continued, "mother
was not well that evening; in fact, she has been ill
ever since. So it is only three weeks."

"Only three weeks!" I echoed.

"Yes," she nodded. "I have not seen the river for
all that time. Is it changed?"

P 2

"Sadly changed."

" How? "

" Perhaps I have changed."

" Well, I hope so," she laughed, " after that wetting;" then, seeing an indignant flash in my eyes, she added quickly, "which you got by so kindly bringing back my boat."

" You have not been rowing to-day?"

" No; see, I have been gathering the last of the May-blossom. May is all but dead."

" And 'Flower of the May'?"

" Please do not remind me of that foolish song. Had I known, I would not have sung it for worlds."

" I would not for worlds have missed it."

Again she frowned and now turned to go. "And you, too, must make these speeches!"

The world of reproach in her tone was at once gall and honey to me. Gall, because the "you too" conjured up a host of jealous imaginings; honey, because it was revealed that of me she had hoped for better. And now like a fool I had flung her good opinion away and she was leaving me.

I made a half-step forward.

" I must go now," she said, and the little hand was held out in token of farewell.

" No! no! I have offended you."

No answer.

" I have offended you," I insisted, still holding her hand.

"I forgive you. But, indeed, I must go." The hand made a faint struggle to be free.

"Why?"

My voice came hard and unnatural. I still held the fingers, and as I did so, felt the embarrassment of utter shyness pass over the bridge of our two hands and settle chokingly upon my heart.

"Why?" I repeated, more hoarsely yet.

"Because—because I must not neglect mother again. She is waiting."

"Then let me go with you."

"Oh, no! Some day—if we meet—I will introduce you."

"Why not now?"

"Because she is not well."

Even my lately-acquired knowledge of the *Materia Medica* scarcely warranted me in offering to cure her. But I did.

She laughed shyly and said, "How, sir; are you a doctor?"

"Tinker, tailor, soldier, sailor, gentleman, apothecary," I said lightly, "neither one nor the other, but that curious compound of the two last—a medical student."

"Then I will not trust you," she answered, smiling.

"Better trust me," I said; and something in my words again made her look down.

"You will trust me?" I pleaded, and the something in my words grew plainer.

Still no answer.

"Oh, trust me!"

The hand quivered in mine an instant, the eyes looked up and laughed once more. "I will trust you," she said—"not to move from this spot until I am out of sight."

Then with a light "Good-bye" she was gone, and I was left to vaguely comprehend my loss.

Before long I had seen her a third time and yet once again. I had learnt her name to be Luttrell—Claire Luttrell; how often did I not say the words over to myself? I had also confided in Tom and received his hearty condolence, Tom being in that stage of youth which despises all of which it knows nothing—love especially, as a thing contrary to nature's uniformity. So Tom was youthfully cynical, and therefore by strange inference put on the airs of superior age; was also sceptical of my description, especially a certain comparison of her eyes to stars, though a very similar trope occurred somewhere in the tragedy. Indeed therein Francesca's eyes were likened to the Pleiads, being apparently (as I pointed out with some asperity) seven in number, and one of them lost.

I had also seen Mrs. Luttrell, a worn and timid woman, with weak blue eyes and all the manner of the professional invalid. I say this now, but in those days she was in my eyes a celestial being mysteriously clothed in earth's infirmities—as how should the mother of Claire be anything else? Somehow I won the favour of this faded creature—chiefly, I suspect, because she liked so well to be left alone. All day long she would sit contentedly watching the river and waiting for Claire, yet only anxious that Claire should be happy. All her heart centred on her child, and often, in spite of our friendliness, I caught her glancing from Claire to me with a jealous look, as though the mother guessed what the child suspected but dimly, if at all.

So the summer slipped away, all too fleetly—to me, as I look back after these weary years, in a day. But nevertheless much happened: not much that need be written down in bald and pitiless prose, but much to me who counted and treasured every moment that held my darling near me. So the Loves through that golden season wound us round with their invisible chains and hovered smiling and waiting. So we drifted week after week upon the river, each time nearer and nearer to the harbour of confession. The end was surely coming, and at last it came.

It was a gorgeous August evening. A week before she had told me that Saturday would be a holiday for her, and had, when pressed, admitted a design of spending it upon the river. Need it be confessed that Saturday saw me also in my boat, expectant? And when she came and feigned pretty astonishment at meeting me, and scepticism as to my doing any work throughout the week, need I say the explanation took time and seemed to me best delivered in a boat? At any rate, so it was; and somehow, the explanation took such a vast amount of time, that the sun was already plunging down the western slope of heaven when we stepped ashore almost on the very spot where first I had heard her voice.

As the first film of evening came creeping over earth, there fell a hush between us. A blackbird—the same, I verily believe—took the opportunity to welcome us. His note was no longer full and unstudied as in May. The summer was nearly over, and with it his voice was failing: but he did his best, and something in the hospitality of his song prompted me to break the silence.

"This is the very spot on which we met for the first time—do you remember?"

"Of course I remember," was the simple answer.

"You do?" I foolishly burned to hear the assurance again.

"Of course—it was such a lovely day."

"A blessed day," I answered, "the most blessed of my life."

There was a long pause here, and even the blackbird could hardly fill it up.

"Do you regret it?"

(Why does man on these occasions ask such a heap of questions?)

"Why should I?"

(Why does woman invariably answer his query with another?)

"I hope there is no reason," I answered, "and yet—

oh, can you not see of what that day was the beginning? Can you not see whither these last four months have carried me?"

The sun struck slanting on the water and ran in tapering lustre to our feet. The gilded ripple slipped and murmured below us; the bronzed leaves overhead bent carefully to veil her answer. The bird within the covert uttered an anxious note.

"They have carried you, it seems," she answered, with eyes gently lowered, "back to the same place."

"They have carried me," I echoed, "from spring to summer. If they have brought me back to this spot, it is because the place and I have changed—Claire!"

As I called her by her Christian name she gave one quick glance, and then turned her eyes away again. I could see the soft rose creeping over her white neck and cheek. Had I offended? Between hope and desperation, I continued—

"Claire—I will call you Claire, for that was the name you told me just four months ago—I am changed, oh, changed past all remembrance! Are you not changed at all? Am I still nothing to you?"

She put up her hand as if to ward off further speech, but spoke no word herself.

"Answer me, Claire; give me some answer if only a word. Am I still no more than the beggar who rescued your boat that day?"

"Of course, you are my friend—now. Please forget that I took you for a beggar."

The words came with effort. Within the bushes the
blackbird still chirped expectant, and the ripple below
murmured to the bank, "The old story—the old story."

"But I am a beggar," I broke out. "Claire, I am
always a beggar on my knees before you. Oh, Claire!"

Her face was yet more averted—the sun kissed her
waving locks with soft lips of gold, the breeze half
stirred the delicate draperies around her. The blackbird's note was broken and halting as my own speech.

"Claire, have you not guessed? will you never
guess? Oh, have pity on me!"

I could see the soft bosom heaving now. The little
hand was pulling at the gown. Her whole sweet shape
drooped away from me in vague alarm—but still no
answer came.

"Courage! Courage!" chirped the bird, and the
river murmured responsive, "Courage!"

"Claire!"—and now there was a ring of agony in
the voice; the tones came alien and scarcely recognised—
"Claire, I have watched and waited for this day, and
now that it has come, for good or for evil, answer me—
I love you!"

O time-honoured and most simple of propositions!
"I love you!" Night after night had I lain upon my
bed rehearsing speeches, tender, passionate and florid,
and lo! to this had it all come—to these three words,
which, as my lips uttered them, made my heart leap in
awe of their crude and naked daring.

And she? The words, as though they smote her,

chased for an instant the rich blood from her cheek. For a moment the bosom heaved wildly, then the colour came slowly back, and ebbed again. A soft tremor shook the bending form, the little hand clutched the gown, but she made no answer.

"Speak to me, Claire! I love you! With my life and soul I love you. Can you not care for me?" I took the little hand. "Claire, my heart is in your hands—do with it what you will, but speak to me. Can you not—do you not—care for me?"

The head drooped lower yet, the warm fingers quivered within mine, then tightened, and—

What was that whisper, that less than whisper, for which I bent my head? Had I heard aright? Or why was it that the figure drooped closer, and the bird's note sprang up jubilant?

"Claire!"

A moment—one tremulous, heart-shaking moment —and then her form bent to me, abandoned, conquered; her face looked up, then sank upon my breast; but before it sank I read upon it a tenderness and a passion infinite, and caught in her eyes the perfect light of love.

As the glory of delight came flooding on my soul, the sun's disc dropped, and the first cold shadow of night fell upon earth. The blackbird uttered a broken "Amen," and was gone no man knew whither. The golden ripple passed up the river, and vanished in a leaden grey. One low shuddering sigh swept through

the trees, then all was dumb. I looked westward.
Towards the horizon the blue of day was fading downwards through indistinguishable zones of purple, ame-
thyst, and palest rose, the whole heaven arching in one
perfect rainbow of love.

But while I looked and listened to the beating of
that beloved heart girdled with my arm, there grew a
something on the western sky that well-nigh turned my
own heart to marble. At first, a lightest shadow—a
mere breath upon heaven's mirror, no more. Then as
I gazed, it deepened, gathering all shadows from around
the pole, heaping, massing, wreathing them around one
spot in the troubled west—a shape that grew and
threatened and still grew, until I looked on—what?

Up from the calm sea of air rose one solitary
island, black and looming, rose and took shape and
stood out—the very form and semblance of Dead Man's
Rock! Sable and real as death it towered there against
the pale evening, until its shadow, falling on my heart
itself and on the soft brown head that bent and nestled
there, lay round us clasped so, and with its frown
cursed the morning of our love.

Something in my heart's beat, or in the stiffening of
my arm, must have startled my darling, for as I gazed
I felt her stir, and, looking down, caught her eyes
turned wistfully upwards. My lips bent to hers.

"Mine, Claire! Mine for ever!"

And there, beneath the shadow of the Rock, our
lips drew closer, met, and were locked in their first kiss.

When I looked up again the shadow had vanished, and the west was grey and clear.

So in the tranquil evening we rowed homewards, our hearts too full for speech. The wan moon rose and trod the waters, but we had no thoughts, no eyes for her. Our eyes were looking into each other's depths, our thoughts no thoughts at all, but rather a dazzled and wondering awe.

Only as a light or two gleamed out, and Streatley twinkled in the distance, Claire said—

"Can it be true? You know nothing of me."

"I know you love me. What more should I know, or wish to know?"

The red lips were pursed in a manner that spoke whole tomes of wisdom.

"You do not know that I work for my living all the week?"

"When you are mine you shall work no more."

"'But sit on a cushion and sew a gold seam'? Ah, no; I have to work. It is strange," she said, musingly, "so strange."

"What is strange, Claire?"

"That you have never seen me except on my holidays—that we have never met. What have you done since you have been in London?"

I thought of my walks and tireless quest in Oxford Street with a kind of shame. That old life was severed from the present by whole worlds.

"I have lived very quietly," I answered. "But is it so strange that we have never met?"

She laughed a low and musical laugh, and as the boat drew shoreward and grounded, replied—

"Perhaps not. Come, let us go to mother—Jasper."

O sweet sound from sweetest lips! We stepped ashore, and hand-in-hand entered the room where her mother sat.

As she looked up and saw us standing there together, she knew the truth in a moment. Her blue eyes filled with sudden fear, her worn hand went upwards to her heart. Until that instant she had not known of my presence there that day, and in a flash divined its meaning.

"I feared it," she answered at length, as I told my story and stood waiting for an answer. "I feared it, and for long have been expecting it. Claire, my love, are you sure? Oh, be quite sure before you leave me."

For answer, Claire only knelt and flung her white arms round her mother's neck, and hid her face upon her mother's bosom.

"You love him now, you think; but, oh, be careful. Search your heart before you rob me of it. I have known love, too, Claire, or thought I did; and indeed it can fade—and then, what anguish, what anguish!"

"Mother, mother! I will never leave you."

Mrs. Luttrell sighed.

" Ah, child, it is your happiness I am thinking of."

" I will never leave you, mother."

" And you, sir," continued Mrs. Luttrell, " are you sure? I am giving you what is dearer than life itself; and as you value her now, treat her worthily hereafter. Swear this to me, if my gift is worth so much in your eyes. Sir, do you know——"

" Mother ! "

Claire drew her mother's head down towards her and whispered in her ear. Mrs. Luttrell frowned, hesitated, and finally said—

" Well, it shall be as you wish—though I doubt if it be wise. God bless you, Claire—and you, sir ; but oh, be certain, be certain ! "

What incoherent speech I made in answer I know not, but my heart was sore for this poor soul. Claire turned her eyes to me and rose, smoothing her mother's grey locks.

" We will not leave her, will we ? Tell her that we will not."

I echoed her words, and stepping to Mrs. Luttrell, took the frail, white hand.

" Sir," she said, " you who take her from me should be my bitterest foe. Yet see, I take you for a son."

*   *   *   *   *

Still rapt with the glory of my great triumph, and drunk with the passion of that farewell kiss, I walked into our lodgings and laid my hand on Tom's shoulder.

" Tom, I have news for you."

Tom started up. " And so have I for you."

" Great news."

" Glorious news ! "

" Tom, listen : I am accepted."

" Bless my soul ! Jasper, so am I."

" You ? "

" Yes."

" When ? Where ? "

" This afternoon. Jasper, our success has come at last : for you the Loves, for me the Muses ; for you the rose, for me the bay. Jasper, dear boy, they have learnt her worth at last."

" Her ! Who ? "

" Francesca. Jasper, in three months I shall be famous ; for next November " Francesca : a Tragedy " will be produced at the Coliseum.

CHAPTER V.

TELLS HOW THE CURTAIN ROSE UPON " FRANCESCA :
A TRAGEDY."

AGAIN my story may hurry, for on the enchanted
weeks that followed it would weary all but lovers
to dwell, and lovers for the most part find their own
matters sufficient food for pondering.   Tom was busy
with the rehearsals at the Coliseum, and I, being left
alone, had little taste for the *Materia Medica*.   On
Sundays only did I see Claire ; for this Mrs. Luttrell
had stipulated, and my love, too, most mysteriously
professed herself busy during the week.   As for me, it
was clear that before marriage could be talked of I
must at least have gained my diplomas, so that the more
work I did during the week the better.   The result of
this was a goodly sowing of resolutions and very little
harvest.   In the evenings, Tom and I would sit together—he tirelessly polishing and pruning the tragedy,
and I for the most part smoking and giving advice
which I am bound to say in duty to the author (" Francesca " having gained some considerable fame since those
days) was invariably rejected.

Tom had been growing silent and moody of late—
a change for which I could find no cause.   He would
answer my questions at random, pause in his work to

Q

gaze long and intently on the ceiling, and altogether
behave in ways unaccountable and strange. The play
had been written at white-hot speed : the corrections proceeded at a snail's pace. The author had also fallen into
a habit of bolting his meals in silence, and, when rebuked,
of slowly bringing his eyes to bear upon me as a person
whose presence was until the moment unsuspected. All
this I saw in mild wonder, but I reflected on certain
moods of my own of late, and held my peace.

The explanation came without my seeking. We
were seated together one evening, he over his everlasting
corrections, and I in some especially herbaceous nook of
the *Materia Medica*, when Tom looked up and said—

"Jasper, I want your opinion on a passage. Listen
to this."

Sick of my flowery solitude, I gave him my attention while he read :—

> "She is no violet to veil and hide
> Before the lusty sun, but as the flower,
> His best-named bride, that leaneth to the light
> And images his look of lordly love
> Yet how I wrong her. She is more a queen
> Than he a king ; and whoso looks must kneel
> And worship, conscious of a Sovranty
> Undreamt in nature, save it be the Heaven
> That minist'ring to all is queen of all,
> And wears the proud sun's self but as a gem
> To grace her girdle, one among the stars.
> Heaven is Francesca, and Francesca Heaven.
> Without her, Heaven is dispossessed of Heaven,
> And Earth, discrowned and disinherited,
> Shall beg in black eclipse, until her eyes——"

"Stay," I interrupted, "unless I am mistaken her eyes are like the Pleiads, a simile to which I have more than once objected."

"If you would only listen you would find those lines cut out," said Tom, pettishly.

"In that case I apologise : nevertheless, if that is your idea of a Francesca, I confess she seems to me a trifle—shall we say?—massive."

"Your Claire, I suppose, is stumpy?"

"My Claire," I replied with dignity, "is neither stumpy nor stupendous."

"In fact, just the right height."

"Well, yes, just the right height."

Tom paid no attention, but went on in full career—

"I hate your Griseldas, your Jessamys, your Mary Anns; give me Semiramis, Dido, Joan of——"

"My dear Tom, not all at once, I hope."

"Bah! you are so taken up with your own choice, that you must needs scoff at anyone who happens to differ. I tell you, woman should be imperial, majestic; should walk as a queen and talk as a goddess. You scoff because you have never seen such; you shut your eyes and go about saying, 'There is no such woman.' By heaven, Jasper, if you could only see——"

At this point Tom suddenly pulled up and blushed like any child.

"Go on—whom shall I see?"

Tom's blush was beautiful to look upon.

"The Lambert, for instance; I meant——"

Q 2

" Who is the Lambert? "

" Do you mean to say you have never heard of Clarissa Lambert, the most glorious actress in London? "

" Never. Is she acting at the Coliseum? "

" Of course she is. She takes Francesca. Oh, Jasper, you should see her, she is divine ! "

Here another blush succeeded.

" So," I said after a pause, " you have taken upon yourself to fall in love with this Clarissa Lambert."

Tom looked unutterably sheepish.

" Is the passion returned ? "

" Jasper, don't talk like that and don't be a fool. Of course I have never breathed a word to her. Why, she hardly knows me, has hardly spoken to me beyond a few simple sentences. How should I, a miserable author without even a name, speak to her? Jasper, do you like the name Clarissa? "

" Not half so well as Claire."

" Nonsense; Claire is well enough as names go, but nothing to Clarissa. Mark how the ending gives it grace and quaintness; what a grand eighteenth-century ring it has! It is superb—so sweet, and at the same time so stately."

" And replaces Francesca so well in scansion."

Tom's face was confession.

" You should see her, Jasper—her eyes. What colour are Claire's? "

" Deep grey."

" Clarissa's are hazel brown : I prefer brown ; in fact

I always thought a woman should have brown eyes; we won't quarrel about inches, but you will give way in the matter of eyes, will you not?"

"Not an inch."

"It really is wonderful," said Tom, "how the mere fact of being in love is apt to corrupt a man's taste. Now in the matter of voice—I dare wager that your Claire speaks in soft and gentle numbers."

"As an Æolian harp," said I, and I spoke truth.

"Of course, unrelieved tenderness and not a high note in the gamut. But you should hear Clarissa; I only ask you to hear her once, and let those glorious accents play upon your crass heart for a moment or two. O Jasper, Jasper, it shakes the very soul!"

Tom was evidently in a very advanced stage of the sickness; I could not find it in my heart to return his flouts of a month before, so I said—

"Very well, my dear Tom, I shall look upon your divinity in November. I do not promise you she will have the effect that you look forward to, but I am glad your Francesca will be worthily played; and, Tom, I am glad you are in love; I think it improves you."

"It is hopeless — absolutely hopeless; she is cold as ice."

"What, with that voice and those eyes? Nonsense, man."

"She is cold as ice," groaned poor Tom; "every-one says so."

"Of course everyone says so; you ought to be glad

of that, for this is the one point on which what every-
one says must from the nature of things be false.
Why, man, if she beamed on the whole world, then I
might believe you."

From which it will be gathered that I had learned
something from being in love.

$$* \qquad * \qquad * \qquad * \qquad *$$

So sad did I consider Tom's case, that I spoke to
Claire about it when I saw her next.

"Claire," I said, "you have often heard me speak
of Tom."

"Really, Jasper, you seldom speak of anybody else.
In fact I am growing quite jealous of this friend."

After the diversion caused by this speech, I resumed—

"But really Tom is the best of fellows, and if I talk
much of him it is because he is my only friend. You
must see him, Claire, and you will be sure to like him.
He is so clever!"

"What is the name of this genius—I mean the other
name?"

"Why, Loveday, of course—Thomas Loveday. Do
you mean to say I have never told you?"

"Never," said Claire, meditatively. "Loveday—
Thomas Loveday—is it a common name?"

"No, I should think not very common. Don't you
like it?"

"It—begins well."

Here followed another diversion.

"But what I was going to say about Tom," I

continued, " is this—he has fallen in love; in fact, I have never seen a man so deeply in love."

" Oh! "

" Anyone else," I corrected, " for of course I was quite as bad; you understand that."

" We were talking of Thomas Loveday."

" Oh, yes, of Tom. Well, Tom, you know—or perhaps you do not. At any rate, Tom has written a tragedy."

" All about love? "

" Well, not quite all; though there is a good deal in it, considering it was written when the author had no idea of what the passion was like. But that is not the point. This tragedy is coming out at the Coliseum in November. Are you not well, Claire? "

" Yes, yes; go on. What has all this to do with Tom's love? "

" I am coming to that. Tom, of course, has been attending the rehearsals lately. He will not let me come until the piece is ready, for he is wonderfully nervous. I am to come and see it on the first night. Well, as I was saying, Tom has been going to rehearsals, and has fallen in love with—guess with whom."

Claire was certainly getting very white.

" Are you sure you are well, Claire? " I asked, anxiously.

" Oh, yes; quite sure. But tell me with whom— how should I guess? "

"Why, with the leading actress; one Clarissa Lambert, is it not?"

"Clarissa—Lambert!"

"Why, Claire, what is the matter? Are you faint?" For my love had turned deathly pale, and seemed as though she would faint indeed.

We were in the old spot so often revisited, though the leaves were yellowing fast, and the blackbird's note had long ceased utterly. I placed my arm around her for support, but my darling unlocked it after a moment, struggled with her pallor, and said—

"No, no; I am better. It was a little faintness, but is passing off. Go on, and tell me about Mr. Loveday."

"I am afraid I bored you. But that is all. Do you know this Clarissa Lambert? Have you seen her?"

"Yes—I have seen her."

"I suppose she is very famous; at least, Tom says so. He also says she is divine; but I expect, from his description, that she is of the usual stamp of Tragedy Queen, tall and loud, with a big voice."

"Did he tell you that?"

"No, of course Tom raves about her. But there is no accounting for what a lover will say." This statement was made with all the sublime assurance of an accepted man. "But you have seen her," I went on, "and can tell me how far his description is true. I suppose she is much the same as other actresses, is she not?"

" Jasper," said Claire, very gently, after a pause, " do you ever go to a theatre ? "

" Very seldom ; in fact, about twice only since I have been in London."

" I suppose you were taught as a boy to hate such things ? "

" Well," I laughed, " I do not expect Uncle Loveday would have approved of Tom's choice, if that is what you mean. But that does not matter, I fear, as Tom swears that his case is hopeless. He worships from afar, and says that she is as cold as ice. In fact, he has never told his love, but lets concealment like a——"

" That is not what I meant. Do you—do you think all actors and actresses wicked ? "

" Of course not. Why should I ? "

" You are going to see——"

" ' Francesca' ? Oh, yes, on the opening night."

" Then possibly we shall meet. Will you look out for me ? "

" Let me take you, Claire. Oh, I am glad indeed ! You will see Tom there, and, I hope, be able to congratulate him on his triumph. So let me take you."

She shook her head.

" No, no."

" Why ? "

" Because that is impossible—really. I shall see you there, and you will see me. Is not that enough ? "

" If you say so, it must be," I answered sadly. " But—— "

"'But me no buts,'" she quoted. "See, it is getting late; we must be going."

A most strange silence fell upon us on the way back to Streatley. Claire's face had not yet wholly regained its colour, and she seemed disinclined to talk. So I had to solace myself by drinking in long draughts of her loveliness, and by whispering to my soul how poorly Tom's Queen of Tragedy would show beside my sweetheart.

O fool and blind!

Presently my love asked musingly—

"Jasper, do you think that you could cease to love me?"

"Claire, how can you ask it?"

"You are quite sure? You remember what mother said?"

"Claire, love is strong as death. How does the text run? 'Many waters cannot quench love, neither can the floods drown it: if a man would give all the substance of his house for love, it would utterly be contemned.' Claire, you must believe that!"

"'Strong as death,'" she murmured. "Yes, I believe it. What a lovely text that is!"

The boat touched shore at Streatley, and we stepped out.

"Jasper," she said again at parting that night, "you have no doubt, no grain of doubt, about my question, and the answer? 'Strong as death,' you are sure?"

For answer I strained her to my heart.
O fool and blind !   O fool and blind !

*   *   *   *   *

The night that was big with Tom's fate had come.
The Coliseum was crowded as we entered. In those
days the theatre had no stalls, so we sat in the front
row of the dress circle, Tom having in his modesty
refused a box. He was behind the scenes until some
five minutes before the play began, so that before he
joined me I had ample time to study the house and look
about for some sign of Claire.

Certainly, the sedulous manner in which the new
tragedy had been advertised was not without result.
To me, unused as I was to theatre-going, the host
of people, the hot air, the glare of the gas-lights
were intoxicating. In a flutter of anxiety for Tom's
success, of sweet perturbation at the prospect of meeting Claire, at first I could grasp but a confused image of
the scene. By degrees, however, I began to look about
me, and then to scan the audience narrowly for sight of
my love.

Surely I should note her at once among thousands.
Yet my first glance was fruitless. I looked again,
examined the house slowly face by face, and again was
baffled. I could see all but a small portion of the pit,
the upper boxes and gallery. Pit and gallery were out
of the question. She might, though it was hardly
likely, be in the tier just above, and I determined to
satisfy myself after the end of Act I. Meantime I

scanned the boxes. There were twelve on either side of the house, and all were full. By degrees I satisfied myself that strangers occupied all of them, except the box nearest the stage on the right of the tier where I was sitting. The occupants of this were out of sight. Only a large yellow and black fan was swaying slowly backwards and forwards to tell me that somebody sat there.

Somehow, the slow, ceaseless motion of this pricked my curiosity. Its pace, as it waved to and fro, was unaltered; the hand that moved it seemingly tireless; but even the hand was hidden. Not a finger could I gain a glimpse of. By some silly freak of fancy I was positively burning with eagerness to see the fan's owner, when Tom returned and took his seat beside me.

"It begins in five minutes; everything is ready," said he, and his voice had a nervous tremor which he sought in vain to hide.

"Courage!" I said; "at least the numbers here should flatter you."

"They frighten me! What shall I do if it fails?"

The overture was drawing to its close. Tom looked anxiously around the house.

"Yes," he said, "it is crowded, indeed. By the way, was not Claire to have been here? Point her out to me."

"She was; but I cannot see her anywhere. Perhaps she is late."

"If so, I cannot see where she is to find a place. Hush! they are ending."

As he spoke, the last strains of the orchestra died slowly and mournfully away, and the curtain rose upon " Francesca : a Tragedy."

This play has since gained such a name, not only from its own merits (which are considerable), but in consequence also of certain circumstances which this story will relate, that it would be not only tedious but unnecessary to follow its action in detail. For the benefit, however, of those who did not see it at the Coliseum, I here subjoin a short sketch of the plot, which the better-informed reader may omit.

Francesca is the daughter of Sebastian, at one time Duke of Bologna, but deposed and driven from his palace by the intrigues of his younger brother Charles. At the time when the action begins, Sebastian is chief of a band of brigands, the remains of his faithful adherents, whom he has taken with him to the fastnesses of the Apennines. Charles, who has already usurped the duchy for some sixteen years, is travelling with his son Valentine, a youth of twenty, near the haunt of his injured brother. Separated from their escort, they are wandering up a pass, when Valentine stops to admire the view, promising his father to join him at the summit. While thus occupied, he is startled by the entrance of Francesca, and, struck with her beauty, accosts her. She, sympathising for so noble a youth, warns him of the banditti, and he hastens on

only to find his father lying at the foot of a precipitous
rock, dead. He supposes him to have fallen, has the
body conveyed back to Bologna, and having by this
time fallen deeply in love with Francesca, prevails on
her to leave her father and come with him. She con-
sents, and flies with him, but after some time finds that
he is deserting her for Julia, daughter of the Duke of
Ferrara. Slighted and driven to desperation, she makes
her way back to her father, is forgiven, and learns that
Charles' death was due to no accident, but to her father's
hand. No sooner is this discovery made than Valentine and Julia are brought in by the banditti, who have
surprised and captured them, but do not know their
rank. The deposed duke, Sebastian, does not recognise
Valentine, and consigns him, with his wife, to a cave,
under guard of the brigands. It is settled by Sebastian
that on the morrow Valentine is to go and fetch a
ransom, leaving his wife behind. Francesca, having
plied the guards with drink, enters by night into the
cave where they lie captive, is recognised by them, and
offers to change dresses with Julia in order that husband
and wife may escape. A fine scene follows of insistence
and self-reproach, but ultimately Francesca prevails.
Valentine and Julia pass out in the grey dawn, and
Francesca, left alone, stabs herself. The play concludes
as her father enters the cave and discovers his daughter's
corpse.

The first scene (which is placed at the court of
Bologna) passed without disaster, and the curtain fell

for a moment before it rose upon the mountain pass. Hitherto the audience had been chilly. They did not hiss, but neither did they applaud; and I could feel, without being able to give any definite reason for the impression, that so far the play had failed. Tom saw it too. I did not dare to look in his face, but could tell his agony by his short and laboured breathing. Luckily his torture did not last long, for the curtain quickly rose for Scene 2.

The scene was beautifully painted and awakened a momentary enthusiasm in the audience. It died away, however, as Sebastian and Valentine entered. The dialogue between them was short, and Valentine was very soon left alone to a rather dull soliloquy (since shortened) which began to weary the audience most unmistakably. I caught the sound of a faint hiss, saw one or two people yawning; and then——

Stealing, rising, swelling, gathering as it thrilled the ear all graces and delights of perfect sound; sweeping the awed heart with touch that set the strings quivering to an ecstasy that was almost pain; breathing through them in passionate whispering; hovering, swaying, soaring upward to the very roof, then shivering down again in celestial shower of silver — there came a voice that trod all conceptions, all comparisons, all dreams to scorn; a voice beyond hope, beyond belief; a voice that in its unimaginable beauty seemed to compel the very heaven to listen.

And yet—surely I knew—surely it could not be—

I must be dreaming—mad! The bare notion was incredible—and even as my heart spoke the words, the theatre grew dim and shadowy ; the vast sea of faces heaved, melted, swam in confusion ; all sound came dull and hoarse upon my ear ; while there—there——

There, in the blaze of light, radiant, lovely, a glorified and triumphant queen, stepped forward before the eyes of that vast multitude—my love, my Claire !

CHAPTER VI.

As I sat stupefied our eyes met. It was but for an instant, but in that instant I saw that she recognised me and mutely challenged my verdict. Then she turned to Valentine.

The theatre rang with tumultuous plaudits as her song ended. I could feel Tom's grasp at my elbow, but I could neither echo the applause nor answer him. It was all so wildly, grotesquely improbable.

This then was my love, this the Claire whom I had wooed and won in the shy covert of Pangbourne Woods —this deified and transfigured being before whom thousands were hushed in awe. Those were the lips that had faltered in sweet confession—those before which the breath of thousands came and went in agitated wonder. It was incredible.

And then, as Tom's hand was laid upon my arm, it flashed upon me that the woman he loved was my plighted bride—and he knew nothing of it. As this broke upon me there swept over me an awful dread lest he should see my face and guess the truth. How could I tell him? Poor Tom! Poor Tom!

R

I turned my eyes upon Claire again. Yes, she was superb : beyond all challenge glorious. And all the more I felt as one who has betrayed his friend and is angry with fate for sealing such betrayal beyond revoke.

Whether Claire misinterpreted my look of utter stupefaction or not, I do not know ; but as she turned and recognised Valentine there was a tremor in her voice which the audience mistook for art, though I knew it to be but too real. I tried to smile and to applaud, but neither eyes nor hand would obey my will; and so even Claire's acting became a reproach and an appeal to me, pleading forgiveness to which my soul cried assent though my voice denied it. Minute after minute I sat beneath an agonising spell I could not hope to break.

*   *   *   *   *

"Congratulate me, Jasper. What do you think of her ? "

It was Tom's voice beside me. Congratulate him ! I felt the meanest among men.

" She is—glorious," I stammered.

" I knew you would say so. Unbeliever, did ever man see such eyes? Confess now, what are Claire's beside them ? "

" Claire's—are—much the same."

" Why, man, Claire's were deep grey but a day or two ago, and Clarissa's are the brownest of brown ; but of course you cannot see from here."

Alas ! I knew too surely the colour of Claire's eyes, so like brown in the blaze of the foot-lights. And her height—Tom had only seen her walk in tragic buskin. How fatally easy had the mistake been!

"Tom, your success is certain now."

"Yes, thanks to her. They were going to damn the play before she entered. I could see it. Did you see, Jasper? She looked this way for a moment. Do you think she meant to encourage me? By the way, have you caught sight of Claire yet?"

Oh, Tom, Tom, let me spare you for this night! My heart throbbed and something in my throat seemed choking me as I muttered, "Yes."

"Then do not stay congratulating me, but fly. Success spoils the lover. Ah, Jasper, if only Clarissa had summoned me! Hasten: I will keep my eye upon you and smile approval on your taste. Where is she?"

Again something seemed to catch me by the throat; I was struggling to answer when I heard a voice behind me say, "For you, sir," and a note was thrust into my hand. With beating heart I opened it, expecting to see Claire's handwriting. But the note was not from her. It was scribbled hastily with pencil in a bold hand, and ran thus :—

"An old friend wishes to see you. Come, if you have time. Box No. 7."

At first I thought the message must have reached me by mistake,· but it was very plainly directed to "J. Trenoweth, Esq." I looked around for the messenger but found him gone, and fell to scanning the boxes once more.

R 2

As before, they were filled with strangers; and, as before, the black and yellow fan was waving slowly to and fro, as though the hand that wielded it was no hand at all, but rather some untiring machine. Still the owner remained invisible. I hesitated, reflected a moment, and decided that even a fool's errand was better than enduring the agony of Tom's rapture. I rose.

"I will be back again directly," I said, and then left him.

Still pondering on the meaning of this message, I made my way down the passages until I came to the doors of the boxes, and stopped opposite that labelled "No. 7." As I did so, it struck me that this, from its position, must be the one which contained the black and yellow fan. By this time thoroughly curious, I knocked.

"Come in," said a low voice which I seemed to remember.

I entered and found myself face to face with the yellow woman—the mistress of the gambling-hell.

She was seated there alone, slightly retired from the view of the house and in the shadow; but her arm, as it rested on the cushion, still swayed the black and yellow fan, and her diamonds sparkled lustrously as ever in the glare that beat into the box. Her dress, as if to emphasise the hideousness of her skin and form a staring contrast with her wrinkled face and white hair, was of black and yellow, in which she seemed some grisly corpse masquerading as youth.

Struck dumb by this apparition, I took the seat into which she motioned me, while her wonderful eyes regarded my face with stony impassiveness. I could hear the hoarse murmurs of the house and feel the stifling heat as it swept upwards from the pit. The strange woman did not stir except to keep up the ceaseless motion of her wrist.

For a full five minutes, as it seemed to me, we sat there silently regarding each other. Then at last she spoke, and the soft voice was as musically sympathetic as ever.

"You seem astonished to see me, Mr. Trenoweth, and yet I have been looking for you for a long time."

I bowed.

"I have been expecting you to give me a chance of redeeming my defeat."

"I am sorry," stammered I, not fully recovered from my surprise, "but that is not likely."

"No? From my point of view it was extremely likely. But somehow I had a suspicion that you would be different from the rest. Perhaps it was because I had set my heart upon your coming."

"I hope," said I, "that the money——"

She smiled and waved her hand slightly.

"Do not trouble about that. Had I chosen, I could have gone on losing to you until this moment. No, perhaps it was simply because you were least likely to do so, that I wished you to come back as all other young men would come back. I hope you reached

home safely with what you won; but I need not ask
that."

"Indeed you need. I was attacked as I left the
room, and but for a lucky accident, should now be
dead."

"Ah," she said placidly; "you suspect me. Don't
say 'no,' for I can see you do. Nevertheless you are
entirely wrong. Why, Mr. Trenoweth, had I chosen,
do you think I could not have had you robbed before
you had gone three paces from the house?"

This was said with such composure, and her eyes
were so absolutely void of emotion, that I could but
sit and gasp. Once more I recalled the moment
when, as I fled down the dark passage, I had seen her
sitting motionless and calm in the light of her countless
candles.

"But do you think I sent for you to tell you that?"
she continued. "I sent for you because you interested
me, and because I want a talk with you. Hush! the
curtain is rising for the second act. Let us resume
when it has finished; you will not deny me that favour
at least."

I bowed again, and was silent as the curtain rose—
and once more Claire's superb voice thrilled the house.
Surely man was seldom more strangely placed than was
I, between the speech of my love and the eyes of this
extraordinary woman. As I sat in the shadow and
listened, I felt those blazing fires burning into my very
soul; yet whenever I looked up and met them, their icy

glitter baffled all interpretation. Still as I sat there, the voice of Claire came to me as though beseeching and praying for my judgment, and rising with the blaze of light and heated atmosphere of the house, swept into the box until I could bear the oppression no longer. She must have looked for me, and seeing my place empty, have guessed that I condemned her. Mad with the thought, I rose to my feet and stood for a minute full in the light of the theatre. It may not have been even a minute, but she saw me, and once more, as our gaze met, faltered for an instant. Then the voice rang out clear and true again, and I knew that all was well between us. Yet in her look there was something which I could not well interpret.

As I sank back in my seat, I met the eyes of my companion still impenetrably regarding me. But as the curtain fell she said quietly—

"So you know Clarissa Lambert?"

I stammered an affirmative.

"Well? You admire her acting?"

"I never saw it until to-night."

"That is strange; and yet you know her?"

I nodded.

"She is a great success—on which I congratulate myself, for I discovered her."

"You!" I could only exclaim.

"Yes, I. Is it so extraordinary? She and I are connected, so to speak; which makes it the more odd that she should never have mentioned you."

The eyes seemed now to be reading me as a book. I summoned all my courage and tried to return their steady stare. There was a pause, broken only by the light *frou-frou* of the fan, as it still waved slowly backwards and forwards. Among all the discoveries of this night, it was hard enough to summon reason, harder to utter speech.

"But you will be leaving me again if I do not explain why I sent for you. You are wondering now on my reasons. They are very simple—professional even, in part. In the first place, I wished to have a good look at you. Do you wonder why an old woman should wish to look upon a comely youth? Do not blush; but listen to my other and professional reason. I should greatly like, if I may, to look upon your talisman—that golden buckle or whatever it was that brought such marvellous luck. Is it on you to-night?"

I wore it, as a matter of fact, in my waistcoat pocket, attached to one end of my chain; but I hesitated for a moment.

"You need not be afraid," she said, and there was a suspicion of mockery in her tone. "I will return it, as I returned it before. But if you are reluctant to let me see it (and remember, I have seen it once), do not hesitate to refuse. I shall not be annoyed."

Reflecting that, after all, her curiosity was certain to be baffled, I handed her the Golden Clasp, with the chain, in silence.

"It is a curious relic," said she, as she slowly

examined it and laid it on her lap for a moment. " If the question be allowed, how did you become possessed of it?"

" It belonged to my father," I answered.

" Excuse me," she said, deliberately, " that is hardly an answer to my question."

During the silence that followed, she took up the clasp again, and studied the writing. As she did so she used her right hand only; indeed, during the whole time, her left had been occupied with her tireless fan. I fancied, though I could not be certain, that it was waving slightly faster than before.

" The writing seems to be nonsense. What is this— ' Moon . end . south—deep . at . point' ? I can make no meaning of it. I suppose there is a meaning?"

" Not to my knowledge," said I, and immediately repented, for once more I seemed to catch that gleam in her eyes which had so baffled me when first she saw the Clasp. The curtain rose upon the third act of " Francesca," and we sat in silence, she with the Clasp lying upon her lap, I wondering by what possibility she could know anything about my father's secret. She could not, I determined. The whole history of the Golden Clasp made it impossible. And yet I repented my rashness. It was too late now, however; so, when the act was over I waited for her to speak.

" So this belonged to your father. Tell me, was he at all like you?"

" He was about my height, I should guess," said

I, wondering at this new question; "but otherwise quite unlike. He was a fair man, I am dark."

"But your grandfather—was he not dark?"

"I believe so," I answered, "but really—"

"You wonder at my questions, of course. Never mind me; think me a witch, if you like. Do I not look a witch?"

Indeed she did, as she sat there. The diamonds flashed and gleamed, lighting up the awful colour of her skin until she seemed a very "Death-in-Life."

"I see that I puzzle you; but your looks, Mr. Trenoweth, are hardly complimentary. However, you are forgiven. Here, take your talisman, and guard it jealously; I thank you for showing it to me, but if I were you I should keep it secret. Shall I see you again? I suppose not. I am afraid I have made you miss some of the tragedy. You must pardon me for that, as I have waited long to see you. At any rate, there is the last act to come. Good-bye, and be careful of your talisman."

As she spoke, she shut her fan with a sharp click, and then it flashed upon me that it had never ceased its pendulous motion until that instant. It was a strange idea to strike me then, but a stranger yet succeeded. Was it that I heard a low mocking laugh within the box as I stepped out into the passage? I cannot clearly tell; perhaps it is but a fancy conjured up by later reflection on that meeting and its consequences. I only know that as I bowed and left her, the vision that I bore away was not of the gleaming gems, the yellow face, the white hair, or waving fan, but of two coal-black and impenetrable eyes.

I sought my place, and dropped into the seat beside Tom. The fourth act was beginning, so that I had time to speculate upon my interview, but could find no hope of solution. Finally, I abandoned guessing, to admire Claire. As the play went on, her acting grew more and more transcendent. Lines which I had heard from Tom's lips and scoffed at, were now fused with subtle meaning and passion. Scenes which I had condemned as awkward and heavy, became instinct with exquisite pathos. There comes a point in acting at which criticism ceases, content to wonder; this point it was clear that my love had touched. The new play was a triumphant success.

" So," said Tom, before the last act, " Claire carries a yellow fan, does she? I looked everywhere for you at first, and only caught sight of you for an instant by the merest chance. You behaved rather shabbily in giving me no chance of criticism, for I never caught a glimpse of her. I hope she admired—— Hallo! she's gone!"

I followed his gaze, and saw that Box No. 7 was no longer occupied by the fan.

" I suppose you saw her off? Well, I do not admire your taste, I must confess—nor Claire's—to go when Francesca was beginning to touch her grandest height. Whew! you lovers make me blush for you."

"Tom," I said, anxious to lead him from all mention of Claire, "you must forgive me for having laughed at your play."

"Forgive you! I will forgive you if you weep during the next act; only on that condition."

How shall I describe the last act? Those who read "Francesca" in its published form can form no adequate idea of the enthusiasm in the Coliseum that night. To them it is a skeleton; then it was clothed with passionate flesh and blood, breathed, sobbed and wept in purest pathos; to me, even now, as I read it again, it is charged with the inspiration of that wonderful art, so true, so tender, that made its last act a miracle. I saw old men sob, and young men bow their heads to hide the emotion which they could not check. I saw that audience which had come to criticise, tremble and break into tumultuous weeping. Beside me, a grey-headed man was crying as any child. Yet why do I go on? No one who saw Clarissa Lambert can ever forget —no one who saw her not can ever imagine.

Tom had bowed his acknowledgments, the last flower had been flung, the last cheer had died away as we stepped out into the Strand together. The street was wrapped in the densest of November fogs. So thick was it that the lamps, the shop windows, came into sight, stared at us in ghostly weakness for a moment, and then were gone, leaving us in Egyptian gloom. I could not hope to see Claire to-night, and Tom was too modest to offer his congratulations until the morning. Both he and I were too shaken by the scene just past for many words, and outside the black fog caught and held us by the throat.

Even in the pitchy gloom I could feel that Tom's step was buoyant. He was treading already in imagination the path of love and fame. How should I have the heart to tell him? How wither the chaplet that already seemed to bind his brow?

Tom was the first to break the silence which had fallen upon us.

"Jasper, did you ever see or hear the like? Can a man help worshipping her? But for her, 'Francesca' would have been hissed. I know it, I could see it, and now, I suppose, I shall be famous.

"Famous!" continued he, soliloquising. "Three months ago I would have given the last drop of my blood for fame; and now, without Clarissa, fame will be a mockery. Do you think I might have any chance, the least chance?"

How could I answer him? The fog caught my breath as I tried to stammer a reply, and Tom, misinterpreting my want of words, read his condemnation.

"You do not? Of course, you do not; and you are right. Success has intoxicated me, I suppose. I am not used to the drink!" and he laughed a joyless laugh.

Then, with a change of mood, he caught my hat from off my head, and set his own in its place.

"We will change characters for the nonce," he said,

"after the fashion of Falstaff and Prince Hal, and I will read myself a chastening discourse on the vanity of human wishes. 'Do thou stand for me, and I'll play my father.' Eh, Jasper?"

"'Well, here I am set,'" quoted I, content to humour him.

"Well, then, I know thee; thou art Thomas Loveday, a beggarly Grub Street author, i' faith, a man of literature, and wouldst set eyes upon one to whom princes fling bouquets; a low Endymion pulling a scrannel pipe, and wouldst call therewith a queen to be thy bride. Out upon thee for such monstrous folly!"

In his voice, as it came to me through the dense gloom, there rang, for all its summoned gaiety, a desperate mockery hideous to hear.

"Behold, success hath turned thy weak brain. But an hour agone enfranchised from Grub Street, thou must sing 'I'd be a butterfly.' Thou art vanity absolute, conceit beyond measure, and presumption out of all whooping. Yea, and but as a fool Pygmalion, not content with loving thine own handiwork, thou must needs fall in love with the goddess that breathed life into its stiff limbs; must yearn, not for Galatea, but for Aphrodite; not for Francesca, but for——Ah!"

What was that? I saw a figure start up as if from below our feet, and Tom's hand go up to his breast. There was a scuffle, a curse, and as I dashed forward, a dull, dim gleam—and Tom, with a groan, sank back into my arms.

That was all. A moment, and all had happened. Yet not all; for as I caught the body of my friend, and saw his face turn ashy white in the gloom, I saw also, saw unmistakably framed for an instant in the blackness of the fog, a face I knew; a face I should know until death robbed my eyes of sight and my brain of remembrance—the face of Simon Colliver.

A moment, and before I could pursue, before I could even shout or utter its name, it had faded into the darkness, and was gone.

CHAPTER VII.

Tom was dying. His depositions had been taken and
signed with his failing hand; the surgeon had given his
judgment, and my friend was lying upon his bed, face
to face with the supreme struggle.

The knife had missed his heart by little more than
an inch, but the inward bleeding was killing him and
there was no hope. He knew it, and though the reason
of that cowardly blow was a mystery to him, he asked
few questions, but faced his fate with the old boyish
pluck. His eyes as they turned to mine were lit with
the old boyish love.

Once only since his evidence was taken had his lips
moved, and then to murmur *her* name. I had sent for
her: a short note with only the words "Tom is dying
and wants to speak with you." So, while we waited, I
sat holding my friend's hand and busy with my own
black thoughts.

I knew that he had received the blow meant for me,
and that the secret of this too, as well as that other
assault in the gambling-den, hung on the Golden Clasp

and the Great Ruby. Whatever that secret was, the
yellow woman knew of it, and held it beneath the glitter of her awful eyes. She it was that had directed
the murderous knife in the hands of Simon Colliver.
Bitterly I cursed the folly which had prompted my rash
words in the theatre, and so sacrificed my friend. With
what passion, even in my despair, I thanked Heaven that
the act which led to Colliver's mistake had been Tom's
and not mine! Yet, what consolation was it? It was
I, not he, that should be lying there. He had given
his life for his friend—a friend who had already robbed
him of his love. O false and traitorous friend!

In my humiliation I would have taken my hand
from his, but a feeble pressure and a look of faint reproach restrained me. So he lay there and I sat beside
him, and both counted the moments until Claire should
come—or death.

A knock at the door outside. Tom heard it and in
his eyes shone a light of ineffable joy. In answer to his
look I dropped his hand and went to meet her.

" Claire, how can I thank you for this speed? "

" How did it happen? "

" Murdered! " said I. " Foully struck down last
night as he left the theatre."

Her eyes looked for a moment as though they would
have questioned me further, but she simply asked—

" Does he want to see me? '

" When he heard he was to die he asked for you.
Claire, if you only knew how he longs to see you; had

s

you only seen his eyes when he heard you come! You
know why——"

She nodded gravely.

" I suppose," she said slowly, " we had better say
nothing of——"

" Nothing," I answered ; " it is better so.   If there
be any knowledge beyond the grave he will know all
soon."

Claire was silent.

" Yes," she assented at length, " it is better so.
Take me to him."

I drew back as Claire approached the bed, dreading
to meet Tom's eyes ; but I saw them welcome her in a
flash of thankful rapture, then slowly close as though
unable wholly to bear this glad vision.

Altogether lovely she was as she bent and lifted his
nerveless hand, with the light of purest compassion on
her face.

" You have come then," said the dying man. "God
bless you for that ! "

" I am come, and oh ! I am so very, very sorry."

" I saw Jasper write and knew he had sent, but I
hardly dared to hope.   I am—very weak—and am
going—fast."

For answer, a tear of infinite pity dropped on the
white hand.

" Don't weep—I can't bear to see you weeping.   It
is all for the best.   I can see that I have had hopes
and visions, but I should never have attained them—

never. Now I shall not have to strive. Better so—better so."

For a moment or two the lips moved inaudibly; then they spoke again—

"It was so good of you—to come; I was afraid—afraid—but you are good. You saved my play last night, but you cannot save—me." A wan smile played over the white face and was gone.

"Better so, for I can speak now and be pardoned. Do you know why I sent for you? I wanted to tell something—before I died. Do not be angry—I shall be dead soon, and in the grave, they say, there is no knowledge. Clarissa! oh, pity me—pity me, if I speak!"

The eyes looked up imploringly and met their pardon.

"I have loved you—yes, loved you. Can you forgive? It need not distress—you—now. It was mad—mad—but I loved you. Jasper, come here."

I stepped to the bed.

"Tell her I loved her, and ask her—to forgive me. Tell her I knew it was hopeless. Tell her so, Jasper."

Powerless to meet those trustful eyes, weary with the anguish of my remorse, I stood there helpless.

"Jasper is too much—upset just now to speak. Never mind, he will tell you later. He is in love himself. I have never seen her, but I hope he may be happier than I. Forgive me for saying that. I am happy now—happy now.

"You do not know Jasper," continued the dying

s 2

man after a pause; "but he saw you last night—and admired—how could he help it? I hope you will be friends—for my sake. Jasper is my only friend."

There was a grey shadow on his face now—the shadow of death. Tom must have felt it draw near, for suddenly raising himself upon his elbow, he cried—

"Ah, I was selfish—I did not think. They are waiting at the theatre—go to them. You will act your best—for my sake. Forget what I have said, if you cannot forgive."

"Oh, why will you think that?"

"You do forgive? Oh, God bless you, God bless you for it! Clarissa, if that be so, grant one thing more of your infinite mercy. Kiss me once—once only—on the lips. I shall die happier so. Will you—can you—do this?"

The film was gathering fast upon those eyes once so full of laughter; but through it they gazed in passionate appeal. For answer, my love bent gravely over the bed and with her lips met his; then, still clasping his hand, sank on her knees beside the bed.

"Thank God! My love—oh, let me call you that—you cannot—help—my loving you. Do not pray—I am happy now and—they are waiting for you."

Slowly Claire arose to her feet and stood waiting for his last word—

"They are waiting—waiting. Good-bye, Jasper—old friend—and Clarissa—Clarissa—my love—they are waiting—I cannot come—Clar——"

Slowly Claire bent and once more touched his lips, then without a word passed slowly out. As she went Death entered and found on its victim's face a changeless, rapturous smile.

So "Francesca" was played a second time and, as the papers said next morning, with even more perfect art and amid more awed enthusiasm than on the first night. But as the piece went on, a rumour passed through the house that its young author was dead—suddenly and mysteriously dead while the dawn of his fame was yet breaking—struck down, some said, outside the theatre by a rival, while others whispered that he had taken poison, but none knew for certain. Only, as Claire passed from one heart-shaking scene to another, the rumour grew and grew, so that when the curtain fell the audience parted in awed and murmured speculations.

And all the while I was kneeling beside the body of my murdered friend.

*   *   *   *   *

A week had passed and I was standing with Claire beside Tom's grave. We had met and spoken at the funeral, but some restraint had lain upon our tongues. For myself, I was still as one who had sold his brother for a price, and Claire had forborne from questioning my grief.

The coroner's jury had brought in a verdict of "Murder by a certain person unknown," and now the police were occupied in following such clues as I could give them. All the daily papers assigned robbery as the

motive, and the disappearance of Tom's watch-chain gave
plausibility to the theory.   But I knew too well why
that chain had disappeared, and even in my grief found
consolation in the thought of Colliver's impotent rage
when he should come to examine his prize.   I had described the face and figure of my enemy and had even
identified him with the long-missing sailor Georgio
Rhodojani, so that they promised to lay hands on him
in a very short space.   But the public knew nothing of
this.   The only effect of the newspapers' version of the
murder was to send the town crowding in greater numbers than ever to see the dead man's play.

Since the first night of " Francesca," Claire and I
had only met by Tom's bedside and at his funeral.   But
as I entered the gloomy cemetery that afternoon I spied
a figure draped in black beside the yet unsettled mound,
and as I drew near knew it to be Claire.

So we stood there facing one another for a full
minute, at a loss for words.   A wreath of *immortelles*
lay upon the grave.   In my heart I thanked her for the
gift, but could not speak.   It seemed as though the
hillock that parted us were some impassable barrier to
words.   Had I but guessed the truth I should have
known that, unseen and unsuspected, across that foot or
two of turf was stretched a gulf we were never more to
cross : between our lives lay the body of my friend ;
and not his only, but many a pallid corpse that with its
mute lips cursed our loves.

Presently Claire raised her head and spoke.

" Jasper, you have much to forgive me, and I hardly dare ask your forgiveness. It is too late to ask forgiveness of a dead man, but could he hear now I would entreat him to pardon the folly that wrought this cruel mistake."

" Claire, you could not know. How was it possible to guess ? "

" That is true, but it is no less cruel. And I deceived you. Can you ever forgive ? "

" Forgive ! forgive what ? That I found my love peerless among women ? Oh, Claire, Claire, ' forgive ' ? "

" Yes; what matters it that for the moment I have what is called fame ? I deceived you—yet, believe me, it was only because I thought to make the surprise more pleasant. I thought—but it is too late. Only believe I had no other thought, no other wish. My poor scheme seemed so harmless at first: then as the days went on I began to doubt. But until you told me, as we stood beside the river, of—*him*, I never guessed ; —oh, believe me, I never guessed ! "

" Love, do not accuse yourself in this way. It hurts me to hear you speak so. If there was any fault it was mine ; but the Fates blinded us. If you had known Tom, you would know that he would forgive could he hear us now. For me, Claire, what have I to pardon ? "

Claire did not answer for a moment. There was still a trouble in her face, as though something yet remained to be said and she had not the courage to utter it.

"Jasper, there is something besides, which you have to pardon if you can."

"My love!"

"Do you remember what I asked you that night, when you first told me about *him*?"

"You asked me a foolish question, if I remember rightly. You asked if I could ever cease to love you."

"No, not foolish; I really meant it seriously, and I believed you when you answered me. Are you of the same mind now? Believe me, I am not asking lightly."

"I answer you as I answered you then: 'Love is strong as death.' My love, put away these thoughts and be sure that I love you as my own soul."

"But perhaps, even so, you might be so angry that —Oh, Jasper, how can I tell you?"

"Tell me all, Claire."

"I told you I was called, or that they called me Claire. Were you not surprised when you saw my name as Clarissa Lambert?"

"Is that all?" I cried. "Why, of course, I knew how common it is for actresses to take another name. I was even glad of it; for the name I know, your own name, is now a secret, and all the sweeter so. All the world admires Clarissa Lambert, but I alone love Claire Luttrell, and know that Claire Luttrell loves me."

"But that is not all," she expostulated, whilst the trouble in her eyes grew deeper. "Oh, why will you make it so hard for me to explain? I never thought, when I told you so carelessly on that night when we met for the first time, that you would grow to care for me at all. And it was the same afterwards, when I introduced you to my mother; I gave you the name Luttrell, without ever dreaming——"

"Was Luttrell not your mother's name?" I asked, perplexed.

"That is the name by which she is always called now; and I am always called Claire; in fact, it is my name, but I have another, and I ought to have told you."

"Why, as Claire I know you, and as Claire I shall always love you. What does it matter if your real name be Lambert? You will change it, love, soon, I trust."

But my poor little jest woke no mirth in her eyes.

"No, it is not Lambert. That is only the name I took when I went on the stage. Nor am I called Luttrell. It is a sad story; but let me tell it now, and put an end to all deception. I meant to do so long ago; but lately I thought I would wait until after you had seen me on the stage; I thought I would explain all together, not knowing that *he*——but it has all gone wrong. Jasper, I know you will pity poor mother, even though she had allowed you to be deceived. She has been so unhappy. But let me tell it first, and then you will judge. She calls herself Luttrell to avoid persecution; to avoid a man who is——"

"A villain, I am sure."

"A villain, yes; but worse. He is her husband;

not my father, but a second husband. My father died when I was quite a little child, and she married again. Ever since that day she has been miserable. I remember her face—oh, so well! when she first discovered the real character of the man. For years she suffered—we were abroad then—until at last she could bear it no longer, so she fled—fled back to England, and took me with her. I think, but I am not sure, that her husband did not dare to follow her to England, because he had done something against the laws. I only guess this, for I never dare to ask mother about him. I did so once, and shall never forget the look of terror that came into her eyes. I only guess he has some strong reason for avoiding England, for I remember we went abroad hastily, almost directly after that night when mother first discovered that she had been deceived. However that may be, we came to England, mother and I, and changed our name to Luttrell, which was her maiden name. After this, our life became one perpetual dread of discovery. We were miserably poor, of course, and I was unable to do anything to help for many years. Mother was so careful; why, she even called me by my second name, so desperately anxious was she to hide all traces from that man. Then suddenly we were discovered—not by him, but by his mother, whom he set to search for us, and she—for she was not wholly bad—promised to make my fortune on the single condition that half my earnings were sent to him. Otherwise, she threatened that mother should have no rest. What could I do? It was the only way to save ourselves. Well, I promised to go upon the stage, for this woman fancied she discovered some talent in me. Why, Jasper, how strangely you are looking!"

"Tell me—tell me," I cried, "who is this woman?"

"You ought to know that, for you were in the box with her during most of the first night of 'Francesca.'"

A horrible, paralysing dread had seized me.

"Her name, and his? Quick—tell me, for God's sake!"

"Colliver. He is called Simon Colliver. But, Jasper, what is it? What——"

I took the chain and Golden Clasp and handed them to Claire without speech.

"Why, what is this?" she cried. "He has a piece exactly like this, the fellow to it; I remember seeing it when I was quite small. Oh, speak! what new mystery, what new trouble is this?"

"Claire, Colliver is here in London, or was but a week ago."

"Here!"

"Yes, Claire; and it was he that murdered Thomas Loveday."

"Murdered Thomas Loveday! I do not understand." She had turned a deathly white, and spread out her hands as if for support. "Tell me——"

"Yes, Claire," I said, as I stepped to her, and put my arm about her; "it is truth, as I stand here. Colliver, your mother's husband, foully murdered my innocent friend for the sake of that piece of gold; and more, Simon Colliver, for the sake of this same accursed token, murdered my father!"

"Your father!"

She shook off my arm, and stood facing me there, by Tom's grave, with a look of utter horror that froze my blood.

"Yes, my father; or stay, I am wrong. Though Colliver prompted, his was not the hand that did the deed. That he left to a poor wretch whom he afterwards slew himself—one Railton—John Railton."

"What!"

"Why, Claire, Claire! What is it? Speak!"

"I am Janet Railton!"

CHAPTER VIII.

FOR a moment I staggered back as though buffeted in the face, then, as our eyes met and read in each other the desperate truth, I sprang forward just in time to catch her as she fell. Blindly, as if in some hideous trance, reeling and stumbling over the graves, I carried her in my arms to the cemetery gate and stood there panting and bewildered.

Cold and white as marble she lay in my arms, so that for one terrible moment I thought her dead. "Better so," my heart had cried, and then I laughed aloud (God forgive me!) at the utter cruelty of it all. But she was not dead. As I watched the lovely ashen face, the slow blood came trickling back and throbbed faintly at her temples, the light breath flickered and went and came once more. Feebly and with wonder the dark eyes opened to the light of day, then closed again as the lips parted in a moaning whisper.

"Claire!" I cried, and my voice seemed to come from far away, so hollow and unnatural was it, "I must take you to your home; are you well enough to go?"

I had laid her on the stone upon which the bearers

were used to set down the coffins when weary. Scarcely
a week ago, poor Tom's corpse had rested for a moment
upon this grim stone. As I bent to catch the answer,
and saw how like to death her face was, I thought how
well it were for both of us, should we be resting there
so together; not leaving the acre of the dead, but
entering it as rightful heirs of its oblivion.

After a while, as I repeated my question, the lips
again parted and I heard.

I looked down the road. The cemetery lay far out
in one of the northern suburbs, and just now the neighbourhood seemed utterly deserted. By good chance,
however, I spied an old four-wheeler crawling along in
the distance. I ran after it, hailed it, brought it back,
and with the help of the wondering driver, placed my
love inside; then I gave the man the address, and bidding him drive with all speed, sprang in beside Claire.

Still faint, she was lying back against the cushion.
The cab crawled along at a snail's pace, but long as the
journey was, it was passed in utter silence. She never
opened her eyes, and as for me, what comfortable words
could I speak? Yet as I saw the soft rise and fall of
her breast, I longed for words, Heaven knows how
madly! But none came, and in silence we drew up at
length before a modest doorway in Old Kensington.

Here Claire summoned all her strength lest her
mother should be frightened. Still keeping her eyes
averted, she stepped as bravely as she could from the
cab, and laid her hand upon the door-handle.

I made as if to follow.

"No, no," she said hastily, "leave me to myself—I will write to-morrow and perhaps see you; but, oh, pray, not to-day!"

Before I could answer she had passed into the house.

*   *   *   *   *

Twenty-four hours had passed and left me as they found me, in torture. Despite my doubt, I swore she should not cast me off; then knelt and prayed as I had never prayed before, that Heaven would deny some of its cruelty to my darling. In the abandonment of my supplication, I was ready to fling the secret from me and forgive all, to forgive my father's murderer, my life-long enemy, and let him go unsought, rather than give up Claire. Yet as I prayed, my entreaties and my tears went up to no compassionate God, but beat themselves upon the adamantine face of Dead Man's Rock that still rose inexorable between me and Heaven.

That night the crowd that gathered in the Coliseum to see the new play, went away angry and disappointed; for Clarissa Lambert was not acting. Another actress took her part—but how differently! And all the while she, for whose sake they had come, was on her knees wrestling with a grimmer tragedy than "Francesca," with no other audience than the angels of pity.

Twenty-four hours had passed, and found me hastening towards Old Kensington; for in my pocket lay a note bearing only the words "Come at 3.30—Claire," and on my heart rested a load of suspense unbearable.

For many minutes beforehand, I paced up and down outside the house in an agony, and as my watch pointed to the half-hour, knocked and was admitted.

Mrs. Luttrell met me in the passage. She seemed most terribly white and worn, so that I was astonished when she simply said, "Claire is slightly unwell, and in fact could not act last night, but she wishes to see you for some reason."

Wondering why Claire's mother should look so strangely if she guessed nothing of what had happened, but supposing illness to be the reason, I stopped for an instant to ask.

"Am I pale?" she answered. "It is nothing—nothing—do not take any notice of it. I am rather weaker than usual to-day, that is all—a mere nothing. You will find Claire in the drawing-room there." And so she left me.

I knocked at the drawing-room door, and hearing a faint voice inside, entered. As I did so, Claire rose to meet me. She was very pale, and the dark circles around her eyes told of a long vigil; but her manner at first was composed and even cold.

"Claire!" I cried, and stretched out my hands.

"Not yet," she said, and motioned me to a chair. "I sent for you because I have been thinking of—of—what happened yesterday, and I want you to tell me all; the whole story from beginning to end."

"But——"

"There is no 'but' in the case, Jasper. I am Janet

Railton, and you say that my father killed yours. Tell me how it was."

Her manner was so calm that I hesitated at first, bewildered. Then, finding that she waited for me to speak, I sat down facing her and began my story.

I told it through, without suppression or concealment, from the time when my father started to seek the treasure, down to the cowardly blow that had taken my friend's life. During the whole narrative she never took her eyes from my face for more than a moment. Her very lips were bloodless, but her manner was as quiet as though I were reading her some story of people who had never lived. Once only she interrupted me. I was repeating the conversation between her father and Simon Colliver upon Dead Man's Rock.

" You are quite sure," she asked, " of the words ? You are positive he said, ' Captain, it was your knife'?"

" Certain," I answered sadly.

" You are giving the very words they both used ? "

" As well as I can remember ; and I have cause for a good memory."

" Go on," she replied simply.

So I unrolled the whole chronicle of our unhappy fates, and even read to her Lucy Railton's letter which I had brought with me. Then, as I ceased, for full a minute we sat in absolute silence, reading each other's gaze.

" Let me see the letter," she said, and held out her hand for it.

T

I gave it to her. She read it slowly through and handed it back.

"Yes, it is my mother's letter," she said, slowly.

Then again silence fell upon us. I could hear the clock tick slowly on the mantelpiece, and the beating of my own heart that raced and outstripped it. That was all; until at length the slow, measured footfall of the timepiece grew maddening to hear; it seemed a symbol of the unrelenting doom pursuing us, and I longed to rise and break it to atoms.

I could stand it no longer.

"Claire, tell me that this will not—cannot alter you —that you are mine yet, as you were before."

"This is impossible," she said, very gravely and quietly.

"Impossible? Oh, no, no; do not say that! You cannot, you must not say that!"

"Yes, Jasper," she repeated, and her face was pallid as snow; "it is impossible."

But as I heard my doom, I arose and fought it with blind despair.

"Claire, you do not know what you are saying. You love me, Claire; you have told me so, and I love you as my very soul. Surely, then, you will not say this thing. How were we to know? How could you have told? Oh, Claire! is it that you do not love me?"

Her eyes were full of infinite compassion and tenderness, but her lips were firm and cold.

"You know that I love you."

"Then, oh, my love! how can this come between us? What does it matter that our fathers fought and killed each other, if only we love? Surely, surely Heaven cannot fix the seal of this crime upon us for ever? Speak, Claire, and tell me that you will be mine in spite of all!"

"It cannot be," she answered, very gently.

"Cannot be!" I echoed. "Then I was right, and you do not love, but fancied that you did for a while. Love, love, was that fair? No power on earth—no, nor in heaven—should have made me cast you off so."

My rage died out before the mute reproach of those lovely eyes. I caught the white hand.

"Forgive me, Claire; I was desperate, and knew not what I was saying. I know you love me—you have said so, and you are truth itself; truth and all goodness. But if you have loved, then you can love me still. Remember our text, Claire, 'Love is strong as death.' Strong as death, and can it be overcome so easily?"

She was trembling terribly, and from the little hand within mine I could feel her agitation. But though the soft eyes spoke appealingly as they were raised in answer, I could see, behind all their anguish, an immutable resolve.

"No, Jasper; it can never be—never. Do you think I am not suffering—that it is nothing to me to lose you? Try to think better of me. Oh, Jasper, it is hard indeed for me, and—I love you so.

"No, no," she went on; "do not make the task harder for me. Why can you not curse me? It would be easier then. Why can you not hate me as you ought? Oh, if you would but strike me and go, I could better bear this hour!"

There was such abandonment of entreaty in her tones that my heart bled for her; yet I could only answer—

"Claire, I will not give you up; not though you went [on your knees and implored it. Death alone can divide us now; and even death will never kill my love."

"Death!" she answered. "Think, then, that I am dead; think of me as under the mould. Ah, love, hearts do not break so easily. You would grieve at first, but in a little while I should be forgotten."

"Claire!"

"Forgive me, love; not forgotten. I wronged you when I said the word. Believe me, Jasper, that if there be any gleam of day in the blackness that surrounds me it is the thought that you so love me; and yet it would have been far easier otherwise—far easier."

Little by little my hope was slipping from me; but still I strove with her as a man battles for his life. I raved, protested, called earth and heaven to witness her cruelty; but all in vain.

"It would be a sin—a horrible sin!" she kept saying. "God would never forgive it. No, no; do not try to persuade me—it is horrible!" and she shuddered.

Utterly beaten at last by her obstinacy, I said—

" I will leave you now to think it over. Let me call again and hear that you repent."

" No, love; we must never meet again. This must be our last good-bye. Stay!" and she smiled for the first time since that meeting in the cemetery. " Come to ' Francesca ' to-night; I am going to act."

" What ! to-night ?"

" Yes. One must live, you see, even though one suffers. See, I have a ticket for you—for a box. You will come? Promise me."

" Never, Claire."

" Yes, promise me. Do me this last favour; I shall never ask another."

I took the card in silence.

" And now," she said, " you may kiss me. Kiss me on the lips for the last time, and may God bless you, my love."

Quite calmly and gently she lifted her lips to mine, and on her face was the glory of unutterable tenderness.

"Claire ! My love, my love!" My arms were round her, her whole form yielded helplessly to mine, and as our lips met in that one passionate, shuddering caress, sank on my breast.

" You will not leave me ?" I cried.

And through her sobs came the answer—

" Yes, yes; it must be, it must be."

Then drawing herself up, she held out her hand and said—

" To-night, remember, and so—farewell."

And so, in the fading light of that grey December afternoon I left her standing there.

*　　　*　　　*　　　*　　　*

Mad and distraught with the passion of that parting, I sat that evening in the shadow of my box and waited for the curtain to rise upon " Francesca." The Coliseum was crowded to the roof, for it was known that Clarissa Lambert's illness had been merely a slight indisposition, and to-night she would again be acting. I was too busy with my own hard thoughts to pay much attention at first, but I noticed that my box was the one nearest to the stage, in the tier next above it. So that once more I should hear my darling's voice, and see her form close to me. Once or twice I vaguely scanned the audience. The boxes opposite were full; but, of course, I could see nothing of my own side of the theatre. After a moment's listless glance, I leaned back in the shadow and waited.

I do not know who composed the overture. It is haunted by one exquisite air, repeated, fading into variations, then rising once more only to sink into the tender sorrow of a minor key. I have heard it but twice in my life, but the music of it is with me to this day. Then, as I heard it, it carried me back to the hour when Tom and I sat expectant in this same theatre, he trembling for his play's success, I for the sight of my love. Poor Tom! The sad melody wailed upwards as though it were the voice of the wind playing about his grave, every note breathing pathos or suspiring in tremulous anguish.

Poor Tom! Yet your love was happier than mine; better to die with Claire's kiss warm upon the lips than to live with but the memory of it.

The throbbing music had ended, and the play began. As before, the audience were without enthusiasm at first, but to-night they knew they had but to wait, and they did so patiently; so that when at last Claire's voice died softly away at the close of her opening song, the hushed house was suddenly shaken to its roof with the storm and tumult of applause.

There she stood, serene and glowing, as one that had never known pain. My very eyes doubted. On her face was no sign of suffering, no trace of a tear. Was she, then, utterly without heart? In my memory I retraced the scene of that afternoon, and all my reason acquitted her. Yet, as she stood there in her glorious epiphany, illumined with the blazing lights, and radiant in the joy and freshness of youth, I could have doubted whether, after all, Clarissa Lambert and Claire Luttrell were one and the same.

There was one thing which I did not fail, however, to note as strange. She did not once glance in the direction of my box, but kept her eyes steadily averted. And it then suddenly dawned upon me that she must be playing with a purpose; but what that purpose was I could not guess.

Whatever it was, she was acting magnificently and had for the present completely surrendered herself to her art. Grand as that art had been on the first night of

" Francesca," the power of that performance was utterly eclipsed to-night. Once between the acts I heard two voices in the passage outside my box—

" What do you think of it ? " said the first.

" What can I ? " answered the other. " And how can I tell you ? It is altogether above words."

He was right. It was not so much admiration as awe and worship that held the house that night. I have heard a man say since that he wonders how the play could ever have raised anything beyond a laugh. He should have heard the sobs that every now and then would break uncontrollably forth, even whilst Claire was speaking. He should have felt the hush that followed every scene before the audience could recollect itself and pay its thunderous tribute.

Still she never looked towards me, though all the while my eyes were following my lost love. Her purpose—and somehow in my heart I grew more and more convinced that some purpose lay beneath this transcendent display—was waiting for its accomplishment, and in the ringing triumph of her voice I felt it coming nearer—nearer—until at last it came.

The tragedy was nearly over. Francesca had dismissed her old lover and his new bride from their captivity and was now left alone upon the stage. The last expectant hush had fallen upon the house. Then she stepped slowly forward in the dead silence, and as she spoke the opening lines, for the first time our eyes met.

" Here then all ends :—all love, all hate, all vows,
All vain reproaches. Aye, 'tis better so.
So shall he best forgive and I forget,
Who else had chained him to a life-long curse,
Who else had sought forgiveness, given in vain
While life remained that made forgiveness dear.
Far better to release him—loving more
Now love denies its love and he is free,
Than should it by enjoyment wreck his joy,
Blighting his life for whom alone I lived.

" No, no. As God is just, it could not be.
Yet, oh, my love, be happy in the days
I may not share, with her whose present lips
Usurp the rights of my lost sovranty.
I would not have thee think—save now and then
As in a dream that is not all a dream—
On her whose love was sunshine for an hour,
Then died or e'er its beams could blast thy life.
Be happy and forget what might have been,
Forget my dear embraces in her arms,
My lips in hers, my children in her sons,
While I——
　　　　　Dear love, it is not hard to die
Now once the path is plain. See, I accept
And step as gladly to the sacrifice
As any maid upon her bridal morn—
One little stroke—one tiny touch of pain
And I am quit of pain for evermore.
It needs no bravery. Wert thou here to see,
I would not have thee weep, but look—one stroke,
And thus——"

What was that shriek far back there in the house?
What was that at sight of which the audience rose white
and aghast from their seats ? What was it that made
Sebastian as he entered rush suddenly forward and fall
with awful cry before Francesca's body ? What was

that trickling down the folds of her white dress? Blood?

Yes, blood! In an instant I put my hand upon the cushion of the box, vaulted down to the stage and was kneeling beside my dying love. But as the clamorous bell rang down the curtain, I heard above its noise a light and silvery laugh, and looking up saw in the box next to mine the coal-black devilish eyes of the yellow woman.

Then the curtain fell.

CHAPTER IX.

TELLS HOW TWO VOICES LED ME TO BOARD A SCHOONER; AND WHAT BEFELL THERE.

SHE died without speech. Only, as I knelt beside her and strove to staunch that cruel stream of blood, her beautiful eyes sought mine in utter love and, as the last agony shook her frame, strove to rend the filmy veil of death and speak to me still. Then, with one long, contented sigh, my love was dead. It was scarcely a minute before all was over. I pressed one last kiss upon the yet warm lips, tenderly drew her white mantle across the pallid face, and staggered from the theatre.

I had not raved or protested as I had done that same afternoon. Fate had no power to make me feel now; the point of anguish was passed, and in its place succeeded a numb stupidity more terrible by far, though far more blessed.

My love was dead. Then I was dead for any sensibility to suffering that I possessed. Hatless and cloakless I stepped out into the freezing night air, and regardless of the curious looks of the passing throng I turned and walked rapidly westward up the Strand. There was a large and eager crowd outside the Coliseum,

for already the news was spreading; but something in
my face made them give room, and I passed through
them as a man in a trance.

The white orb of the moon was high in heaven; the
frozen pavement sounded hollow under-foot; the long
street stood out, for all its yellow gas-light, white and
distinct against the clear air; but I marked nothing of
this. I went westward because my home lay westward,
and some instinct took my hurrying feet thither. I had
no purpose, no sensation. For aught I know, that night
London might have been a city of the dead.

Suddenly I halted beneath a lamp-post and began
dimly to think. My love was dead:—that was the one
fact that filled my thoughts at first, and so I strove to
image it upon my brain, but could not. But as I stood
there feebly struggling with the thought another took
its place. Why should I live? Of course not; better
end it all at once—and possessed with this idea I started
off once more.

By degrees, as I walked, a plan shaped itself before
me. I would go home, get my grandfather's key, together with the tin box containing my father's Journal,
and then make for the river. That would be an easy
death, and I could sink for ever, before I perished, all
trace of the black secret which had pursued my life. I
and the mystery would end together—so best. Then,
without pain, almost with ghastly merriment, I thought
that this was the same river which had murmured so
sweetly to my love. Well, no doubt its voice would be

just as musical over my grave. The same river:—but nearer the sea now—nearer the infinite sea.

As I reflected, the idea took yet stronger possession of me. Yes, it was in all respects the best. The curse should end now. "Even as the Heart of the Ruby is Blood and its Eyes a Flaming Fire, so shall it be for them that would possess it: Fire shall be their portion and Blood their inheritance for ever." For ever? No: the river should wash the blood away and quench the fire. Then arose another text and hammered at the door of my remembrance. "Many waters cannot quench love, neither can the floods drown it." "Many waters"— "many waters":—the words whispered appealingly, invitingly, in my ears. "Many waters." My feet beat a tune to the words.

I reached my lodgings, ran upstairs, took out the key and the tin box, and descended again into the hall. My landlord was slipping down the latch. He stared at seeing me.

"Do not latch the door just yet: I am going out again," I said simply.

"Going out! I thought, sir, it was you as just now come in."

"Yes, but I must go out again:—it is important."

He evidently thought me mad; and so indeed I was.

"What, sir, in that dress? You've got no hat— no——"

I had forgotten. "True," I said; "get me a hat and coat."

He stared and then ran upstairs for them. Returning he said, "I have got you these, sir; but I can't find them as you usually wears."

"Those will do," I answered. "I must have left the others at the theatre."

This reduced him to utter speechlessness. Mutely he helped me to don the cloak over my thin evening dress. I slipped the tin box and the key into the pockets. As I stepped out once more into the night, my landlord found his speech.

"When will you be back, sir?"

The question startled me for a moment; for a second or two I hesitated.

"I asked because you have no latch-key, as I suppose you left it in your other coat. So that——"

"It does not matter," I answered. "Do not sit up. I shall not be back before morning;" and with that I left him still standing at the door, and listening to my footsteps as they hurried down the street.

"Before morning!" Before morning I should be in another world, if there were another world. And then it struck me that Claire and I might meet. She had taken her own life and so should I. But no, no—Heaven would forgive her that; it could not condemn my saint to the pit where I should lie: it could not be so kindly cruel; and then I laughed a loud and bitter laugh.

Still in my dull stupor I found myself nearing the river. I have not mentioned it before, but I must explain now, that during the summer I had purchased a boat, in which my Claire and I were used to row idly between Streatley and Pangbourne, or whithersoever love guided our oars. This boat, with the approach of winter, I had caused to be brought down the river and had housed in a waterman's shed just above Westminster, until the return of spring should bring back once more the happy days of its employment.

In my heart I blessed the chance that had stored it ready to my hand.

Stumbling through dark and tortuous streets where the moon's frosty brilliance was almost completely hidden, I came at last to the waterman's door and knocked.

He was in bed and for some time my summons was in vain. At last I heard a sound in the room above, the window was let down and a sulky voice said, "Who's there?"

"Is that you, Bagnell?" I answered. "Come down. It is I, Mr. Trenoweth, and I want you."

There was a low cursing, a long pause broken by a muttered dispute upstairs, and then the street door opened and Bagnell appeared with a lantern.

"Bagnell, I want my boat."

"To-night, sir? And at this hour?"

"Yes, to-night. I want it particularly."

"But it is put away behind a dozen others, and can't be got."

"Never mind. I will help if you want assistance, but I must have it."

Bagnell looked at me for a minute and I could see that he was cursing under his breath.

"Is it serious, sir? You're not——"

"I am not drunk, if that is what you mean, but perfectly serious, and I must have my boat."

"Won't another do as well?"

"No, it will not." I felt in my pockets and found two sovereigns and a few shillings. "Look here," I said, "I will give you two pounds if you get this boat out for me."

This conquered his reluctance. He stared for a moment as I mentioned the amount, and then hastily deciding that I was stark mad, but that it was none of his business, put on his hat and led the way down to his boat-yard.

Stumbling in the uncertain light over innumerable timbers, spars, and old oars, we reached the shed at length and together managed, after much delay, to get out the light boat and let her down to the water. I gave him the two sovereigns as well as the few shillings that remained in my pocket, and as I descended, reflected grimly that after all they were better in his possession; the man who should find my body would have so much the less spoil. We had scarcely spoken whilst we were getting the boat out, and what words we used were uttered in that whisper which night always enforces; but as I clambered down (for the tide was now far out) and Bagnell passed down the sculls, he asked—

"When will you be back, sir?"

The same question! I gave it the same answer.
"Not before morning," I said, and with a few strokes
was out upon the tide and pulling down the river. I
saw him standing there above in the moonlight, still
wondering, until he faded in the dim haze behind. My
boat was a light Thames dingey, so that although I felt
the tide running up against me, it nevertheless made
fair progress. What decided me to pull against the
tide rather than float quietly upwards I do not know to
this day. So deadened and vague was all my thought,
that it probably never occurred to me to correct the
direction in which the first few strokes had taken me.
I was conscious of nothing but a row of lights gliding
past me on either hand, of here and there a tower or tall
building, that stood up for an instant against the sky
and then swam slowly out of sight, of the creaking of
my sculls in the ungreased rowlocks, and, above all, the
white shimmer of the moon following my boat as it
swung downwards.

I remember now that, in a childish way, I tried to
escape this persistent brilliance that still clung to my
boat's side with every stroke I took; that somehow a
dull triumph possessed me when for a moment I slipped
beneath the shadow of a bridge, or crept behind a black
and silent hull. All this I can recall now, and wonder
at the trivial nature of the thought. Then I caught
the scent of white rose, and fell to wondering how it
came there. There had been the same scent in the
drawing-room that afternoon, I remembered, when Claire

U

had said good-bye for ever. How had it followed me? After this I set myself aimlessly to count the lights that passed, lost count, and began again. And all the time the white glimmer hung at my side.

I was still wrapped up in my cloak, though the cape was flung back to give my arms free play. Rowing so, I must quickly have been warm; but I felt it no more than I had felt the cold as I walked home from the theatre. My boat was creeping along the Middlesex shore, by the old Temple stairs, and presently threaded its way through more crowded channels, and passed under the blackness of London Bridge.

How far below this I went, I cannot clearly call to mind; of distance, as well as of time, I had lost all calculation. I recollect making a circuit to avoid the press of boats waiting for the early dawn by Billingsgate Market, and have a vision of the White Tower against the heavens. But my next impression of any clearness is that of rowing under the shadow of a black three-masted schooner that lay close under shore, tilted over on her port side in the low water. As my dingey floated out again from beneath the overhanging hull, I looked up and saw the words, *Water-Witch*, painted in white upon her pitch-dark bows.

By this time I was among the tiers of shipping. I looked back over my shoulder, and saw their countless masts looming up as far as eye could see in the dim light, and their lamps flickering and wavering upon the water. I rowed about a score of strokes, and then

stopped. Why go further? This place would serve as
well as any other. No one was likely to hear my splash
as I went overboard, and even if heard it would not be
interpreted. I was still near enough to the Middlesex
bank to be out of the broad moonlight that lit up
the middle of the river. I took the tin box out of
my cloak and stowed it for a moment in the stern.
I would sink it with the key before I flung myself in.
So, pulling the key out of the other pocket, I took
off the cloak, then my dress-coat and waistcoat, folded
them carefully, and placed them on the stern seat.
This done, I slipped the key into one pocket of my
trousers, my watch and chain into the other. I would
do all quietly and in order, I reflected. I was silently
kicking off my shoes, when a thought struck me.
In my last struggles it was possible that the desire of
life would master me, and almost unconsciously I
might take to swimming. In the old days at Lizard
Town swimming had been as natural to me as walking, and I had no doubt that as soon as in the water
I should begin to strike out. Could I count upon
determination enough to withhold my arms and let
myself slowly drown?

Here was a difficulty; but I resolved to make
everything sure. I took my handkerchief out of the
coat pocket, and bent down to tie my feet firmly together.
All this I did quite calmly and mechanically. As far as
one can be certain of anything at this distance of time,
I am certain of this, that no thought of hesitation came

u 2

into my head. It was not that I overcame any doubts; they never occurred to me.

I was stooping down, and had already bound the handkerchief once around my ankles, when my boat grated softly against something. I looked up, and saw once more above me a dark ship's hull, and right above my head the white letters, *Water-Witch*.

This would never do. My boat had drifted up the river again with the tide, stern foremost, but a little aslant, and had run against the warp by the schooner's bows. I must pull out again, for otherwise the people on board would hear me. I pushed gently off from the warp and took the sculls, when suddenly I heard voices back towards the stern.

My first impulse was to get away with all speed, and I had already taken half a stroke, when something caused my hands to drop and my heart to give one wild leap.

What was it? Something in the voices? Yes; something that brushed my stupor from me as though it were a cobweb; something that made me hush my breath, and strain with all my ears to listen.

The two voices were those of man and woman. They were slightly raised, as if in a quarrel; the woman's pleading and entreating, the man's threatening and stern. But that was not the reason that suddenly set my heart uncontrollably beating and all the blood rushing and surging to my temples.

For in those two voices I recognised Mrs. Luttrell and Simon Colliver!

" Have you not done enough ? " the woman's voice was saying. " Has your cruelty no end, that you must pursue me so ? Take this money, and let me go."

" I must have more," was the answer.

" Indeed, I have no more just now. Go, only go, and I will send you some. I swear it."

" I cannot go," said the man.

" Why ? "

" Never mind. I am watched." Here the voice muttered some words which I could not catch. " So that unless you wish to see your husband swing—and believe me, my confession and last dying speech would not omit to mention the kind aid I had received from you and Clar——"

" Hush ! oh, hush ! If I get you this money, will you leave us in peace for a time ? Knowing your nature, I will not ask for pity—only for a short respite. I must tell Claire, poor girl ; she does not know yet—"

Quite softly my boat had drifted once more across the schooner's bows. I pulled it round until its nose touched the anchor chain, and made the painter fast. Then slipping my hand up the chain, I stood with my shoeless feet upon the gunwale by the bows. Still grasping the chain, I sprang and swung myself out to the jibboom that, with the cant of the vessel, was not far above the water : then pressed my left foot in between the stay and the brace, while I hung for a moment to listen.

They had not heard, for I could still catch the

murmur of their voices. The creak of the jibboom and the swish of my own boat beneath had frightened me at first. It seemed impossible that it should not disturb them. But after a moment my courage returned, and I pulled myself up on to the bowsprit, and lying almost at full length along it, for fear of being spied, crawled slowly along, and dropped noiselessly on to the deck.

They were standing together by the mizzen-mast, he with his back turned full towards me, she less entirely averted, so that I could see a part of her face in the moonlight, and the silvery gleam of her grey hair. Yes, it was they, surely enough; and they had not seen me. My revenge, long waited for, was in my grasp at last.

Suddenly, as I stood there watching them, I remembered my knife—the blade which had slain my father. I had left it below—fool that I was!—in the tin box. Could I creep back again, and return without attracting their attention? Should I hazard the attempt for the sake of planting that piece of steel in Simon Colliver's black heart?

It was a foolish thought, but my whole soul was set upon murder now, and the chance of slaying him with the very knife left in my father's wound seemed too dear to be lightly given up. Most likely he was armed now, whilst I had no weapon but the naked hand. Yet I did not think of this. It never even occurred to me that he would defend himself. Still, the thought of that knife was sweet to me as I crouched there beneath the shadow of the bulwarks. Should I go, or not? I paused for a moment, undecided; then rose slowly erect.

As I did so Mrs. Luttrell turned for an instant and saw me.

As I stood there, bareheaded, with the moonlight shining full upon my white shirt-sleeves, I must have seemed a very ghost; for a look of abject terror swept across her face; her voice broke off and both her hands were flung up for mercy—

"Oh, God! Look! look!"

As I rushed forward he turned, and then, with the spring of a wild cat, was upon me. Even as he leapt, my foot slipped upon the greasy deck; I staggered backward one step—two steps—and then fell with a crash down the unguarded forecastle ladder.

CHAPTER X.

TELLS IN WHAT MANNER I LEARNT THE SECRET OF THE GREAT KEY.

As my senses came gradually back I could distinguish a narrow, dingy cabin, dimly lit by one flickering oil-lamp which swung from a rafter above. Its faint ray just revealed the furniture of the room, which consisted of a seaman's chest standing in the middle, and two gaunt stools. On one of these I was seated, propped against the cabin wall, or rather partition, and as I attempted to move I learnt that I was bound hand and foot.

On the other stool opposite me and beside the chest, sat Simon Colliver, silently eyeing me. The lamplight as it flared and wavered cast grotesque and dancing shadows of the man upon the wall behind, made of his matted hair black caves under which his eyes gleamed red as fire, and glinted lastly upon something bright lying on the chest before him.

For a minute or so after my eyes first opened no word was said. Still dizzy with my fall, I stared for a moment at the man, then at the chest, and saw that the bright objects gleaming there were my grandfather's key and my watch-chain, at the end of which hung the

Golden Clasp. But now the clasp was fitted to its fellow and the whole buckle lay united upon the board.

Though the bonds around my arms, wrists, and ankles caused me intolerable pain, yet my first feeling was rather of abject humiliation. To be caught thus easily, to be lying here like any rat in a gin ! this was the agonising thought. Nor was this all. There on the chest lay the Golden Clasp united at last—the work completed which was begun with that unholy massacre on board the *Belle Fortune*. I had played straight into Colliver's hand.

He was in no hurry, but sat and watched me there with those intolerably evil eyes. His left hand was thrust carelessly into his pocket, and as he tilted back upon the stool and surveyed me, his right was playing with the clasp upon the chest. As I painfully turned my head a drop of blood came trickling down into my eyes from a cut in my forehead ; I saw, however, that the door was bolted. An empty bottle and a plate of broken victuals lay carelessly thrust in a corner, and a villainous smell from the lamp filled the whole room and almost choked me ; but the only sound in the dead stillness of the place was the monotonous tick-tick of my watch as it lay upon the chest.

How long I had lain there I could not guess, but I noticed that the floor slanted much less than when I first scrambled on deck, so guessed that the tide must have risen considerably. Then having exhausted my wonder

I looked again at Colliver, and began to speculate how he would kill me and how long he would take about it.

I found his wolfish eyes still regarding me, and for a minute or two we studied each other in silence. Then without removing his gaze he tilted his stool forward, slowly drew a short heavy knife from his waist-band, slipped it out of its sheath—still without taking his left hand from his pocket—laid it on the table and leant back again.

" I suppose," he said at last and very deliberately as if chewing his words, " you know that if you attempt to cry out or summon help, you are a dead man that instant."

" Well, well," he continued, after waiting a moment for my reply, " as long as you understand that, it does not matter. I confess I should have preferred to talk with you and not merely to you. However, before I kill you—and I suppose you guess that I am going to kill you as soon as I've done with you—I wish to have just a word, Master Jasper Trenoweth."

From the tone in which he said the words he might have been congratulating me on some great good fortune. He paused awhile as if to allow the full force of them to sink in, and then took up the Golden Clasp. Holding the pieces together with the fore-finger and thumb of his right hand, he advanced and thrust it right under my sight—

" Do you see that? Can you read it? "

As I was still mute he walked back to the chest and laid the clasp down again.

"Aha!" he exclaimed with a short laugh horrible to hear, "you won't speak. But there have been times, Mr. Jasper Trenoweth, when you would have given your soul to lay hands upon this piece of gold and read what is written upon it. It is a pity your hands are tied—a thousand pities. But I do not wish to be hard on you, and so I don't mind reading out what is written here. The secret will be safe with you, don't you see? Quite—safe—with—you."

He rolled out these last words, one by one, with infinite relish; and the mockery in the depths of those eyes scared me far more than my bonds. After watching the effect of his taunt he resumed his seat upon the stool, pulled the clasp towards him and said—

"People might call me rash for entrusting these confidences to you. But I do not mind admitting that I owe you some reparation—some anterior reparation. So, as I don't wish you to die cursing me, I will be generous. Listen!"

He held the buckle down upon the table and read out the inscription as follows :—

START	.	AT	.	FULL	.	MOON	.	END	.	SOUTH.
POINT	.	27	.	FEET	.	N.N.W.	. .	22	.	FEET.
W.	.	OF	.	RING	.	NORTH	.	SIDE	.	4.
FEET	.	6	.	INCHES.		DEEP	.	AT	.	POINT.
OF	.	MEETING	.	LOW	.	WATER	.	$1\frac{1}{2}$	.	HOURS.

He read it through twice very slowly, and each time as he ceased looked up to see how I took it.

"It does not seem to make much sense, does it?" he asked. "But wait a moment and let me parcel it out into sentences. I should not like you to miss any of its meaning. Listen again." He divided the writing up thus :—

"Start at full moon.
End South Point 27 feet N.N.W.
22 feet W. of Ring. North Side.
4 feet 6 inches deep at point of meeting.
Low water 1½ hours."

"You still seem puzzled, Mr. Trenoweth. Very well, I will even go on to explain further. The person who engraved this clasp meant to tell us that something —let us say treasure, for sake of argument—could be found by anyone who drew two lines from some place unknown : one 27 feet in length in direction N.N.W. from the South Point of that place; the other 22 feet due West of a certain Ring on the North side of that same place. So far I trust I make my meaning clear. That which we have agreed to call the treasure lies buried at a depth of 4 feet 6 inches on the spot where these two lines intersect. But the person (you or I, for the sake of argument) who seeks this treasure must start at full moon. Why? Obviously because the spring tides occur with a full moon, consequently the low ebb. We must expect, then, to find our treasure buried in a spot which is only uncovered at dead low water; and to this conclusion I am also helped by the last sentence, which says, " Low water 1½ hours." It is then, I submit, Mr. Trenoweth, in some such place that we must look for our treasure; the only question being, ' Where is that place?' "

I was waiting for this, and a great tide of joy swept over me as I reflected that after all he had not solved the mystery. The clasp told nothing, the key told nothing. The secret was safe as yet.

He must have read my thoughts, for he looked steadily at me out of those dark eyes of his, and then said very slowly and deliberately—

" Mr. Trenoweth, it grieves me to taunt your miserable case; but do you mind my saying that you are a fool?"

I simply stared in answer.

" Your father was a fool—a pitiful fool; and you are a fool. Which would lead me, did I not know better, to believe that your grandfather, Amos Trenoweth, was a fool also. I should wrong him if I called him that. He was a villain, a black-hearted, murderous, cold-blooded, damnable villain; but he was only a fool for once in his life, and that was when he trusted in the sense of his descendants."

His voice, as he spoke of my grandfather, grew suddenly shrill and discordant, while his eyes blazed up in furious wrath. In a second or two, however, he calmed himself again and went on quietly as before.

"You wonder, perhaps, why I call you a fool. It is because you have lived for fourteen years with your hand upon riches that would make a king jealous, and have never had the sense to grasp them; it is because you have shut your eyes when you might have seen, have been a beggar when you might have ridden in a carriage. Upon my word, Mr. Jasper Trenoweth, when I think of your folly I have half a mind to be dog-sick with you myself."

What could the man mean? What was this clue which I had never found?

"And all the time it was written upon this key here, as large as life; not only that, but, to leave you no excuse, Amos Trenoweth actually told you that it was written here."

"What do you mean?" stammered I, forced into speech at last.

"Ah! so you have found your voice, have you? What do I mean? Do you mean to say you do not guess even now? Upon my word, I am loth to kill so fair a fool." He regarded me for a moment with pitying contempt, then stretched out his hand and took up my grandfather's key.

"I read here," he said, "written very clearly and distinctly, certain words. You must know those words; but I will repeat them to you to refresh your memory :—

'THY HOUSE IS SET UPON THE SANDS: AND THY HOPES BY A DEAD MAN.'"

" Well ? " I asked, for—fool that I was—even yet I did not understand.

" Mr. Jasper Trenoweth, did you ever hear tell of such a place as Dead Man's Rock ? "

The truth, the whole horrible certainty of it, struck me as one great wave, and rushed over my bent head as with the whirl and roar of many waters. " Dead Man's Rock ! " " Dead Man's Rock ! " it sang in my ears as it swept me off my feet for a moment and passed, leaving me to sink and battle in the gulf of bottomless despair. And then, as if I really drowned, my past life with all its follies, mistakes, wrecked hopes and baseless dreams, shot swiftly past in one long train. Again I saw my mother's patient, anxious smile, my father's drowned face with the salt drops trickling from his golden hair, the struggle on the rock, the inquest, the awful face at the window, the corpses of my parents stretched side by side upon the bed, the scene in the gambling-hell with all its white and desperate faces, Claire, my lost love, the river, the theatre, Tom's death, and that last dreadful scene, Francesca with the dark blood soaking her white dress and trickling down upon the boards. I tried to put my hands before my eyes, but the cords held and cut my arms like burning steel. Then in a flash I seemed to be striding madly up and down Oxford Street, while still in front of me danced and flew the yellow woman, her every diamond flashing in the gas-light, her cold black eyes, as they turned and mocked me, blazing marsh-lights of doom. Then came the ringing of many bells in my ears, mingled with silvery laughter, as though the fiends were ringing jubilant peals within the pit.

Presently the sights grew dim and died away, but the chiming laughter still continued.

I looked up. It was Colliver laughing, and his face was that of an arch-devil.

"It does me good to see you," he explained; "oh, yes, it is honey to my soul. Fool! and a thousand times fool! that ever I should have lived to triumph thus over you and your accursed house!"

Once more his voice grew shrill and his eyes flashed; once more he collected himself.

"You shall hear it out," he said. "Look here!" and he pulled a greasy book from his pocket. "Here is a nautical almanack. What day is it? December 23rd, or rather some time in the morning of December 24th, Christmas Eve. On the evening of December 24th it is full moon, and dead low water at Falmouth about 11.30 p.m. Fate (do you believe in fate, Mr. Trenoweth?) could not have chosen the time better. In something under twenty hours one of us will have his hands upon the treasure. Which will it be, eh? Which will it be?"

Well I knew which it would be, and the knowledge was bitter as gall.

"A merry Christmas, Mr. Jasper Trenoweth! Peace on earth and good-will—— You will bear no malice by that time. So a merry Christmas, and a merry Christ-

mas-box! likewise the compliments of the season, and
a happy New Year to you! Where are you going to
spend Christmas, Mr. Trenoweth—eh? I am thinking
of passing it by the sea. You will, perhaps, try the sea
too, only you will be *in* it. Thames runs swiftly when
it has a corpse for cargo. Oho!

> " At his red, red lips the merrymaid sips
> For the kiss that his sweetheart stole, my lads—
> Sing ho ! for the bell shall toll!

" I'm afraid no bell will toll for you, Mr. Trenoweth ;
not yet awhile at any rate. Not till your sweetheart is
weary of waiting—

> " And the devil has got his due, my lads—
> Sing ho! but he waits for you !

" Both waiting for you, Mr. Trenoweth, your sweetheart and the devil—which shall have you? 'Ladies
first,' you would say. Aha! I am not so sure. By the
way, might I give a guess at your sweetheart's name?
Might it begin with a C? Might she be a famous
actress? Claire perhaps she calls herself? Aha!
Claire's pretty eyes will go red with watching before
she sets them on you again. Fie on you to keep so
sweet a maiden waiting! And where will you be all
the time, Mr. Jasper Trenoweth?"

He stopped at last, mastered by his ferocity and
almost panting. But I, for the sound of Claire's name
had maddened me, broke out in fury—

" Dog and devil! I shall be lying with all the

v

other victims of your accursed life; dead as my father
whom you foully murdered within sight of his home;
dead as those other poor creatures you slew upon the
Belle Fortune; dead as my mother whose pure mind
fled at sight of your infernal face, whose very life fled
at sight of your handiwork; dead as John Railton whom
you stabbed to death upon——"

"Hush, Mr. Trenoweth! As for your ravings, I love
to hear them, and could listen by the hour, did not time
press. But I cannot have you talking so loudly, you
understand;" and he toyed gently with his knife; "also
remember I must be at Dead Man's Rock by half-past
eleven to-night."

"Fiend!" I continued, "you can kill me if you like,
but I will count your crimes with my last breath. Take
my life as you took my friend Tom Loveday's life—
Tom whom you knifed in the dark, mistaking him for
me. Take it as you took Claire's, if ever man——"

"Claire—Claire dead!" He staggered back a step,
and almost at the same moment I thought I caught a
sound on the other side of the partition at my back. I
listened for a moment, then concluding that my ears had
played me some trick, went on again—

"Yes, dead—she killed herself to-night at the
theatre—stabbed herself—oh, God! Do you think I
care for your knife now? Why, I was going to kill
myself, to drown myself, at the very moment when I
heard your voice and came on board. I came to kill
you. Make the most of it—show me no mercy, for as

there is a God in heaven I would have shown you
none!"

What was that sound again on the other side of the
partition? Whatever it was, Colliver had not heard, for
he was musing darkly and looking fixedly at me.

"No, I will show you no mercy," he answered
quietly, "for I have sworn to show no mercy to your
race, and you are the last of it. But listen, that for a
few moments before you die you may shake off your
smug complacency and learn what this wealth is, and
what kind of brood you Trenoweths are. Dog! The
treasure that lies by Dead Man's Rock is treasure
weighted with dead men's curses and stained with dead
men's blood—wealth won by black piracy upon the high
seas—gold for which many a poor soul walked the plank
and found his end in the deep waters. It is treasure
sacked from many a gallant ship, stripped from many a
rotting corpse by that black hound your grandfather,
Amos Trenoweth. You guessed that? Let me tell you
more.

"There is many a soul crying in heaven and hell
for vengeance on your race; but your death to-night,
Jasper Trenoweth, shall be the peculiar joy of one. You
guessed that your grandfather had crimes upon his
soul; but you did not guess the blackest crime on his
account—the murder of his dearest friend. Listen. I
will be brief with you, but I cannot spare myself the
joy of letting you know this much before you die.
Know then that when your grandfather was a rich man

v 2

by this friend's aid—after, with this friend's help, he had laid hands on the secret of the Great Ruby for which for many a year he had thirsted, in the moment of his triumph he turned and slew that friend in order to keep the Ruby to himself.

"That fool, your father, kept a Journal—which no doubt you have read over and over again. Did he tell you how I caught him upon Adam's Peak, sitting with this clasp in his hands before a hideous, graven stone? That stone was cut in ghastly mockery of that friend's face; the bones that lay beneath it were the bones of that friend. There, on that very spot where I met your father face to face, did his father, Amos Trenoweth, strike down my father Ralph Colliver.

"Ah, light is beginning to dawn on your silly brain at last! Yes, pretending to protect the old priest who had the Ruby, he stabbed my father with the very knife found in your father's heart, stabbed him before his wife's eyes on that little lawn upon the mountain-side; and, when my helpless mother called vengeance upon him, handed the still reeking knife to her and bade her do her worst. Ah, but she kept that knife. Did you mark what was engraved upon the blade? That knife had a good memory, Mr. Jasper Trenoweth.

"Let me go on. As if that deed were not foul enough, he caused the old priest to carve—being skilful with the chisel—that vile distortion of his dead friend's face out of a huge boulder lying by, and then murdered him too for the Ruby's sake, and tumbled their bodies into the trough together. Such was Amos Trenoweth. Are you proud of your descent?

"I never saw my father. I was not born until three months after this, and not until I was ten years old did my mother tell me of his fate.

"Your grandfather was a fool, Jasper Trenoweth, to despise her; for she was young then and she could wait. She was beautiful then, and Amos Trenoweth himself had loved her. What is she now? Speak, for you have seen her."

As he spoke I seemed to see again that yellow face, those awful, soulless eyes, and hear her laugh as she gazed down from the box upon my dying love.

"Ah, beauty goes. It went for ever on that day when Amos Trenoweth spat in her face and taunted her as she clung to the body of her husband. Beauty goes, but revenge can wait; to-night it has come; to-night a thousand dead men's ghosts shall be glad, and point at your body as it goes tossing out to sea. To-night —but let me tell the rest in a word or two, for time presses. How I was brought up, how my mad mother—for she is mad on every point but one—trained me to the sea, how I left it at length and became an attorney's clerk, all this I need not dwell upon. But all this time the thought of revenge never left me for an hour; and if it had, my mother would have recalled it.

"Well, we settled in Plymouth and I was bound a clerk to your grandfather's attorney, still with the same purpose. There I learnt of Amos Trenoweth's affairs, but only to a certain extent; for of the wealth which he had so bloodily won I could discover nothing; and yet I knew he possessed riches which make the heart faint even to think upon. Yet for all I could discover, his possessions were simply those of a struggling farmer, his business absolutely nothing. I was almost desperate, when one day a tall, gaunt and aged man stepped into the office, asked for my employer, and gave the name of Amos Trenoweth. Oh, how I longed to kill him as he stood there! And how little did he guess that the clerk of whom he took no more notice than of a stone, would one day strike his descendants off the face of the earth and inherit the wealth for which he had sold his soul—the great Ruby of Ceylon!

"My voice trembled with hate as I announced him and showed him into the inner room. Then I closed the door and listened. He was uneasy about his Will—the fool—and did not know that all his possessions would necessarily become his son's. In my heart I laughed at his ignorance; but I learnt enough—enough to wait patiently for years and finally to track Ezekiel Trenoweth to his death.

"It was about this time that I fell in love. In this as in everything through life I have been cursed with the foulest luck; but in this as in everything else my patience has won in the end. Lucy Luttrell loved another man called Railton—John Railton. He was another fool—you are all fools—but she married him and had a daughter. I wonder if you can guess who that daughter was?"

He broke off and looked at me with fiendish malice.

" You hound ! " I cried, " she was Janet Railton— Claire Luttrell; and you murdered her father as you say Amos Trenoweth murdered yours."

" Right," he answered coolly. " Quite right. Oh, the arts by which I enticed that man to drink and then to crime! Even now I could sit and laugh over them by the hour. Why, man, there was not a touch of guile in the fellow when I took him in hand, and yet it was he that afterwards took your father's life. He tried it once in Bombay and bungled it sadly : he did it neatly enough, though, on the jib-boom of the *Belle Fortune.* I lent him the knife : I would have done it myself, but Railton was nearer; and besides it is always better to be a witness."

What *was* that rustling sound behind the partition ? Colliver did not hear it, at any rate, but went on with his tale, and though his eyes were dancing flames of hate his voice was calm now as ever.

" I had stolen half the clasp beforehand from the cabin floor where that stupendous idiot, Ezekiel Trenoweth, had dropped it. Railton caught him before he dropped, but I did not know he had time to get the box away, for just then a huge wave broke over us and before the next we both jumped for the Rock. I thought that Railton must have been sucked back, for I only clung on myself by the luckiest chance. It was pitch-dark and impossible to see. I called his name, but he either could not hear for the roar, or did not choose to answer, so after a bit I stopped. I thought him dead, and he no doubt thought me dead, until we met upon Dead Man's Rock.

"Shall I finish? Oh, yes, you shall hear the whole story. After the inquest I escaped back to Plymouth, told Lucy that her husband had been drowned at sea, and finally persuaded her to leave Plymouth and marry me. So I triumphed there, too : oh, yes, I have triumphed throughout."

"You hound!" I cried.

He laughed a low musical laugh and went on again—

"Ah, yes, you are angry of course ; but I let that pass. I have one account to settle with you Trenoweths, and that is enough for me. Three times have I had you in my power, Mr. Jasper Trenoweth—three times or four—and let you escape. Once beneath Dead Man's Rock when I had my fingers on your young weasand and was stopped by those cursed fishermen. Idiots that they were, they thought the sight of me had frightened you and made you faint. Faint! You would have been dead in another half-minute. How I laughed in my sleeve while that uncle of yours was trying to make me understand—me—what was my name then ?—oh, ay, Georgio Rhodojani. However, you escaped that time : and once more you hardly guessed how near you were to death, when I looked in at the window on the night

after the inquest. Why, in my mind I was tossing up
whether or not I should murder you and your white-
faced mother. I should have done so, but thought you
might hold some knowledge of the secret after your
meeting with Railton, so that it seemed better to bide
my time."

"If it be any satisfaction to you," I interrupted, "to
know that had you killed me then you would never have
laid hands on that clasp yonder, you are welcome to it."

"It is," he answered. "I am glad I did not kill
you both: it left your mother time to see her dead
husband, and has given me the pleasure of killing you
now : the treat improves with keeping. Well, let me
go on. After that I was forced to leave the country for
some time——"

"For another piece of villainy, which your wife
discovered."

"How do you know that? Oh, from Claire, I
suppose : however, it does not matter. When I came
back I found you : found you, and struck again. But
again my cursed luck stood in my way and that damned
friend of yours knocked me senseless. Look at this
mark on my cheek."

"Look at the clasp and you will see where your
blow was struck."

"Ah, that was it, was it ? " he said, examining the
clasp slowly. "I suppose you thought it lucky at the
time. So it was—for me. For, though I made another
mistake in the fog that night, I got quits with your

friend at any rate. I have chafed often enough at these failures, but it has all come right in the end. I ought to have killed your father upon Adam's Peak; but he was a big man, while I had no pistol and could not afford to risk a mistake. Everything, they say, comes to the man who can wait. Your father did not escape, neither will you, and when I think of the joy it was to me to know that you and Claire, of all people——"

But I would hear no more. Mad as I was with shame and horror for my grandfather's cruelty, I knew this man, notwithstanding his talk of revenge, to be a vile and treacherous scoundrel. So when he spoke of Claire I burst forth—

"Dog, this is enough! I have listened to your tale. But when you talk of Claire—Claire whom you killed to-night—then, dog, I spit upon you; kill me, and I hope the treasure may curse you as it has cursed me; kill me; use your knife, for I *will* shout——"

With a dreadful snarl he was on me and smote me across the face. Then as I continued to call and shout, struck me one fearful blow behind the ear. I remember that the dim lamp shot out a streak of blood-red flame, the cabin was lit for one brief instant with a flash of fire, a thousand lights darted out, and then—then came utter blackness—a vague sensation of being caught up and carried, of plunging down—down * * * *

CHAPTER XI. AND LAST.

TELLS HOW AT LAST I FOUND MY REVENGE AND THE GREAT RUBY.

"SPEAK—speak to me! Oh, look up and tell me you are not dead!"

Down through the misty defiles and dark gates of the Valley of the Shadow of Death came these words faintly as though spoken far away. So distant did they seem that my eyes opened with vague expectation of another world; opened and then wearily closed again.

For at first they stared into a heaven of dull grey, with but a shadow between them and colourless space. Then they opened once more, and the shadow caught their attention. What was it? Who was I, and how came I to be staring upward so? I let the problem be and fell back into the easeful lap of unconsciousness.

Then the voice spoke again. "He is living yet," it said. "Oh, if he would but speak!"

This time I saw more distinctly. Two eyes were looking into mine—a woman's eyes. Where had I seen that face before? Surely I had known it once, in some other world. Then somehow over my weary mind stole the knowledge that this was Mrs. Luttrell—or was it Claire? No, Claire was dead. "Claire—dead," I seemed to repeat to myself; but how dead or where I could not recall. "Claire—dead;" then this must be her mother, and I, Jasper Trenoweth, was lying here with Claire's mother bending over me. How came we so? What had happened, that—and once more the shadow of oblivion swept down and enfolded me.

She was still there, kneeling beside me, chafing my hands and every now and then speaking words of tender solicitude. How white her hair was! It used not to be so white as this. And where was I lying? In a boat? How my head was aching!

Then remembrance came back. Strange to tell, it began with Claire's death in the theatre, and thence led downwards in broken and interrupted train until Colliver's face suddenly started up before me, and I knew all.

I raised myself on my elbow. My brain was throbbing intolerably, and every pulsation seemed to shoot fire into my temples. Also other bands of fire were clasped about my arms and wrists. So acutely did they burn that I fell back with a low moan and looked helplessly at Mrs. Luttrell.

Although it had been snowing, her bonnet was thrust back from her face and hung by its ribbons which were tied beneath her chin. The breeze was playing with her disordered hair—hair now white as the snow-flakes upon it, though grey when last I had seen it—but it brought no colour to her face. As she bent over me to place her shawl beneath my head, I saw that her blue eyes were strangely bright and prominent.

"Thank God, you are alive! Does the bandage pain you? Can you move?"

I feebly put my hand up and felt a handkerchief bound round my head.

"I was afraid—oh, so afraid!—that I had been too late. Yet God only knows how I got down into your boat—in time—and without his seeing me. I knew what he would do—I was listening behind the partition all the time; but I was afraid he would kill you first."

"Then—you heard?"

"I heard all. Oh, if I were only a man—but can you stand? Are you better now? For we must lose no time."

I weakly stared at her in answer.

"Don't you see? If you can stand and walk, as I pray you can, there is no time to be lost. Morning is already breaking, and by this evening you must catch him."

"Catch him?"

"Yes, yes. He has gone—gone to catch the first train for Cornwall, and will be at Dead Man's Rock to-night. Quick! see if you cannot rise."

I sat up. The water had dripped from me, forming a great pool at our end of the boat. In it she was kneeling, and beside her lay a heavy knife and the cords with which Simon Colliver had bound me.

"Yes," I said, "I will follow. When does the first train leave Paddington?"

"At a quarter past nine," she answered, "and it is now about half-past five. You have time to catch it; but must disguise yourself first. He will travel by it; there is no train before. Come, let me row you ashore."

With this she untied the painter, got out the sculls, sat down upon the thwart opposite, and began to pull desperately for shore. I wondered at her strength and skill with the oar.

"Ah," she said, "I see at what you are wondering. Remember that I was a sailor's wife once, and without strength how should I have dragged you on board this boat?"

"How did you manage it?"

"I cannot tell. I only know that I heard a splash as I waited under the bows there, and then began with my hands to fend the boat around the schooner for dear life. I had to be very silent. At first I could see nothing, for it was dark towards the shore; but I cried to Heaven to spare you for vengeance on that man, and then I saw something black lying across the warp, and knew it was you. I gave a strong push, then rushed to the bows and caught you by the hair. I got you round by the stern as gently as I could, and then pulled you on board somehow—I cannot remember exactly how I did it."

"Did he see you?"

"No, for he must have gone below directly. I

rowed under the shadow of the lighter to which we were tied just now, and as I did so, thought I heard him calling me by name. He must have forgotten me, and then suddenly remembered that as yet I had not given him the money. However, presently I heard him getting into his boat and rowing ashore. He came quite close to us—so close that I could hear him cursing, and crouched down in the shadow for fear of my life. But he passed on, and got out at the steps yonder. It was snowing at the time and that helped me."

She pulled a stroke or two in silence, and then continued—

"When you were in the cabin together I was listening. At one point I think I must have fainted; but it cannot have been for long, for when I came to myself you were still talking about—about John Railton."

I remembered the sound which I had heard, and almost in spite of myself asked, "You heard about—"

"Claire? Yes, I heard." She nodded simply ; but her eyes sought mine, and in them was a gleam that made me start.

Just then the boat touched at a mouldering flight of stairs, crusted with green ooze to high-water mark, and covered now with snow. She made fast the boat.

"This was the way he went," she muttered. "Track him, track him to his death ; spare him no single pang to make that death miserable!" Her low voice positively trembled with concentrated hate. "Stay," she said, "have you money?"

I suddenly remembered that I had given all the
money on me to Bagnell for getting out my boat, and
told her so. At the same moment, too, I thought upon
the tin box still lying under the boat's stern. I stepped
aft and pulled it out.

" Here is money," she said ; " money that I was to
have given him. Fifty pounds it is, in notes—take it
all."

" But you? " I hesitated.

" Never mind me. Take it—take it all. What do
I want with money if only you kill him ? "

I bent and kissed her hand.

" As Heaven is my witness," I said, " it shall be his
life or mine. The soul of one of us shall never see
to-morrow."

Her hand was as cold as ice, and her pale face never
changed.

" Kill him ! " she said, simply.

I turned, and climbed the steps. By this time day
had broken, and the east was streaked with angry flushes
of crimson. The wind swept through my dripping
clothes and froze my aching limbs to the marrow. Up
the river came floating a heavy pall of fog, out of which
the masts showed like grisly skeletons. The snow-storm
had not quite ceased, and a stray flake or two came
brushing across my face. So dawned my Christmas
Eve !

As I gained the top, I turned to look down. She
was still standing there, watching me. Seeing me look,

she waved her arms, and I heard her hoarse whisper,
" Kill him !   Kill him !   Kill him ! "

I left her standing so, and turned away ; but in the
many ghosts that haunt my solitary days, not the least
vivid is the phantom of this white - haired woman
on the black and silent river, eternally beckoning,
" Kill him ! "

I found myself in a yard strewn with timber, spars
and refuse, half hidden beneath the snow. From it a
flight of rickety stone steps led to a rotting door, and
thence into the street. Here I stood for a moment,
pondering on my next step. Not a soul was abroad so
early ; but I must quickly get a change of clothes somewhere ; at present I stood in my torn dress trousers and
soaked shirt. I passed up the street, my shoeless feet
making the first prints in the newly-fallen snow. The
first ? No ; for when I looked more closely I saw other
footprints, already half obliterated, leading up the street.
These must be Simon Colliver's. I followed them for
about a hundred yards past the shuttered windows.

Suddenly they turned into a shop door, and then
seemed to leave it again. The shop was closed, and
above it hung three brass balls, each covered now with
a snowy cap. Above, the blinds were drawn down, but
on looking again, I saw a chink of light between the
shutters. I knocked.

After a short pause, the door was opened. A red-
eyed, villainous face peered out, and seeing me, grew
blank with wonder.

W

"What do you want?" inquired at length the voice belonging to it.

"To buy a fresh suit of clothes. See, I have fallen into the river."

Muttering something beneath his breath, the pawn-broker opened his door, and let me into the shop.

It was a dingy nest, fitted up with the usual furniture of such a place. The one dim candle threw a ghostly light on chairs, clocks, compasses, trinkets, saucepans, watches, piles of china, and suits of left-off clothes arrayed like rows of suicides along the wall. A general air of decay hung over the den. Immediately opposite me, as I entered, a stuffed parrot, dropping slowly into dust, glared at me with one malevolent eye of glass, while a hideous Chinese idol, behind the counter, poked out his tongue in a very frenzy of malignity. But my eye wandered past these, and was fixed in a moment upon something that glittered upon the counter. That something was my own watch.

Following my gaze, the man gave me a quick, suspicious glance, hastily caught up the watch, and was bestowing it on one of his shelves, when I said—

"Where did you get that?"

"Quite innocently, sir, I swear. I bought it of a gentleman who came in just now, and would not pawn it. I thought it was his, so that if you belong to the Force, I hope——"

"Gently, my friend," said I; "I am not in the police, so you need not be in such a fright. Nevertheless, that watch is mine; I can tell you the number, if you don't believe it."

He pushed the watch across to me and said, still greatly frightened—

" I am sure you may see it, sir, with all my heart. I wouldn't for worlds——"

" What did you give for it?"

He hesitated a moment, and then, as greed overmastered fear, replied—

" Fifteen pounds, sir; and the man would not take a penny less. Fifteen good pounds! I swear it, as I am alive!"

Although I saw that the man lied, I drew out three five-pound notes, laid them on the table, and took my watch. This done, I said—

" Now I want you to sell me a suit of clothes, and aid me to disguise myself. Otherwise——"

" Don't talk, sir, about 'otherwise.' I'm sure I shall only be too glad to rig you out to catch the thief. You can take your pick of the suits here; they are mostly seamen's, to be sure; but you'll find others as well. While as for disguises, I flatter myself that for getting up a face——"

Here he stopped suddenly.

" How long has he been gone?"

" About half an hour, sir, before you came. But no doubt you know where he'd be likely to go; and I won't be more than twenty minutes setting you completely to rights."

w 2

In less than half an hour afterwards, I stepped out into the street so completely disguised that none of my friends—that is, if I had possessed a friend in the world—would have recognised me. I had chosen a sailor's suit, that being the character I knew myself best able to sustain. My pale face had turned to a bronze red, while over its smoothly - shaven surface now grew the roughest of untrimmed beards. Snow was falling still, so that Colliver's footprints were entirely obliterated. But I wanted them no longer. He would be at Paddington, I knew; and accordingly I turned my feet in that direction, and walked rapidly westward.

My chase had begun. I had before me plenty of time in which to reach Paddington, and the exercise of walking did me good, relaxing my stiffened limbs until at length I scarcely felt the pain of the weals where the cords had cut me. It was snowing persistently, but I hardly noticed it. Through the chill and sullen morning I held doggedly on my way, past St. Katharine's Wharf, the Tower, through Gracechurch Street, and out into St. Paul's Churchyard. Traffic was already beginning here, and thickened as I passed down Ludgate Hill and climbed up to Holborn. Already the white snow was being churned and trodden into hideous slush in which my feet slipped and stumbled. My coat and sailor's cap were covered with powdery flakes, and I had to hold my head down for fear lest the drifting moisture should wash any of the colouring off my face. So my feet carried me once more into Oxford Street. How well remembered was every house, every lamp-post, every flag of the pavement almost! I was on my last quest now.

"To-night! to-night!" whispered my heart : then came back the words of Claire's mother—"Kill him! Kill him!" and still I tramped westward, as westward lay my revenge.

Suddenly a hansom cab shot past me. It came up silently on the slushy street, and it was only when it was close behind that I heard the muffled sound of its wheels. It was early yet for cabs, so that I turned my head at the sound. It passed in a flash, and gave me but a glimpse of the occupant : but in that moment I had time to catch sight of a pair of eyes, and knew now that my journey would not be in vain. They were the eyes of Simon Colliver.

So then in Oxford Street, after all, I had met him. He was cleverly disguised—as I guessed, by the same hands that had painted my own face—and looked to the casual eye but an ordinary bagman. But art could not change those marvellous eyes, and I knew him in an instant. My heart leapt wildly for a moment—my hands were clenched and my teeth shut tight; but the next, I was plodding after him as before. I could wait now.

Before I reached Paddington I met the cab returning empty, and on gaining the station at first saw nothing of my man. Though as yet it was early, the

platform was already crowded with holiday-makers:
a few country dames laden with countless bundles,
careworn workers preparing to spend Christmas with
friends or parents in their village home, a sprinkling of
schoolboys chafing at the slowness of the clock. After
a minute or so, I spied Simon Colliver moving among
this happy and innocent crowd like an evil spirit. I
flung myself down upon a bench, and under pretence of
sleeping, quietly observed him. Once or twice, as he
passed to and fro before me, he almost brushed my knee,
so close was he—so close that I had to clutch the bench
tightly for fear I should leap up and throttle him. He
did not notice me. Doubtless he thought me already
tossing out to sea with the gulls swooping over me, and
the waves merrily dashing over my dead face. The
waiting game had changed hands now.

I heard him demand a ticket for Penryn, and, after
waiting until he had left the booking office, took one
myself for the same station. I watched him as he
chose his compartment, and then entered the next.
It was crowded, of course, with holiday-seekers; but
the only person that I noticed at first was the man
sitting directly opposite to me—an honest, red-faced
countryman, evidently on his way home from town, and
at present deeply occupied with a morning paper which
seemed to have a peculiar fascination for him, for as he
raised his face his round eyes were full of horror. I
paid little attention to him, however, but, having the
corner seat facing the engine, watched to see that Colliver

did not change his compartment. He did not appear
again, and in a minute or two the whistle shrieked and
we were off.

At first the countryman opposite made such a prodigious to-do with his piece of news that I could not
help watching him. Then my attention wandered from
him to the country through which we were flying.
Slowly I pondered over the many events that had passed
since, not many months before, I had travelled up from
Cornwall to win my fortune. My fortune! To what
had it all come? I had won a golden month or two of
love, and lo! my darling was dead. Dead also was the
friend who had travelled up with me, so full of boyish
hope: both dead; the one in the full blaze of her
triumph, the other in the first dawn of his young
success: both dead—and, but for me, both living yet
and happy.

Suddenly the countryman looked up and spoke.

"Hav'ee seen this bit o' news? Astonishin'! And
her so pretty too!"

"What is it?" I asked vacantly.

For answer he pushed the paper into my hands,
and with his thumb-nail pointed to a column headed
"TERRIBLE TRAGEDY IN A THEATRE."

"An' to think," he continued reflectively, "as how
I saw her wi' my own eyes but three nights back—an'
actin' so pretty, too! Lord! It made me cry like any
sucking child: beautiful it was — just beau-ti-ful!
Here's a story to tell my missus!"

I took the paper and read—

"TERRIBLE TRAGEDY IN A THEATRE. SUICIDE OF A FAMOUS ACTRESS.—Last evening, the performance of the new and popular tragedy, *Francesca*, at the Coliseum, was interrupted by a scene perhaps the most awful that has ever been presented to the play-going public. A sinister fate seems to have pursued this play from the outset. It will be within the memory of all that its young and gifted author was, on the very night of its production, struck down suddenly in the street by an unknown hand which the police have not yet succeeded in tracing. Last night's tragedy was even more terrible. Clarissa Lambert, whose name——"

But I wanted to read no more. To the country-man's astonishment the paper slipped from my listless fingers, and once more my gaze turned to the carriage window. On we tore through the snow that raced horizontally by the pane, through the white and peaceful country—homeward. Homeward to welcome whom? Whom but the man now sitting, it might be, within a foot of me? To my heart I hugged the thought of him, sitting there and gloating over the morrow.

The morrow! Somehow my own horizon did not stretch as far: it was bounded by to-night. Before to-morrow one of us two should be a dead man; perhaps both. So best: the world with its loves and hatreds would end to-night. So westward we sped in the grey light beneath which the snowy fields gleamed unnaturally — westward while the sun above showed only as a crimson ball, an orb of blood, travelling westward too. At Bristol it glared through a murky veil of smoke, at Exeter and through the frozen pastures and

leafless woodlands of Devon dropped swiftly towards
my goal, beckoning with blood-stained hand across the
sky. Past the angry sea we tore, and then again into
the whitened fields now growing dim in the twilight.
In the carriage the talk was unceasing—talk of home,
of expectant friends, of Christmas meetings and festivi-
ties. Every station was thronged, and many a happy
welcome I witnessed as I sat there with no friend but
hate. Friends! What had I to do with such? I had
a friend once, but he was dead. Friend, parents, love
—all dead by one man's hand, and he—— But a little
while now; but a little while!

We reached Plymouth shortly after five—the train
being late—and here the crowd in the carriages grew
greater. It was dark, but the moon was not yet up—
the full moon by which the treasure was to be sought.
How slowly the train dragged through Cornwall! It
would be eight before we reached Penryn, and low water
was at half-past eleven. Should we be in time?

The snow had ceased to fall : a clear north-east wind
had chased the clouds from heaven, and scarcely had we
passed Saltash before a silver rim came slowly rising
above the black woods on the river's opposite bank.
Clear into the frosty night it rose, and I fell to wondering savagely with what thoughts Colliver saluted it.

It was already half-past eight as we changed our
train at Truro, and here again more time was wasted.
Upon the platform I saw him again. He was heavily
cloaked and muffled now, for it was freezing hard ; but

beneath the low brim of his hat I saw the deep, black eyes gleaming with impatience. So at last once more we started.

" Penryn ! "

I looked at my watch. It was nine o'clock; more than an hour and a half late. By the light from the carriage window I saw him step out into the shadow of the platform. I followed. Here also was a large crowd bound for Helston, and the coach that waited outside was quickly thronged inside and out. Colliver was outside the station in a moment, and in another had jumped into a carriage waiting there with two horses, and was gone up the hill beneath the shadow of the bridge. In my folly I had forgotten that he might have telegraphed for horses to meet him. However, the coach was fast and I could post from Helston. I clambered up to the top, where for want of a better seat I propped myself up on a pile of luggage, and waited whilst box after box, amid vociferous cursing, was piled up beside me. At length, just as I was beginning to despair of ever starting at all, with a few final curses directed at the bystanders generally, the driver mounted the box, shook his reins, and we were off.

The load was so heavy that at first five horses were used, but we left one with his postillion at the top of the hill and swung down at a canter into the level country. The snow lay fairly deep, and the horses' hoofs were soundless as we plunged through the crisp and tingling air. The wind raced past me as

I sat perched on my rickety seat, swaying wildly with every lurch of the coach. With every gust I seemed to drink in fresh strength and felt the very motion and swiftness enter into my blood. Across the white waste we tore, up a stiff ascent and down across the moorland again—still westward; and now across the stretches of the moor I could catch the strong scent of the sea upon the wind. Along the level we sped, silent and swift beneath the moon. Here a white house by the roadside glimmered out and was gone; there a mine-chimney shot up against the sky and faded back again. We were going now at a gallop, and from my perch I could see the yellow light of the lamps on the sweating necks of the leaders.

There was a company of sailors with me on the coach-top—smoking, talking, and shouting. Once or twice one of them would address a word or two to me, but got scanty answers. I was looking intently along the road for a sign of Colliver's carriage. He must have ordered good horses, for I saw no sign of him as yet. Stay! As we swept round a sharp corner and swung on to the straight road again, I thought I spied far in front a black object moving on the universal white. Yes, it must be he: and again on the wings of the wind I heard the call, "To-night! to-night! Kill him! kill him! kill——"

Crash! With a heavy and sickening lurch sideways, the coach hung for an instant, tottered, and then plunged over on its side, flinging me clear of the luggage which pounded and rattled after. As I struggled to my feet, half dazed, I saw a confused medley of struggling horses, frightened passengers and scattered boxes. Collecting my senses I rushed to help those inside the coach and then amid the moaning, cursing and general dismay, sought out my bundle, grasped it tightly and set off at a run down the heavy road. I could wait now for no man.

Panting, spent, my sore limbs weighted with snow, I gained the top of the hill and plunged down the steep street into Helston. There, at "the Angel" I got a post-chaise and pair, and set off once more. At first, seeing my dress and wondering what a sailor could want with post-chaises at that hour, they demurred, but the money quickly persuaded them. They told me also that a gentleman had changed horses there about half an hour before and gone towards the Lizard, after borrowing a pickaxe and spade. Half an hour: should I yet be in time?

I leant back in the chaise and pondered. I knew by heart the shortest cuts across the downs. When I reached them I would stop the carriage and take to my feet once more. The fresh horses were travelling fast, and as we drew near the sea I dimly noted a hundred familiar landmarks, and in each a fresh memory of Tom. How affectionately we had taken leave of them, one by one, on our journey to London! Now each seemed to cry, "What have you done with your friend?" This was my home-coming.

At the beginning of the downs I stopped the carriage, paid and dismissed the astonished post-boy and started off alone at a swinging trot across the snow. Southward hung the white moon, now high in heaven. It must be almost time. Along the old track I ran, still clutching my bundle, over the frozen ruts, stumbling, slipping, but with set teeth and straining muscles, skirted the hill above Polkimbra with just a glimpse of the cottage roofs shining in the hollow below, and raced along the cliffs towards Lantrig. I guessed that Colliver would come across Polkimbra Beach, so had determined to approach the rock from the northern side, over Ready-Money Cove.

Lantrig, my old home, was merrily lit up this Christmas Eve, and the sight of it gave me one swift, sharp pang of anguish as I stole cautiously downwards to the sands. At the cliff's foot I paused and looked across the Cove.

Sable and gloomy as ever, Dead Man's Rock soared up against the moon, the grim reality of that dark shadow which had lain upon all my life. From it had my hate started; to it was I now at the last returning. There it stood, the stern warder of that treasure for which my grandfather had sold his soul, my father had given his life, and I had lost all that made both life and soul worth having. " Blood shall be their inheritance, and Fire their portion for ever." The curse had lain upon us all.

Creeping along the shadow, I crossed the little Cove

and peered through the archway on to Polkimbra Sands,
now sparkling in the moonlight.

Not a soul in sight!   As far as eye could see the
beach was utterly deserted and peaceful.   I stepped
down to a small pool, left by the receding tide in the
rock's shadow, removed my false hair and beard, and
carefully washed away all traces of paint from my face.
This done, I slipped off my shoes and holding them with
the bundle in my right hand, began softly and carefully
to ascend the rock.   I gained the first ledge ; crept
out along it as far as the ring mentioned on the clasp,
and then began to climb again.   This needed care, for
the ascent on the north side was harder at first than
on the other, and I could use but one hand with ease.
Slowly, however, and with effort I pulled myself up
and then stole out towards the face until I could command a view of Polkimbra Beach.   Still I could see
nobody, only the lights of the little church - town
twinkling across the beach and, far beyond, the shadowy
cliffs of Kynance.   I pulled out my watch.   It was
close on half-past eleven, the hour of dead low water.

As I looked up again I thought I saw a speck
approaching over the sands.   Yes, I was not mistaken.
I set my teeth and crouched down nearer to the rock.
Over the sands, beneath the shadow of the cliffs he came,
and as he drew nearer, I saw that he carried something
on his shoulder, doubtless the spade and pickaxe.   A
moment more and he turned to see that no one was
following.   As he did so, the moon shone full in his

face, and I saw, stripped now of all disguises, the features of my enemy.

I opened the tin box and took out my knife. I had caused the thin sharp blade, found in my dead father's heart, to be fitted to a horn handle into which it shut with an ordinary spring-clasp. As I opened it, the moonlight glittered down the steel and lit up the letters " Ricordati."

Still in the shadow, he crept down by the rock, and once more looked about him. No single soul was abroad at that hour to see; none but the witness crouching there above. I gripped the knife tighter as he disappeared beneath the ledge on which I hung.

A low curse or two, and then silence. I held my breath and waited. Presently he reappeared, with compass in one hand and measuring-tape in the other, and stood there for a moment looking about him. Still I waited.

About forty feet from the breakers now crisply splashing on the sand, Dead Man's Rock suddenly ended on the southern side in a thin black ridge that broke off with a drop of some ten feet. This ridge was, of course, covered at high water, and upon it the *Belle Fortune* had doubtless struck before she reeled back and settled in deep water. This was the " south point " mentioned on the clasp. Fixing his compass carefully, he drew out the tape, and slowly began to measure towards the north-west. " End South Point, 27 feet," I remembered that the clasp said. He measured it out to the end, and then, digging with his heel a small hole in the sand, began to walk back towards the rock, this time to the north side. And still I waited.

Again I could hear him searching for the mark—an old iron ring, once used for mooring boats—and cursing because he could not find it. After a minute or two, however, he came into sight again, drawing his line now straight out from the cliff, due west. He was very slow, and every now and then, as he bent over his task, would look swiftly about him with a hunted air, and then set to work again. Still there was no sight but the round moon overhead, the sparkling stretch of sand, and the gleam of the waves as they broke in curving lines of silver: no sound but the sigh of the night breeze.

Apparently his measurements were successful, for the tape led him once more to the hole he had marked in the sand. He paused for a moment or two, drew out the clasp, which shot out a sudden gleam as he turned it in his hand, and consulted it carefully. Presumably satisfied, he walked back to the rock to fetch his tools. And still I crouched, waiting, with knife in hand.

Arrived once more at the point where the two lines met, he threw a hasty glance around, and began to dig rapidly. He faced the sea now, and had his back turned to me, so that I could straighten myself up, and watch at greater ease. He dug rapidly, and the pit, as his spade threw out heap after heap of soft sand, grew quickly bigger. If treasure really lay there, it would soon be disclosed.

Presently I heard his spade strike against something
hard. Surely he had not yet dug deeply enough. The
clasp had said " four feet six inches," and the pit could
not yet be more than three feet in depth. Colliver bent
down and drew something out, then examined it intently.
As I strained forward to look, he half turned, and I saw
between his hands—a human skull. Whose? Doubtless, some victim's of those many that went down in the
Belle Fortune; or perhaps the skull of John Railton,
sunk here above the treasure to gain which he had taken
the lives of other men and lost in the end his own. It
was a grisly thought, but apparently troubled Colliver
little, for with a jerk of his arm he sent it bowling
down the sands towards the breakers. A bound or two,
a splash, and it was swallowed up once more by the
insatiate sea.

With this he fell to digging anew, and I to watching.
For a full twenty minutes he laboured, flinging out the
sand to right and left, and every now and then stopping
for a moment to measure his progress. By this time,
I judged, he must have dug below the depth pointed out
upon the clasp, for once or twice he drew it out and
paused in his work to consult it.

He was just resuming, after one of these rests, when
his spade grated against something. He bent low to
examine it, and then began to shovel out the sand with
inconceivable rapidity.

The treasure was found !

Like a madman he worked ; so that even from where

x

I stood I could hear his breath coming hard and fast. At length, with one last glance around, he knelt down and disappeared from my view.

My time was come.

Knife in hand, I softly clambered down the south side of the rock, and dropped upon the sand.

The pit lay rather to the north, so that by creeping behind the ridge on the south side I could get close up to him unobserved, even should he look. But he was absorbed now in his prize, so that I stole noiselessly out across the strip of sand between us until within about ten feet of him; then, on hands and knees, I crawled and pulled myself to the trench's lip and peered over.

There, below me, within grasp, he sat, his back still turned towards me. The moon was full in front, so that it cast no shadow of me across him. There he sat, and in front of him lay, imbedded in the sand, a huge iron chest, bound round with a broad band of iron, and secured with an enormous padlock. On the rusty top I could even trace the rudely-cut initials A. T.

I held my breath as he drew from his pocket my grandfather's key and inserted it in the lock, after first carefully clearing away the sand. The stubborn lock creaked heavily as at last and with difficulty he managed to turn the key. And still I knelt above him, knife in hand.

Then, with a long, shuddering sigh, he lifted and threw back the groaning lid. We both gazed, and as we gazed were well-nigh blinded.

For this is what we saw :—

At first, only a blaze of darting rays that beneath the moon gleamed, sparkled and shot out a myriad scintillations of colour—red, violet, orange, green and deepest crimson. Then by degrees I saw that all these flashing hues came from one jumbled heap of gems— some large, some small, but together in value beyond a king's ransom.

I caught my breath and looked again. Diamonds, rubies, sapphires, amethysts, opals, emeralds, turquoises, and innumerable other stones lay thus roughly heaped together and glittering as though for joy to see the light of heaven once more. Some polished, some uncut, some strung on necklaces and chains, others gleaming in rings and bracelets and barbaric ornaments; there they lay—wealth beyond the hope of man, the dreams of princes.

The chest measured some five feet by three, and these jewels evidently lay in a kind of sunken drawer, or tray, of iron. In the corner of this was a small space of about four inches square, covered with an iron lid. As we gazed with straining eyes, Colliver drew one more long sigh of satisfied avarice, and lifted this smaller lid.

Instantly a full rich flood of crimson light welled up, serene and glorious, with luminous shafts of splendour, that, as we looked, met and concentred in one glowing heart of flame—met in one translucent, ineffable depth of purple-red. Calm and radiant it lay there, as though no curse lay in its deep hollows, no passion had ever fed its flames with blood; stronger than the centuries, imperishably and triumphantly cruel—the Great Ruby of Ceylon!

With a short gasp of delight, Colliver was stretching out his hand towards it, when I laid mine heavily on his shoulder, then sprang to my feet. My waiting was over.

He gave one start of uttermost terror, leapt to his feet, and in an instant was facing me. Already his knife was half out of his waist-band; already he had taken half a leap forwards, when he saw me standing there above him.

Bareheaded I stood in the moonlight, the white ray glittering up my knife and lighting up my bared chest and set stern face. Bareheaded, with the light breeze fanning my curls, I stood there and waited for his leap. But that leap never came.

One step forward he took and then looked, and looking, staggered back with hands thrown up before his face. Slowly, as he cowered back with hands upraised and straining eyeballs, I saw those eyeballs grow rigid, freeze and turn to stone, while through his gaping, bloodless lips came a hoarse and gasping sound that had neither words nor meaning.

Then as I still watched, with murderous purpose on my face, there came one awful cry, a scream that startled the gulls from slumber and awoke echo after echo along the shore—a scream like no sound in earth or heaven—a scream inhuman and appalling.

Then followed silence, and as the last echo died away, he fell.

As he collapsed within the pit, I made a step forward to the brink and looked. He was now upon his hands and knees before the chest, bathing his hands in the gleaming heap of gems, catching them up in handfuls, and as they ran like sparkling rain through his fingers, muttering incoherently to himself and humming wild snatches of song.

"Colliver—Simon Colliver!" I called.

He paid no attention, but went on tossing up the diamonds and rubies in his hands and watching them as they rattled down again upon the heap.

"Simon Colliver!"

I leapt down into the pit beside him, and laid my hand upon his shoulder. He paused for a moment, and looked up with a vacant gleam in his deep eyes.

"Colliver, I have to speak a word with you."

"Oh, yes, I know you. Trenoweth, of course: Ezekiel Trenoweth come back again after the treasure. But you are too late, too late, too late! You are dead now—ha, ha! dead and rotting.

"For his glittering eyes are the salt sea's prize,
     And his fingers clutch the sand, my lads.

"Aha! his fingers clutch the sand. Here's pretty sand for you! sand of all colours; look, look, there's a brave sparkle!" And again he ran the priceless shower through his fingers.

"Oh, yes," he continued after a moment, looking up, "oh, yes, I know you—Ezekiel Trenoweth, of course; or is it Amos, or Jasper? No matter, you are all dead. I killed the last of you last year—no, last night; all dead,

"And the devil has got his due, my lads!

"His due, his due! Look at it! look again! I had a skull just now. John Railton's skull, no eyes in it though,

"For his glittering eyes are the salt sea's——

"Where is the skull? Let me fit it with a bonny pair of eyes here—here they are, or here, look, here's a pair that change colour when they move. Where is the skull? Give it me. Oh, I forgot, I lost it. Never mind, find it, find it. Here's plenty of eyes when you find it. Or give it this big, red one. Here's a flaming, fiery eye!"

As he stretched out his hand over the Great Ruby, I caught him by the wrist. But he was too quick for me, and with a sharp snarl and click of his teeth, had whipped his hand round to his back.

Then in a flash, as I grappled with him, he thrust me back with his left palm, and, with a sweep of his right, hurled the great jewel far out into the sea. I saw it rise and curve in one long, sparkling arch of flame, then fall with a dropping line of fire down into the billows. A splash—a jet of light, and it was gone:—gone perhaps to hide amid the rotting timbers of what was once

the *Belle Fortune*, or among the bones of her drowned
crew to watch with its blood-red tireless eye the ex-
tremity of its handiwork. There, for aught I know,
it lies to-day, and there, for aught I care, beneath
the waters it shall treasure its infernal loveliness for
ever.

Into its red heart I have looked once, and this was
what I read :—of treachery, lust and rapine ; of battle
and murder and sudden death ; of midnight outcries, and
poison in the guest-cup ; of a curse that said, "Even as
the Heart of the Ruby is Blood and its Eyes a Flaming
Fire, so shall it be for them that would possess it : Fire
shall be their portion, and Blood their inheritance for
ever." Of that quest and that curse we were the two
survivors. And what were we, that night, as we stood
upon the sands with that last hellish glitter still dancing
in our eyes ? The one, a lonely and broken man ; the
other——

I turned to look at Colliver. He was huddled
against the pit's side, with his dark eyes gazing wistfully up at me. In their shining depths there lurked
no more sanity than in the heart of the Great Ruby. As
I looked, I knew him to be a hopeless madman, and
knew also that my revenge had slipped from me for
ever.

We were still standing so when a soft wave came
stealing up the beach and flung the lip of its foam over
the pit's edge into the chest. I turned round. The tide
was rising fast, and in a minute or so would be upon us.

Catching Colliver by the shoulder, I pointed and tried to make him understand; but the maniac had again fallen to playing with the jewels. I shook him; he did not stir, only sat there jabbering and singing. And now wave after wave came splashing over us, soaking us through, and hissing in phosphorescent pools among the gems.

There was no time to be lost. I tore the madman back, stamped down the lid, locked it, and took out the key; then caught Colliver in my arms and heaved him bodily out of the trench. Jumping out beside him, I caught up the spade and shovelled back the wet sand as fast as I could, until the tide drove us back. Colliver stood quite tamely beside me all this while and watched the treasure disappearing from his view; only every now and then he would chatter a few wild words, and with that break off again in vacant wonder at my work.

When all was done that could be, I took my companion's hand, led him up the sands beyond high-water mark, and then sat down beside him, waiting for the dawn.

And there, next morning, by Dead Man's Rock they found us, while across the beach came the faint music of Polkimbra bells as they rang their Christmas peal, "Peace on earth and goodwill toward men."

    *   *   *   *   *

There is little more to tell. Next day, at low ebb, with the aid of Joe Roscorla (still hale and hearty)

and a few Polkimbra fishermen whom I knew, the rest
of my grandfather's treasure was secured and carried
up from the sea. In the iron chest, besides the gems
already spoken of, and beneath the iron tray containing
them, was a prodigious quantity of gold and silver,
partly in ingots, partly in coinage. This last was of
all nationalities : moidores, dollars, rupees, doubloons,
guineas, crown-pieces, louis, besides an amount of
coins which I could not trace, the whole proving a
most catholic taste in buccaneering. So much did it
all weigh, that we found it impossible to stir the
chest as it stood, and therefore secured the prize piece-
meal. Strangest of all, however, was a folded parchment which we discovered beneath the tray of gems and
above the coins. It contained but few words, which ran
as follows—

FAIR FORTUNE WRECKED, FAIR
FORTUNE FOUND,
AND ALL BUT THE FINDER UNDER-
GROUND.—A. T.

This, as far as I know, was my grandfather's one
and only attempt at verse; and its apparent application
to the wreck of the *Belle Fortune* is a coincidence which
puzzles me to this day.

The reader will search the chronicles of wrecks in
vain for the story of that ill-fated ship. But if he
comes upon the record of a certain vessel, the *James and
Elizabeth*, wrecked upon the Cornish coast on the night

of October 11th, 1849, he may know it to be the same.
For that was the name given by the only survivor, one
Georgio Rhodojani, a Greek sailor, and as the *James and
Elizabeth* she stands entered to this day.

If, however, his curiosity lead him further to inquire
into the after-history of this same Georgio Rhodojani,
let him go on a fine summer day to the County Lunatic
Asylum at Bodmin, and, with permission, enter the
grounds set apart for private patients. There he may
chance to see a strange sight.

On a garden seat against the sunny wall sit two
persons—a man and a woman. The man is decrepit and
worn, being apparently about sixty-seven or eight years
old; but the woman, as the keepers will tell, is ninety.
She is his mother, and as they sit together, she feeds
him with sweets and fruit as tenderly as though he were
a child. He takes them, but never notices her, and
when he has had enough, rises abruptly and walks away
humming a song which runs—

> "So it's hey! for the homeward bound, my lads!
>   And ho! for the drunken crew,
> For his mess-mates round lie dead and drowned,
> And the devil has got his due, my lads—
>   Sing ho! but he waits for you!"

This is his only song now, and he will walk round
the gravel paths by the hour, singing it softly and
muttering. Sometimes, however, he will sit for long
beside his mother and let her pat his hand. They
never speak.

Folks say that she is as mad as her son, but she lodges in the town outside the walls and comes to see him every day. Certainly she is as remarkable to look upon, for her skin is of a brilliant and startling yellow, and her withered hands are loaded with diamonds. As you pass, she will stare at you with eyes absolutely passionless and vague; but see them as she sighs and turns to go, see them as she watches for a responsive touch of love on her son's face, and you may find some meaning in them then.

Mrs. Luttrell was never seen again from the hour when she stood below the river steps and waved her white arms to me, crying "Kill him! kill him!" I made every inquiry but could learn nothing, save that my boat had been found floating below Gravesend, quite empty. She can scarcely be alive, so that is yet one soul more added to the account of the Great Ruby.

Failing to find her mother, I had Claire's body conveyed to Polkimbra. She lies buried beside my father and mother in the little churchyard there. Above her head stands a white stone with the simple words, "In memory of C. L., died Dec. 23rd, 1863. 'Love is strong as death.'"

The folk at Polkimbra have many a fable about this grave, but if pressed will shake their heads sagely and refer you to "Master Trenoweth up yonder at Lantrig. Folks say she was a play-actor and he loved her. Anyway you may see him up in the churchyard most days, but dont'ee go nigh him then, unless you baint afeard of th' evil eye."

And I? After the treasure was divided with Government, I still had for my share what I suppose would be called a considerable fortune. The only use to which I put it, however, was to buy back Lantrig, the home of a stock that will die out with me. There again from the middle beam in the front parlour hangs my grandfather's key, covered with cobwebs as thickly as on the day when my father went forth to seek the treasure. There I live a solitary life—an old man, though scarcely yet past middle age. For all my hopes are buried in the grave where sleeps my lost love, and my soul shall lie for ever under the curse, engulfed and hidden as deeply as the Great Ruby beneath the shadow of Dead Man's Rock.

THE END.

PRINTED BY CASSELL & COMPANY, LIMITED, LA BELLE SAUVAGE, LONDON, E.C

Crown 8vo. Cloth. Price 3s. 6d. each Volume.

A Tragic Mystery ... ... By JULIAN HAWTHORNE.

The Yoke of the Thorah .... By SIDNEY LUSKA.

Two Gentlemen of Gotham ... By C. and C.

Who is John Noman? ... By C. H. BECKETT.

The Tragedy of Brinkwater... By MARTHA L. MOODEY.

The Great Bank Robbery ... By JULIAN HAWTHORNE.

POPULAR NOVELS.

By G. MANVILLE FENN.

In cloth, 2s. each.

The Vicar's People. | My Patients.
Sweet Mace. | The Parson o' Dumford.
Dutch the Diver. | Poverty Corner.

"Mr. Manville Fenn is one of the rare novelists who practise a delicate profession conscientiously. His successive books show unmistakable progress."—*The Times.*

POPULAR NOVELS.

By WILLIAM WESTALL.

e Old Factory. *Cheap Edition*, cloth. **2s.**

Red Ryvington. *Cheap Edition*, cloth. **2s.**

Ralph Norbreck's Trust. *Cheap Edition.* **2s.**

"There is invention, and spirit, and 'go' in Mr. Westall's novels, as well as an invariably healthy tone and a sufficiently close adh·rence to the ways and habits of man, as actually observed, to justify them from the charge of unreality."—*Manchester Guardian.*

CASSELL & COMPANY, LIMITED, *Ludgate Hill, London.*

3

4

Illustrated, Fine-Art, and other Volumes.

Abbeys and Churches of England and Wales, The: Descriptive,
Historical, Pictorial. 21s.
After London; or, Wild England. By RICHARD JEFFERIES. 3s. 6d.
Along Alaska's Great River. By F. SCHWATKA. Illustrated. 12s. 6d.
American Yachts and Yachting. Illustrated. 6s.
Arabian Nights Entertainments, The (Cassell's Pictorial Edition).
With about 400 Illustrations. 10s. 6d.
Artists, Some Modern. With highly-finished Engravings. 12s. 6d.
Art, The Magazine of. Yearly Vol. With 500 choice Engravings. 15s.
A Tragic Mystery. By JULIAN HAWTHORNE. 3s. 6d.
Behind Time. By GEORGE PARSONS LATHROP. Illustrated. 2s. 6d
Bimetallism, The Theory of. By D. BARBOUR. 6s.
Bismarck, Prince. By CHARLES LOWE, M.A. Two Vols. *Cheap
Edition.* 10s. 6d.
Bright, John, Life and Times of. By W. ROBERTSON. 7s. 6d.
British Ballads. With 275 Original Illustrations. Two Vols. 7s. 6d. each.
British Battles on Land and Sea. By the late JAMES GRANT. With
about 600 Illustrations. Three Vols., 4to, £1 7s.; Library Edition, £1 10s.
British Battles, Recent. Illustrated. 4to, 9s.; Library Edition, 10s.
British Empire, The. By Sir GEORGE CAMPBELL, M.P. 3s.
Browning, An Introduction to the Study of. By A. SYMONS. 2s. 6d.
Butterflies and Moths, European. By W. F. KIRBY. With 62
Coloured Plates. Demy 4to, 35s.
Canaries and Cage-Birds, The Illustrated Book of. By W. A.
BLAKSTON, W. SWAYSLAND, and A. F. WIENER. With 56 Fac-simile
Coloured Plates, 35s. Half-morocco, £2 5s.
Cannibals and Convicts. By JULIAN THOMAS ("The Vagabond").
Cheap Edition. 5s.
Cassell's Family Magazine. Yearly Vol. Illustrated. 9s.
Cathedral Churches of England and Wales. Illustrated. 21s.
Celebrities of the Century: being a Dictionary of Men and
Women of the Nineteenth Century. 21s.; Roxburgh, 25s.
Chess Problem, The. A Text-Book, with Illustrations. 7s. 6d.
Children of the Cold, The. By Lieut. SCHWATKA. 2s. 6d.
Choice Poems by H. W. Longfellow. Illustrated from Paintings
by his Son, ERNEST W. LONGFELLOW. Small 4to, cloth, 6s.
Choice Dishes at Small Cost. By A. G. PAYNE. 1s.
Christmas in the Olden Time. By Sir WALTER SCOTT, with Original
Illustrations. 7s. 6d.
Cities of the World. Three Vols. Illustrated. 7s. 6d. each.
Civil Service, Guide to Employment in the. 3s. 6d.
Civil Service.—Guide to Female Employment in Government
Offices. 1s.
Clinical Manuals for Practitioners and Students of Medicine. A
List of Volumes forwarded post free on application to the Publishers.
Clothing, The Influence of, on Health. By F. TREVES, F.R.C.S. 2s.
Colonies and India, Our, How we Got Them, and Why we Keep
Them. By Prof. C. RANSOME. 1s.
Colour. By Prof. A. H. CHURCH. *New and Enlarged Edition,* with
Coloured Plates. 3s. 6d.
Columbus, Christopher, The Life and Voyages of. By WASHINGTON
IRVING. Three Vols. 7s. 6d.
Cookery, Cassell's Dictionary of. Containing about Nine Thousand
Recipes. 7s. 6d.; Roxburgh, 10s. 6d.
Co-operators, Working Men: What they have Done, and What
they are Doing. By A. H. DYKE-ACLAND, M.P., and B. JONES. 1s.
Cookery, A Year's. By PHYLLIS BROWNE. 3s. 6d.
Cook Book, Catherine Owen's New. 4s.

Countries of the World, The. By ROBERT BROWN, M.A., Ph.D., &c. Complete in Six Vols., with about 750 Illustrations. 4to. 7s. 6d. each.

Cromwell, Oliver: The Man and his Mission. By J. ALLANSON PICTON, M.P. Cloth, 7s. 6d.; morocco, cloth sides, 9s.

Cyclopædia, Cassell's Concise. With 12,000 subjects, brought down to the latest date. With about 600 Illustrations, 15s.; Roxburgh, 18s.

Dairy Farming. By Prof. J. P. SHELDON. With 25 Fac-simile Coloured Plates. Cloth, 31s. 6d.; half-morocco, 42s.

Dead Man's Rock. A Romance. By "Q." 5s.

Decisive Events in History. By THOMAS ARCHER. With Sixteen Illustrations. Boards, 3s. 6d.; cloth, 5s.

Decorative Design. By CHRISTOPHER DRESSER, Ph.D. Illustrated. 5s.

Deserted Village Series, The. Consisting of *Editions de luxe* of the most favourite poems of Standard Authors. Illustrated. 2s. 6d. each.

| SONGS FROM SHAKESPEARE. | GOLDSMITH'S DESERTED VILLAGE. |
| MILTON'S L'ALLEGRO AND IL PENSEROSO. | WORDSWORTH'S ODE ON IMMORTALITY, AND LINES ON TINTERN ABBEY. |

Dickens, Character Sketches from. FIRST, SECOND, and THIRD SERIES. With Six Original Drawings in each by F. BARNARD. In Portfolio, 21s. each.

Diary of Two Parliaments. By W. H. LUCY. Vol. I.: The Disraeli Parliament. Vol. II.: The Gladstone Parliament. 12s. each.

Dog, The. By IDSTONE. Illustrated. 2s. 6d.

Dog, Illustrated Book of the. By VERO SHAW, B.A. With 28 Coloured Plates. Cloth bevelled, 35s.; half-morocco, 45s.

Domestic Dictionary, The. Illustrated. Cloth, 7s. 6d.

Doré's Adventures of Munchausen. Illustrated by GUSTAVE DORÉ. 5s.

Doré's Dante's Inferno. Illustrated by GUSTAVE DORÉ. 21s.

Doré's Dante's Purgatorio and Paradiso. Illustrated by GUSTAVE DORÉ. *Popular Edition.* 21s.

Doré's Fairy Tales Told Again. With Engravings by DORÉ. 5s.

Doré Gallery, The. With 250 Illustrations by DORÉ. 4to, 42s.

Doré's Milton's Paradise Lost. Illustrated by DORÉ. 4to, 21s.

Earth, Our, and its Story. By Dr. ROBERT BROWN, F.L.S. Vol. I. With Coloured Plates and numerous Wood Engravings. 9s.

Edinburgh, Old and New. Three Vols. With 600 Illustrations. 9s. each.

Egypt: Descriptive, Historical, and Picturesque. By Prof. G. EBERS. Translated by CLARA BELL, with Notes by SAMUEL BIRCH, LL.D., &c. With 800 Original Engravings. *Popular Edition.* In Two Vols. 42s.

Electricity in the Service of Man. With nearly 850 Illustrations. 21s.

Electricity, Practical. By Prof. W. E. AYRTON. 7s. 6d.

Electricity, Age of, from Amber Soul to Telephone. By PARK BENJAMIN, Ph.D. 7s. 6d.

Electrician's Pocket-Book, The. By GORDON WIGAN, M.A. 5s.

Encyclopædic Dictionary, The. A New and Original Work of Reference to all the Words in the English Language. Twelve Divisional Vols. now ready, 10s. 6d. each; or the Double Divisional Vols., half-morocco, 21s. each.

England, Cassell's Illustrated History of. With 2,000 Illustrations. Ten Vols., 4to, 9s. each. *New and Revised Edition.* Vol. I. 9s.

English History, The Dictionary of. Cloth, 21s.; Roxburgh, 25s.

English Literature, Library of. By Prof. HENRY MORLEY. Five Vols., 7s. 6d. each.

    VOL. I.—SHORTER ENGLISH POEMS.
    VOL. II.—ILLUSTRATIONS OF ENGLISH RELIGION.
    VOL. III.—ENGLISH PLAYS.
    VOL. IV.—SHORTER WORKS IN ENGLISH PROSE.
    VOL. V.—SKETCHES OF LONGER WORKS IN ENGLISH VERSE AND PROSE.

English Literature, The Story of. By ANNA BUCKLAND. 3s. 6d.

English Literature, Morley's First Sketch of. *Revised Edition,* 7s. 6d.
English Literature, Dictionary of. By W. DAVENPORT ADAMS. *Cheap Edition,* 7s. 6d. ; Roxburgh, 10s. 6d.
English Poetesses. By ERIC S. ROBERTSON, M.A. 5s.
English Writers. By Prof. HENRY MORLEY. Vols. I. and II. Crown 8vo, 5s. each.
Æsop's Fables. Illustrated throughout by ERNEST GRISET. *Cheap Edition.* Cloth, 3s. 6d.
Etching. By S. K. KOEHLER. With 30 Full-Page Plates by Old and Modern Etchers. £4 4s.
Etiquette of Good Society. 1s. ; cloth, 1s. 6d.
Eye, Ear, and Throat, The Management of the. 3s. 6d.
False Hopes. By Prof. GOLDWIN SMITH, M.A., LL.D., D.C.L. 6d.
Fair Trade Unmasked. By GEORGE W. MEDLEY. 6d.
Family Physician, The. By Eminent PHYSICIANS and SURGEONS. Cloth, 21s. ; half-morocco, 25s.
Fenn, G. Manville, Works by. Cloth boards, 2s. each.

SWEET MACE.	THE VICAR'S PEOPLE.
DUTCH THE DIVER.	COBWEB'S FATHER.
MY PATIENTS. Being the Notes of a Navy Surgeon.	THE PARSON O' DUMFORD.
	POVERTY CORNER.

Ferns, European. By JAMES BRITTEN, F.L.S. With 30 Fac-simile Coloured Plates by D. BLAIR, F.L.S. 21s.
Field Naturalist's Handbook, The. By the Rev. J. G. WOOD and THEODORE WOOD. 5s.
Figuier's Popular Scientific Works. With Several Hundred Illustrations in each. 3s. 6d. each.

THE HUMAN RACE.	THE OCEAN WORLD.
WORLD BEFORE THE DELUGE.	THE VEGETABLE WORLD.
REPTILES AND BIRDS.	THE INSECT WORLD.
MAMMALIA.	

Fine-Art Library, The. Edited by JOHN SPARKES, Principal of the South Kensington Art Schools. Each Book contains about 100 Illustrations. 5s. each.

ENGRAVING. By Le Vicomte Henri Delaborde. Translated by R. A. M. Stevenson.	THE EDUCATION OF THE ARTIST. By Ernest Chesneau. Translated by Clara Bell. (Not illustrated.)
TAPESTRY. By Eugène Müntz. Translated by Miss L. J. Davis.	GREEK ARCHÆOLOGY. By Maxime Collignon. Translated by Dr. J. H. Wright.
THE ENGLISH SCHOOL OF PAINTING. By E. Chesneau. Translated by L. N. Etherington. With an Introduction by Prof. Ruskin.	ARTISTIC ANATOMY. By Prof. Duval. Translated by F. E. Fenton.
THE FLEMISH SCHOOL OF PAINTING. By A. J. Wauters. Translated by Mrs. Henry Rossel.	THE DUTCH SCHOOL OF PAINTING. By Henry Havard. Translated by G. Powell.

Fisheries of the World, The. Illustrated. 4to. 9s.
Five Pound Note, The, and other Stories. By G. S. JEALOUS. 1s.
Flower Painting, Elementary. With Eight Coloured Plates. 3s.
Flowers, and How to Paint Them. By MAUD NAFTEL. With Coloured Plates. 5s.
Forging of the Anchor, The. A Poem. By the late Sir SAMUEL FERGUSON, LL.D. With 20 Original Illustrations. Gilt edges, 5s.
Fossil Reptiles, A History of British. By Sir RICHARD OWEN, K.C.B., F.R.S., &c. With 268 Plates. In Four Vols., £12 12s.
Franco-German War, Cassell's History of the. Two Vols. With 500 Illustrations. 9s. each.
Fresh-water Fishes of Europe, The. By Prof. H. G. SEELEY, F.R.S. *Cheap Edition.* 7s. 6d.
From Gold to Grey. Being Poems and Pictures of Life and Nature. By MARY D. BRINE. Illustrated. 7s. 6d.

Garden Flowers, Familiar. By SHIRLEY HIBBERD. With Coloured Plates by F. E. HULME, F.L.S. Complete in Five Series. 12s. 6d. each.

Gardening, Cassell's Popular. Illustrated. 4 vols., 5s. each.

Geometrical Drawing for Army Candidates. By H. T. LILLEY, M.A. 2s.

Geometry, Practical Solid. By MAJOR ROSS. 2s.

Gladstone, Life of W. E. By G. BARNETT SMITH. With Portrait. 3s. 6d.

Gleanings from Popular Authors. Two Vols. With Original Illustrations. 4to, 9s. each. Two Vols. in One, 15s.

Great Industries of Great Britain. Three Vols. With about 400 Illustrations. 4to, cloth, 7s. 6d. each.

Great Painters of Christendom, The, from Cimabue to Wilkie. By JOHN FORBES-ROBERTSON. Illustrated throughout. 12s. 6d.

Great Northern Railway, The Official Illustrated Guide to the. 1s.; or in cloth, 2s.

Great Western Railway, The Official Illustrated Guide to the. *New and Revised Edition.* With Illustrations, 1s.; cloth, 2s.

Gulliver's Travels. With 88 Engravings by MORTEN. *Cheap Edition.* Cloth, 3s. 6d.; cloth gilt, 5s.

Gun and its Development, The. By W. W. GREENER. With 500 Illustrations. 10s. 6d.

Health, The Book of. By Eminent Physicians and Surgeons. Cloth, 21s.; Roxburgh, 25s.

Health, The Influence of Clothing on. By F. TREVES, F.R.G.S. 2s.

Health at School. By CLEMENT DUKES, M.D., B.S. 7s. 6d.

Heavens, The Story of the. By Sir ROBERT STAWELL BALL, F.R.S., F.R.A.S. With Coloured Plates and Wood Engravings. 31s. 6d.

Heroes of Britain in Peace and War. In Two Vols., with 300 Original Illustrations. 5s. each; or One Vol., library binding, 10s. 6d.

Holy Land and the Bible, The. By the Rev. CUNNINGHAM GEIKIE, D.D. With Map. Two Vols. 24s.

Homes, Our, and How to Make them Healthy. By Eminent Authorities. Illustrated. 15s.; Roxburgh, 18s.

Horse Keeper, The Practical. By GEORGE FLEMING, LL.D., F.R.C.V.S. Illustrated. 7s. 6d.

Horse, The Book of the. By SAMUEL SIDNEY. With 28 *fac-simile* Coloured Plates. *Enlarged Edition.* Demy 4to, 35s.; half-morocco, 45s.

Horses, The Simple Ailments of. By W. F. Illustrated. 5s.

Household Guide, Cassell's. With Illustrations and Coloured Plates. *New and Cheap Edition*, in Four Vols., 20s.

How Dante Climbed the Mountain. By ROSE EMILY SELFE. With Eight Full-page Engravings by GUSTAVE DORÉ. 2s.

How Women may Earn a Living. By MERCY GROGAN. 1s.

Imperial White Books. In Quarterly Vols. 10s. 6d. per annum, post free; separately, 3s. 6d. each.

India, The Coming Struggle for. By Prof. VAMBÉRY. 5s.

India, Cassell's History of. By the late JAMES GRANT. With about 400 Illustrations. Library binding. One Vol. 15s.

India: the Land and the People. By Sir J. CAIRD, K.C.B. 10s. 6d.

Indoor Amusements, Card Games, and Fireside Fun, Cassell's Book of. Illustrated. 3s. 6d.

Invisible Life, Vignettes from. By JOHN BADCOCK, F.R.M.S. Illustrated. 3s. 6d.

Irish Parliament, The; What it Was and What it Did. By J. G. SWIFT MACNEILL, M.A., M.P. 1s.

John Parmelee's Curse. By JULIAN HAWTHORNE. 2s. 6d.

Kennel Guide, The Practical. By Dr. GORDON STABLES. Illustrated. *Cheap Edition.* 1s.

Khiva, A Ride to. By the late Col. FRED. BURNABY. 1s. 6d.

Kidnapped. By R. L. STEVENSON. *Illustrated Edition.* 5s.

King Solomon's Mines. By H. RIDER HAGGARD. 5s.

Ladies' Physician, The. A Guide for Women in the Treatment of their Ailments. By a Physician. 6s.

Lady's World, The. An Illustrated Magazine of Fashion and Society. Yearly Vol. 18s.

Land Question, The. By Prof. J. ELLIOT, M.R.A.C. 10s. 6d.

Landscape Painting in Oils, A Course of Lessons in. By A. F. GRACE. With Nine Reproductions in Colour. *Cheap Edition*, 25s.

Law, About Going to. By A. J. WILLIAMS, M.P. 2s. 6d.

Letts's Diaries and other Time-saving Publications are now published exclusively by CASSELL & COMPANY. (*A list sent post free on application.*)

Local Dual Standards. Gold and Silver Currencies. By JOHN HENRY NORMAN. 1s.

London and North Western Railway, The Official Illustrated Guide to the. 1s.; cloth, 2s.

London and South Western Railway, The Official Illustrated Guide to the. 1s.; cloth, 2s.

London, Greater. By EDWARD WALFORD. Two Vols. With about 400 Illustrations. 9s. each.

London, Old and New. Six Vols., each containing about 200 Illustrations and Maps. Cloth, 9s. each.

Longfellow's Poetical Works. Illustrated throughout, £3 3s.; *Popular Edition*, 16s.

Love's Extremes, At. By MAURICE THOMPSON. 5s.

Luther, Martin: His Life and Times. By PETER BAYNE, LL.D. Two Vols., demy 8vo, 1,040 pages. Cloth, 24s.

Mechanics, The Practical Dictionary of. Containing 15,000 Drawings. Four Vols. 21s. each.

Medicine, Manuals for Students of. (*A List forwarded post free.*)

Midland Railway, Official Illustrated Guide to the. *New and Revised Edition.* 1s.; cloth, 2s.

Modern Europe, A History of. By C. A. FYFFE, M.A. Vol. I., from 1792 to 1814. 12s. Vol. II., from 1814 to 1848. 12s.

Music, Illustrated History of. By EMIL NAUMANN. Edited by the Rev. Sir F. A. GORE OUSELEY, Bart. Illustrated. Two Vols. 31s. 6d.

National Library, Cassell's. In Weekly Volumes, each containing about 192 pages. Paper covers, 3d.; cloth, 6d. (*A List of the Volumes already issued sent post free on application.*)

Natural History, Cassell's Concise. By E. PERCEVAL WRIGHT, M.A., M.D., F.L.S. With several Hundred Illustrations. 7s. 6d.

Natural History, Cassell's New. Edited by Prof. P. MARTIN DUNCAN, M.B., F.R.S., F.G.S. With Contributions by Eminent Scientific Writers. Complete in Six Vols. With about 2,000 high-class Illustrations. Extra crown 4to, cloth, 9s. each.

Nimrod in the North; or, Hunting and Fishing Adventures in the Arctic Regions. By F. SCHWATKA. Illustrated. 7s. 6d.

Nursing for the Home and for the Hospital, A Handbook of. By CATHERINE J. WOOD. *Cheap Edition.* 1s. 6d.; cloth, 2s.

Oil Painting, A Manual of. By the Hon. JOHN COLLIER. 2s. 6d.

Our Own Country. Six Vols. With 1,200 Illustrations. 7s. 6d. each.

Painting, Practical Guides to. With Coloured Plates and full instructions:—Animal Painting, 5s.—China Painting, 5s.—Figure Painting, 7s. 6d.—Elementary Flower Painting, 3s.—Flower Painting, 2 Books, 5s. each.—Tree Painting, 5s.—Water-Colour Painting, 5s.—Neutral Tint, 5s.—Sepia, in 2 Vols., 3s. each; or in One Vol., 5s.—Flowers, and How to Paint Them, 5s.

Paris, Cassell's Illustrated Guide to. 1s.; cloth, 2s.

Parliaments, A Diary of Two. By H. W. Lucy. The Disraeli Parliament, 1874—1880. 12s. The Gladstone Parliament, 1881—1886. 12s.

Paxton's Flower Garden. By Sir Joseph Paxton and Prof. Lindley. Three Vols. With 100 Coloured Plates. £1 1s. each.

Peoples of the World, The. In Six Vols. By Dr. Robert Brown. Illustrated. 7s. 6d. each.

Phantom City, The. By W. Westall. 5s.

Photography for Amateurs. By T. C. Hepworth. Illustrated. 1s.; or cloth, 1s. 6d.

Phrase and Fable, Dictionary of. By the Rev. Dr. Brewer. *Cheap Edition, Enlarged*, cloth, 3s. 6d. ; or with leather back, 4s. 6d.

Picturesque America. Complete in Four Vols., with 48 Exquisite Steel Plates and about 800 Original Wood Engravings. £2 2s. each.

Picturesque Canada. With 600 Original Illustrations. Two Vols. £3 3s. each.

Picturesque Europe. Complete in Five Vols. Each containing 13 Exquisite Steel Plates, from Original Drawings, and nearly 200 Original Illustrations. £10 10s. The Popular Edition is published in Five Vols., 18s. each.

Pigeon Keeper, The Practical. By Lewis Wright. Illustrated. 3s. 6d.

Pigeons, The Book of. By Robert Fulton. Edited and Arranged by L. Wright. With 50 Coloured Plates, 31s. 6d. ; half-morocco, £2 2s.

Poets, Cassell's Miniature Library of the :-

Burns. Two Vols. 2s. 6d.	Milton. Two Vols. 2s. 6d.
Byron. Two Vols. 2s. 6d.	Scott. Two Vols. 2s. 6d. [2s. 6d.
Hood. Two Vols. 2s. 6d.	Sheridan and Goldsmith. 2 Vols.
Longfellow. Two Vols. 2s. 6d.	Wordsworth. Two Vols. 2s. 6d.

Shakespeare. Twelve Vols., in Case, 15s.

. *The above are also publishing in cloth, 1s. each Vol.*

Police Code, and Manual of the Criminal Law. By C. E. Howard Vincent, M.P. 2s.

Popular Library, Cassell's. Cloth, 1s. each.

The Russian Empire.	The Story of the English Jacobins.
The Religious Revolution in the 16th Century.	Domestic Folk Lore.
English Journalism.	The Rev. Rowland Hill: Preacher and Wit.
Our Colonial Empire.	Bishop and Johnson : their Com-
John Wesley.	panions and Contemporaries.
The Young Man in the Battle of Life.	History of the Free-Trade Move- ment in England.

Post Office of Fifty Years Ago, The. 1s.

Poultry Keeper, The Practical. By Lewis Wright. With Coloured Plates and Illustrations. 3s. 6d.

Poultry, The Illustrated Book of. By Lewis Wright. With Fifty Coloured Plates. Cloth, 31s. 6d. ; half-morocco, £2 2s.

Poultry, The Book of. By Lewis Wright. *Popular Edition.* 10s. 6d.

Pre-Raphaelites, The Italian, in the National Gallery. By Cosmo Monkhouse. Illustrated. 1s.

Queen Victoria, The Life and Times of. By Robert Wilson. With numerous Illustrations, representing the Chief Events in the Life of the Queen, and Portraits of the Leading Celebrities of her Reign. Volume I., extra crown 4to, cloth gilt, 9s.

Quiver Yearly Volume, The. With about 300 Original Contributions by Eminent Divines and Popular Authors, and upwards of 250 high-class Illustrations. 7s. 6d.

Rabbit-Keeper, The Practical. By Cuniculus. Illustrated. 3s. 6d.

Representative Poems of Living Poets American and English. Selected by the Poets themselves. 15s.

Royal River, The : The Thames from Source to Sea. With Descriptive Text and a Series of beautiful Engravings. £2 2s.

Red Library, Cassell's. Stiff covers, 1s. each; cloth, 2s. each: or half-calf, marbled edges, 5s. each.

Selections from Hood's Works.
Longfellow's Prose Works.
Sense and Sensibility.
Lytton's Plays. [Harte.
Tales, Poems, and Sketches. Bret
Martin Chuzzlewit (2 Vols.).
The Prince of the House of David.
Sheridan's Plays.
Uncle Tom's Cabin.
Deerslayer.
Eugene Aram.
Jack Hinton, the Guardsman.
Rome and the Early Christians.
The Trials of Margaret Lyndsay.
Poe's Works.
Old Mortality.
The Hour and the Man.

Handy Andy.
Scarlet Letter.
Pickwick (2 Vols.)
Last of the Mohicans.
Pride and Prejudice.
Yellowplush Papers.
Tales of the Borders.
Last Days of Palmyra. [Book.
Washington Irving's Sketch-
The Talisman.
Rienzi.
Old Curiosity Shop.
Heart of Midlothian.
Last Days of Pompeii.
American Humour.
Sketches by Boz. [Essays.
Macaulay's Lays and Selected
Harry Lorrequer.

Russia. By Sir DONALD MACKENZIE WALLACE, M.A. 5s.

Russo-Turkish War, Cassell's History of. With about 500 Illustrations. Two Vols., 9s. each.

Saturday Journal, Cassell's. Yearly Volume. 6s.

Science for All. Edited by Dr. ROBERT BROWN, M.A., F.L.S., &c. With 1,500 Illustrations. Five Vols. 9s. each.

Sea, The: Its Stirring Story of Adventure, Peril, and Heroism. By F. WHYMPER. With 400 Illustrations. Four Vols., 7s. 6d. each.

Sent Back by the Angels. And other Ballads. By FREDERICK LANG-BRIDGE, M.A. Cloth, 4s. 6d.

Shaftesbury, The Seventh Earl of, K.G., The Life and Work of. By EDWIN HODDER. With Portraits. Three Vols., 36s. *Popular Edition.* In One Vol., 7s. 6d.

Shakspere, The Leopold. With 400 Illustrations. Cloth, 6s.; cloth gilt, 7s. 6d.; half-morocco, 10s. 6d. *Cheap Edition.* 3s. 6d.

Shakspere, The Royal. With Steel Plates and Wood Engravings. Three Vols. 15s. each.

Shakespeare, Cassell's Quarto Edition. Edited by CHARLES and MARY COWDEN CLARKE, and containing about 600 Illustrations by H. C. SELOUS. Complete in Three Vols., cloth gilt, £3 3s.

Shakespeare, The International. *Edition de Luxe.* "King Henry IV.," Illustrated by Herr EDUARD GRUTZNER, £3 10s.; "As You Like It," Illustrated by Mons. EMILE BAYARD, £3 10s.; "Romeo and Juliet," Illustrated by FRANK DICKSEE, A.R.A., £5 5s.

Shakespearean Scenes and Characters. With 30 Steel Plates and 10 Wood Engravings. The Text written by AUSTIN BRERETON. 21s.

Short Studies from Nature. With Full-page Illustrations. *Cheap Edition.* 2s. 6d.

Sketching from Nature in Water Colours. By AARON PENLEY. With Illustrations in Chromo-Lithography. 15s.

Skin and Hair, The Management of the. By MALCOLM MORRIS, F.R.C.S. 2s.

Sports and Pastimes, Cassell's Book of. With more than 800 Illustrations and Coloured Frontispiece. 768 pages. *New Edition.* 9s. (Can be had separately thus: Outdoor Sports, 7s. 6d.; Indoor Amusements, 3s. 6d.)

Steam Engine, The Theory and Action of the: for Practical Men. By W. H. NORTHCOTT, C.E. 3s. 6d.

Stock Exchange Year-Book, The. By THOMAS SKINNER. 10s. 6d.

"Stories from Cassell's." A Series of Seven Books. 6d. each; cloth lettered, 9d. each.

Sunlight and Shade. With numerous Exquisite Engravings. 7s. 6d.

Surgery, Memorials of the Craft of, in England. With an Introduction by Sir JAMES PAGET. 21s.

Thackeray, Character Sketches from. Six New and Original Drawings by FREDERICK BARNARD, reproduced in Photogravure. 21s.
Trajan. An American Novel. By H. F. KEENAN. 7s. 6d.
Transformations of Insects, The. By Prof. P. MARTIN DUNCAN, M.B., F.R.S. With 240 Illustrations. 6s.
Treasure Island. By R. L. STEVENSON. Illustrated. 5s.
Treatment, The Year-Book of. A Critical Review for Practitioners of Medicine and Surgery. 5s.
Trees, Familiar. First Series. By G. S. BOULGER, F.L.S. With 40 full-page Coloured Plates, from Original Paintings by W. H. J. BOOT. 12s. 6d.
Twenty Photogravures of Pictures in the Salon of 1885, by the leading French Artists.
Two Gentlemen of Gotham. By C. C. 3s. 6d.
"Unicode": the Universal Telegraphic Phrase Book. *Desk and Pocket Editions.* 2s. 6d. each.
United States, Cassell's History of the. By the late EDMUND OLLIER. With 600 Illustrations. Three Vols. 9s. each.
United States, The Youth's History of the. By EDWARD S. ELLIS. Illustrated. Four Volumes. 36s.
Universal History, Cassell's Illustrated. Four Vols. 9s. each.
Vicar of Wakefield and other Works by OLIVER GOLDSMITH. Illustrated. 3s. 6d.; cloth, gilt edges, 5s.
Westall, W., Novels by. *Popular Editions.* Cloth, 2s. each.
    RALPH NORBRECK'S TRUST.
    THE OLD FACTORY. | RED RYVINGTON.
What Girls Can Do. By PHYLLIS BROWNE. 2s. 6d.
Who Is John Noman? By CHARLES HENRY BECKETT. 3s. 6d.
Wild Birds, Familiar. First, Second, and Third Series. By W. SWAYSLAND. With 40 Coloured Plates in each. 12s. 6d. each.
Wild Flowers, Familiar. By F. E. HULME, F.L.S., F.S.A. Five Series. With 40 Coloured Plates in each. 12s. 6d. each.
Wise Woman, The. By GEORGE MACDONALD. 2s. 6d.
World of the Sea. Translated from the French of MOQUIN TANDON, by the Very Rev. H. MARTYN HART, M.A. Illustrated. Morocco, cloth sides, 9s.
World of Wit and Humour, The. With 400 Illustrations. Cloth, 7s. 6d.; cloth gilt, gilt edges, 10s. 6d.
World of Wonders. Two Vols. With 400 Illustrations. 7s. 6d. each.
Yoke of the Thorah, The. By SIDNEY LUSKA. 3s. 6d.
Yule Tide. Cassell's Christmas Annual. 1s.

MAGAZINES.

The Quiver, for Sunday Reading. Monthly, 6d.
Cassell's Family Magazine. Monthly, 7d.
"Little Folks" Magazine. Monthly, 6d.
The Magazine of Art. Monthly, 1s.
The Lady's World. Monthly, 1s.
Cassell's Saturday Journal. Weekly, 1d.; Monthly, 6d.

Catalogues of CASSELL & COMPANY'S PUBLICATIONS, which may be had at all Booksellers', or will be sent post free on application to the publishers :—

    CASSELL'S COMPLETE CATALOGUE, containing particulars of upwards of One Thousand Volumes.
    CASSELL'S CLASSIFIED CATALOGUE, in which their Works are arranged according to price, from *Threepence to Twenty-five Guineas.*
    CASSELL'S EDUCATIONAL CATALOGUE, containing particulars of CASSELL & COMPANY'S Educational Works and Students' Manuals.

CASSELL & COMPANY, LIMITED, *Ludgate Hill, London.*

Bibles and Religious Works.

Bible, The Crown Illustrated. With about 1,000 Original Illustrations. With References, &c. 1,248 pages, crown 4to, cloth, 7s. 6d.

Bible, Cassell's Illustrated Family. With 900 Illustrations. Leather, gilt edges, £2 10s.

Bible Dictionary, Cassell's. With nearly 600 Illustrations. 7s. 6d.

Bible Educator, The. Edited by the Very Rev. Dean PLUMPTRE, D.D., Wells. With Illustrations, Maps, &c. Four Vols., cloth, 6s. each.

Bible Work at Home and Abroad. Volume. Illustrated. 3s.

Bunyan's Pilgrim's Progress (Cassell's Illustrated). 4to. 7s. 6d.

Bunyan's Pilgrim's Progress. With Illustrations. Cloth, 3s. 6d.

Child's Life of Christ, The. With 200 Illustrations. 21s.

Child's Bible, The. With 200 Illustrations. 143*rd Thousand.* 7s. 6d.

Church at Home, The. A Series of Short Sermons. By the Rt. Rev. ROWLEY HILL, D.D., Bishop of Sodor and Man. 5s.

Dictionary of Religion, The. An Encyclopædia of Christian and other Religious Doctrines, Denominations, Sects, Heresies, Ecclesiastical Terms, History, Biography, &c. &c. By the Rev. WILLIAM BENHAM, B.D. Cloth, 21s. ; Roxburgh, 25s.

Doré Bible. With 230 Illustrations by GUSTAVE DORÉ. Cloth, £2 10s.

Err'y Days of Christianity, The. By the Ven. Archdeacon FARRAR, D.D., F.R.S.
> LIBRARY EDITION. Two Vols., 24s. ; morocco, £2 2s.
> POPULAR EDITION. Complete in One Volume, cloth, 6s. ; cloth, gilt edges, 7s. 6d. ; Persian morocco, 10s. 6d. ; tree-calf, 15s.

Family Prayer-Book, The. Edited by Rev. Canon GARBETT, M.A., and Rev. S. MARTIN. Extra crown 4to, cloth, 5s. ; morocco, 18s.

Geikie, Cunningham, D.D., Works by :—
> THE HOLY LAND AND THE BIBLE. A Book of Scripture Illustrations gathered in Palestine. Two Vols., demy 8vo, with Map. 24s.
> HOURS WITH THE BIBLE. Six Vols., 6s. each.
> ENTERING ON LIFE. 3s. 6d.
> THE PRECIOUS PROMISES. 2s. 6d.
> THE ENGLISH REFORMATION. 5s.
> OLD TESTAMENT CHARACTERS. 6s.
> THE LIFE AND WORDS OF CHRIST. *Illustrated Edition*—Two Vols., 30s. ; *Library Edition*—Two Vols., 30s. ; *Students' Edition*—Two Vols., 16s. ; *Cheap Edition*—One Vol., 7s. 6d.

Glories of the Man of Sorrows, The. Sermons preached at St. James's, Piccadilly. By Rev. H. G. BONAVIA HUNT, Mus.D., F.R.S., Ed. 2s. 6d.

Gospel of Grace, The. By a LINDESIE. Cloth, 3s. 6d.

"Heart Chords." A Series of Works by Eminent Divines. Bound in cloth, red edges, One Shilling each.

My Father.	My Aspirations.	My Hereafter.
My Bible.	My Emotional Life.	My Walk with God.
My Work for God.	My Body.	My Aids to the Divine Life.
My Object in Life.	My Soul.	My Sources of Strength.
	My Growth in Divine Life.	

Helps to Belief. A Series of Helpful Manuals on the Religious Difficulties of the Day. Edited by the Rev. TEIGNMOUTH SHORE, M.A., Chaplain-in-Ordinary to the Queen. Cloth, 1s. each.

CREATION. By the Lord Bishop of Carlisle.	MIRACLES. By the Rev. Brownlow Maitland, M.A.
THE DIVINITY OF OUR LORD. By the Lord Bishop of Derry.	PRAYER. By the Rev. T. Teignmouth Shore, M.A.
THE MORALITY OF THE OLD TESTAMENT. By the Rev. Newman Smyth, D.D.	THE RESURRECTION. By the Lord Archbishop of York.
	THE ATONEMENT. By the Lord Bishop of Peterborough.

Life of Christ, The. By the Ven. Archdeacon FARRAR, D.D., F.R.S.
ILLUSTRATED EDITION, with about 300 Original Illustrations.
Extra crown 4to, cloth, gilt edges, 21s. ; morocco antique, 42s.
LIBRARY EDITION. Two Vols. Cloth, 24s. ; morocco, 42s.
BIJOU EDITION. Five Volumes, in box, 10s. 6d. the set.
POPULAR EDITION, in One Vol. 8vo, cloth, 6s. ; cloth, gilt edges,
7s. 6d. ; Persian morocco, gilt edges, 10s. 6d. ; tree-calf, 15s.

Marriage Ring, The. By WILLIAM LANDELS, D.D. Bound in white
leatherette, gilt edges, in box, 6s. ; morocco, 8s. 6d.

Moses and Geology ; or, The Harmony of the Bible with Science.
By the Rev. SAMUEL KINNS, Ph.D., F.R.A.S. Illustrated. *Cheap
Edition.* 6s.

New Testament Commentary for English Readers, The. Edited
by the Rt. Rev. C. J. ELLICOTT, D.D., Lord Bishop of Gloucester
and Bristol. In Three Volumes, 21s. each.
Vol. I.—The Four Gospels.
Vol. II.—The Acts, Romans, Corinthians, Galatians.
Vol. III.—The remaining Books of the New Testament.

Old Testament Commentary for English Readers, The. Edited
by the Right Rev. C. J. ELLICOTT, D.D., Lord Bishop of Gloucester
and Bristol. Complete in 5 Vols., 21s. each.
Vol. I.—Genesis to Numbers.   Vol. III.—Kings I. to Esther.
Vol. II.—Deuteronomy to   Vol. IV.—Job to Isaiah.
    Samuel II.   Vol. V.—Jeremiah to Malachi.

Patriarchs, The. By the late Rev. W. HANNA, D.D., and the Ven.
Archdeacon NORRIS, B.D. 2s. 6d.

Protestantism, The History of. By the Rev. J. A. WYLIE, LL.D.
Containing upwards of 600 Original Illustrations. Three Vols., 27s.

Quiver Yearly Volume, The. 250 high-class Illustrations. 7s. 6d.

Sacred Poems, The Book of. Edited by the Rev. Canon BAYNES, M.A.
With Illustrations. Cloth, gilt edges, 5s.

St. George for England ; and other Sermons preached to Children. By
the Rev. T. TEIGNMOUTH SHORE, M.A. 5s.

St. Paul, The Life and Work of. By the Ven. Archdeacon FARRAR,
D.D., F.R.S., Chaplain-in-Ordinary to the Queen.
LIBRARY EDITION. Two Vols., cloth, 24s. ; morocco, 42s.
ILLUSTRATED EDITION, complete in One Volume, with about 300
Illustrations, £1 1s. ; morocco, £2 2s.
POPULAR EDITION. One Volume, 8vo, cloth, 6s. ; cloth, gilt edges,
7s. 6d. ; Persian morocco, 10s. 6d. ; tree-calf, 15s.

Secular Life, The Gospel of the. Sermons preached at Oxford. By
the Hon. W. H. FREMANTLE, Canon of Canterbury. 5s.

Shall We Know One Another ? By the Rt. Rev. J. C RYLE, D.D.,
Bishop of Liverpool. *New and Enlarged Edition.* Cloth limp, 1s.

Simon Peter: His Life, Times, and Friends. By E. HODDER. 5s.

**Twilight of Life, The. Words of Counsel and Comfort for the
Aged.** By the Rev. JOHN ELLERTON, M.A. 1s. 6d.

Voice of Time, The. By JOHN STROUD. Cloth gilt, 1s.

Educational Works and Students' Manuals.

Alphabet, Cassell's Pictorial. 3s. 6d.

Algebra, The Elements of. By Prof. WALLACE, M.A. 1s.

Arithmetics, The Modern School. By GEORGE RICKS, B.Sc. Lond. With Test Cards. (*List on application.*)

Book-Keeping. By THEODORE JONES. For Schools, 2s. ; cloth, 3s. For the Million, 2s. ; cloth, 3s. Books for Jones's System. 2s.

Chemistry, The Public School. By J. H. ANDERSON, M.A. 2s. 6d.

Commentary, The New Testament. Edited by the Lord Bishop of GLOUCESTER and BRISTOL. Handy Volume Edition.
St. Matthew, 3s. 6d. St. Mark, 3s. St. Luke, 3s. 6d. St. John, 3s. 6d. The Acts of the Apostles, 3s. 6d. Romans, 2s. 6d. Corinthians I. and II., 3s. Galatians, Ephesians, and Philippians, 3s. Colossians, Thessalonians, and Timothy, 3s. Titus, Philemon, Hebrews, and James, 3s. Peter, Jude, and John, 3s. The Revelation, 3s. An Introduction to the New Testament, 3s. 6d.

Commentary, Old Testament. Edited by Bishop ELLICOTT. Handy Volume Edition. Genesis, 3s. 6d. Exodus, 3s. Leviticus, 3s. Numbers, 2s. 6d. Deuteronomy, 2s. 6d.

Copy-Books, Cassell's Graduated. *Eighteen Books.* 2d. each.

Copy-Books, The Modern School. *Twelve Books.* 2d. each.

Drawing Books, Cassell's New Standard. 7 Books. 2d. each.

Drawing Copies, Cassell's Modern School Freehand. First Grade, 1s. ; Second Grade, 2s.

Drawing Copies, Cassell's New Standard. Seven Books. 2d. each.

Drawing Copies, The Standard. Adapted to the higher Standards. Seven Books, 3d. each.

Electricity, Practical. By Prof. W. E. AYRTON. 7s. 6d.

Energy and Motion: A Text-Book of Elementary Mechanics. By WILLIAM PAICE, M.A. Illustrated. 1s. 6d.

English Literature, First Sketch of. *New and Enlarged Edition.* By Prof. MORLEY. 7s. 6d.

Euclid, Cassell's. Edited by Prof. WALLACE, M.A. 1s.

Euclid, The First Four Books of. In paper, 6d. ; cloth, 9d.

Flower Painting, Elementary. With Eight Coloured Plates and Wood Engravings. Crown 4to, cloth, 3s.

French Reader, Cassell's Public School. By GUILLAUME S. CONRAD. 2s. 6d.

French, Cassell's Lessons in. *New and Revised Edition.* Parts I. and II., each 2s. 6d. ; complete, 4s. 6d. Key, 1s. 6d.

French-English and English-French Dictionary. *Entirely New and Enlarged Edition.* 1,150 pages, 8vo, cloth, 3s. 6d.

Galbraith and Haughton's Scientific Manuals. By the Rev. Prof. GALBRAITH, M.A., and the Rev. Prof. HAUGHTON, M.D., D.C.L. Arithmetic, 3s. 6d.—Plane Trigonometry, 2s. 6d.—Euclid, Books I., II., III., 2s. 6d.—Books IV., V., VI., 2s. 6d.—Mathematical Tables, 3s. 6d.—Mechanics, 3s. 6d.—Natural Philosophy, 3s. 6d.—Optics, 2s. 6d.—Hydrostatics, 3s. 6d.—Astronomy, 5s.—Steam Engine, 3s. 6d. —Algebra, Part I., cloth, 2s. 6d. ; Complete, 7s. 6d.—Tides and Tidal Currents, with Tidal Cards, 3s.

German-English and English-German Dictionary. *Entirely New and Revised Edition.* 3s. 6d.

German Reading, First Lessons in. By A. JAGST. Illustrated. 1s.

German of To-Day. By Dr. HEINEMANN. 1s. 6d.

Handbook of New Code of Regulations. By JOHN F. MOSS. 1s.

Historical Course for Schools, Cassell's. Illustrated throughout. I.—Stories from English History, 1s. II.—The Simple Outline of English History, 1s. 3d. III.—The Class History of England, 2s. 6d.

Latin-English Dictionary, Cassell's. By J. R. V. MARCHANT, M.A. 3s. 6d.

Latin-English and English-Latin Dictionary. By J. R. BEARD, D.D., and C. BEARD, B.A. Crown 8vo, 914 pp., 3s. 6d.

Lay Texts for the Young. In English and French. By Mrs. RICHARD STRACHEY. 2s. 6d.

Little Folks' History of England. By ISA CRAIG-KNOX. With 30 Illustrations. 1s. 6d.

Making of the Home, The: A Book of Domestic Economy for School and Home Use. By Mrs. SAMUEL A. BARNETT. 1s. 6d.

Marlborough Books:—Arithmetic Examples, 3s. Arithmetic Rules, 1s. 6d. French Exercises, 3s. 6d. French Grammar, 2s. 6d. German Grammar, 3s. 6d.

Music, An Elementary Manual of. By HENRY LESLIE. 1s.

New Code, Handbook of. By J. MOSS. 1s.; cloth, 2s.

Popular Educator, Cassell's. *New and Thoroughly Revised Edition.* Illustrated throughout. Complete in Six Vols., 5s. each.

Readers, Cassell's Readable. Carefully graduated, extremely interesting, and illustrated throughout. (*List on application.*)

Readers, Cassell's Historical. Illustrated throughout, printed on superior paper, and strongly bound in cloth. (*List on application.*)

Readers for Infant Schools, Coloured. Three Books. Each containing 48 pages, including 8 pages in colours. 4d. each.

Reader, The Citizen. By H. O. ARNOLD-FORSTER, with Preface by the late Right Hon. W. E. FORSTER, M.P. 1s. 6d.

Readers, The Modern Geographical, illustrated throughout, and strongly bound in cloth. (*List on application.*)

Readers, The Modern School. Illustrated. (*List on application.*)

Reading and Spelling Book, Cassell's Illustrated. 1s.

Right Lines; or, Form and Colour. With Illustrations. 1s.

School Bank Manual. By AGNES LAMBERT. Price 6d.

School Manager's Manual. By F. C. MILLS, M.A. 1s.

Shakspere's Plays for School Use. 5 Books. Illustrated, 6d. each.

Shakspere Reading Book, The. By H. COURTHOPE BOWEN, M.A. Illustrated. 3s. 6d. Also issued in Three Books, 1s. each.

Spelling, A Complete Manual of. By J. D. MORELL, LL.D. 1s.

Technical Manuals, Cassell's. Illustrated throughout:—
Handrailing and Staircasing, 3s. 6d. Bricklayers, Drawing for, 3s.—Building Construction, 2s. Cabinet-Makers, Drawing for, 3s. Carpenters and Joiners, Drawing for, 3s. 6d.—Gothic Stonework, 3s.—Linear Drawing and Practical Geometry, 2s.—Linear Drawing and Projection. The Two Vols. in One, 3s. 6d.—Machinists and Engineers, Drawing for, 4s. 6d. Metal Plate Workers, Drawing for, 3s.—Model Drawing, 3s.—Orthographical and Isometrical Projection, 2s.—Practical Perspective, 3s.—Stonemasons, Drawing for, 3s.—Applied Mechanics, by Sir R. S. Ball, LL.D., 2s.—Systematic Drawing and Shading, 2s.

Technical Educator, Cassell's. *New Edition,* in Four Vols., 5s. each.

Technology, Manuals of. Edited by Prof. AYRTON, F.R.S., and RICHARD WORMELL, D.Sc., M.A. Illustrated throughout:—
The Dyeing of Textile Fabrics, by Prof. Hummel, 5s.—Watch and Clock Making, by D. Glasgow, 4s. 6d.—Steel and Iron, by W. H. Greenwood, F.C.S., M.I.C.E., &c., 5s.—Spinning Woollen and Worsted, by W. S. Bright McLaren, 4s. 6d.—Design in Textile Fabrics, by T. R. Ashenhurst, 4s. 6d.—Practical Mechanics, by Prof. Perry, M.E., 3s. 6d.—Cutting Tools Worked by Hand and Machine, by Prof. Smith, 3s. 6d. *A Prospectus on application.*

Test Cards, Cassell's Combination. In sets, 1s. each.

CASSELL & COMPANY, LIMITED, *Ludgate Hill, London.*

Books for Young People.

Books for Young People. Illustrated. Cloth gilt, 5s. each.

The Palace Beautiful. By L. T. Meade.

Under Bayard's Banner. By Henry Frith.

The King's Command: A Story for Girls. By Maggie Symington.

For Fortune and Glory: a Story of the Soudan War. By Lewis Hough.

" Follow My Leader;" or, the Boys of Templeton. By Talbot Baines Reed.

The Tales of the Sixty Mandarins. By P. V. Ramaswami Raju. With an Introduction by Prof. Henry Morley.

The Romance of Invention. By James Burnley.

The Champion of Odin: or, Viking Life in the Days of Old. By J. Fred. Hodgetts.

Bound by a Spell: or, the Hunted Witch of the Forest. By the Hon. Mrs. Greene.

Books for Young People. Illustrated. Price 3s. 6d. each.

The Cost of a Mistake. By Sarah Pitt.

A World of Girls: The Story of a School. By L. T. Meade.

Lost among White Africans: A Boy's Adventures on the Upper Congo. By David Ker.

Freedom's Sword: A Story of the Days of Wallace and Bruce. By Annie S. Swan.

On Board the "Esmeralda;" or, Martin Leigh's Log. By John C. Hutcheson.

In Quest of Gold: or, Under the Whanga Falls. By Alfred St. Johnston.

For Queen and King: or, the Loyal 'Prentice. By Henry Frith.

Perils Afloat and Brigands Ashore. By Alfred Elwes.

The "Cross and Crown" Series. Consisting of Stories founded on incidents which occurred during Religious Persecutions of Past Days. With Illustrations in each Book, printed on a tint. 2s. 6d. each.

Strong to Suffer: A Story of the Jews. By E. Wynne.

Heroes of the Indian Empire; or, Stories of Valour and Victory. By Ernest Foster.

In Letters of Flame: A Story of the Waldenses. By C. L. Matéaux.

Through Trial to Triumph. By Madeline B. Hunt.

By Fire and Sword: A Story of the Huguenots. By Thomas Archer.

Adam Hepburn's Vow: A Tale of Kirk and Covenant. By Annie S. Swan.

No. XIII.; or, The Story of the Lost Vestal. A Tale of Early Christian Days. By Emma Marshall.

The "Log Cabin" Series. By EDWARD S. ELLIS. With Four Full-page Illustrations in each. Crown 8vo, cloth, 2s. 6d. each.

The Lost Trail. | Camp-Fire and Wigwam. | Footprints in the Forest.

The "Great River" Series (uniform with the "Log Cabin" Series) By EDWARD S. ELLIS. Illustrated. Crown 8vo, cloth, bevelled boards, 2s. 6d. each.

Down the Mississippi. | Lost in the Wilds.
Up the Tapajos; or, Adventures in Brazil.

The "Boy Pioneer" Series. By EDWARD S. ELLIS. With Four Full-page Illustrations in each Book. Crown 8vo, cloth, 2s. 6d. each.

Ned in the Woods. A Tale of Early Days in the West. | Ned on the River. A Tale of Indian River Warfare.
Ned in the Block House. A Story of Pioneer Life in Kentucky.

"Golden Mottoes" Series, The. Each Book containing 208 pages, with Four full-page Original Illustrations. Crown 8vo, cloth gilt, 2s. each.

"Nil Desperandum." By the Rev. F. Langbridge.

"Bear and Forbear." By Sarah Pitt.

"Foremost if I Can." By Helen Atteridge.

"Honour is my Guide." By Jeanie Hering (Mrs. Adams-Acton).

"Aim at the Sure End." By Emilie Searchfield.

"He Conquers who Endures." By the Author of "May Cunningham's Trial," &c.

www.ingramcontent.com/pod-product-compliance
Lightning Source LLC
Chambersburg PA
CBHW021529110726
47902CB00004B/810